IN THE
WAKE OF GODS

THE GODLESS TRILOGY | BOOK ONE

CHRISTOPHER MONTEAGLE

Black Rose Writing | Texas

ISBN: 978-1-68433-482-7 (Paperback), 978-1-68513-787-8 (Hardcover)
PUBLISHED BY BLACK ROSE WRITING
www.blackrosewriting.com

Printed in the United States of America
Suggested Retail Price (SRP) $20.95 (Paperback), $24.95 (Hardcover)

In the Wake of Gods is printed in Calluna
Map art credited to Edwin Menzo @ fantasymapshop

*As a planet-friendly publisher, Black Rose Writing does its best to eliminate unnecessary waste to reduce paper usage and energy costs, while never compromising the reading experience. As a result, the final word count vs. page count may not meet common expectations.

For my wife, Anya.

Without you this book simply would never have happened.

Iron Union

Kovalith

Alovat

Grand Duchy
of Joana

Ironhelm

Ciro

The Shield

Klyph
(Malene's Fall)

Mac-Soldai

Fortress of Krág

Hammerfall

Dark Spires

Arbek

Rhaskitov

Greuud

Barrens of Silence

Kardak

The Render

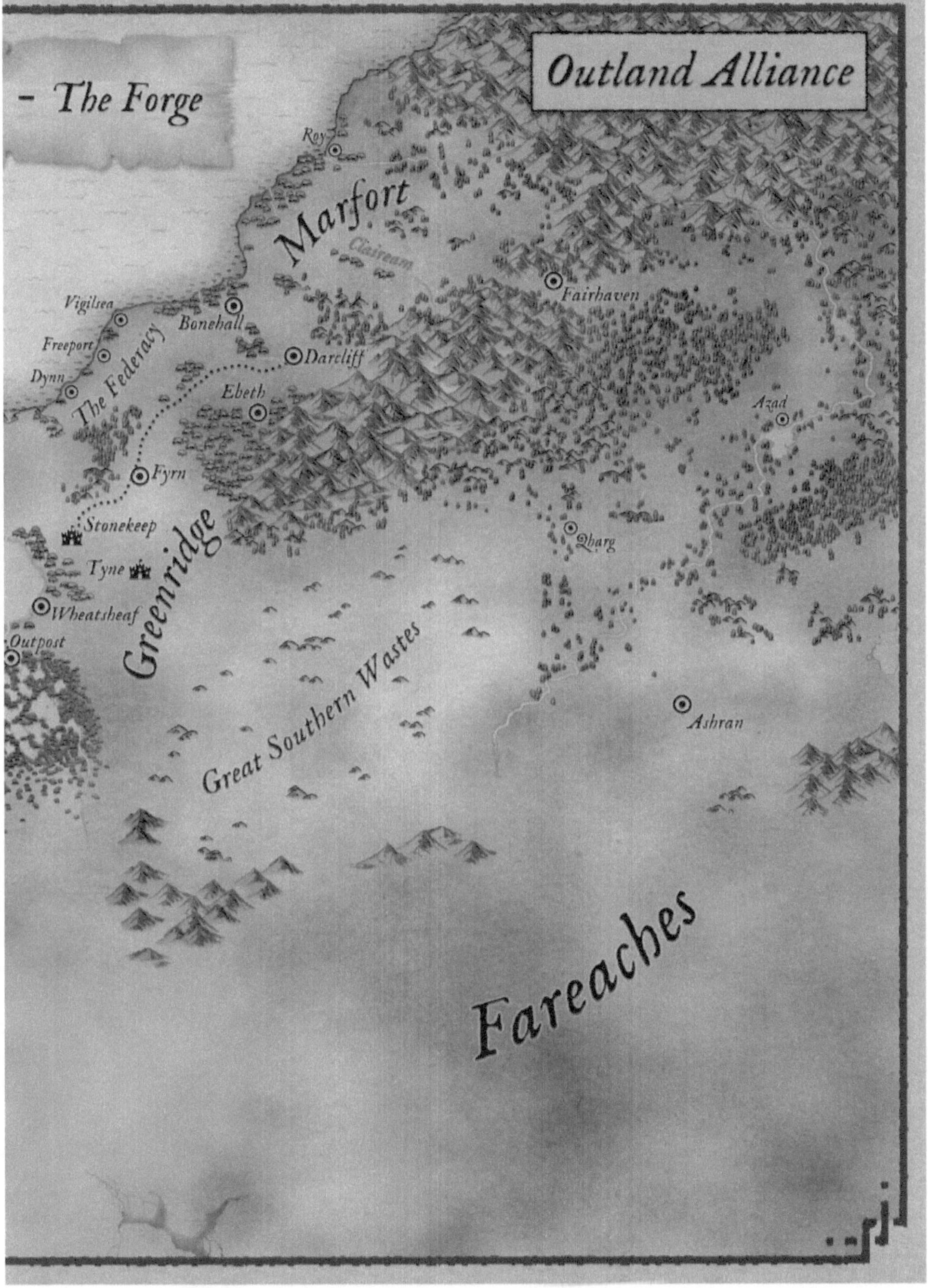

- The Forge
Outland Alliance
Roy
Marfort
Clairean
Fairhaven
Vigilsea
Boneball
Freeport
The Federacy
Darcliff
Dynn
Ebeth
Azad
Fyrn
Stonekeep
Greenridge
Qharg
Tyne
Wheatsheaf
Outpost
Great Southern Wastes
Ashran
Fareaches

IN THE
WAKE OF GODS

THE GODLESS TRILOGY | BOOK ONE

BOOK 1
REDISCOVERY

CHAPTER 1

"Our gods have left us.

After centuries of guidance and leadership, they simply vanished, leaving only two behind: Bythe of the Iron Union and Maelene the Blessed Mother.

Peace held for a time. The Iron Union existed statically, as did the Outer Wild – but one lesson the gods have no doubt learned from this world, is that life is not static. It cannot be. Life will bring growth, growth will bring change, and change will bring conflict. As the diametrically opposed influences of both Bythe and Maelene came into contact, conflict and disagreement was inevitable. One might have hoped that the gods had learned wisdom, restraint, and even maturity in their dealings with their kin. This is not so.

For it would seem that the gods created us very much in their own image."

~Aleasea of the Ageless

Her town was burning. Elyn was sprinting down a laneway between two stone buildings. She was oblivious to the rubbish that cracked underfoot and sent fragments of wood and glass painfully into her shins. All that mattered was escape. Behind her were truly dreadful sounds. Men were dying. Elyn had never had to endure those sounds before, but in that moment of desperate flight it seemed like those terrible screams would never again leave her thoughts.

The town of Outpost was finally under siege from the Iron Union – and while the people of her hometown had feared this day might come, they were completely unprepared for the swiftness and ferocity of the assault. No one in the Council had seriously expected the Iron Union's Helmsguard to move against the town so soon. Even if the Union finally decided to attack, everyone had thought there would be plenty of warning, sights of troop movements, or the usual intelligence that would seep into the community and give everyone time enough to stage an orderly evacuation.

Everyone had been wrong.

An entire army of the Helmsguard had crashed upon the ramshackle town of Outpost just after dawn, and the result had been devastating. Captain Drake's men had been surprised, and they paid for it. Hopelessly outnumbered, they still tried to plan an organized resistance as the invaders began cutting them down.

For her part, Elyn had been alone praying in the Chapel of Maelene when she first heard the shouts. At sixteen, society expected the sandy-haired young woman to pray to the Blessed Mother Maelene at least twice a week, and Elyn was always diligent with her duties. She had been kneeling before the small stone statue of a beautiful woman, praying for the usual things a young woman might pray for: her family – in this case her father, Leon – and her training. She also couldn't help adding in the slightly selfish request that she might figure out how to get herself noticed in the same way everybody noticed her beautiful friend, Nadine.

A man's distant scream had shaken her out of those prayers. Elyn had realized that it was one of those truly awful screams that communicates a primal terror – the type of sound that warns the listener on an instinctive level that something dreadful has happened. When she emerged from the small stone building, she felt an icy shard of dread stab into her stomach. Further up the road to her right, men in black metal armor were moving in an ordered line toward the chapel. Their weapons were like nothing Elyn had ever seen, long, polished sabers of shining silver metal that seemed to curve with a cruel, malicious edge. The black armor of the invaders was equally impressive, with each soldier covered head to foot in a seamless carapace of overlapping iron plates. Metal. The hallmark of the Iron Union.

By contrast, the town's defenders were almost shamefully equipped in their padded blue leather and crude shortswords. As Elyn stood at the door to the chapel, she watched as six of the town guard rushed past her door and down the street to intercept the invaders. An act that could only have one outcome. Elyn felt a compelling need to watch this disaster unfold before she shook off the thought and started to move.

Run!

It was an internal instruction to her unwilling feet. She found that she had to push them into action. As if they had lost all feeling and had declared autonomy from her body. Elyn quelled the internal insurrection and forced her feet into action. She abandoned her sanctuary and started running as hard as she could in the direction away from the soldiers. Elyn's physical limitations didn't seem to apply when she was running in fear of her life – a secret only revealed to a person facing their moment of terror. The buildings rushed past her as an indistinct blur, and every stride stretched her hamstrings to their limit as she moved her legs faster than she ever had. The pain never registered, only survival mattered. She knew that if she slowed for a second, her life could end. It was as simple as that.

She continued down the street only to raise her eyes and take in a terrible sight before her. At least a dozen more men in jet-black armor were fighting men in blue only a hundred feet away. She skidded to a halt and watched in dismay as men in blue were cut down while several more lay dying in the dirt, bloody hands clutching at terrible red gashes. Beyond them was a scene of pure mayhem. People were running in panic. Townsfolk were screaming for children, some men were attempting to attack the Helmsguard in a pitiful gesture of defiance, but most had the good sense to just run.

Scanning left and right, Elyn spied an alleyway and wasted no time heading for it. She pelted down the rubbish-strewn alley with the same superhuman gait that sheer terror seemed to gift her. Her only thoughts were to find her father. Find Leon. Leon would know what to do. He always did. She desperately hoped he was alright. At sixty-three years old, Leon had begun to show signs of frailty and Elyn feared that he might not escape this.

Put it out of your head, Elyn. Focus on the problem!

She knew that's what Leon would say. With this conviction in mind, she rounded the corner of the alley and collided with a figure. Elyn was sent sprawling in the dirt, and she tumbled limb over limb until she came to rest on her back. She looked up to see who she'd hit – certain it was a Helmsguard soldier. Certain she was caught.

It was worse than that.

Standing around her were three men dressed in the ragged and threadbare garb of Outpost's street thieves. One of them was taking the possessions of a well-dressed corpse, while the second was breaking open his rucksack and pilfering through the contents. Looters. The third man was slowly getting to his feet after Elyn had knocked him down and was fixing her with a look that could only be described as murderous. He was tall and skinny with a pock-marked face and a cruel glint in his eyes. The kind of man who would laugh at beggars and spit in their faces as they asked for money – the obvious irony never occurring to him in his arrogance.

"Grab 'er," he snarled and before Elyn could rise, she felt her arms and legs seized in the firm grip of desperate men.

"Just a girl, Ray!" said the shorter man who had stopped sifting through the corpse's pockets and grabbed Elyn's feet.

"Shut up!" spat the man called Ray as he stood over Elyn with a sneer twisting his upper lip. "No one hits me, not even girls."

Somewhere in Elyn's mind, she realized that she was witnessing the universal display of the posturing braggart, and somehow, she recognised the absurdity of it all – but that didn't help her. When Ray produced the large cleaver from behind his back, Elyn felt cold dread sweep through her body.

"No, no, please! I'm sorry. I was running from the Helmsguard! They're here!" Elyn blurted out in desperation, but Ray appeared unmoved.

"Doesn't matter. No one disrespects me. You'll remember that next time you try to run without a foot."

Elyn cried out. It was a guttural and desperate thing. It was the second scream of truly primal terror she had heard that morning. It was one that saved her life.

· · ·

Commander Vale surveyed her troops as they moved swiftly under her command. The town of Outpost spread out before her like a rotting cancer, and Vale regarded the scene with mild disgust. She had expected the town to be an unruly hovel, but the sheer filth and stench of chaos turned her stomach. She leaned forward in her saddle and watched her third company moving up to support the troops engaging the enemy at the southern side of the city. The oiled metal plates in her black armor barely sounded, as she shifted her weight with the well-practised movements of a military officer. Gold engraving laced the plates at their edges, and thick, black chainmail protected the joints of the arms and legs, or any other parts that were not covered for the sake of mobility. Despite her very young age of sixteen, Vale had already risen to become a Commander of an army in the Iron Union. Most people knew why.

"Charming little rat-hole, isn't it?" A man's voice rang out almost cheerfully as a red-headed man in almost identical black armor, but for the silver engravings, rode up beside her.

"All of our planning just to claim a place like this, Ethan?" she answered without taking her eyes off the town. "Look at them running in terror from us! We're better off leaving them to fend for themselves. We're risking the lives of our men...for this?"

"Ah, no! We risk them for the pride of the Union, my lady," Ethan replied with heavy sarcasm. "Outpost must be retaken to restore our rightful borders against the Outer Wild."

"You're bordering on treasonous thoughts there, Baron," Vale mocked with a deadpan expression, then let out a heavy sigh. "Ethan, what are we doing here?"

Vale's friend turned in his saddle to look at her. "You know why we're here, my lady."

Vale met Ethan's gaze and understood his meaning. Ethan was a tall young man of twenty, with the noble features befitting a man of his excellent background. With a casual glance he verified that they couldn't be overheard, then gracefully moved his horse a step closer to Vale's, speaking in lower tones.

"Don't forsake this opportunity, Vale, there are many Commanders in the Ironhelm who would give anything for this chance."

Vale met his gaze but didn't reply. She knew how much it might have rankled this fine, young aristocrat to be taking orders from someone not only younger than him, but from the only female Commander in the Helmsguard. But in all the time Ethan had served as her second-in-command, he had never shown the slightest hint of resentment or insubordination. Ethan would almost certainly have relished this opportunity to win valour in the courts of the Iron Union, had it been granted to him. Vale realized she was dishonoring her friend with her own sullenness and snapped herself out of her mood.

"Prepare the company. I want to head in there myself," Vale spoke with the clear and commanding voice of a military chief once more.

Ethan stiffened in his saddle and saluted with a mailed fist across his plated chest. He turned his horse around and began to bark orders at the lieutenants behind them. Vale watched him for a moment then turned her attention back to the town before her.

Outpost.

Appropriately named, it stood on the borderlands between the Iron Union and the Outer Wild. It had once served as the border position for the Iron Union, but over the years the town had fallen into enemy hands. Now that the powers of the Ageless were faltering, the time had come to retake the city. A symbolic gesture to be sure, but an important one. However, as a potential gateway to the empire, it would serve as a very poor example. Years of war had taken a toll on the town and what had once been a thriving populace was now a collection of slums and temporary buildings.

Vale regarded the scene from atop her horse. Below her plains stretched out to the horizon. Dry grasslands swept the vista, but for a thin crack of water that broke the land from south to north. Along this river sat the town, where people scurried about like roaches at the sight of the oncoming soldiers. No matter that her men would be their protectors, they seemed panicked by the thought of such a display of power. No doubt every tavern owner, whore, or gaming den patron was fretting that the might of the Iron Union was about to kick over the rubbish of their lives and unearth their dirty little secrets. Vale felt a sudden urge to order her men to raze the town to the ground.

"My lady," Ethan interrupted. "The company awaits your command."

Vale gave the order and a group of forty armed men began marching down the dry grasslands. The vanguard moved before her, under Ethan's watchful eye, dutifully ensuring that no surprise or rogue attacker would threaten their Commander. Vale rode protected in the center of the formation, a position that irritated her – as if even her own men doubted her ability to defend herself. That insecurity still nagged at her.

"Any sign of the Ageless?" Vale asked Ethan as they approached the outskirts of the town.

"None, my lady," he replied with a small shake of his head.

Vale tightened her jaw. Did this mean that the Ageless had left this town undefended, or were they waiting to spring an ambush? Vale knew the intentions of the Ageless could never be predicted, but it didn't stop her analytical mind from working on the problem. Just as their goddess, Maelene, had long since fallen, it didn't stop them from trying to avenge her sacrifice.

"Stay alert then, Ethan," Vale replied. "I want our men to raise the alarm at the first sign of a green cloak. We've lost enough good men to those zealots."

Ethan gave an affirmation then turned to see the instruction carried out. The verbal order swept through the soldiers like a wave, and Vale was reminded of the efficiency of her men and of her lieutenants. The Iron Union trained their soldiers well. No, the Iron Union trained their soldiers perfectly. There was simply no comparison in all the lands – both within the Iron Union and the Outlands. Within minutes, they had passed through the outskirts and beheld the prize they had come so far to claim.

The town was a mess.

Old rubbish lay strewn across the open dirt road, and Vale knew that this wasn't simply the result of her attack. The few sturdy buildings were decrepit from years of clear neglect, and the air seemed to smell of cabbage and sour milk. Occasionally, a dirty face with matted hair would appear in between the heaps of trash, only to vanish as soon as they sighted it. Human rats. Vale wondered how a city – no matter how remote – could sit in such a state. Before long the dilapidated structures and slums gave way to buildings of slightly better integrity. The road widened and the faces of townsfolk replaced the faces of beggars in alleys in windows, still as curious as their predecessors, but at least with an improved odor. In the distance, Vale could hear the unmistakable sounds of battle.

"We've pushed the town guard to the east. They're giving us some resistance, but they're in steady retreat. Our losses have been light." Ethan turned and favored Vale with a warm smile. "Your plan was perfect, Vale, well done."

Vale returned the smile. The plan had been a great risk; avoid the early warning posts by bringing her army through the marshlands to the south. It could have just as easily turned to disaster – her campaign brought to a halt by disease, dehydration, and drownings – but Vale never left a variable to chance. She had spent weeks studying every scrap of detail about the marshes and ignoring the persistently conventional wisdom of her military advisors – much to their obvious frustration. Over that time, she became convinced that a path through the marshes was not only possible, but likely, given the timing was right. She then realized that if she approached Outpost from the south under darkness, she could catch the town's sentry posts off guard from the rear. The town guard could be ambushed. They could not only be taken with devastating swiftness, they could also be taken with minimal losses.

"We've both done well, Ethan. I couldn't have done this without you."

Ethan nodded his head in a sign of mutual respect. He was an excellent officer, yet he was a better friend.

There was a sound of clashing metal and renewed cries of men. Ethan signalled to the company, and within seconds, they had swept into position in the dirt road before them.

"There's still skirmishes nearby, my lady," Ethan explained somewhat redundantly. "Stay here for a moment while we secure the surrounds."

Vale felt that irritating insecurity rise within her once more but managed to suppress the mutiny. Did they really need to protect her so completely? Was she more of an intellectual tactician than a real battlefield commander to them?

She'd watched them move down the street for no more than a few moments when Vale, alone, heard another cry to her right. It wasn't the usual battlefield scream that was soaking the air. This had the edge of pure terror. She turned in her saddle and searched for the source, finding it almost immediately. In a narrow alley formed by two lopsided buildings, Vale could make out a young woman pinned to the ground by a gang of three larger men. The woman was clearly defenseless, a fact that was apparently lost on the others as they leaned over her with weapons in their hands and sneers on their faces. Criminals.

Cowards.

Then Vale was moving without thinking. She dismounted her horse and, with three great strides, she halved the distance between herself and her quarry, drawing a dagger from her belt with her left hand while raising her saber behind her head with her right. The three men snapped their heads around, and a cry went up from one as they leapt to their feet in the blink of an eye. Somewhere in the back of her mind, Vale recalled Yvorre's warnings that three men were near-impossible odds, even for the best fighter. Once the third opponent got behind you, the fight was over.

Vale still didn't hesitate.

The largest man barely had time to raise the cleaver in his hand before Vale was upon him, her saber arcing horizontally as its sharp blade slashed across the man's throat. Blood shot out from the wound as the man's face froze in an expression of shock. He staggered half a step before crashing to the ground without a sound, as blood continued to spray from the fatal injury.

But Vale saw none of it.

She had already stepped forward to engage the second man, who seemed stunned at the sight of his leader cut down so efficiently by such a young attacker, staring in horror with his hands swinging by his side. Vale seized the initiative. With no time to reverse her blade for a second slash, she instead drew her saber toward him and pushed off the ground with her rear foot, thrusting her weapon outward in a deadly lunge. Before the second man could react, the sword's pointed tip buried itself deep in his chest. The victim barely had time to open his mouth in a silent scream as he started to fall backward.

The third man, however, was not as slow as his companions, and he launched himself at Vale before the young Commander could withdraw her saber from her victim. Sensing the opportunity, the wiry man leapt at Vale, his blade ready to thrust into the weaker chain links at her side. Vale's instinct told her to abandon her first weapon, and she let it fall to the ground with its now screaming victim. Instead, she turned to face her attacker and raised the long dagger in her left hand, turning her opponent's blade with a downward swing so that the short sword passed inches from her abdomen. The failed lunge made the two fighters collide, but Vale was ready. She reached with her free right hand, grabbed her enemy's extended weapon arm, and with a turn of her own body, jerked him forward and off balance. The criminal stumbled over his opponent's legs and fell face first into the dirt. In a heartbeat, Vale thrust her armored knee into the man's spine and pinned him to the ground. Without a thought, the young warrior wrenched the man's head back to expose his neck, and with her other hand, quickly plunged her dagger into the vulnerable flesh. For the second time in less than half a minute, blood shot across the small alleyway and a man died without so much as a cry; but still Vale did not breathe easy or let her cold mindset drop. She jumped to her feet and scanned the alley on all sides, looking for other men running to aid or fleeing in terror back to their hovels.

There were none.

Methodically she raised herself to her full height and gave the three corpses a final glance, as if she half expected them to twitch or moan, as if she had not so decisively ended their lives mere moments before. If her handiwork satisfied her, she gave no indication. Her blank expression perfectly reflected her state of mind.

Vale began to break the grip on her concentration and the details of her surrounds started to come back into focus. Her head seemed light and her arms tingled from her fingers to her shoulders, but despite the mortal struggle, her breathing was steady and her heartbeat firm. It was only then she noticed the young woman lying at the center of the dirt alley and staring at her with an expression of open surprise on her face. And then Vale mirrored the expression.

• • •

Elyn had been bracing herself for agony when she realized that Ray was no longer fixing his glare on her. Instead his gaze had moved to something over Elyn's head and his expression was changing from self-important rage to something like incredulity. Elyn watched as Ray and his two associates had jumped to their feet, only to be met by a smaller figure in the black armor of the Helmsguard. Elyn lay helpless as the interloper moved with a speed and grace that she'd never beheld in a fighting man. With clinical efficiency, the three attackers had simply been killed. No sprawling battle or clumsy street brawl. It was almost an execution. Elyn had never seen a man killed in her life, let alone three men violently killed within seconds – so the experience had a somewhat bewildering effect on her. Elyn continued to lie in the dirt as the young soldier cast an efficient glance around him before seeming to relax a fraction. The solider turned to Elyn and revealed his face.

It was a young woman's face. It was Elyn's own face.

Elyn felt a surreal sensation, as if she had just awoken from a dream with the feelings fresh in her mind. The face that looked back at her own was an almost perfect copy, except for the eyes. The face of the woman in armor bore eyes of shining blue, whereas Elyn knew her eyes were the darkest of brown. Yet everything else looked identical. The youthful pale face with the narrow chin and high cheekbones. Elyn could even detect the strands of sandy colored hair showing from beneath her black helm. And while this bizarre paradox shocked her, it seemed to have quite the equal effect on the other. The woman in the black armor was staring at her as if she was transfixed. She stood rooted to the spot with confusion flaring in those piercing blue eyes.

Elyn recovered first and climbed to her feet, mindful of the still bleeding corpses around her. The movement seemed to jolt the warrior from her fixation.

"Wait!" the soldier commanded.

Elyn wasn't at all sure what her voice sounded like to others, but this woman's voice sounded strange – yet also familiar – to her own ears. She took an involuntary step backward at the sound and the soldier reached out to detain her.

It was at that moment that something happened. Elyn wasn't quite sure what it was, and she'd struggle to recall it later, but there was a sense of vertigo combined with a strange sense of displacement. There was also a surge of something else. Euphoria? Adrenaline? It was there in an instant and gone a second later, as Elyn felt something crash into her from behind. It knocked the air from her lungs and all she could see was the sky. It took Elyn a moment to realize that she was lying on her back.

She sat up, head spinning, and saw her strange twin also lying in the dirt some thirty feet away. It seemed to Elyn that they'd both been repelled the instant they had come into contact with each other. She didn't know why; at that moment, she didn't actually care. Maybe later she'd regret her haste, but at the time, all she knew was that a soldier from the Iron Union bore her face and wanted to detain her.

She jumped to her feet and saw the other woman starting to move her arms in a groggy fashion, as if dazed by the shock but quickly coming around. Elyn didn't wait. She turned and ran back down the alley in the direction she had come. She knew there might be Helmsguard waiting for her, but at that moment, it was her only option. Sprinting back into the open street, she felt a surge of relief to find it empty – the resistance having apparently been pushed back some distance. Elyn turned left and continued her flight. She was aware that she was now probably behind the lines of the invaders, but that was alright. In fact, it gave her one advantage – they would be preoccupied subduing the resistance and would not yet have time to manage the population now at their back. That gave her a slim window of opportunity to escape the city.

She hurried up the street and within moments, she'd slipped down another side alley, then another. She'd not grown up in this town without learning the shortcuts. Moving almost instinctively, she navigated the labyrinth of laneways that crisscrossed the makeshift town and headed toward the river. She prayed to Maelene – if the god was watching over her – that she'd find what she needed.

It seemed that Maelene was still watching over her.

Elyn emerged from between two warehouses to run onto the decrepit docks and straight into a scene of frantic riverside evacuation. The river was choked with a flotilla of boats, small and large, all burdened with people and belongings sailing northward. Clearly, the Helmsguard hadn't yet blockaded the river, although Elyn suspected they might solve that problem at any moment. Elyn ran through the crowd of residents about to become refugees. She saw, to her rising alarm, that many of the boats had already cast off and the few that remained were already starting to swamp with people. Spot-fires of raised voices and even raised fists were peppering the docks as tempers flared and desperation boiled over.

Somewhere behind her, a woman screamed and then another took up the call. Looters or Helmsguard? It didn't matter. Elyn didn't want to find out. She started running toward the nearest vessel – a skiff boat barely capable of holding a dozen people. She'd scarcely closed within twenty feet of the boat when she caught the attention of a large man with a clean-shaven head and a somewhat bedraggled beard. With a speed that belied his bulk, he swung his body around to face Elyn and brandished a sword in an accusatory gesture that needed no interpretation. Elyn quickly pulled up at the greeting.

"Please…" she attempted. "I've got nowhere…"

"Get out of here, piss-ant!" came the reply with such a ferocious and sincere promise of violence that Elyn knew there would be no further warnings. Almost stumbling backward, Elyn turned and heard more screams from further up the docks. Helmsguard almost certainly. They would have this dock secured in minutes. Elyn looked up and down the boardwalk that lined the foul-smelling river and counted her options. Assuming these few remaining boats would be as fiercely defended for the next few minutes before they cast off, she seemed to have no options left at all.

"Elyn!" called a female voice over the tumult. Elyn clung to the offered sound like it was a lifeline thrown to her in a torrent.

"Nadine?" she replied in confusion. She turned in the direction of the voice, eyes scanning the throng of people for the owner.

"Elyn!" the voice repeated in a louder and far more impatient tone.

She turned her attention toward a medium-sized boat tethered further down the boardwalk. Elyn could see a small crowd of people held at bay by two armed manservants. Safely in the boat and beyond the crowd, Elyn could see the familiar figure of a slender, blonde-haired female. She wasted little time beyond basic recognition before she was moving through the rapidly thinning crowd toward the boat. Behind her, Elyn could hear more screams as the Helmsguard were doubtless continuing their advance onto the docks.

"Hurry, Elyn, we're leaving," Nadine's voice now drifted to her carrying a note of desperation.

Elyn reached the small crowd and began to shoulder her way through, insensitive to the curses and blows that were thrown at her, and only stopping when she found herself at the pointed end of a weapon for the second time within minutes. The manservant wielding the weapon may have looked a little more refined than the previous aggressor, but Elyn didn't doubt that his resolve was as strong.

"Vander, wait!" Nadine ordered her servant in the slightly imperious manner that seemed to belong to certain social classes. The man named Vander risked a glance in her direction to confirm the validity of the instructions.

"My lady?" the red-faced servant enquired. Although he was doing a more than adequate job defending the boat, Elyn still suspected that wielding a sword was not one of his common duties.

"Let her through," came a commanding male voice. Elyn glanced up to see a tall man with well-groomed hair and a fine moustache had walked up alongside his daughter. "She's one of Nadine's friends. Quickly! We're casting off right now!"

Without even waiting for Vander to step aside, Elyn launched herself across the narrow gap between the dock and the boat and landed on the deck. Instantly, she was enveloped by slender arms and the scent of flowers.

"Thank gods you're alright!" Nadine gushed. Elyn couldn't help but blurt a strangled laugh at the absurdity of the comment.

"I'm alright thanks to you!" She hugged her friend back. "Where did you come from?"

They separated with a lurch as the boat pulled away from the dock and starting to catch the current. Vander and the other unnamed manservant abandoned their short careers as armed protectors and leaped to the safety of the boat. In the distance, Elyn could now make out armored figures advancing through the docks, starting to move upon the few unfortunate vessels that had not made their escape in time.

"Gods..." Elyn whispered as she watched the scenes from the dock start to diminish in clarity. "How did this happen?"

"I know," Nadine replied as she watched beside her. For a moment, with the immediate threat of capture or death removed, they both seemed to lapse into a state of shocked silence as they bore witness to the fall of their childhood home. It only then occurred to Elyn that this would be even harder for Nadine as the daughter of a wealthy river trader. It was very possible that her family had lost everything this morning. Not that she hadn't lost everything herself, it's just that when you're the daughter of a records clerk, you don't really have that much to lose.

Leon!

The thought jolted her from her melancholy mood harder than a slap. In her confusion after her encounter with her strange twin and her preoccupation with her own personal safety thereafter, Elyn realized she had completely forgotten about her father. The guilt that then flooded her was nauseating. She opened her mouth to ask the futile question when she was grasped violently and spun around in place. Leon's familiar arms enveloped Elyn as firmly as Nadine's had moments before. Elyn found she could measure the intensity of her father's distress by the way he was squeezing the life out of her.

"Elyn!" Leon choked through tears. "Oh, Elyn thank gods...thank gods..."

She felt a bewildering mix of confusion, relief, and exhaustion as she sank into the embrace of her father. Tears welled behind her closed lids and began to spill down her cheeks in hot streams. After a moment, Leon broke the embrace and looked her over with an appraising eye. Elyn had grown taller than Leon last summer, but somehow his hugs still made her feel like she was half his size.

"Are you hurt?" he asked with a father's genuine concern.

Leon was a short and portly man. He wore a full head of silver hair and a round face that was careworn by years of parenthood.

"No, Pa, I'm alright. I was in the chapel when they attacked... I managed to get to the docks when Nadine found me."

For a moment, she wanted to tell Leon about her near capture with Ray and the Helmsguard, particularly the encounter with her young twin, but she somehow knew this wasn't the right time for that conversation. Leon looked half out of his wits with worry, and Elyn suspected he didn't need the additional problems laid on him right then and there. Leon looked at his daughter, and for a moment, Elyn thought he was going to press her further, but he just nodded. Perhaps he likewise thought better of raising a question, or perhaps he sensed nothing – Elyn always found herself a little off balance around her father's probing looks. Eager to deflect the unspoken question, she changed the subject.

"What are you doing here?"

The question earned an unexpected expression of guilt and shame from Leon. Elyn immediately regretted asking.

"I was with the Council processing an application for a renewed trade permit for Nadine's family when news of the attack hit. They took me with them. I tried to get someone to find you, but the Helmsguard came at us from everywhere and there was no time to do anything but run. Before I knew what had happened, I was on the boat... I didn't know where you were. I wasn't going to leave without you, Elyn, I promise."

Elyn reached out and touched her father on the shoulder. "It's alright, I know."

Leon calmed himself before continuing, as if steadied by the reassurance. A parent's endless guilt assuaged for the moment.

"And then without warning, you were next to me as if placed there by Maelene Herself. She's been watching over us today." Leon placed an arm around his daughter and turned to face Nadine. "Also, we've had some more direct assistance. Young lady, we owe your father our lives. We simply will never be able to repay what you've done for us today."

Nadine smiled faintly and wiped at a small tear as she looked back at the swarming soldiers on the docks. "I think we've all lost too much today, sir," she replied, respecting an elder despite her superior social station.

They all stood in silence for a moment as Outpost faded from view. Elyn was surprised at how swift the ship was. The household staff that had served as armed bodyguards were now running back and forth across the deck to manipulate the rigging. Within moments, the mainsail was lowered, and the boat lurched again as the added wind bolstered the speed afforded by the steady current.

"What do we do now?" Elyn asked.

Leon sighed. "Well, the Helmsguard are no good on water so we'll run. There's always been a rendezvous location agreed for the day we'd have to flee from the Iron Union. I just hoped that we'd never have to use it."

Nadine's father had returned with blankets which he distributed to all three of them. Elyn hadn't realized how cold it had become on the open river and wrapped one around her shoulders.

"We'll have to see how many got out," Nadine's father said. "This was a blow."

"Where will we go, Father?" Nadine hugged her arms around him as he gently placed the blanket around her.

"Well, like Leon said, we'll regroup at Wheatsheaf, but we won't be able to stay there. It's not exactly a secure position, and I don't think the fortresses like Bonehall will take us in. No, I think we're going to have to retreat to Fairhaven."

They all looked at him. Even Leon seemed surprised.

"Fairhaven, Paeter? Will it come to that?"

Nadine's father shrugged. "I honestly don't **think** we have much of a choice. We're going to need to find a settlement that'll take us, and Fairhaven's one of the only places left, unless we want to stay close to the front line."

There was a pause.

"What about the Ageless?" Elyn asked. It was the obvious question even if it had been unspoken. Elyn and Nadine's respective fathers shared a look.

"They're Maelene's disciples, Elyn," Leon answered. "They're our protectors. If we need them, then they'll take us in. You don't have to worry."

Elyn and Nadine shared a look of their own. The look shared by daughters who don't quite believe what their fathers tell them. Paeter kissed his daughter on her forehead, then turned to walk back to his servants. his commanding voice calling out instructions before he had even reached them.

Elyn turned back to the water. Outpost had faded from sight already, a bend in the river obliterating the dismal view. She wanted to think about Fairhaven. She wanted to think about the Ageless and how they would react to their arrival.

But she couldn't.

As she stared out across the water, all she could think about was that sharp image of a face. A face like so much like her own – but with piercing blue eyes.

CHAPTER 2

"The war between Bythe's Iron Union and Maelene's alliance of settlements in the Outlands raged for decades. In hindsight, it was little more than a waste of the precious lives both gods had vowed to protect. Neither Bythe nor Maelene were able to gain a permanent advantage over the other.

It was not until Maelene was betrayed and murdered, that the Iron Union began to enjoy a long period of success."

~Aleasea of the Ageless

The sounds of celebration filled the night. The grounds that had served as a disciplined military encampment that morning had now become transformed into a raucous field of festivity, and the sky glowed orange with the light of dozens of bonfires. Vale scanned the scene in front of her as her party rode into camp.

She was not pleased.

The men were behaving as if they had won an entire campaign instead of one decrepit township. As always, Vale had remained behind to oversee the route and capture of the remaining enemy soldiers. Most of Outpost's leaders had managed to escape via the river or were killed in battle, but there were still senior soldiers to question. There were also the dead and the dying to attend to. Although Vale had won a decisive victory, several of her men had still lost their lives – far too many men. She had walked through the streets after they had secured the town, staring down onto the faces of soldiers she had used as weapons. They were no different from the sword she had used to kill the looters earlier that morning. Tools. Devices to achieve a goal.

However, now that the battle was over, Vale found herself in a far more difficult situation. Social occasions never made her comfortable. She recognised the raucous drinking and celebrations as an invaluable part of a soldier's life after a battle – yet still, she had no interest for such social rituals. Or so she told herself, as she urged her horse on through the camp.

Two men staggered alongside each other, arms around each other's shoulders as much for support as it was for a show of friendship. They passed a sodden wineskin between them as they bellowed some old pub ballad at the top of their lungs, oblivious to the fact that no one could recognise whatever song it was they were trying to recite. They glanced up as Vale rode by and gave a cry of praise. One man tried to disentangle himself from his drinking partner to offer his lady a drink from the putrid wineskin. Vale nudged her horse on more quickly.

She found her command tent mercifully quickly and dismounted, handing her reins to a waiting squire. Too tired to acknowledge his salute, Vale removed her helmet and brushed aside the flap to her tent. It surprised her to find the interior buzzing with the conversations of a dozen men who were standing about with goblets and food in hand – senior command officers enjoying their own celebration. Vale hesitated and almost turned to leave, but an officer saw her and immediately raised the alarm. A second later, all faces turned and cheers assailed her.

"All praise, Commander Vale!" bellowed a short, squat officer nearby. Vale knew him as Morbus, a Knight-General under her command. A confident and ambitious man in his early thirties who had been passed over for further promotion more than once. Vale had often noted that he seemed better suited to a life of politics instead of the battlefield.

"Lady Vale!" the collection of officers shouted in unison.

Goblets upraised. Vale waved her hand in an effort to fend off the attention. She looked over the beaming faces of her senior officers, some flushed with too much wine.

How many of you doubted my youth today?

Morbus had for certain. She remembered the short officer's exasperated face, as he openly shared his concerns with his Lieutenant at briefing two days earlier. How many others had worn similar faces? How many had hoped to see her fail so that they might rise higher? She felt a wave of revulsion and an urge to wheel about and storm from the tent.

Instead, she held her resolve and raised her palm toward the sycophants before her in a gesture of silence.

"My commanders, I just don't have the words to describe you," she announced with all sincerity and with confidence that the irony would be lost on her audience. "With the recapture of Outpost, the natural borders of the Iron Union have been fully restored."

A cheer went up inside the tent. Here and there throughout the tent were shouts of "Hail, Bythe." Vale gestured for silence once again.

"You have all conducted yourself with honor today and you have served the Iron Union with pride, but more importantly, the fall of Outpost has given the Ageless an insult they cannot conceal. We have taken something dear from them and we have done it with ease. Today we have humbled them for all to see!"

Another cheer erupted, this one significantly louder than the first. Vale allowed herself a feeling of satisfaction. She knew what to say to these men. She was an excellent speaker regardless of her age.

"Men, the path east is open to us at last. Thanks to you, our lord Bythe will be free to send his mighty Helmsguard to the front steps of the enemy and to kick their rotting doors down. Hail, Lord Bythe!"

The echoed response was almost deafening. Vale raised her fist in the obligatory salute then let it drop. She tried to keep the mask from slipping from her face. She could feel no elation, only weariness and exhaustion, and she looked for an escape from the crowd moving expectantly toward her.

"My lady," Ethan's familiar voice cut through the din, much to her relief. "My lady," he repeated, shouldering his way through the crowd to stand in front of his friend. "There is a messenger from Ironhelm here for you."

"Very well. Let's have it."

Ethan hesitated. "My lady, the courier demands to speak to you and you alone."

Vale raised an eyebrow. "Presumptuous, is he? Then let him wait. I'm in no mood for more orders or dispatches tonight, no matter where they came from." She started to remove her gauntlets.

Ethan looked uneasy and took a step closer to speak quietly into her ear. "The courier is no man."

A quick glance of understanding passed between them.

"Where is she?" Vale asked.

"She ordered the guards to take her to your quarters to await you."

Vale felt her jaw clench. Frustration flooded back into her chest. "Did she now?"

Flinging her gauntlets onto the table, she turned and stalked out of the tent, ignoring the curious glances from her waiting officers. Ethan hustled to catch up in silence. Within moments, the pair had crossed the makeshift parade grounds and stood before the tent that served as Vale's personal quarters.

The usual Helmsguard sentries were gone, replaced by two most unnatural men – if men was even the right word for them. They stood tall and silent, dressed in robes of deep crimson. On their heads, they wore helms of dark-scarlet metal, their human features lost to darkness but for a laboured breathing that emanated from somewhere within. They both turned their heads to appraise Vale as she approached. She paused to address them, when she realized that she was about to seek permission to enter her own personal quarters. Fury boiled within her again and she strode past the two guards and into the tent without a word. Ethan checked himself and decided to remain outside.

The interior of the tent was dimly lit by a coal brazier in the center of the floor. A straw mattress and a chest lay against the far wall and a table and chairs were adjacent to them. Standing in the rear of the tent, partially obscured by shadows, was a tall man garbed head to toe in white. A plain white mask covered his face save for two eye-slits. He stood tall and imposing in an odd posture, a mix of casual indifference and intense readiness. His name was Imbatal, and Vale was always completely unsure what to make of him.

But it was the figure seated at the table that commanded attention. The figure was female, that much was certain but little else was. She was incredibly gaunt. Her arms – too long for her body – stretched out on the table in front of her. Her gnarled and ancient hands were clasped together, her skin greyish, wrinkled, and sickly. The dark robes covered her from head to toe but, unlike her soldier, she did not hide her features.

Vale wished she had.

Her age was impossible to determine; however, she looked like a woman who had lived far past her natural time. Her heavily wrinkled face was long and thin, and her grey hair hung around her face like a wretched mane. But her eyes – sunk deep into dark, shadowed pits in her face – were piercing and cold. They stared out ruthlessly from under her black hood, probing the hearts of anyone they fell upon. All was laid bare before her.

She was Yvorre – Mistress of Spies and Assassins and Royal Counsel to Lord Bythe the Immortal. There were few more dangerous people alive.

According to some stories she was a witch who had discovered the secret to immortality. In others, she was an ancient demon whose powers over darkness challenged even Bythe when he was a younger god. They said that Bythe had tamed her in her dungeon of Kardak and then honored her as a trusted agent within his kingdom. What was known for certain was that she had served Bythe for decades and had leave to come and go as she pleased, to speak to whomever she pleased, and to dispense a god's justice as she saw fit.

And she had been Vale's teacher.

Vale stood there for a moment and regarded the old woman. She raised her ruined face and look at Vale silently in return. Vale knew that protocol demanded she speak first, and yet some sullen and petty part of her resisted. A thin smile crept across Yvorre's face as though she could sense Vale's petulance and was enjoying it.

"Commander Vale," Yvorre's voice cracked and sighed like old, brittle paper. "The Iron Union congratulates you on a well-earned victory today." Yvorre did not look up.

"Thank you, Mistress Yvorre," Vale replied formally. "I honor the Union and Lord Bythe the Immortal."

"Indeed, you do, my young lady, indeed you do..." Yvorre's voice trailed off disinterestedly or disdainfully. She was impossible to read. "Come sit by me." She gestured to a chair opposite.

Vale would have preferred to sit further away; however, she invoked a soldier's discipline and took the seat that was offered to her. The smell was disturbing. Old. Decayed. Diseased. The scent of something unpleasant that she could not quite place. They sat in silence for a few moments as she continued to stare at her own hands clasped in front of her. Vale knew this was a game to throw her off guard, but she did not have the patience to wait it out.

"You have made quite a journey, Mistress," she ventured to break the silence. Yvorre returned her eyes to Vale's. The stare was a cold one.

"Facile pleasantries, Commander Vale? Is that how you intend to lead this discussion?"

Vale felt frustration surge within her once more. Yvorre was always playing games with her. Sometimes as a lesson, but she suspected it had often been more out of cruelty than out of any genuine desire to help her grow. She sighed to calm herself, remembering that she shouldn't let these little games rattle her – that was exactly what Yvorre wanted.

"Very well, Mistress," she rejoined in a more forthright tone. "Outpost has fallen, as I planned. The town was taken completely by surprise, with a bare minimum of casualties. My strategy of an ambush from the south was vindicated, despite the opposition of Morbus and the other Generals who foresaw my doom. Tell me this pleases you at last? Tell me this finally pleases my father?"

Yvorre nodded.

"It does please me, to an extent, and I would imagine Lord Bythe will be likewise pleased once your report reaches him. You should go and celebrate with your commanders."

Vale snorted and looked away. Yvorre knew very well how Vale felt about such insincere gestures and ceremonies – both when they are made and likewise received.

"So, tell me, Mistress, what was the point of this exercise? Now that I've managed to achieve the task that Bythe set me—"

"Lord Bythe," Yvorre corrected her sharply. "Illegitimate daughter or not, you have no right to blaspheme against the last god in this world."

"So, now that I've managed to achieve the task that Lord Bythe has set me," Vale corrected herself, "will I now get an explanation as to why it was necessary? Outpost is nothing more than a small border town. Strategically, it holds no value since it's all but impossible to defend. It was a lawless home for the rabbles of the Outlands."

"And as you said to your men mere moments ago, now it has fallen and opened up the path to the Outer Wild in the east."

Vale rolled her eyes. "Please, Mistress, that was a speech. We both know that Lord Bythe could take Outpost through sheer force whenever he chose to. The ancient alliances of the Ageless have been breaking down for years. Their entire eastern line is now vulnerable. Why the complications? Why was it so important that I personally take the town so efficiently? Was this just another of your tests of my skills?"

Yvorre smiled again. It was a grotesque thing.

"No, Vale, although I admit that it was my desire for you to do so." She leaned forward across the table and her putrid odor increased along with her presence. "You tell me you took the town efficiently, yet how many escaped today?"

Vale looked at her in confusion. "Some of the civilians and merchants made their escape via the river, we can't be certain how many, but we closed the docks within fifteen minutes." She looked at Yvorre closely. "Is that what this is about? Civilians?"

"Your orders were to minimize any and all refugees. Your brilliant tactical mind did not account for their escape via water to the north it seems."

Vale felt anger flow within her once more. It was just like Yvorre's tutelage of her as a child. She never completed a task to Yvorre's satisfaction. There was always a flaw in the execution, and the flaw was always her. In her youth, she had stood for it and accepted it silently, if not meekly. But today something stirred within her. Vale had felt unsettled since the contact with her strange twin earlier in the day. She stood up. Vale saw Imbatal straighten at this sudden movement, but she was too frustrated to care what that strange bodyguard might do. Yvorre did not move an inch.

"And am I now to blame for the seafaring inadequacies of the Iron Union? It's always been our weakness and the Ageless know it. Does Lord Bythe now expect me to overcome a tactical deficiency that he left unaddressed for centuries?"

"You let too many escape." Yvorre's quiet tone made Vale's own frustration escalate by comparison.

"It's not enough that I take the entire town guard by surprise and lose only a handful of my own men – our own men. Now you're displeased because I didn't find a way to secretly blockade the river in advance? You're asking the impossible."

Yvorre shrugged in reply. "You were given your orders; the execution was entirely at your discretion. You simply did not achieve all of your objectives, Commander Vale."

There was that mocking tone in her words again. Not overt but there all the same. Vale took a breath and tried to calm herself. It was strangely difficult to control her surging emotions today, and she suspected she knew why. After a moment, she picked up her chair where it had toppled over and returned to her seat.

"Very well, Mistress," she formally replied. "I will also send out scouts tonight to ride upstream and—"

Yvorre cut her off with an upraised palm.

"You will do nothing more. I have already dispatched my spies to gather intelligence on those who are attempting to flee. I will know where they go."

Vale paused, momentarily confused and attempting to piece together the moves Yvorre was laying out before her. "Then what is it you really want to know from me, Mistress?"

"I want you to interrogate the townsfolk and compile a list of those who are missing or are known to have fled. I shall stay here for a while; this town and its people are of interest to me."

"Of interest to you?" Vale repeated with surprise bordering on amusement. "What about this hovel could possibly captivate your interest?"

Yvorre smiled back in her insincere fashion as if a predatory thought had just occurred to her. "Young woman, have I taught you so poorly? Are you still so distracted with appearances that you fail to behold the powers and opportunities that lie beneath? Your poorly veiled revulsion of me only reminds me of your own limited potential. For as long as you fail to see things as they truly are, you will remain little more than an untamed bitch."

Vale looked away. Her confidence wasn't hurt directly – she was too strong for that now – but Yvorre knew those words would still find their mark within her. Why the god Bythe had delegated the raising of his mortal daughter to Yvorre was a question that still festered within her. She felt the urge to use something against her teacher, but like always, she had nothing. Yvorre was an emotional fortress. Vale got to her feet, hoping she could end the interview and get Yvorre to leave.

"Very well, Mistress. I'll arrange an immediate cataloguing of the town and its residents. We will report those who are missing."

"And those who remain are to be detained here, Vale," Yvorre added in a quiet voice. "My Inquisitor will review them all."

Vale sighed. "Very well." She had no idea what Yvorre was getting at and at that moment, she realized she no longer cared. The rigours of the day were starting to descend upon her, and all she wanted was her bed.

"Of course, my young lady, you must be tired," Yvorre observed without moving. She studied Vale with those unblinking eyes for a moment. "Tell me, Vale, have you seen or heard of anything...unusual...in this place? Any odd reports from your men or possibly even something you may have witnessed yourself?"

For a moment Vale had no idea what to say. She was sure that even Yvorre wasn't capable of reading a person's thoughts, but Yvorre had an uncanny way of knowing what you were thinking. Immediately, Vale's mind turned to the strange encounter with the young woman who wore her face and their inexplicable experience when they had made physical contact. That certainly met the definition of unusual. She opened her mouth to reply when a sudden thought gave her pause.

She doesn't know.

Vale felt a surge of triumph as she realized that she finally had a small piece of intelligence that Yvorre lacked. This unexpected reversal of knowledge was satisfying, and Vale saw no reason to hand the advantage back.

"I'm afraid I don't know what you mean, Mistress."

The equivocal nature of her response brought a flash of anger to Yvorre's eyes. It was a very unsettling expression on her ancient face.

"Do not toy with me, Vale," she warned. "If you have seen or heard of anything that is out of place or unusual, then you are to report it to me. I have been entrusted with the defense of the Iron Union by your father. You have been placed at my disposal. Is this how you repay the training I have given you? With petulant games?"

Vale's patience evaporated into the stale air of the tent. "Training? My father discarded me to you instead of openly acknowledging me as his heir, and you think I should feel gratitude toward you? I should be commanding the Iron Union at his side, not stuck in this backwater town taking rubbish from you. I've led my men to an incredible victory today, and this is how you reward me? What hells have you come from?"

Vale turned to leave when she felt a stunning shock to the side of her face. She staggered back a step, her vision swimming. Vaguely, she could make out the tall figure in white advancing toward her. His blank mask impassive and intimidating. Vale raised her hands to defend herself, but they would not respond quickly enough. A second blow cracked across her jaw and the ground rushed up to meet her. Blood filled her mouth as she lay there. When she opened her eyes, she could see two figures standing over her, one in white, the other in black.

"Shall I have Imbatal kill you now?" Yvorre asked quietly. "Do you realize your father wouldn't stop me? I doubt he would even care."

Yvorre leaned over so her ancient and creviced face filled Vale's vision. She stank of fever and nightmares.

"Heed me, Vale, you live or die by my whim and at my discretion. Godling or not, I will tolerate no disrespect from you."

Vale tried to respond but found that she couldn't. Her head was spinning. Yvorre seemed satisfied that her point was made and straightened herself. From Vale's prone position, Yvorre looked something like an enormous stick insect.

"Since you seem to be in a strangely uncooperative mood, I will relieve you from this assignment and place you somewhere less important. I will discover this town's secrets without you, girl, and you can reflect on your actions this night as you watch your career aspirations slowly dissolve."

Yvorre looked down at Vale with contempt on her face and then left without another word. The tall figure in white lingered a moment longer, regarding Vale's damaged figure from behind his mask. Mocking, intimidating, or merely curious – it was impossible to tell. Then he too was gone. And the world around Vale dissolved into oblivion.

CHAPTER 3

"Fairhaven had earned its name. A beautiful city nestled deep in the mountains of the Outlands, it sometimes seems to have been grown naturally instead of constructed artificially. Yet do not be fooled by its tranquil appearance. Its remote location and unique inhabitants render it a truly resilient target for any potential aggressors."

~Aleasea of the Ageless

Elyn walked in silence and in solitude. She always preferred it this way, just herself and the tall trees of the surrounding forest. Haere-Est was the name given to it by the people of Fairhaven, and while she'd heard stories about the impossibly tall trees in the Outer Wild, she had been unprepared for their natural magnificence when she first beheld them. They were immense, not only in height but also in girth. They stretched hundreds of feet into the air and were so wide that over twenty men would be needed to link arms around their base. It was these trees that Elyn and Leon had first noticed when they arrived at Fairhaven almost two years ago. It was slightly ironic that Elyn seemed to always feel more at home wandering beneath the canopy of Haere-Est than she did inside the city walls. After all, wasn't Fairhaven supposed to be their protective refuge?

No. Not really. Elyn knew that she'd never felt comfortable there and it was hardly surprising. Allies against the Iron Union or not, the people of Fairhaven were understandably put out by a few hundred refugees from Outpost arriving on their doorstep. While they weren't hostile or rude, they also weren't exactly warm in their welcoming. The threat of the Iron

Union's increasing presence in the Outer Wild had cast a stifling blanket over the mood of the city ever since their arrival, and that mood of oppression was only getting heavier. Every month seemed to bring another story of the Helmsguard taking another town or securing another small victory. Even Wheatsheaf had been raided by pursuing soldiers a mere three days after they had fled there from Outpost. Fortunately, Nadine's father had had the good sense, and the good means, to secure their escape via horseback the day earlier. However, they still would have fallen capture to the Helmsguard had not the towns of Stonekeep and Tyne rallied their forces and pushed the Iron Union back to Outpost – at least for a while.

Elyn paused to look about her. She'd been wandering for what seemed like a very long time, and she wasn't quite sure of her exact location. She walked over to a break in the massive trees that lined the path and climbed a steep embankment to get a better look. The Black Ridge of the western edge of Haere-Est stretched out before her, roughly ninety minutes' walk from home on a good day. Elyn estimated that it would be at least two hours before she would return, and judging by the sun, she'd best not wait too long if she wanted to avoid thumping on the town gates, begging the guards to let her in. Considering the number of warnings they had given the youths about getting back to Fairhaven before nightfall, there was every chance Captain Lewis would make an example of her and force her to spend the night outside the walls.

Elyn looked about her again – she was alone. She was as certain as she could possibly be that there wasn't another living being within eyesight, if not within miles. There was another reason she sought solitude like this, beyond the alienation she experienced from the other young women her age – the young women who seemed to regard her as an immigrant with some kind of infectious disease. This was the only place where she could risk turning her thoughts to Outpost, back to that day and the encounter in the alley. The woman with her own face.

"Who were you?" she asked the trees around her in what had become something of a ritual for her now.

She had told Leon once they'd arrived at Fairhaven and were out of danger. Leon had listened with intense interest and questioned every detail, then after weighing all the evidence, had assured Elyn with a perfectly reasonable answer.

"You were in shock, Elyn," Leon had told her with a warm smile. "It happens to everyone. You'd just had your entire world turned upside down by an invading army, there was killing all around you, and, to top it all off, you'd just escaped being murdered yourself a few moments earlier. People see things on the battlefield – they have visions of their own fears or desires come to life. It's a way of the mind coping with something it can't quite handle, I guess. I have no doubt that your mind placed your own face onto the person who saved your life, then you blacked out for a few moments. It's normal, Elyn."

Leon's words had been so reassuring that Elyn had wanted to believe them. For a short time, she actually did, but there had been some kind of strange discordance between Leon's face and his words. It had been something very subtle, so subtle that Elyn hadn't recognised it at first. Instead, it had sat in her unconscious mind, working its way through to her consciousness, until one morning Elyn had awoken to the realization that Leon hadn't truly believed his own explanation. On that morning, Elyn had opened the box of anxiety in her mind once more, and the questions spilled out like serpents. It had been at that moment, lying on her bed with her mind replaying the moment at Outpost and a cold uncertainty bleeding into her stomach, that she had first felt the connection.

It had been brief and sharp like a slap, but it had been there – just for a second. An image of a young woman in a Commander's uniform looking over a map. Elyn could feel her – focused, dedicated, and full of confidence.

Vale.

In that moment, Elyn knew the woman's name. She wasn't sure how she knew this, but it was an instinctive sensation, then it was gone. Elyn hadn't been sure what to do. Was this another hallucination? Was the battlefield horror having a permanent impression on her? Was she slowly going mad, like she'd heard some soldiers do? She wanted to tell Leon, but she found that she couldn't. That look of uncertainty in her father's eyes, that fleeting sensation of discordance, had given Elyn pause. Leon had been worried for her.

For a young woman, that was sometimes all that was needed to completely shatter your certainty.

So Elyn had told no one of this alien feeling. Not her father, not her friend Jason, certainly not Nadine. How could she risk it? Over time she realized that she could contain the feelings – provided that her thoughts didn't stray to Outpost. She also learned that when her thoughts went in that direction, something would happen to her. It was like someone had opened a door in her mind and she had but to step through and see what was waiting on the other side, but she dared not try.

At least she dared not try it in Fairhaven.

A full year had passed before Elyn had first developed the courage to try to understand what had happened to her, but she had been determined to do so on her own, and her walks into the depths of Haere-Est had presented the perfect opportunity. Slowly, over months, Elyn had become more adept at finding that sense and following the path to her twin. In that time, she hadn't manufactured any direct dialogue between them, but the contact was becoming stronger.

Now, safely in the isolation of the forest once more, Elyn closed her eyes and focused on the name.

"Vale."

She recalled the morning when she lay in that alley in Outpost and replayed the moments in her head. She dredged up that feeling of pure terror, when she thought for certain she would die, followed by the surprise and relief of the armored figure cutting down Ray and his crew. The memories stirred feelings and physical sensations, as if it were happening to her all over again, and with those feelings came something else. Another presence starting to flitter on the periphery of her awareness.

She only felt Vale at first — like the existence of another mind pressing against her own. Elyn closed her eyes and focused on the sensation, and in a rush, that small fleeting presence grew in size and intensity in her consciousness until she could see the figure of Vale in her mind's eye. The woman looked almost exactly the same as she had one year ago. Sandy hair over a face with blue eyes. Her jet-black armor polished to a brilliant shine. She was outside. Elyn could discern that the sun was reflecting off the metal plates and the wind ruffled her hair. There was a thrill of excitement as she'd never dared to visualise Vale this clearly.

"*Vale. Can you hear me?*"

Elyn wasn't sure how she did it, but she pushed the thought across the gap between the two young women and sent it toward her twin. The figure in armor looked unsettled and began to glance around, as if she were trying to remember something.

Elyn pushed harder and could now feel the other mind reaching back in her direction. It was instinctive, almost like an animal sensing a scent on the breeze and searching for the trail. Then they made contact.

One moment Vale was casting her eyes around, looking through Elyn as if she wasn't there, the next her eyes came in to sharp focus on Elyn's.

"*Elyn...?*" came the uncertain reply.

For a moment they simply looked at each other. Now that Elyn had achieved contact with her twin, she found that she had absolutely no idea what to do next.

"*Elyn...who are you? How are you doing this?*"

Vale's questions rushed at Elyn like a wind. It was as if Vale's curiosity bore down on her as one physical force. Elyn struggled to maintain contact, but the strength of Vale's will was immense. It buffeted Elyn, and she felt her own will detach itself from Vale's. The figure of the woman in black armor faded from her mind's eye and was replaced with the void.

Elyn sighed in frustration and opened her eyes to behold a scene of the forest bathed in fading twilight. She took in a sharp breath and looked about herself in a complete circle. Disbelief flooded her. The daylight was almost gone, which meant that the brief contact she'd shared with Vale must have taken almost two full hours. She swore. There was now no chance of reaching Fairhaven before nightfall, which would mean an almost certain confrontation with the guards if she was lucky, or a night in the cells if she was unlucky.

She wasted no more time on dwelling on possible outcomes and instead, cast around for the path leading back to Fairhaven. The sun's light was now almost completely gone and the first of the evening's stars were appearing. Elyn quickened her pace a fraction. She told herself that it was to help fight the growing chill, but deep down she knew that she had no great love of the outdoors after dark. The deep forest of Haere-Est was beautiful and mysterious by day, but by night the wilderness took on a sinister air. It almost seemed that the trees around her knew that she wasn't supposed to be there and were doing their best to make her feel unwelcome. She descended the Black Ridge and, with little trouble, found the walking trail that would lead back to Fairhaven. She tried her best to avoid thinking of the consequences that now lay in wait.

• • •

Over two hours later, Elyn was limping behind a soldier as he led the way across the Fairhaven military base toward the command building. The brisk walk back had taken its toll on her, and a single misstep in the treacherous dark of Haere-Est was all it had taken to twist her ankle in a direction that it clearly hadn't been designed to go. She had become a sorry and bedraggled sight by the time she had stumbled across a patrol of soldiers dressed in the blue livery of Fairhaven two hours later. They had been firm but not unkind – even taking the time to splint and bandage her twisted ankle before leading her back home.

Now that they were back, Elyn found her fears confirmed as she noticed the remaining escort was not leading her in the direction of home, but instead toward the command headquarters of Captain Lewis. The Fairhaven military base was large. Elyn had been told that it was the largest one in the entire Outland alliance, even rivalling some of the bases of the Iron Union. It occupied almost a third of Fairhaven's outer circle, which spanned the distance between the old wall of the city and the newer outer wall. The parade ground was dark and quiet, and no lights burned in the barracks halls. The only light came from the torches in the North Tower, high on the outer wall, and from a few half-shuttered lanterns hanging on their brackets. Here and there, guards stood a silent watch or paced without a sound in their nightly patrol.

Elyn's guide led her past the armory and into a large double story stone building that was the central command for Fairhaven's defenses. They walked straight through a dark and empty foyer to march up a broad flight of stairs, and then down a series of equally dark hallways before stopping in front of a closed door. The guard rapped twice on the wood with sharp, loud knocks and a muffled voice replied.

"Enter."

Elyn found herself stepping into a modest-sized office dominated by a large oak desk, behind which hung the bright-blue banner of Fairhaven, covering almost the entire wall. Two large maps covered the wall to her right. One was a map of Fairhaven showing the layout of the city, including the Claiream River running through the center, the old wall which now enclosed the inner town, and the four towers that defended the ramparts of the outer wall. The second was a map of Kovalith, the Outer Wilderness surrounding Fairhaven in the east and the Iron Union in the west. Two halves of a world almost completely split by a wedge of ocean. She was so engrossed by it, she had failed to even notice the one man in the room, who deserved her full attention.

"I ought to have a copy made up for you," an icy voice cut through Elyn's concentration, "if it will prevent me from having to mobilise almost half the Fairhaven defense force in future."

With a start, Elyn broke away from the map and realized that the guard had already been dismissed, and that she was alone with a man sitting behind the desk.

"Stand at attention when I address you!"

Elyn quickly stepped into the center of the room and did her best to stand at attention, if anyone can stand at attention with a bandaged foot and a crutch. She managed an awkward pose balancing on one foot, so she looked more like a terrified flamingo than a soldier at attention. However, if Captain Lewis was amused, he certainly didn't show it. He was glaring at Elyn with a well-practiced intensity that made seasoned soldiers feel uncomfortable. Elyn felt like she would be executed at any moment.

"Three hundred men." Lewis spat out each word. "That's how many soldiers I had to divert from the defense of this town to go looking for a careless girl who had gone wandering in the forest." The Captain rose to his feet and paced over to an open window, hands clasped behind his back, his entire posture one of military discipline.

"I always believe in giving my men a chance to explain themselves before I pass judgment." Lewis spoke to the open window, staring out into the night. "So, I want you to tell me now, why it was necessary for me to endanger the safety of this town and its citizens by sending troops away from these walls and out into the wild."

Elyn stammered and then began recounting the events of the previous eight hours. She omitted the truth of her seemingly magical encounter with a member of the enemy forces bent on their destruction – as she had the nagging feeling this information would not be well received.

Throughout the narrative Lewis stood stoic and unmoving by the window, listening to every word, giving Elyn every chance to fully explain her actions. Although Elyn's less-than-honest telling was muddled and confusing, often requiring her to stop and backtrack several times, Lewis listened with patience and never motioned for her to hurry along or showed frustration at the confusing account. His face, heavily lined for a man of his forty-six years, was completely impassive and betrayed no reaction to any events in Elyn's story. When she reached the end, a silence hung in the air while Lewis gave her a chance to be sure she was finished or add any final details.

"Are you finished?" Lewis asked.

"Yes, sir."

Lewis turned away from the windows and faced Elyn, his eyes maintaining their intensity. "You, like everyone else in this town, were given clear instructions to return to the walls well before nightfall. Am I correct?"

Elyn felt her heart sink. "Yes, sir."

"These orders are not issued lightly or needlessly. I am charged with the responsibility of safeguarding the lives of over five thousand civilians, and the only way I can protect you is if you follow my orders." Lewis enunciated the last few words as he paced around Elyn, so that he stood behind her.

"Surely you are aware of the increased presence of the Iron Union in the Outlands since your hometown fell? Surely, you know that the wild nomads to our north are taking advantage of this by raiding our citizens at any opportunity? That is why the curfew has been enforced, that is why you were told to return before dark – so that you can be protected." Captain Lewis was building his argument, making sure Elyn realized that the reason for the night's turmoil lay solely with her carelessness. She felt like a trap was closing around her and wished an army of the Helmsguard would invade the barracks that moment and spare her any further torture. It didn't happen.

"But seeing as you did not return well before curfew," Lewis continued, "you found yourself in the exact situation we wanted you to avoid. Not only were you in needless danger from nomads – if not the Helmsguard – but we were forced to send over three hundred soldiers off to find you." Lewis' speech was now starting to hit full stride, and he stepped around Elyn so he stood only a few inches from her face. He glared down at her with such ferocity that Elyn wondered if the Captain was about to strike her.

"What would have happened if the Northmen had taken advantage of the situation and chosen to attack us tonight? You, of all people, should know how quickly an enemy can take everything from you if they're given just a moment of opportunity. I'm disgusted that you would put the innocents of this town at risk through your thoughtlessness!"

Elyn winced. It hadn't occurred to her that experimentation with things she didn't understand could have such unforeseen consequences – although it should have. The memories of Outpost were still too fresh, and Elyn suffered a deep surge of shame. Upon seeing that he had made his point, Lewis abruptly turned away and marched back behind his desk.

"You should be thankful you have such a caring father. If it wasn't for Leon's..." Lewis hesitated as if searching for the right word, "...influence, we would have waited until morning to look for you, Northmen and all!" The words hung in the air as the two of them stood there in silence. Elyn stared ahead, praying to any or all gods that the torment would end, that she could receive her punishment and leave the presence of this man.

"Do you have anything to say for yourself?"

Elyn didn't know what to say, but she knew she should offer something. Some sort of explanation or apology, no matter how feeble, but how could she explain this communion that she couldn't even understand? A communion with an enemy officer of all people.

"Sir...I'm sorry. I lost track of time. When I tried to find my way back...well, the forest was frightening. I wasn't sure what to do—"

Captain Lewis seemed to lose his composure, and slammed his palm on the desktop, cutting Elyn off mid-sentence.

"You sound like a child! It was a forest. Are you going to spend your whole life jumping at shadows? What's wrong with you?"

Elyn felt cold shame welling in her stomach. Now that she was back in the safety of the town, her fear seemed foolish. She knew he was right. Even most of the girls of Fairhaven were trained and confident fighters by her age, but Elyn had never had the ability nor the stomach for conflict. It sickened her. Elyn sensed incredulity emanating from Lewis. As if he struggled to understand how such a young woman could be so helpless and weak. If Elyn had felt bad before, she was now humiliated. Lewis sighed and moved his hand over his eyes, rubbing his brow. When he continued speaking, his tone was less harsh.

"It's been a long night for both of us. I think you've learned your lesson enough. Do you agree?"

"Yes, sir. It won't happen again, sir," Elyn mumbled.

"Then go home."

CHAPTER 4

"It is said that the Helmsguard were crafted from Bythe's own image. Men clad in the iron forged by their own god. The strength of the metal that Lord Bythe had created gave the Helmsguard a unique advantage over every other fighting force in the lands. Many spears had shattered against the black iron shields of the Helmsguard, and many wildmen had fallen under their sabers, as they carved an unstoppable path through undefended lands. It was not until the Ageless stood before them that they first tasted defeat."

~Aleasea of the Ageless

Vale stared out over the rough-hewed land that formed the south steppes of the Southern Wastes. The land was broken. A mash of desert waste interrupted by towering shards of rock that speared outward from the ground and jutted high into the air. She had seen nothing like it before. The battlegrounds of the gods. At least that's what they had taught her. A land shattered by Dazh and Narak as they'd fought and sparred for centuries, ripping up the land in the wake of their never-ending battles with one another.

What gods they must have been.

Primal fighters. Warriors. There was honor in following a god like that. A god that was clear and simple. To fight purely for the sake of fighting and nothing else. Vale felt envious. It was, of course, a life that she had no logical right to claim – but she indulged the thought nonetheless. She had walked up here to watch the dawn – at least that was the initial motivation.

But then it had happened. That same feeling she had experienced twice before over the past two years since the day in Outpost. She could sense someone else pressing on her mind.

It had been an alarming feeling. As if someone was entering her head and invading the most precious corners of who she was. Vale had experienced a cold wave of shock both times it had happened. This time she had stood on the crest of a hill watching the first light of dawn creeping over the horizon, then in the next moment the sun had already started its long climb into the sky. And in between? That same cold wave of shock. A few moments of contact – nothing more. Although those few moments of conversation in her mind had clearly taken hours to pass.

Elyn.

She took one glance at the vista in front of her and, noting the retreating shadows formed by the rising sun, realized she'd already spent enough time away from her duties. She brushed her loose hair from her eyes and turned to stride back to the western side of the hilltop.

Who was Elyn?

Yvorre had hoped to discover her that day in Outpost, although Vale's victory at withholding the secret of their meeting quickly proved to be somewhat pyrrhic. She still had no answers, and to make matters worse, she'd now been banished to this gods-forsaken corner of the campaign against the Ageless. As if these setbacks weren't enough of a problem, Vale now found that she was becoming haunted by visions of this strange twin. A ploy of Yvorre? Possibly. But there was something unique about the connection between them that was almost personal. Yvorre – for all of her power and knowledge – was certainly no master of personal intimacy. No, this was not her doing. Vale was certain of that. Yvorre had interrogated dozens of innocents at Outpost, but from what Vale had heard, none seemed to satisfy her. That gave her a strange feeling of comfort although it didn't help.

Clearing the small rocky outcrop and the clump of trees that had obscured her view of the western plains, Vale took in a sight that was a stark contrast to the serenity she had observed moments earlier. The scene demanded respect. No matter how many times in her life she beheld it. No longer muted by the outcrop, a wave of noise swept over Vale as she looked down on a horde of warriors massing. Sunlight glinted off hundreds upon hundreds of polished-black-armored figures in a dazzling display, and the dull roar of men marching and shouting was a sound that could be heard nowhere else in a natural world. As she watched, the tiny figures started to organize themselves into ordered lines. Already more than half of the men had grouped into these regiments, and the rest were marching into well practised formations.

The young warrior allowed herself a few moments to watch the small army group themselves to prepare for battle as she retied her long, fair hair into a neat ponytail. Mounted cavalry groups were waiting toward the rear of the assembly, while more heavily armored infantry with large black and gold shields were gathering in front of them. On either flank of the main body stood formations of archers already in position, and even from this distance, Vale could make out their massive longbows at the ready. She smiled to herself as she noted the total discipline and professionalism of her soldiers on display. Even in her absence, her officers needed no orders or guidance to prepare the troops for battle, and the soldiers followed their standing orders without question. The Helmsguard were the most effective and most feared army in all the known lands, and today yet another gang of savages was about to be reminded of that.

Vale turned away from the spectacle in front of her and started down the narrow trail. The slope became steeper as the path twisted north and led her into a sparse collection of withering trees. Here in the southern plains of Greenridge, the proximity of the Great Southern Wastes was having its detrimental effect on the nearby environment. Where once the grounds had been green and fertile, the encroaching desert was slowly rendering them dry and barren.

Fitting. Even Maelene seems to have deserted her followers in death.

The proud clans of the wastes were now vulnerable, and Vale had been ordered to subdue them. It was a trivial assignment. Not because the Men of the Wastes were no challenge – indeed the very opposite was true. The clans that roamed these lands were as hardened as the warmongering gods who had sired them centuries ago. No, it was a trivial assignment because it was far from the main campaign back in the north, where the Helmsguard were pushing the spearhead of their advance into the Outlands. That was where Vale wanted to be. Where she should have been. Not here, where Yvorre had banished her for the affront two years earlier.

She continued striding down the steep slope, never once faltering or breaking pace on the uneven ground. Within moments, Vale was striding past her encampment's perimeter guard, acknowledging the soldier as he saluted with his left fist pressed flat against his armored breast. She walked through the rows of tents, each of them pure white but for the emblem of a black helm emblazoned onto the side. The morning was already warming even though the sun was not yet an hour over the horizon and the day threatened to be hot, a factor that would favor the wild men who were used to such conditions.

All the more reason to be away sooner.

Vale unconsciously quickened her pace. She soon cleared the main camp and walked out onto a broad field of brown grass which would have stretched as far as her eyes could tell were it not for the thousands of soldiers standing on the field at attention or moving quickly into lines. If the sight had been impressive from the hilltop, then at a close distance, it was almost overwhelming. Thousands of soldiers wearing black plates of armor stood ready to be commanded. Here and there, squires and servants ran to quickly fetch something that had been forgotten or to attend to some final arrangements, while the solders that were already in position stood silent and unmoving.

Vale noticed none of it. She marched up to a large white marquee that stood pitched apart from the others and thrust aside the canvas flap. Immediately, two soldiers standing guard inside snapped to attention, thumping their fists against their chest as she entered. The interior of the spacious tent encompassed a large wooden table upon which lay a campaign map with several brightly colored wooden pieces to denote various troop positions. Ethan had been bent over the map but straightened as Vale entered and offered the same salute as his guards, only he decorated his with a slight grin.

"Ah, here she is," Ethan greeted her. "I was starting to get concerned, You've been standing up on that hill for so long I was tempted to come up and join you. Are the Southern Wastes really that impressive?"

Vale glanced at the map. "I needed time to clear my head. This battle shouldn't be underestimated."

Ethan smiled and nodded. "Of course, my lady."

Vale waited a moment to see if Ethan would pursue the matter further, but he remained silent and respectfully awaited his commander's direction.

"So then." Vale crossed over to the large map on the table, eager to change the subject. "What do we know of our friends in the Rak'Tunga clan this morning?"

"Well, they're certainly not shy. The scouts have returned with reports that the enemy remain assembled fifty miles due southeast and that they appear to be preparing to march. If they set out immediately, they will reach us within two days."

"As we expected." Vale regarded the positions of the wooden markers on the map. Three different colors indicated their infantry, archers, and cavalry, all grouped together in five separate brigades. Fifty miles away the map displayed another army, the wooden pieces were also colored various hues to denote the different categories of archers, infantry, and cavalry.

"We've received word of their formations?" Vale asked with interest.

"Yes. While you were off admiring the view, the first of our infiltration scouts returned. I've spent the last hour trying to make sense of what they've reported. I have to admit I'm a little puzzled."

"Really?" Vale asked, relieved to have something to occupy her full attention.

Ethan gestured to the map where the various markers had been meticulously laid out. "The reports have been confirmed by two scouts, but they're a little unusual."

Vale scanned the map and spotted the inconsistency before her deputy could voice it. "The cavalry formations. There's too many of them and they're too far from the main lines." Her brow furrowed in concentration. This was unusual.

"They're most likely mounted phasmida warriors," Ethan answered.

"And that's even more unusual," Vale continued, circling the map as she pondered the inconsistency. The phasmida were horrendous creatures, much like giant stick insects the size of a horse, but they were not commonly found among the Rak'Tunga clan. It was very unusual to have so many assembled for one army and for them to be so dispersed. Something didn't feel right to Vale.

"I've ordered another deployment of scouts. There may be something wrong with these reports."

Vale nodded absently. "That's possible," she agreed, "but there may be another explanation."

"Another explanation?" an imperious voice inquired. Vale and Ethan both turned to see that Morbus had quietly entered the tent while they were bent over the map. "Are we now to be subjected to more of your insights, Commander Vale?"

Ethan stiffened at the remark but held his tongue. Vale looked up from the map. Morbus stood before them, unarmored and dressed instead in a lavish uniform of black silk with an embroidered white cravat tied around his throat.

"Bureaucrator Morbus," Vale answered, acknowledging the man's recent promotion. "How can I help you?"

Morbus's face broke into an insincere grin as he crossed the tent to stand between them. "I noticed that you returned from your long wanderings on the hilltop, and I merely wondered if you were now ready to return your attention to the task at hand. I have a report to file to Yvorre before sunset today, and she keenly awaits word on our progress here – oh, I mean on your progress here."

Vale suppressed the rising frustration. She would not let Morbus bait her. Upon their return to the Ironhelm two years earlier, Morbus had quickly been promoted to the role of Bureaucrator and assigned to Vale's army. Ever since, he had monitored and reported directly to Yvorre regarding Vale's leadership and her plans. He also rarely failed to remind Vale of his new authority over her. While a Bureaucrator was not in command in a technical sense, one had the authority to monitor and report on the behaviour of any and all Helmsguard within his direct jurisdiction – regardless of rank. In addition, Yvorre had taken the unusual step of granting Morbus veto discretion over Vale's command decisions, should Morbus judge them too unconventional. This insult had infuriated Ethan, but Vale had no choice but to accept it. The only alternative would be insubordination, and Vale suspected that such an action would satisfy both Morbus and Yvorre alike.

"Our progress continues on schedule, Bureaucrator," Vale replied.

"So what's the cause of these furrowed brows then? Not thinking about another unique and spontaneous tactic like you employed at Outpost, I hope? We all know how popular that was with the Mistress Yvorre." Morbus's question had all the outward merits of a friendly jibe and yet no one was fooled by the tone. Morbus revelled in these moments.

Don't be baited.

Vale forced her attention back to the map with a significant act of will.

"The Rak'Tunga have never before employed phasmida in such numbers, but the Paephu clan do," said Vale.

"The Paephu are miles to the east," Ethan replied in surprise. "You think they're here?"

Vale nodded, her eyes looking through the map as her mind worked on the shape of the puzzle. "Yes, I think they are. The explanation fits."

Morbus snorted. "Explanation? You have but a theory. An untested and unproven theory at that."

Ethan levelled a cool stare at the Bureaucrator. "Commander Vale has an excellent tactical mind and proven battlefield experience. Her instincts are known to be reliable."

"Well, yes, that's true, but they're not always in the best interests of the Iron Union, are they? If they were, then our Lord Bythe wouldn't have assigned me to keep a watch over things here."

"Yvorre," Vale corrected.

"I'm sorry?" answered Morbus.

"Mistress Yvorre assigned you, not my father."

Morbus's face hardened at the correction. "It matters little, Commander Vale. What matters is that it's been proven that your instincts require supervision." He stepped closer to the map and made a great show of examining the markings and troop positioning. Ethan and Vale shared a knowing look while he did so. At length, he straightened. "I see nothing too concerning here, the intelligence reports are clearly confused, and I concur with Baron Ethan. You should dispatch scouts to correct the report and all will become clear."

"That will take at least twenty-four hours, probably more. In the meantime, we risk losing the initiative," Vale replied.

"What initiative? The plan is to set up a defensive position and hold here. The Rak'Tunga will come to us in a few days, and we will use our superior skills and cavalry to defeat them from a defensible position."

"No," Vale replied. "We need to break camp and take the battle to them as soon as we can." She walked around the map and pointed to the clusters of markings denoting the phasmida units. "These are not Rak'Tunga, they are the Paephu clan."

A patronising look smeared Morbus's round and well-fed face. "Nonsense! The Paephu are blood rivals of the Rak'Tunga, my young Vale, and they've never allied themselves for as long as I've been alive."

"That doesn't mean it's unheard of. The Men of the Wastes have allied themselves before in different ways, and we're now punching into the heart of their homelands. We are pushing them to take extreme actions in defense, including reluctant alliances. If we take the fight to them, we can exploit this alliance to our advantage. They aren't comfortable fighting alongside each other."

Morbus sighed and walked to stand alongside Vale. "Look, young lady, I understand that someone in your position feels a need to...prove that she can invent something new. These feelings you have are a function of your inexperience, not of some unique insight. The truth is, there's little here that hasn't been seen before."

Vale forcefully pointed to the phasmida units. "Look at them, Bureaucrator. They're positioned in a flanking formation three miles on either side of the main force. These are disbursed cavalry tactics used by the Paephu clan. On the other hand, the Rak'Tunga always use close infantry formations to move slowly and protect their numbers – they never spread out. These additional units are not Rak'Tunga, they are Paephu."

The logic of Vale's observations caused a flash of uncertainty to flicker on Morbus's face. He looked again at the board and regarded it anew. Triumph emerged on his face as a new thought struck him.

"Well...maybe you're right and they're Paephu. There's still no evidence that they're uncomfortable fighting alongside each other." When he turned his gaze back to Vale, his chubby face was all but gloating "In Bythe's name, why would any responsible commander spontaneously change a battle strategy based solely on a fantasy that you've concocted on assumptions! You see, it's a good thing Yvorre had the wisdom to place me here. Your inexperience will cost the Union more lives and result in another failure like Outpost."

"Outpost was not a failure," Vale said in a low voice.

"Tell that to the dead soldiers. Yvorre did not achieve her goals. I hear even Lord Bythe was displeased."

Vale didn't believe a word that Morbus uttered. She knew Yvorre well enough to be sure that she would keep Morbus in the dark regarding her true plans, but that didn't stop him from lying to the rest of the men about his importance. It stung Vale that her own soldiers would be repeating these lies to each other in their mess halls and tents. She breathed in gently and forced her voice to calm, but when she spoke it still had the edge of a blade.

"The Paephu and the Rak'Tunga are not working well together. We have evidence," Vale repeated.

"What evidence? Your gut feelings are not evidence, I'm afraid," Morbus replied.

"Tell me, Bureaucrator, what is the recommended formation distance of a cavalry unit?"

Morbus's eye narrowed in pudgy sockets. He sensed Vale's attempt to expose his lack of military knowledge but was prepared to thwart her. "No more than three hundred feet," he replied with satisfaction. "Any experienced commander knows to keep his cavalry close to the infantry so the units can protect each other."

"Even at rest?"

"My dear Vale, especially at rest. That is when cavalry is most vulnerable."

Vale slammed her palm onto the map in a display so unexpected it made Morbus start. "Then why is their cavalry positioned three miles away from the infantry? Are you suggesting that the seasoned warriors of the Rak'Tunga know less about basic military tactics than you do? Or might it be that these formations are necessary because they can't risk intermingling the armies of sworn rivals?"

Morbus opened his mouth and then closed it again as his slower mind tried to grasp the logic that Vale had outlined. Ethan simply looked impressed with the insight.

"The Paephu's presence resolves the question of the cavalry numbers, and their disunity also explains their dispersed formations. If we move out now, we have a chance to put them on the back foot before they can overcome their disadvantage. If an enemy is unsure of himself, then an unexpected attack will only inflame his uncertainty. They won't be this vulnerable when they form up to attack in two days' time."

Morbus was silent for a few moments. When he replied, there was a sullen quality to his words. "Still a theory. Nothing more. I will not authorise such irresponsible tactics based purely on your whims, Commander Vale. You may dispatch the scouts and we'll wait for their report."

"Bureaucrator, by then it will be too late. We risk losing the initiative if..." Vale began, but Morbus raised his voice to an almost shrill pitch.

"We risk losing lives, Commander Vale! I will hear no more of your instincts. Dispatch the scouts and then let us see the evidence with rational minds. That is what responsible grown men do, my good Commander. I would hope that you would be learning that by now. Good day to you." He nodded and all but stormed out of the tent. His humiliation was clear on his face.

"What a fool," Ethan cursed.

"Maybe, but he's right about one thing. I can't execute my plan without his approval." Vale sighed and leaned on the table. Why was it always so hard? Were they trying to break her? "Redeploy the scouts. Then let's wait another day to learn what we already know."

Ethan saluted and left the tent without a word. He knew his friend, and he knew that in moments like this, it was best to leave the daughter of Bythe to her own black mood.

CHAPTER 5

"Many years ago, the Council established its own means of supplying food to the thousands of Fairhaven inhabitants, rather than relying solely on the farmers and merchants. The Council warehouses would purchase a farmer's produce and distribute it fairly through food halls and soup kitchens throughout the city. Although a farmer could do far better by selling his stock at the market, and the goods at the market were always of a higher quality than the food halls, the system made sure that no resident of Fairhaven ever starved or went hungry."

~Aleasea of the Ageless

The twisted ankle throbbed, but Elyn tried her best to ignore it. The fact that the book she was studying held absolutely no interest for her didn't make that an easy task. It seemed that almost anything could tug her attention away from what she was supposed to be doing. Tynel had given her the task of studying the scintillating topic of how to fertilise Fairhaven's silver rose bushes in the springtime. At least the groundskeeper had allowed her to read the chapters wherever she pleased, instead of remaining cooped up in the appallingly humid greenhouse, which doubled as her classroom.

Instead, she was sitting on a small wooden bench under the shade of a large tree that was shielding her very well from the early afternoon sun. The warmth combined with what little sleep she had had the night before was making her drowsy, and she brought her hand up to stifle a yawn. She placed the open book down on her lap and stared out across the rolling green pastures for what must have been the hundredth time. The farmlands and grazing fields stretched for miles around Fairhaven in all directions, work sheds and fences marking where one farmer's claim ended and another's began, and while there were several small huts dotting the landscape, no farmhouses were to be seen. No one would dare live outside the protection of the city walls this close to the mountains and the Northmen.

Elyn was still feeling sheepish after her encounter the night before. It surprised her that the gruff, old caretaker hadn't mentioned a word about the previous night's commotion and **had** thrust the book into her hands with a mumbled order to read the first three chapters somewhere outside. Surprised, but not concerned; they were both beginning to realize that Elyn had little talent or interest in gardening.

"Well, well... a beautiful day and guess who's reading a book outdoors?" a familiar voice called out.

Elyn smiled to herself but refused to give her heckler the satisfaction of turning her head and instead, pretended to take a feverish interest in the correct ingredients of compost. Within moments a large youth with closely shaved white hair came jogging over and threw himself onto the bench, deliberately jostling Elyn as he did. He was of the same age as Elyn, but was taller and appeared well built beneath his pale-blue uniform of a Fairhaven Military Cadet.

"Y'know," Elyn commented dryly without looking up from her book, "those of us who actually know how to read occasionally like to do so."

The white-haired boy snatched the book from Elyn's hands and glanced at the pages. "Oh right, I'm sure flower-potting is considered the conversation topic of choice among Fairhaven's intellectual elite."

Elyn shook her head but made no attempt to reclaim the book and instead, shifted across the bench to make room for her friend. "So why are you out here? Are you thinking of a rewarding career in botany?"

Jason grunted in disgust and thrust the book back into Elyn's hands. "From what I've been hearing this morning, you should be in the stocks rather than sitting here reading books. Why am I hearing that you've been out all night wreaking havoc?"

Now it was Elyn's turn to grunt in disgust. She was trying her best to forget about her ordeal, but she should have realized she was going to be forced to relive it countless times over the next few days. What made it worse was that her best friend was now looking at her expectantly, as if she was some kind of brave rebel. For a moment, she considered changing the story, making it sound like there had been some dramatic encounter with the Northmen. But Jason and Elyn had been friends since she arrived in Fairhaven, and she couldn't lie to him. She drew a deep breath and started to recount the tale in all of its unglamorous detail – omitting the contact with Vale. Unfortunately, this simply made Elyn appear even more the complete fool of the story, since she didn't even possess a valid reason for losing track of time. When she was done, Jason shrugged and turned his attention to something on the horizon.

"Ah, who cares? Don't worry about what anyone says. It'll be forgotten by the end of the week, probably sooner."

Elyn sighed but smiled at him. Jason always stuck by her no matter what. Within the first week of her arrival as a refugee, they struck up a friendship. They had sent most of the younger refugees to the stockyards to join the apprenticeship training with the other youths. The task of the week had been animal husbandry, and Elyn was to understand what it meant to milk a very irritable and unforgiving goat. Within hours, it had become obvious to Elyn that a clear pecking order was established among the groups and that there was a distinction between the native children of Fairhaven and the refugees. A distinction that had been reinforced by a lanky young man named Nathan. Nathan was the sort of boy that seemed to labour under the bizarre fantasy that his level of attractiveness was somehow stronger to women new to him. So Elyn bit her lip when he swaggered over to compliment her on her skills at milking body parts. Elyn couldn't tell if he had been attempting witty banter or inappropriate condescension, but she'd tried to ignore him in the hope that he'd lose interest. He didn't. At the detection of her passive and unaggressive posture, Nathan's observations became increasingly bold. None of the others helped. They well knew Nathan as a spoiled son from one of Fairhaven's wealthier families. By contrast, her designation as an outsider gave Nathan free reign without fear of interference. At least, that had been the expectation.

"Hey, Nathan, if you're after a partner, the cows are waiting for you in the pens as usual."

The unexpected jibe had sparked a rustle of laughter among the others. Nathan had turned in outrage but froze when he saw the much larger figure of Jason walking over to him.

"C'mon, off you go. I don't think you're her type," Jason had said with a quick wink at Elyn before turning his grin back to Nathan. After an all-too-obvious moment of hesitation, Nathan had pretended to lose interest in Elyn in an attempt to salvage his dignity before walking away.

Jason was the son of a modest clockmaker – one of the few in Outpost – and while his father had tried to school him in the arts of this complex and somewhat cerebral craft, it had quickly become obvious that his son's talent lay in more physical areas. It had not surprised anyone when Jason found himself accepted into a cadetship within Fairhaven's military, while most of the other youths had been enrolled in the usual series of mundane apprenticeships. His presence in the stockyards that day had been pure co-incidence, but his status as a cadet, along with his obvious physical capability, meant that the others always viewed him with respect.

Their friendship grew from that first chance meeting, and Jason seemed to view her as something like a younger sister – despite their identical age. Elyn never quite connected with the other girls in her age group, and Nadine's status as a noble meant that she was rarely around the common girls, so Jason soon became her frequent companion.

"C'mon, Elyn," Jason suddenly sounded cheery, as if he had decided to try to take Elyn's mind off her troubles, "if you've finished memorising the art of shrub pruning, let's go and do something else."

"Sure, let me drop off these books at home first," Elyn replied as they both got off the bench and started walking back toward the city walls.

"So how long are you going to be walking like an old woman for?" Jason asked, noticing her walking crutch for the first time.

"Only for a couple of days."

"Good, then you won't have to miss out on the tournament, will you?" Jason commented with his mischievous grin.

Elyn groaned – she had forgotten about the Wellspring Festival, which was due to be held at the end of the week. The event marked the annual ascension of Fairhaven's youth to the age of adulthood. There was all manner of dances, songs and performances by the girls and boys becoming adults this year. Every Ascendant was required to take part in what was supposed to be a friendly contest of weapons skill but in reality, had become a fierce test of physical strength and skill among the city's youth. Both the males and females competed, as everyone in Fairhaven was expected to defend at arms if called upon. Every year, the entire population of the city gathered to watch as the Ascendants dueled each other in pools and rounds of elimination until they announced a champion. That Ascendant would then be regarded as something of a local hero for the next few months, and he or she was usually elevated to a ranking officer not long afterwards.

Unfortunately, Elyn's skill at swordplay was worse than her knowledge of botany, and all she had to look forward to was a day of humiliation as she was eliminated in the first round in front of a crowd of people.

"Maybe I can keep this bandage on for a bit longer," she mumbled. Jason laughed and nudged her lightly in the ribs.

"Oh no! You'll have to compete with the rest of us. It's only fair."

"Fair?" Elyn glared at him. "What do you know about fair? You've known how to swing a blade since you were child. I'm surprised the Council didn't rewrite the city laws to allow you in as a cadet the moment you were old enough to walk! You're the favorite to win. The actual contest is just a formality for you!"

Jason laughed as the two of them passed under the thick stone arch in the city wall that formed the west gate. Wooden warehouses and storage yards dominated the outer west side of Fairhaven. Horse-drawn carts laden with sacks of grain or vegetables rumbled over unpaved streets, and workmen scurried back and forth to keep the supply of food and materials flowing into the heart of the town. Old farmers in wide hats pushed wooden barrows of tomatoes and turnips and potatoes into several Council-owned warehouses that would purchase their goods for a fair price.

"Well, I wish I had your confidence, but we're not talking about me. C'mon, Elyn, let's get you down to the practice yards. I could probably make a decent soldier out of you before the tournament."

Elyn turned her head away and stared at the rows of wooden warehouses lining the dirt-packed street. "There's no point – you know that. I think I set the record as the most inept soldier-in-training when I did my time at the base last year."

Like most of the other youths who were not accepted as cadets when they reached fifteen, Elyn had only been given three months of compulsory weapons training and during that time, had managed to inflict more damage on herself than anyone else.

"I think the quicker I can be out of that tournament, the better it'll be for everyone." Elyn turned back and gave her friend a grin. "Why would I want to prolong everyone's agony by trying to stay in there longer than I have to?"

Jason rolled his eyes in mock disgust. "Well then, I hope I get to face you in the first round. I'll toy with you for so long you'll have to end up hitting yourself in order to be disqualified."

"I don't think that's going to be a problem," she deadpanned. Jason snorted a chuckle, Elyn's composure broke a moment later and both of them began to laugh loudly as they turned down another dirt street.

After a further few minutes of walking through the narrow streets, they passed under one of the many arches in what had once been the wall around the Old City and passed into the inner ring of Fairhaven that now housed its population. Here the streets were lined with smaller buildings one or two stories high and all squeezed together. The cobblestone streets became even narrower as Elyn started to lead the way through the maze of small alleyways toward her home. Leon lived in the very modest apartments afforded to most Council clerks and bureaucrats.

As they walked, Elyn glanced up the quiet alleyway toward her house and froze. A figure had emerged from the door to her house and was now retreating down an alley to the right. Elyn's shock was at the figure itself. It was shrouded in a deep-violet cloak that seemed to billow about his feet as if touched by an unfelt breeze. Elyn clutched at Jason's elbow, halting him in his tracks.

"Jason, look!" she hissed. "Ageless!"

Jason's head whipped up as he too froze in place.

"Damn me!" Jason whispered in awe. "What's he doing here?"

Elyn didn't answer. She had seen a member of the Ageless only a handful of occasions in the time she had been in Fairhaven, and on those rare occasions, there had been only a single figure, robed head to foot in deep violet, standing in the distance. She had seen one last year, standing beyond the crowd, when Lieutenant Lewis was promoted to Captain, but she had not laid eyes on one since then and certainly never this close. Elyn watched as the figure rounded a corner at the end of the alley and vanished from sight before she realized that her arm was being tugged toward the alley.

"C'mon, Elyn. Let's follow," Jason whispered. Elyn was too shocked to respond and was dragged halfway down the narrow lane as a result.

"Wait! What are we doing?" Elyn hissed as she tugged her arm free. "Have you lost your mind? You know how dangerous they are!"

Jason grinned in reply and jogged to the end of the alleyway, leaving Elyn to glare after him in frustration. Jason had always been the one to drag them into trouble since she arrived from Outpost, daring her to siphon ale from the taverns' barrels or seeing if he could convince her to clamber into one of the watchposts to see what the guards kept up there. Elyn was always afraid, but somehow Jason's encouraging smile gave her the confidence she'd needed to be foolish.

So, despite Elyn's burning desire to find out what the Ageless was doing in her home, she was not surprised when she found herself hobbling to join Jason on the corner. She craned her neck to peer over his shoulder and saw the robed figure gliding down another long, narrow laneway between two large stone buildings. The deep violet robe seemed impossibly long as it billowed out both before and behind the magician, apparently never touching the cobblestones. The figure seemed to glide along the path with unerring grace, and within moments, it had reached another corner and disappeared.

"He's floating," Jason mumbled and looked at Elyn. "I didn't know they floated?"

Elyn rolled her eyes and elbowed him in the ribs. "How should I know? Come on, let's head back"

In reply, Jason rounded the corner and ran further up the alleyway, motioning for Elyn to follow. By the time she limped to the next corner, Jason had already been crouched there for a few moments, and he raised his palm in warning as Elyn approached. She hesitated before creeping the last couple of feet and looked at him.

"He's stopped," Jason whispered in a barely audible hiss. He crouched, as if he was halfway in deciding between getting ready to follow the Ageless in one direction and bolting for his life in the other. Elyn held her breath and noticed her heart thudding like a war drum in her chest. Why was she doing this? Inviting even more trouble onto herself after the incident last night? But then, what was the Ageless doing visiting Leon? She craned her neck around the corner to peer down a slightly wider alleyway that was packed with barrels and littered with hay and other rubbish. The Ageless stood still and silent in the middle of the lane, nearly twenty feet from them. He might have been a statue had it not been for the robes that continued to billow on an absent wind. A thought cut through Elyn like ice.

It knows we're here!

Her heart started to pound even harder, and she wanted to be far away from that alley. She tapped Jason on the shoulder and jerked her thumb back in the direction they'd come. To her surprise, Jason nodded and started to back away from the corner, hooking Elyn's arm over his shoulder as he did so. Together they trotted back up the alley toward the safety of the main street. Elyn's injured ankle started to throb under the strain of jogging, but she paid it no mind. All that mattered was getting away from whatever was under that purple cloak. As they reached the corner leading back to the street, Elyn glanced over her shoulder and her blood froze – the figure was now standing at the spot where they had knelt moments before. She could feel its unseen eyes boring into them under the shadowed hood. Elyn gripped her friends' shoulder and let out a strangled cry. Jason didn't look back and started running to the safety of the street, half dragging Elyn alongside him until they burst onto the wide, cobbled road. For minutes they continued to lurch down the street, pushing past farmers and merchants, oblivious to their complaints and curses until Jason untangled himself from Elyn and collapsed onto his hands and knees. Elyn immediately joined him on the side of the road, sucking in as much air as her lungs would hold, her ankle burning as bad as it had the night before. She glanced up, seeking a robed stalker, but saw only the throng of working men moving up and down the street.

"Don't tell me he followed us, please," Jason wheezed without looking up.

"I don't think he came past the alley," Elyn replied after a moment. "Damn me! That was stupid. And damn you!"

Jason only shook his head in reply, but he still didn't look up.

"It's going to be a bloody miracle if I'm not hauled up in front of Captain Lewis again – that's if those bloody Ageless don't come for us themselves," Elyn added.

She was getting angry now that the fear was subsiding. What was Jason thinking, dragging her into more trouble after everything that had happened last night? That Ageless had known they were following him, had actually looked right at them. If half the rumours she heard about them were true, then it was best that she and Jason flee Fairhaven that minute. The Ageless tolerated neither intrusion nor interference into their affairs, and everyone knew the fate of those who had tried.

Why were the Ageless visiting her father? Did they know about the strange visions Elyn had been experiencing? What had her father told them? She felt sick.

"I'm sorry, Elyn," Jason muttered at the ground.

This suddenly seemed very different to stealing beer or sneaking into watchposts. This time there was no sense of bravado among either of them, only blessed relief that they had managed to escape. For Elyn, it was a familiar feeling. She glanced over at her friend and sighed.

"Forget about it, Jase." She tried to make her voice sound lighter than she felt. She was desperate to get home to find out what had happened. "I think I'm going to go home."

Jason said something in reply, but Elyn didn't hear it. She was limping back down the street toward her home as quickly as she could. Frustrating minutes later, she was fumbling with the latch on the wooden door of her house. Someone had locked it.

"Pa," Elyn called as she thumped on the door. "It's me. Open the door."

Moments later the latch clicked, and the door moved open to reveal Leon's round face masked with concern.

"Elyn? What are you doing back? Is everything alright?"

Elyn looked incredulous.

"What do you mean? Are you alright? Pa...the Ageless..." She pushed past her father as she half-stumbled into the small apartment. Leon closed the door behind them and relatched it. "I saw him leaving. What was he doing here?"

A strange look passed over Leon's face as he crossed the small room and returned to his seat at the table. Various papers and council records were strewn across its surface, and an ink-stained writing brush lay atop an ink pot. As a clerk for Fairhaven's Hall of Records, Leon received these modest accommodations in a respectable, if not affluent, section of the town. The building that housed them was of a far better standard than many people had to settle for. Although the rooms were of a modest size, the two of them had done quite well at making the space homely. Several large rugs covered the bare stone floor, and two padded and comfortable-looking chairs were positioned in front of a crackling fireplace opposite the door. The small table where Leon now sat, occupied the right wall next to the door, and a small door leading into their shared sleeping quarters occupied the left wall.

Leon didn't answer as he took up the brush and began scanning the papers as if looking to get back to work.

"What are you doing back from your lessons so soon? You haven't been sneaking off again have you?"

The blatant attempt to turn the subject caused a welling of frustration in her.

"Leon!"

The use of his first name made Elyn's father look up with raised eyebrows, then he sighed and replaced the brush atop the ink pot.

"Elyn, don't overreact. The Ageless protect this city and watch over all of us. Just because they aren't often seen doesn't mean they're not there. You shouldn't get excited at the sight of one."

"Yes, but why was it here?"

Leon paused for a moment as if choosing his words. "You know that we're still considered newcomers to this place, even after two years. I have a responsibility – we all have a responsibility – to the Ageless and to the townsfolk to help them however we can. Trust isn't easily granted in these times, Elyn."

"You mean they spy on us?"

Leon smiled. "Not spy, Elyn, No. But they do expect information and questions answered whenever they see fit, and it's our duty to give it to them, freely and honestly. This is how we help repay them for their protection from Bythe."

"So, what did they want?" Elyn ventured. "Was this about last night?"

Leon gave Elyn a level stare. "Sit down," he said in a quiet voice and Elyn pulled out the second chair. "I'm not going to lie to you – bless Maelene there's enough of that in these times – but there're some things in life a man just isn't at liberty to discuss – not even with his daughter."

Elyn opened her mouth to reply but Leon stopped her with an upraised palm.

"I know you've got questions and I honestly want to answer them, but you're going to learn that a father has obligations that go beyond what he wants. When we arrived here from Outpost two years ago, there were people that didn't want us here. A lot of people. The war against Bythe and his Iron Union has taken a toll on them. They're just not as open or as helpful as they used to be."

Elyn laughed. "Yeah, I've noticed."

"You can't really blame them, Elyn," Leon continued with a patient smile. "Think about it. Bythe betrayed and killed their god. The Ageless have tried to carry on in Maelene's absence but they're not enough. The war is going badly. The Iron Union is taking territory to the south. The Northmen have taken advantage of the situation and started resuming their raids to the north. People are just losing hope. I've taken on some responsibilities in life, and I'm going to see them through to the end. One day you might too, and when that happens, you'll probably understand.

Just remember that I'd never let anyone hurt you, Elyn. No one has the right to ask that of a father. So you have nothing to worry about."

It was classic Leon. Principled and noble – and today it was a strangely unsatisfying thing to hear. Elyn felt odd. As if something were pressing against her mind. A peculiar feeling of abandonment quickly swept over her. She felt a sudden need to be alone and got to her feet.

"Elyn?" Leon asked with a slight frown creasing his brow.

"Sure. Fine. You don't have to tell me anything. I'm sorry for being worried about you."

"Elyn! You know that's not what I meant."

Deep down Elyn knew she was being unfair, but at that moment she also realized that she didn't want to be nice. She felt a spike of resentment toward her father and wasn't quite sure why.

"Alright," Elyn replied in a petulant tone. She hobbled over to the door leading to their sleeping chambers. "My ankle's hurting. I'm going to lie down."

"Are you feeling alright?" Leon asked. The genuine concern in his voice only inflamed Elyn's resentment. She didn't reply. Instead, she awkwardly shuffled through the door and closed it behind her. She didn't turn her head. She didn't dare confront the expression of dismay on her father's face. She bolted the door and lay on the straw mattress, wishing her mind was as simple a thing to close.

CHAPTER 6

"If there were ever two gods that could be called brothers, it was Dazh and Narak. They chose the form of monstrous men with muscled bodies over twelve feet tall. And what did they do with these gifts? They played and fought as brothers do. They sparred and wrestled for centuries, bringing down entire mountains in their struggles and laying waste to much of the south. It was said their taunts and laughter could be heard as far as the Ironhelm. It was also said that the hardy warriors of the Southern Wastes – who worship them to this day – are direct results of the brothers' amorous bouts with mortals. So great was the bond between these two brothers that when Dazh accidentally killed Narak in their combat, the offending brother took his own life that same day, so they might continue their battles in the heavens."

~Aleasea of the Ageless

The Shrine of the Lord Bythe held a special place among the Helmsguard. Not only did it clearly serve as a sign of worship to their god and protector, it also served as a symbol of conquest whenever the Iron Union seized land that had belonged to the followers of another god. Of course, those other gods had long since departed Kovalith, but that did not make the Shrine of the Lord Bythe any less of an affront to the followers they left behind.

In this case, the Helmsguard had taken a little too much pleasure in first finding, then desecrating a shrine to the god Narak by replacing his statue with the trappings of Bythe the Conqueror. Someone had carved the shrine into a shallow cave in the side of a small hill. As soon as Helmsguard patrols had found it next to their staging grounds, word quickly spread, and the more zealous followers had taken to work. The statue of the well-muscled young man clad only in a loincloth was unceremoniously ripped from its base and tossed into the long grass nearby. Shortly afterwards, cloths of black and red were draped over the cave walls, and someone had located a large-horned helm of black iron to place on the dais of the shrine – the universally recognised emblem of the god Bythe.

Vale now stood at the rear of the cave facing the icon of her father. She wasn't sure what she wanted to do. At the front of the shrine, two young men knelt with their heads bowed in silent prayer. Each of them had one fist pressed against the left side of his chest in the Iron Union salute. Vale watched them pray to her father with a surreal feeling. Men like that would stay there for hours, praying for what? Success? Honor? Happiness? How many of those aspirations were deceitfully incompatible with each other? Would her father tell that to his devout followers? Would he tell them anything at all?

Vale shuffled her feet, allowing the oiled plates of armor to grate in the absolute stillness of the shrine. It had the desired effect as one of the soldiers opened his eyes to see the new visitor before clambering to his feet and alerting his colleague. Within seconds the two of them were at attention, fists still at their chests, only now they addressed the daughter instead of the father. The unrecognised daughter. The illegitimate daughter.

"I'd like a moment, if you please. Ensure that I'm not disturbed." Vale asked the soldiers with a respect and politeness that was obviously unnecessary.

The two men bowed low – too low for Vale's comfort – then left as swiftly as decorum would permit. To these men Vale was more than their commander. Dishonored or not, she was something greater. Vale walked slowly toward the helm on the shrine. She felt uncertainty start to seep through her heart with every step. Why was she here? She never prayed and yet her feet had brought her here today.

My god.

My father.

It had been years since she received any message from her father and well over a decade since she last saw him. How long had it been? She couldn't say. Vale realized that she couldn't even remember the last time they'd met. All she had in her mind was an impression. A god. A father.

Weren't they the same thing to a child? She knelt at the base of the shrine the same way the other men had.

Father.

She bowed her head and closed her eyes.

Father, where are you?

She waited in silence. There was no answer. Vale felt warm tears welling within her closed lids and she was gratified that she'd placed the guards outside. Why was this happening? Her life was once so full of promise. A young officer in training. A daughter of a ruler – unrecognised of course – but that still should have guaranteed her a noble career within the Union. Why did all of that change? Why was she suddenly discarded and left to the cruel whims of Yvorre?

What did I do wrong?

There was no answer.

Alright then, a better question. Why did you desert me?

The second silence that followed her question was as pitiless as the first. Vale sniffed and rubbed her fingers across her eyes in an almost violent movement. This was foolish. Juvenile. She stood to leave when a sensation flooded her. Unexpected, but not unfamiliar.

"*Bythe is your father?*"

Elyn's thoughts rushed through Vale's mind like wind through a door left open. Vale was momentarily stunned. She hadn't expected an answer from her prayers. She certainly hadn't expected contact with Elyn.

"*Elyn,*" Vale silently replied. "*Elyn, how are you doing this?*"

"*I'm not doing anything,*" the young voice answered. "*I'm lying on my bed trying to find peace, and you've forced your way into my head...again.*"

The words surprised Vale. "*Again? You've been listening to me?*"

"*Sometimes I can hear you, but never like this. I've tried to reach you before. Sometimes I feel like I've gotten so close, but I could never break through.*" There was a pause. "*What's different this time?*"

Vale regarded the cold iron helmet of her father and brushed again at the tears that traced her cheeks. She felt naked and exposed. She tried to push aside the emotion that roiled within her, but it was too late.

"*Your father?*" Elyn said. "*You miss him?*"

Vale laughed despite herself. "*Miss him? I never knew him. You'd have to have a meaningful relationship with someone before you missed them, don't you think?*"

"*I'm sorry,*" Elyn replied. "*I've always been close to my father. I couldn't imagine how it would be without him.*"

Vale caught herself. What was she doing? Why was she discussing such intimate details with this stranger? She steadied her mind and prepared to launch into an interrogation, but Elyn spoke first.

"*Vale, who are you?*"

"*Who am I?*" Vale instinctively deflected. "*Who are you? Why do you have my face? Why is Yvorre looking for you?*"

"*Your face? You're wearing my face! You're the one who invaded my home then tried to capture me if you remember? And who's Yvorre?*"

Vale stopped in surprise. It was clear that Elyn knew as little about this as she did. She felt the press of frustration and confusion. She didn't know why she'd expected Elyn to have answers, she'd just assumed that Elyn would know something, but she didn't. Vale could sense Elyn's confusion mirroring her own.

"*Stop that,*" Elyn snapped.

"*Stop what?*"

"*I can feel you pressing through my feelings. It's like you're reading me.*"

"*Elyn,*" Vale began, trying to force a sense of sincerity into her thoughts. "*I don't know what I'm doing. I'm sorry, but I'm as much confused about this as you are.*"

At that moment, Vale could also feel a surge of presence in her mind, as if for a moment, her feelings became magnified before returning to their normal state.

"*You're not lying,*" Elyn answered, and Vale knew that Elyn had also been reading her. This made her uneasy. She tried to process and catalogue the facts before her, but even as she started to do so, she could feel Elyn's presence dispersing through her mind like water seeking out cracks and rivulets in a pathway.

"*Elyn, wait! What are you doing?*"

"*I don't know,*" Elyn said. "*I can't stop it.*"

Elyn was right. Vale sensed Elyn's thoughts creeping deeper into her own. She tried to push back using her own will, but something unexpected happened – Vale's mind pressed deeper into Elyn's. Panic started to swell in both of them. Vale could feel it. She could also sense other things. A middle-aged man with a careworn face. Leon. So much love shared between them. A young man with white hair and a devilish grin. A friend. A town high in the mountains surrounded by trees of impossible size. Fairhaven. Elyn had fled to Fairhaven. Other thoughts were flooding in as well, moving too rapidly for Vale to understand. It felt as if a dam were bursting and an increasing flood of memory were pouring between them – in both directions.

"*Stop!*" Elyn all but shouted into Vale's mind.

What if they couldn't stop this? Vale gathered her wits and forced her mind to a state of calm. It was like trying to stand still in the middle of a raging storm.

"*Elyn! Enough!*"

With nothing less than a supreme push of her mind, Vale forced a momentary break in the clouds of the storm and felt the panic bleed away from both of them. In the brief respite that followed, Vale seized the opportunity and pushed again. Hard. This time she sensed Elyn fly backward from her mind – just like they had in Outpost. And she was gone.

Vale got to her feet. She felt dizzy. Remembering where she was, she looked around, hoping that no one had been watching her. How long had she been here? Hours? She crossed to the entrance of the shrine and lifted the curtain. Outside, the two sentries still stood guard against the midafternoon sky that looked much the same as it had when Vale entered. Upon hearing Vale's movements, both guards turned to attend her. Vale stood watching them in silence for a moment, wondering how to broach the question.

"Thank you both. I... hope I didn't detain you long."

They both shared a questioning look before the taller man spoke.

"My lady, we serve at your command. Take as long as you need and do not leave so early on our account."

Vale felt a wave of relief. The stronger bond had not taken so long to establish. In fact, Vale now suspected the entire exchange had taken mere seconds. She nodded to the guards and walked past them both. She marched toward the tents, anxious to understand what had happened to her – to them.

Leon. Jason. Fairhaven. These names swirled in her mind. How many names were floating through Elyn's thoughts at that same moment? She needed to understand this, but there was no one she could turn to. Yvorre was clearly desperate to find Elyn. Was this why? Was she another daughter of Bythe? Was that why they shared this strange connection? But no, she'd mentioned her own father. She needed a moment to sift through these thoughts. A moment to find the logic here.

"My lady," a voice interrupted her thoughts.

"Yes? What?" Vale snapped as she looked up at the young messenger. Irritation was clear upon Vale's face, and the boy looked uneasy.

"My lady, Bureaucrator Morbus orders your presence in the command tent at once."

Fury rose within her. "He *orders* me?" Vale's words were cold, and the messenger looked distressed.

"I'm sorry, my lady. I was only given a message to relay. He said to tell you clearly that—"

"Let me make this clear to you, squire," Vale spat the words as she advanced to stand within inches of the boys terrified face. "I am in command of this army and no one besides Lord Bythe himself can order me about. Do you understand?"

The messenger went pale. "Of course, my lady."

"You're on half-rations for the next week, squire. See to it."

"Yes, Commander!" The young man stiffened and saluted with his fist across his chest.

"Leave."

The man turned and marched away without a word. Vale felt a touch of guilt at reprimanding a relatively innocent messenger, but the frustration she felt toward Morbus eclipsed it. If she allowed Morbus to sow insubordination among her own men, then she may as well forfeit her command that moment. Anger roiling within, Vale turned and stalked to the command tent. She roughly shoved the tent flap aside and found both Morbus and Ethan studying the map.

"Bureaucrator," Vale declared as she marched into the tent. "You *ordered* me to attend you?" The venom in Vale's voice was clear. Ethan turned to face Morbus with a dark look.

"Oh, my Commander, do calm yourself," Morbus chuckled. "The page overspoke. I merely requested your attendance at your earliest convenience, which is now, I take it?"

Vale glowered at the pudgy man. "I'm here. What do you need?"

Morbus continued smiling as he gestured to the map on the table. "You'll be pleased to learn that the scouts have returned, and they've confirmed the troop deployments as reported yesterday."

Vale crossed to the map. "Then we were right? They're phasmida cavalry units from the Paephu clan?"

"It's unfortunate that we didn't have the opportunity to take advantage of your plan, my lady." Ethan addressed Vale, yet his eyes remained impassively fixed on Morbus. "Had we seized the initiative, we might have put them on a defensive footing, where the phasmida are far less effective in battle."

Morbus's smile melted into a sneer as he turned to Ethan. "Well you needn't fear, Baron. I've put your tactical ideas to good use."

"What do you mean?" asked Vale.

"I mean," Morbus continued, the smile returning to his face, "that I agree with your assessments. The Rak'Tunga will be here within two days. I think they should be attacked and placed on the defensive if we're going to negate their natural speed and aggression."

Vale suppressed a sigh of frustration and forced her voice to a neutral tone. "Bureaucrator, it's too late for that. If they're on the march here, it means that they'll have altered their formations for the march and prepared for battle. Their cavalry will no longer be exposed, and we'll have little advantage to exploit when they get here."

Morbus raised an eyebrow in an expression of surprise that was far from sincere. "You disappoint me, Commander. I would have thought a woman of your vision would be capable of discerning a suitable alternative tactic."

"There is no suitable alternative. We lost the initiative," Ethan shot back in a voice that bridled with frustration. Vale raised a hand to calm her friend to silence. Morbus simply ignored him and instead pointed a stubby finger to the map where the Iron Union army was positioned.

"We will form up here on the plains as planned. When the enemy arrive and take up position to the north, we'll do what they do not expect. We'll launch a series of offensives against their position before they have a chance to launch an attack on us. This move will catch them by surprise and will also force them to take a defensive posture, which will blunt any use of their cavalry." Morbus turned back to them with a face filled with satisfaction.

Ethan shot Vale a look that required no vocalisation.

"Morbus," Vale started, searching for the right words, "this plan will not be as effective as you think. The enemy outmatch us by sheer weight of numbers. If we follow this plan, they will almost certainly form a defensive wall and simply wait for us to exhaust our men while they whittle down our numbers with each failed attack."

Morbus looked as if Vale had slapped him. "What are you talking about, Vale? Of course, it will work. You suggested this yourself."

Vale shook her head and reached for all the diplomacy her frayed temper could afford her. "Morbus, I suggested a full advance while they were unprepared and their units out of position. What you suggest now is a half-measure."

"Half-measure?" Morbus seemed genuinely offended at the term. Vale reflected that as far as diplomacy was concerned, she made an excellent warrior. She knew at that moment that her comments had backed Morbus into a corner, and there was now no way out for him besides escalation. She opened her mouth to remedy the dilemma, but Ethan spoke first.

"Yes, my *lord,*" Ethan spoke the title with sarcasm. "Your plan will be nothing more than a suicide run for those we send out."

Vale clenched her jaw and motioned again for him to fall silent. She knew that Ethan was trying to help, but Vale would have given anything for him to have kept his tongue at that moment. Regrettably, she knew that all hope of negotiation had passed the moment she returned her eyes to Morbus's face. He was now intractable.

"We will see who is correct. This is the only battle plan that I will approve."

"Commander Vale is in charge! She decides the battle plan." Ethan's voice was now almost openly hostile.

"And her plans are subject to my approval!" Morbus shouted back, his injured ego now poisoning his mood.

"You are subverting my lady's authority."

"Are you accusing me of Insurrection, Baron Ethan?" Morbus replied in a low voice.

"Enough!" Vale interjected. "Ethan stand down. Morbus, with respect, you must understand how much risk there is. Any commander who leads these offensives against the enemy will be risking annihilation of men for questionable gain."

A malicious light sparked to life in Morbus's eyes.

"Then I suggest you appoint Baron Ethan to the task. He seems eminently qualified in battlefield knowledge, doesn't he? He certainly has no qualms when it comes to questioning his betters. Let him prove his worth on the field. Perhaps then he may earn his right to speak his mind."

Vale was shocked into silence. Ethan seemed caught between objecting to the lunacy of the plan and the preservation of his honor.

"Yes," Morbus continued, his demeanour now descending into clear hostility. "This is the plan I wish to approve, Commander Vale. You will make the preparations immediately. Should you attempt to subvert my will in this matter, I will see to it that Mistress Yvorre has all the evidence she requires to have you finally charged as a traitor."

Vale felt trapped. She knew that Morbus was overstepping his authority. She also knew that Yvorre was looking for any excuse to formally charge Vale. Fury began to mount.

"He's baiting you both. Don't give him what he wants."

Elyn's voice was a cold shock but a welcome one. Vale felt a strange sense of calm wash over her at these words. Morbus – perhaps mistaking the sudden silence for acquiescence – smiled at them both before sweeping his well-fed figure from the tent without another word.

"I'll commence the planning, my lady," Ethan said.

Vale recovered and shook her head. "Don't be ridiculous, Ethan. I'll figure something out."

"I'm not being ridiculous, Vale." Ethan dropped all formality and looked at her plainly. "This isn't about me, it's about you. If we don't execute this plan, then he's got all the justification he needs to have you arrested today. By the time I've lodged a protest with the Ironhelm, it'll be too late. Yvorre will have you at her mercy in Kardak."

"It's better than sending you to your death."

Ethan smiled in a good-humoured way. "You have a low opinion of my leadership skills, don't you? I'll be fine."

"You'll be slaughtered!"

"No, I won't." Ethan walked over and placed a hand on her shoulder. "It's not going to be easy, but I'll lead the charge. Once the assault fails and everyone can see how futile it is, Morbus will be humiliated and have no choice but to allow you to call off the attack. Even his ego can't excuse sending his troops to slaughter. If he resists in the face of such carnage, then you'll have all the justification you need to defy him. Yvorre's protection only reaches so far."

Elyn still lingered on the edge of Vale's mind. It was a strangely anchoring presence. Vale met Ethan's eyes and nodded. As much as she hated the thought of risking her best and only friend, if they followed his plan, they could expose Morbus and even have him removed from his position – without breaking any laws. It was a clever solution to a difficult problem.

"I'll watch over you Ethan, you have my word. I won't allow any harm to come to you."

"You'd better not. Why do I always do these things for you, Vale?" Ethan replied with a smile. Vale couldn't help but return it.

"Vale, is he in love with you?"

Elyn's thoughts again broke into Vale's mind and her smile fell. Ethan's smile also dropped as he saw the strange look on her face. Misinterpreting her expression, Ethan now seemed embarrassed.

"You'd better see to the arrangements, Baron. We only have two days," Vale said, eager to be alone.

For a moment, Ethan hesitated, as if he were about to say something more, then he simply nodded and left the tent. When Vale certain that she was alone, she turned her attention inward.

"Elyn, who are you? How are you doing this?"

Vale reached out with her feelings and felt a tendril of emotion from her twin. Fear.

"I don't know what's happening, Vale, so yes, I'm afraid." Elyn replied. *"You should be too."*

Vale no longer felt fear. She had driven it out of her heart in the cold towers of the Ironhelm a long time ago. At least, that's what she liked to believe. But today she knew different. Today, for the first time in years, she remembered that feeling. A very cold feeling from her childhood.

CHAPTER 7

"*When our Blessed Mother created Sanctuary, it was not long before she drew followers and disciples to her side. The faithful pilgrims built the town of Fairhaven and strove to adhere to the principles that the name suggests. Fairhaven was a refuge where all could come to be treated equally and justly. The young boys and girls of the town were all enrolled in training and apprenticeships, so that they could choose the vocation best suited to their natural abilities. When the youths came of age, the town would unite in celebration of the Wellspring Festival to usher in their transition to adulthood.*

However, as the war with the Iron Union progressed and the number of refugees grew, Fairhaven's tolerance for outsiders began to wane."

~Aleasea of the Ageless

The following days after the accident seemed to pass quickly for Elyn. Her ankle healed itself well, and the bandages came off sooner than she expected – much to her disappointment, since she was still hoping to avoid the Wellspring Tournament. Tynel, the groundskeeper, had dismissed her from his classes early by politely telling Elyn that he had taught her all he could. Elyn realized that this statement could be interpreted in different ways but decided against clarifying what he had meant. The rest of Fairhaven was bustling with preparations for the festival, as it was every year. The city seemed to adopt a cheerful atmosphere as everyone prepared to accept another generation of men and women into their fold. Bright banners decorated the streets around the center of Fairhaven and fresh flowers hung from shopfronts and decorated the windows of houses.

The day prior to the tournament, Elyn stood in the square opposite the massive edifice of the Temple of Maelene. Despite the fact she'd lived in Fairhaven for some time now, the building never failed to make an impression on her. Resting her eyes on the structure felt easy, as if it were a place safe and familiar and good. Elyn supposed that was the entire point of the design. It was built from the dark grey stone of the nearby mountains, yet it seemed to glimmer in the sun with a hue that may have hinted of blue and green, but Elyn found the color wasn't quite there if she ever tried to focus on it. Vines and foliage had entwined themselves around the façade a long time ago, giving the building a look that seemed almost natural. As if it had grown there without help. Elyn also supposed that impression was intentional. The Temple formed the center of the town, all roads leading outward from this magnificent centerpiece like the rays of a sun in a child's drawing. It was also the home of the Ageless.

Elyn could feel Vale stirring within her mind. Ever since they had established their first rapport in Bythe's temple two days earlier, Elyn had found their contact was now almost constant. Not that Vale was always present and active in her head, but Elyn could somehow feel her presence lingering there like a weight. Elyn knew things about Vale as well. She could see the towers of the Ironhelm in Vale's memory and the years of training under Yvorre. They had both reached out to each other over the past two days, yet despite their brief exchanges and shared memories, neither of them understood their relationship any better.

"*It's less impressive than I expected it to be,*" Vale broke through.

"*It's not the soaring towers of the Ironhelm, no. Not all of us have a god as our town planner, you know?*"

"*So, this is the home of the all-powerful Ageless,*" Vale continued. "*You shouldn't be letting me see this. You know we're coming for them.*"

"*It's not like I can keep you out of my head, even if I tried to. We both have that problem now, don't we? Unless we want to lock ourselves in our bedrooms, it looks like we're both unwilling spies for the enemy.*"

Vale was silent for a moment before voicing her thoughts again.

"*The Ageless kill people. They've killed innocent civilians in our towns. They're agents of terror. You know that, don't you?*"

Elyn sent the emotional approximation of a shrug back in Vale's direction.

"The only agents of terror I know are the ones that invaded my hometown and took all we had. I seem to remember them killing civilians too. Perhaps you need to look in a mirror sometime?"

If Vale tried to reply, Elyn couldn't hear it. Instead, her attention was stolen by the sneering drone of a familiar voice.

"Look, it's my favorite woman."

The comment sliced through Elyn's thoughts and she stiffened. The slender, white-haired figure of Nathan was walking down the path from the temple toward her. A tall boy who Elyn instantly recognised as Shane accompanied him. He was thick with muscle and wore a cruel face with short spiky hair. Unlike Nathan, Shane had come from the streets where he had learned that his natural size and strength gave him power over others, and Elyn had seen him viciously beat other boys for little or no reason.

"What are you doing out here, Elyn? Would you like to come and join us for a drink?" he asked with a slightly sinister air. Ever since their first encounter, Nathan had never forgiven Elyn for his humiliation at the hands of Jason, and, given that Nathan hadn't the courage to redress this with him directly, Elyn had become the surrogate target for his wounded pride.

Elyn resisted the temptation to say anything. She knew only too well that anything she said would either sound weak and humiliating if it was conciliatory or be used as an excuse for escalation if it was aggressive. Silence – as always – seemed the safest option. Nathan wasn't dissuaded so easily.

"What's wrong, Elyn? Are you too good for the local boys?" he took a step closer to her and forced her to meet his eyes.

"No...I'm just waiting for my friends," Elyn replied neutrally. Diplomatically. Carefully.

Sensing that he was not going to get the fight that a stronger girl might give him, Nathan pushed.

"You're waiting for a customer, aren't you? You know that's all you're going to be good for now that you've come of age. You're just going to be another whore on our streets. Still, at least that's something for us to look forward to."

He placed a hand on Elyn's shoulder. Elyn took an involuntary step backward. Her mind worked furiously for something to say but she couldn't think of anything. She could feel Vale pressing against her mind – speaking to her – only the words were washed away in a flood of rising fear.

"Come on, Nathan," Elyn ventured. "Why can't you just leave me alone? What have I ever done to you?"

Negotiation. Again, the safe approach.

"That's the problem. You haven't done anything to me yet. I think it's time we changed that, don't you?" Nathan moved his hand down from her shoulder and ran it gently over her breasts. "I know what I'm going to do to you soon," he said in a softer voice.

Fear stopped her from answering. The less provocation she gave them, the sooner it would be over.

"Is that the girl who had half the guards looking for her the other night?" said Shane standing behind Nathan's shoulder.

"That's right. Now Captain Lewis hates her as much as everyone else," Nathan said. "Maybe he'll draft her to service the regiments. Know what I mean? What do you think? Right?"

Shane laughed but without too much interest. He looked at Elyn as if she were a passing curiosity before glancing around impatiently. "C'mon, Nate, I want to get to the pub."

Realizing that his moment was over, Nathan quickly fell in line, suddenly pretending that Elyn wasn't worth his effort. "Yeah, me too. Let's get out of here."

He winked at Elyn before walking off with Shane in the lead. Elyn watched them walk down the dirt road away from her, laughing and joking among themselves, their torment forgotten. She only wished she could feel the same. Her heart began to slow, and the sickening fear began to subside only to be replaced with shame.

"*Why didn't you do something?*" Vale's judgment flooded in and Elyn's humiliation was complete.

"*I didn't want to,*" was all Elyn could manage in reply.

Confusion surged from Vale. "*I don't understand, Elyn. How could you just stand there and let him do that to you? How do you control your temper like that?*

Elyn smiled at the misguided praise.

"*I can't control something that isn't there, Vale. I don't feel anger when something like that happens, I only feel fear. I wish I could feel anger – it'd be useful – but it just doesn't come.*"

Vale was silent for a while. Elyn slowly turned back to the Temple and glimpsed something that she feared even more than Nathan's gang – Jason's eyes. He was crossing the square with Nadine by his side, concern and anger written on his face.

"What was that about?" he asked as they approached.

"Nothing. She's fine," Nadine answered for her. An understanding look passed between the two young women, one that was completely lost on Jason.

"If they're taking it too far, Elyn, then say the word," Jason glowered at the retreating backs of Nathan's friends. "I'll sort it out. You don't need to put up with that."

"C'mon, Jason, leave her alone," said Nadine. It was different for her. Nadine seemed to have that effortless gift of respect and acceptance no matter whose company she shared. Nathan had never dared approach her. Nadine wasn't alone in this. Like any hostile ecosystem, a pecking order had to be established, and the youth of Fairhaven would either assert their position and have it respected, or they would find a position imposed upon them. Elyn clearly fell into the latter category. The fact that Nadine couldn't directly help Elyn was a source of both awkwardness and shame for both of them. Elyn knew that Nadine had worked hard to earn the acceptance of Fairhaven's wealthy families and their daughters – no small achievement given that she was an outsider. They both knew that Nadine's hard-won acceptance could be shattered in an instant if she agitated too hard in defense of an outsider who was generally looked down upon due to her meek demeanour. Fairhaven valued strength and courage in all citizens, values that were very painfully absent in Elyn. Nadine had tried urging Elyn to be more like her, more confident and forthright, but words are so easy when you don't have a torrent of fear crippling you from within. Over time Nadine relented when she realized she was only making Elyn feel worse.

Jason shook his head in disbelief but surrendered to the secret and eccentric customs of women. He walked over to sit on the low stone wall that bordered the River Claiream. "So, are we all ready for tomorrow?" he asked of everyone and no one in particular.

"Pretty much," Elyn answered, relieved for the opportunity to shift the conversation. "Well, as ready as I'm going to be."

Jason flashed her a grin in reply. "Remember, Elyn, it's the participation that matters," he added in the tone of a teacher.

"Sometimes I'm not sure why we're even bothering," Nadine sighed. She also brought herself alongside Jason, so the three of them now sat along the wall. "It's been two years and they still haven't fully accepted all of us. What's the point in pretending that we're all one happy community when half of them would like nothing more than to hand us over to the Union?"

Jason shrugged. "I dunno. It's not just you. There's been what...three other settlements that've fallen in the past two years? And Bonehall won't take refugees, so most of them seem to make their way here."

"Nice to know their hatred isn't personal," Elyn observed.

"Well, I think that you probably need to cut them a break," Jason continued, ignoring the quip. "The war isn't going well in the south, and now the Northmen have decided to take advantage of the situation and start up their raids again. On top of all that, they still haven't gotten over Maelene's fall. They're not ready for this. They're scared."

"You're right," Nadine sighed. "When did you get so mature and level-headed?"

"What about the Ageless?" Elyn broke in with a heavier tone than she intended. "Where are they in all of this? Skulking about in their temple and sneaking around people's homes?" Nadine – knowing nothing of the encounter with the cloaked figure two days ago – looked at Elyn in faint surprise. Jason also glanced at Elyn with a stern look.

"Well, I don't know much about them, but I believe people when they tell me it's not a good idea to talk about them – especially in a bad way."

Elyn shrugged and stared at the mighty structure of the temple. "Plenty of people used to say things about them in Outpost and nothing mysterious happened to them. Let's be honest, it's not like the Ageless were a great help to us."

Now it was Jason's turn to shrug. "Maybe that's why they didn't help you? Too many smart-mouths like you in Outpost?" he answered with a grin.

Elyn smiled. She suddenly had a bizarre urge to tell her friends the truth. That she harboured visions of their enemy in her head. That she thought the visions and voices were real. That she could actually see through another woman's eyes into the enemy camp at times. What would they say? She honestly didn't know, but she felt that she needed to tell somebody.

"*No. Not yet,*" Vale insisted. "*We need to understand this ourselves first. Once a single person knows, then it's no longer our secret and it takes options from us.*"

She was right of course. Elyn knew that Vale had resisted similar temptations. Yvorre was searching for her – the gods only knew why – but the wrong, well-intended words to the wrong person could have disastrous consequences. She returned her focus to the conversation, thankful that her internal reflections and exchanges with Vale now seemed to take no time at all.

"I'm sure the Ageless know what they're doing," Nadine was reassuring them.

"You have to wonder how they handled it, the fall of Maelene I mean," Elyn said, her eyes remaining fixed on the temple.

Nadine shrugged. "Well, it was a hundred years ago, so hopefully they got over it. Now they're like the rest of us, aren't they? Their god has left them and they're just going to have to deal with it."

"Well, Maelene was all that stood between Bythe and the free world, so we all have to deal with it," Jason added.

"*Lies.*"

"Do you think it's true?" Nadine asked, her eyes also fixed on the temple. "Do you think Bythe killed her after luring her into a peace conference to end the war?"

"*Lies.*"

Jason shook his head. "Who knows? It's what we're taught, isn't it? I don't think we'll ever really learn what happened at Klyph. It's not like we have a right to, anyway. They're the gods."

"They were the gods. Now they're gone," Nadine added.

"Exactly," said Jason. "And you wonder why people don't welcome strangers like family? We're all on our own now. It's every man for himself. Every town stands alone. I think the sooner you accept that you're owed nothing, the sooner you'll start fitting in."

Nadine glanced at Jason with an unusual look in her eyes but said nothing.

"Well, maybe you can cheer us up by winning the tournament tomorrow?" Elyn asked.

Nadine laughed and turned to Jason with mock enthusiasm. "Oh, yes, the charming young man with the dashing smile and lethal sword. I'm sure you'll be the most popular Ascendant in town. We can all bask in your glory."

Nadine's sarcasm was affectionate, but Jason still flushed.

"Well, I don't know!" Jason retorted with a grin. "Maybe when they accept me as an officer, I could teach Captain Lewis a few things."

His friends laughed at him now.

"Maybe you should tell him that," Elyn suggested. "He seemed like a man open to advice."

"Yes, Jason, please do that," Nadine agreed.

Jason simply kept on grinning with the air of a kid who could take on the world.

"I'll think about it," he replied with mock modesty.

"Well," Nadine sighed, jumping down off the wall. "I think we should mark this occasion ourselves before tomorrow."

"And what did you have in mind?" asked Jason, also dismounting the wall.

"I know that some of the girls are planning a little party," she suggested. Parties were frowned upon before Ascension and were technically forbidden; however, they were also accepted as a somewhat unofficial tradition and most of them went strangely unnoticed by those whose job it was to notice them.

"Really?" Jason answered with an equally playful smile. "Well, I happen to know that some of the boys might have found out about this little indiscretion."

"Well..." Nadine continued as if following a complex train of thought. "Maybe we should go and make sure no one breaks any rules or gets into trouble?" She wound her arm around Jason's, an imitation of a woman needing a chaperone.

"Very responsible of you," agreed Jason with a smile.

"I might head home," said Elyn as she also slid off the wall. She liked her friends, but she had no real enjoyment of parties.

"Oh no, Elyn," Nadine scolded. "This is the last night of your childhood and you're not going to spend it alone at home. I won't allow it."

Elyn sighed and felt herself starting to relent.

"Come on, Elyn," Jason clapped her on the shoulder. "Relax and lighten up. Tonight is going to be the beginning of the rest of your life."

Elyn smiled and allowed herself to be guided by them toward the evening festivities.

They walked as innocent friends into the city for the last time.

CHAPTER 8

"Once the gods had deserted us, Bythe discovered that there was very little preventing him from extending his influence throughout the rest of Kovalith. He strengthened his Helmsguard and sent them on campaign after campaign. Over decades, and then centuries, the territory of the Iron Union grew, as Bythe subjugated the settlements of abandoned men, bringing them into his fold and further increasing his power. Under Bythe's direct tutelage, his commanders quickly became known for their tactical brilliance, often overcoming superior numbers through cunning and inventive maneuverrs on the battlefield."

~Aleasea of the Ageless

The sun was climbing toward its peak as the army approached. The brown grass stretched to the horizon in all directions with only the gentle rising and falling of slopes to break the monotony. Vale watched from atop her warhorse as her men started to disperse into groups and take up positions for the coming battle. They had spent the past two days preparing for the foolhardy tactic that Morbus had forced upon them. Ethan had drafted the plans as promised and presented them to Vale and her war council that evening. Vale had marked the muted surprise from two of her older Knight-Generals, both of them veterans with hard faces. Yet Vale also felt a perverse sense of pride at their discipline. While they had shared a glance and Knight-General Salus had pointed out the obvious risk to the plan, they offered no further objection and set to completing their assigned tasks. But rumblings persisted among the men. Vale had heard that there was anxiety at the plan – as there most certainly should be – yet Ethan had made sure that the architect of this plan was known throughout the command. A testament to the brilliant, tactical mind of their Bureaucrator. Vale reflected on Ethan's guile and smiled.

From the crowded hillock that served as her own command post, Vale had a clear view of the field as it dipped then ascended into another gentle rise where the enemy now stood ready. Their forces looked imposing, eight thousand infantry and archers standing in a sea of brown and green robes with brightly colored banners flying overhead. Upon their approach, Vale had noted the various colors of each banner and had counted five distinct clans. As she had hoped, the clans appeared to be grouped under their own banners and there was a discreet distance between each; however, her hope now seemed a trivial detail in the presence of such an army. Although they may have been divided, they still outnumbered her force by at least two thousand men. Over the plain, she could hear the war drums and the roars of the Men of the Wastes, and Vale was forced to remember that – disjointed or not – this was no chaotic rabble. The clans were true warriors and what they may have lacked in discipline they would make up for with courage and honor.

Vale turned and surveyed her own lines. Banners of black and gold fluttered in the breeze as well-ordered rows of infantry and cavalry stood in unison as if they were on a parade ground instead of preparing for battle. The air was filled with the sounds of officers shouting orders and the din of the marching feet of those units that were still forming up. Groups of archers clustered on both flanks, and lines of cavalry created a wall in front of the infantry. Ethan shouted an order to Knight-General Salus, who in turn passed it to his subordinate and less than a minute later a messenger cantered up to Ethan. Words were exchanged in the din and then Ethan rode to join Vale on the hill.

"Five banners fly on their command post, my lady. You were correct. They appear to share command between several clans."

Vale didn't reply. Her cold, blue eyes were scanning the enemy lines, trying to drink up as much information as possible before the battle.

"It changes nothing," Morbus said in an almost cheerful tone. He rode up to join the command post on a horse that looked utterly miserable under the mass of his rider. "You had better prepare the infantry, Baron."

Ethan said nothing but fixed Morbus with a look of sheer contempt before turning his attention to his Commander. "With your permission, my lady, I will make ready the advance."

"Take utmost care, Baron Ethan. My men are not disposable," Vale answered in a clear voice that carried to the rest of the men at the command post. Ethan nodded his head once in affirmation, saluted with his fist across his chest then rode down the slope.

"Your youth makes you far too sentimental," said Morbus as he rode up alongside Vale. "He will earn his reputation and prove his valour on today's field of battle, or he will fail in disgrace and be forgotten. This is the way the Union has always been."

"*Don't let him bait you,*" Elyn pushed into her mind. Elyn was enjoying the Wellspring Festival and the pleasant feelings of a festive day unexpectedly flooded into Vale's heart.

"*Not now, Elyn,*" Vale replied, and she pushed the distractions away with a deliberate act of will. She turned away from the repugnant face of the Bureaucrator. She closed her eyes and concentrated on a calm lake at the center of her being. Slowly, the uncertainty began to fade, and all other emotions started to drain away with it. Her concern and anxiety felt as if they were evaporating, leaving her numb inside. A calm lake, a surface like glass. She opened her eyes and spoke an order – clear and bright – across the clamour of the command post. At the order, all fell silent but for Knight-General Salus, who repeated the order to a Captain, and within moments, a clear horn sounded over the din. The note was repeated from another horn near the front lines and the army parted like a wave, allowing two groups of foot soldiers to march forward through the gap. The two battalions marched clear of the main group, and then the cluster of over one thousand men halted as if they were no more than a handful of soldiers. They stood frozen, hands on their sword hilts, banners waving in the breeze, waiting for their next orders.

"*Will Ethan be alright?*" Elyn asked. The smooth lake in Vale's mind was marred by the ripples of a thrown pebble.

"*We have to trust him now. Be quiet, please.*"

She nodded to her Knight-General. Moments later, the same horn sounded for the second time and again it was repeated by its counterpart among the infantry. Ethan stood at the front of the column. He cried an order that was lost to Vale's ears and hundreds of soldiers drew swords, held them high over their heads in salute, and began to march across the field. Vale could see the enemy's forward lines forming a wall with their large wooden shields while archers took up positions behind them. She noted the worried expressions that flickered over the faces of some of her officers. Without warning, a cloud of arrows shot up from behind the enemy's shield wall and rained down upon the advancing Helmsguard. Black shields were thrust skyward and for a moment the battalion looked like a giant scaled insect crawling toward the defenders. Arrows shattered and bounced off the hardened steel, but many found their mark and men fell to the ground screaming. Vale could feel Elyn's concern, but she held the feeling at bay. Another cloud of arrows flew, and again more men fell victim, and again the two battalions continued to advance, leaving their dead and wounded in their wake. A loud cry went up from the advancing Helmsguard, and they charged before the enemy could fire a third volley. With a crash of sword upon shield, the wave of black armor smashed upon the defensive wall and fiercely tried to break through. Sabers slashed at the men behind the huge round shields but with little effect. Wild men with spears stood behind the defenders, thrusting and stabbing at the Helmsguard as they tried to breach the defense. Here and there, a small pocket of infantry would break through only to be thrown back again by sheer weight of numbers. Within moments, Vale knew that the first charge had failed.

"Bring them back, Salus," she ordered.

"So soon?" Morbus asked, but Vale knew he didn't want an answer.

"They're going to be killed, Vale."

The horn sounded, and the infantry started to break away. They moved back until they were out of range of the spears, and then quickly reorganized themselves into ranks while the front lines held the enemy at bay. Shields held aloft, they slowly retreated across the plain as more arrows broke upon their armor. A great cheer rose from the wild men to mark their first victory. Vale ignored it and watched her men as they regrouped out of the archers' range.

"Your orders, my lady?" Salus had ridden up beside him and was waiting. Morbus looked on expectantly.

"Advance again."

There was neither a moment's hesitation, nor the slightest note of uncertainty in Salus's voice when he replied.

For the second time, the horn called out the advance, and for the second time, the two battalions marched forth. As before, the attackers were met with a hail of arrows which were deflected with shields and armor, and as before, they charged the enemy's defenses with little success.

Vale let the fighting continue for a while longer before signalling the withdrawal and as before, the enemy host erupted with a mighty roar as they celebrated their second victory.

"Reinforce them and advance again." Vale's voice was flat. She could not afford to show or feel any emotion now; too much depended on cold discipline. Inside, Elyn's frustration grew and surged and pulsed. A company of soldiers marched out and joined one of the battalions in the field to rejuvenate their numbers, and moments later, they were advancing again. Some officers nearby Vale started to exchange worried looks, and some murmuring had broken out further down the command post. Without a word, Salus wheeled about on his horse and rode down the line, staring hard at each officer in turn as he did so. The message was silent and clear. A wake of calm followed the old General when he returned to his commander's side.

"*Call this off,*" Elyn protested.

"*Not yet. It's too early.*"

Half an hour passed, and they repeated the same routine over and over. The Helmsguard would assail the enemy's shield wall with little success and be driven back. Each time, they lost more men. Each time, Salus would ask for orders. Each time, Vale would order another attack, and each time, the officers in the command post grew a little more restless. After the sixth failed assault, Salus came again.

"Your orders, my lady?"

"*Stop this, Vale!*"

Vale turned her face to Morbus but answered the General. "Enough. Bring them back, Salus."

Morbus's face darkened and spoke a pre-rehearsed speech in a clear voice. "This was not the plan we discussed, Commander Vale. Panicked improvisation is not the answer. It will lead to the death of your men."

Soft murmurs broke out among the commanders but this time Salus didn't quell them. He was glaring at Morbus with eyes that were almost hateful.

"Bureaucrator," Vale answered in an even voice. "This *approved* plan is clearly not effective. Persistence will only result in more casualties. A new approach is called for."

"Nonsense! You've barely given the plan a chance. Have patience."

The murmurs increased at this open act of disrespect, and this time, Salus tore his baleful glare away from Morbus and fixed it on his Captains.

Vale held the gaze of Morbus for a moment longer before turning back to the Knight-General.

"Advance again," Vale ordered. Salus paused as if about to speak before recovering his discipline and carrying out the order.

The Helmsguard advanced for the seventh time and raced into the enemy's wooden shields. Like so many times before, a wall of black armored figures crashed against a wall of wood and neither moved, but this time Vale did not call them back right away. Toward the northern end of the line, a pocket of armored men forced their way through the defender's shields and started to engage the spearmen behind. Long spears proved to be a disadvantage before the sabers of the Helmsguard in closer quarters and they were quickly forced back. Dark-skinned men dressed in the dark-brown robes of the Rak'Tunga raced through to join the battle, their short swords and brute strength halting the soldiers' advance.

But the Helmsguard did not fall back.

"What are you doing? Pull them back!" Elyn insisted.

"No, I need to end this. Trust me, Elyn."

Shoulder to shoulder, they formed a wall of their own and by inches, began to force a wedge of iron shields into the mass of the enemy. The thick shields easily turned the short swords of the Rak'Tunga, and the wild men began to fall under the overhead slashes of long sabers. With a guttural bark, a huge insect with a man atop its back, forced its way over the Rak'Tunga and onto the soldiers. The creature looked like a scaled, brown stick insect but was as high as a horse and twice as long. Its head, small for its body, extended on a thin neck the length of a man, but its blank and bulbous eyes betrayed cunning intelligence. It leaped through the remaining men, crushing several allies as it landed face to face with the Helmsguard. With the speed of a killing insect, it thrust out its long neck to latch its ferocious mandibles in the neck of the nearest soldier. He gurgled and shuddered as powerful jaws bit through his chainmail and crushed his throat. Before anyone could react, it had grabbed a second man and was killing him when more of the phasmida creatures launched over the crowd to join the battle. The Rak'Tunga gave way as the giant beasts charged through the stricken Helmsguard, crushing many under powerful legs the size of small tree trunks. Vale's eyes glittered.

"Sound the retreat, Salus. Now!"

A high-pitched note rang out over and over. The wall of black armor pulled away and began to hurry from the enemy. Whereas the previous withdrawals had been ordered and controlled, this was almost a panic.

Different groups of soldiers broke away at different paces, some carefully rear-guarding, some running blindly. Toward the north, dozens of the mounted phasmida were breaking though and giving pursuit, snatching up men as they chased them down. Wild shouting erupted within the command camp as the beginning of a massacre began to unfold. The Helmsguard were trying to retreat westward toward their own lines but the phasmida were bearing down from the north. From her position Vale could see that the creatures would cut her men off before they could reach safety. She turned to Morbus who's look of smug overconfidence had drained from his face. Another cheer came up from the wild men and groups began to charge forth to join the rampaging beasts. Hundreds of men threw down their shields in exchange for swords and raced down the slope, exulting in their first major victory of the day. Another group of phasmida broke away from the south and raced to pincer the fleeing soldiers between themselves and the northern group. Vale reckoned there were nearly two hundred of the beasts and almost two thousand soldiers on the battlefield – it was time.

"General Salus. Order them to hold! Now!" Vale shouted with the first open display of emotion since the battle began.

"What are you doing?" Morbus blurted. Vale ignored him.

Salus screamed the order, and the horn sounded a note, long and low, which was soon echoed by its mate on the field. Vale watched with anxiety, trying to find Ethan's familiar figure in the mess of bodies. She found him when the crowd of soldiers ceased its flight and started to reform itself into ordered lines around a clear leader.

"*How are they regrouping so quickly?*" Elyn asked.

"*Pay attention.*"

"*You planned this?*" The surprise was more of a shared feeling than a question, but Vale took some satisfaction, nonetheless.

"*To a point. I know how people will act. I know Ethan, I know the discipline of my men, and I study the actions of my enemies.*"

The Helmsguard managed to form a large circle with a wall of iron shields facing outward before a flood of phasmida surrounded them. The Paephu clansmen who rode the beasts hesitated and reined in their mounts; they had not expected this latest maneuver, and more than a few questioning glances were exchanged between the riders.

"Commander Vale!" Morbus spat with careful outrage. "What are you playing at? Those are your men down there and your panicked orders have now gotten them surrounded. Have you no concern?"

"To hell with you, Morbus!" Vale replied and the satisfaction of those words filled both her and Elyn alike. Morbus's mouth formed a perfect 'O' as he struggled to form a response to Vale's succinct expression of feeling. "You want to command? You can earn it like the rest of us." She turned to Salus and when she spoke, her voice was hard and clear. "General, I want your best riders in there now! Run down the swine!"

"Yes, my lady!" Salus all but shouted, and the horn sounded again. Seconds later the air was filled with the thunder of horses.

The Paephu and their fellow wild men watched in horror as hundreds of armored cavalry came rumbling upon them from both north and south, with lances the color of night levelled in front of them. The phasmida barked in protest as their riders tried to quickly turn them around to face the new threat. The hundreds of foot soldiers who had been rushing to assist in an easy slaughter, stumbled to a halt and now tried to scurry back in the opposite direction. Half of the cavalry peeled away and gave pursuit to the soldiers desperately trying to flee, while the remainder tightened their formation and slammed into the rabble of phasmida. The clash was sickening as lances pierced leather armor like butter and horses in black armor rode over the giant, scaled stick insects. Men screamed and the air was thick with the din of battle. Ethan's battalion – which had been all but captured moments ago – now leapt up and attacked the beasts that had turned away from them, pulling their riders from their mounts and ending their lives quickly. The Paephu were outnumbered and the skirmish was mercifully short.

The second group of cavalry dashed eastward to cut off the fleeing wild men. A stream of black riders scythed across the path of the footmen, bringing them tumbling over each other as they halted to avoid the deadly hoofs. The men looked about them in a panic as the scythe turned into a surrounding circle of armored horsemen. Some men panicked and tried to break through the circle only to be trampled. Others tried to signal their clansmen in the lines for aid, but the ranks of the Men of the Wastes were in uproar.

"I'll see you executed for this, you whelp," Morbus hissed to Vale in a voice barely audible above the clatter.

"General, have the Bureaucrator escorted to his tent for his own safety in battle," Vale ordered in a tone that was completely indifferent. Salus said nothing yet the satisfaction in his eyes was completely undisguised. He gestured to three soldiers and within seconds the protesting figure of Morbus was receding down the hill toward the apparent protection of the camp.

"Won't this be a problem for you?" Elyn asked.

"He's tomorrow's problem. Today I deal with this one."

Vale could see that the enemy command post was chaotic. From her viewpoint, she watched the hurried movement among the officers and even fancied she could discern the figures of arguing men. Some groups of soldiers were preparing to march to aid their comrades, while others milled about uselessly. A handful of men in tan robes even broke away and started to flee south, and moments later, they were chased and set upon by men wearing brown. All the while, the circle of cavalry was tightening its noose around the wild men and as each moment passed, dozens more men fell victim to their lances and sabers. Vale waited until her first group of horsemen had dealt with the phasmida before issuing her next order.

"Regroup and charge, Salus. Run them all down."

It was almost cruel to see the encircling cavalry break away and regroup, giving the wild men a fleeting hope of escape. It was almost brutal to see a thousand horsemen charge back eastward and wash over the footmen, wheeling about and regrouping as a few riders finished off the handful of soldiers running for safety in vain. Vale could almost pity them as they tried to outrun the riders bearing down upon them with sabers raised. But pity was not a desirable quality in a general at war.

"No discipline," Vale said quietly. "No soldier from the Union would have broken formation and given chase so recklessly."

"No, my lady," Salus replied as he watched the masterstroke unfold, eyes shining with respect.

"Let's finish this. Send them in."

A great roar came up from the legions of footmen below as they charged the enemy by the thousands in a cloud of dust. A feeble smattering of arrows met their advance to no avail – Vale had finally unleashed her might. The Helmsguard shattered the weakened shield wall, black armor bleeding into the lines of the defenders. The fighting was ferocious. Spearmen threw their weapons into the breasts of the Helmsguard only to be cut down in reply. The brown=robed Rak'Tunga tried to stand their ground, but now the weight of numbers lay with their enemy and they could only scream defiance as a wave passed over them. Their alliance was shattered, and instead of fighting as one force, they became a rabble. One by one the men in the command post abandoned their station and their alliance, calling for their own men to retreat while doing so.

"*You are indeed your father' s daughter.*"

Vale allowed herself the luxury of a smile under her visor.

CHAPTER 9

"The Outer Wild had long stood opposed to the industrialised might of the Iron Union. The confederacy of towns and villages in the east protected each other with the help of Maelene and her immortal Ageless. United, this alliance was not only capable of repelling Bythe's invasions but was also able to strike into the Iron Union at will. However, after the fall of Maelene, the Outland alliances found themselves increasingly vulnerable."

~Aleasea of the Ageless

It had been a perfect day.

Despite her nerves and misgivings, Elyn found that she actually enjoyed herself more than she ever had. The Wellspring Festival seemed to grant everyone a euphoric mood, so much that she found herself on the receiving end of several awkward and unexpected hugs from weepy-eyed fellow Ascendants, many of whom she barely knew, but she was more than happy to receive the affection, nonetheless. The morning's speeches and processions were formal, but at noon the mood lightened as the celebrations began and all of Fairhaven breathed as one and that the breath was one of merriment and laughter. Leon had come with her that morning and Elyn couldn't remember him ever looking so proud. He had watched the morning's formalities from the back with the other parents and relatives, never once taking his gaze from his daughter. The misadventures with the town guard seemed ages past. Then Vale's battle had pushed into Elyn's mind with an intensity so fierce she worried that she might lose all composure and betray their secret. While she knew little of Vale's friends, their strange bond caused them to share their feelings, and Elyn now worried for Ethan as if he were a brother. Her distraction during the lunchtime feast was noticed by Leon, who seemed to put it down to pre-tournament nerves. This conclusion led Leon into a long and winding recounting of his own misspent youth in an effort to distract his daughter from her anxiety. Thankfully, this allowed Elyn the time she needed as Vale's own victory was secured and the feelings of euphoria then returned tenfold. Leon seemed pleased that his stories had inflated his daughter's spirits and asked no further questions.

After the lunchtime feasting came the tournament and, as expected, Elyn was eliminated quickly in the first round, but not even this could dent her spirits. Rather it allowed her to quickly rejoin Leon and Nadine and the rest of the festivities, her responsibilities lifted. Nadine looked radiant. Her status among the nobility meant that she was exempt from competing alongside the other young women. She instead watched Elyn compete and was there along with Leon to congratulate her when she was eliminated. Then they had remained together to watch Jason, as he rapidly cut a swathe through his competitors on his way to the final bouts. Elyn found herself glancing at Jason more than once throughout the afternoon. She caught herself fantasizing that today, in the joy of the moment, he might find the opportunity to kiss her. While the moment for a kiss didn't come, it was equally satisfying to watch Jason as he fought his way to the final bout where he faced Nathan's friend, Shane. Despite a significant difference in size between the two young men, Jason had used guile and cunning to lure his brutish opponent into overconfidence. Elyn had cheered louder than she ever had at the moment Jason lured Shane into a blustering charge. Jason had fallen to the dirt and appeared helpless, only to quickly regain his footing and step aside like a dance, slapping Shane's backside with the flat of his wooden sword as he passed by.

"*When outmatched by strength, lure your foe into overconfidence.*" Vale's sense of admiration had been matched only by the sense of complete shock on Shane's face.

Sometime later – after the awards and the cheers and the endless congratulations – Jason found his way over to where Elyn, Nadine, and Leon waited. He hugged them all, and they all offered him more congratulations. He was beaming with pride, and Elyn struggled to remember a time when she had ever seen him this happy.

"Look at what my father gave me," Jason announced to the group after the hugging was over. He held out a beautiful golden circle on a chain. When he pressed a small button set into the side, the cover flipped over to reveal an intricate watch of incredible workmanship.

"That's beautiful," gasped Nadine.

"I know," replied Jason with genuine pride on his face. "He'd been working on it for years behind my back. Waiting for today."

"That's some remarkable workmanship, Jason," Leon agreed as he took the watch for a closer inspection. "Martin's a great man at what he does."

"Yeah," Jason answered almost sheepishly.

"He loves you a lot, you know," Leon continued with a smile, handing the watch back to its new owner. Jason took it and flushed with the embarrassment felt by adolescent boys when confronting genuine affection. Leon seemed to sense this and decided to save Jason from any further awkwardness.

"Alright everyone now what? You're all adults. You've come of age. What should we do about it?"

Elyn glanced at Jason – who was looking at his watch with an odd expression on his face – then at Nadine who shrugged.

"I don't have to be home until later," she answered. Nadine's parents had paid their respects earlier in the day, but had to leave to attend their businesses on what would be one of the busiest days of the year for them. Elyn thought Nadine had seemed a little disappointed at this, but she said nothing.

"Well, given that you're all adults, I'm thinking that it might be proper if I bought you all your first round of beer," Leon announced.

Elyn and Jason smiled. This wouldn't have been their first taste of beer and they were pretty sure Leon knew it, but they thanked him and accepted, nonetheless. Even Nadine agreed.

"Alright then, let's go," Leon declared.

The four of them walked the thinning tournament grounds and toward the heart of the Old City. Their path took them through the warehouse district, and the warehouses loomed on either side of them in the fading afternoon light. Jason seemed to have regained some of his old cocky self, and he nudged Elyn as they walked alongside each other.

"So... did you see that move I used on Shane? Not too bad, huh?"

"What?" Elyn replied evenly. "The one where you got laid out on your back?"

Leon and Nadine laughed.

"Yeah, that's the one," Jason answered.

"It was very impressive, Jason," Nadine cut in. "I don't think Shane saw it coming."

"Truth is, I don't think I saw it coming either," said Jason. "I didn't really have a lot of other options when I was down there."

Elyn smiled at him. "Well, I think you've wiped the smirk off his face for a while – Nathan's too. I think I owe you for that."

Jason put his arm around her. "Well, a bit of that was for you too."

Elyn laughed and felt a sudden and unexpected surge of love. She saw Leon shoot them both an approving look as they continued walking with Jason's arm over her shoulders. She glanced up the road to see a tall, brutish figure standing over the bleeding bodies of a young couple.

What happened next would always be unclear to Elyn.

She lost the exact order of events in the sheer panic and confusion of what unfolded. The first indicator that all was not well was the surreal scream of Nadine. The figure ahead turned and regarded them with wild eyes. Blood stained the leather padding he wore as armor and the crude spear he carried in his hand. Suddenly Jason was standing in front of them, pushing Nadine and Elyn back behind him. He was saying something – his lips were moving. Elyn would never remember what those words were. A crash and a guttural cry came from an alley to their left as two of the Northmen came charging out, their bloodied weapons drawn. Then at some point they were everywhere. Masked men in armor, wild men with spears and clubs, all looking to slaughter anyone they could find. People screamed. Axes fell with a sickly sound, like something heavy hitting mud – only it was far worse to her ears. Nadine was still screaming. Jason was still yelling something at them. A hand grabbed Elyn's shoulder, and it was Leon who dragged her backward toward the parade grounds. They ran. Jason stayed. Elyn saw the wild man approaching him with his spear, but then she turned her face back to the road ahead and saw no more. The Northmen roared behind her. Others started to appear in the street ahead.

"How is this happening? How did they break through the walls?" Vale was asking.

It didn't matter. More were emerging with every passing second, and it soon became obvious that they blocked the road ahead.

"Hide, Elyn!"

"Here!" Leon screamed and led them both into a small warehouse off to the side of the road. They fell in among the boxes and barrels and struggled to find somewhere to hide. Leon found a gap behind a bench and hissed at them to hide. The three of them had only just ducked behind when two warriors and a third man burst into the small area in pursuit. He dressed differently from the other two nomads, with no mask to cover a round face flushed with excitement, and he did not carry himself with the same warrior's air of his companions. They set to searching the surrounds, overturning empty barrels and boxes. Elyn felt panic rise, Nadine was biting her fist so hard that she was bleeding. Leon was hunched over both of them. Cradling them like children.

"*Stay calm, Elyn. Help will be coming.*"

Vale's reassuring words seemed fainter now. The sound of heavy mail boots approaching the bench obliterated them. Elyn knew that Leon's hope of escape had failed. Leon squeezed Elyn on the shoulder and raised himself to his feet, his palms held up in a sign of surrender.

"Wait! Please!" he cried. The round-faced man approaching the bench raised his spear in surprise, and the other two warriors wheeled about with a grunt.

"Please!" Leon repeated. "They are only children."

"Where are they?" demanded the wild man. He was short – so that his companions were taller than him – and fat, with a weak face and a shock of red curly hair. For some strange reason Elyn took the impression that he was not truly one of the Northmen although she couldn't say why. Leon slowly lowered his hands and took Elyn and Nadine by the arm and pulled them both to their feet. Nadine was sobbing now. Tears ran down her red cheeks and her breath was ragged. The two Northmen jeered when they saw her, and the short man looked at her greedily. Inside Elyn, Vale was raging with fury.

"Ahh, aren't these pretty little sluts?" said the short man. The nomads barked something behind their shrouds in a guttural tongue, but the man didn't answer.

"Please!" Leon repeated with a chilling desperation in his voice. "Please spare them. They're just children, they won't harm you."

"Oh, really?" mocked the short man in a high-pitched voice. "How kind of you to reassure us. Yet you dogs are happy to kill us year on year, aren't you? And one day soon these little kids will pick up a weapon and come looking for us just like the rest of you weak little pigs."

He was cocky and full of bravado, putting on a show in front of the two warriors. In the midst of this danger, it occurred to Elyn that she'd seen this behaviour with Nathan only the day before. She realized that this little man would probably carry little respect among his peers and that this was his rare opportunity to show off using weaker prey. Elyn now felt Vale's disgust and contempt bubbling within her own fear.

"But wait." Leon took a slow step forward, his palms outstretched. "Wait one moment. I know that wrong has been done to you. The gods know that we haven't always been kind to each other, but please don't let these children suffer for our mistakes."

The man looked Leon in the eye with a strange expression dawning on his face. The Northmen muttered something unintelligible, but the man standing in front of them was regarding Leon in silence.

"But you attack us!" The fat man blurted after a moment. "You kill my brothers and raid us in our homes! How can you talk of mercy now?"

"I know," Leon replied and took another gentle step forward. "I know we wrong you. But please give me this chance. There is no honor in killing these children."

The wild man looked thoughtfully at Elyn, then at Nadine, and then back to Leon.

"No. There is no honor." He repeated and then plunged his spear deep into Leon's stomach.

Nadine screamed. Elyn found she couldn't speak. The fat man laughed a high-pitched and feminine-sounding giggle.

"Honor?" he mocked. "Honor?" He turned to the warriors as if seeking their approval. They gurgled a coarse rasping sound that sounded like a perverse mockery of a laugh. Having won his desired effect, the wild man turned his attention back to Leon.

"Here's my honor, old man," he shrilled and with that he thrust his spear deeper into Leon's guts, causing him to stagger backward. Elyn watched as her father fell to his knees, and she felt something cold clench at her heart. The Northmen were advancing now, still making their perverse laughing noises. The fat man was grinning triumphantly. Vale shouted something within Elyn's mind. Nadine was screaming, but the sounds were far off in the distance. All that mattered in the world was kneeling in front of her, bleeding onto the dirt. Then hands grabbed her by the shirt-front and she found herself face to face with the man's puffy and scowling face.

"You and your friend are coming with us. We need some company in the mountains."

He was sneering inches away from Elyn's face. His breath stank, but Elyn wasn't paying attention. Her eyes were fixed on her dying father. Vale was screaming in her head. Pushing against her mind. Her heart was pounding in her ears. It was getting louder and louder. Vale was reaching for her. She could feel Vale trying to break through. She wanted to reach back.

She opened her mind as far as she could.

Elyn turned to cast her eyes on the pathetic little worm trying to hold her and something in that look made the wild man pause. Without warning, he released his hold on Elyn and jumped back like someone had struck him. A shocked expression seized his ugly little face. Elyn continued to stare into his eyes, the pounding of drums still deafening in her ears. Vale's voice was gone now. All Elyn could see or hear or smell was this man. It was like everything else had faded from sight. Thoughts and images then came trickling into her mind. A few at first, then increasing like the onset of heavy rain. Sounds, smells, words, and memories started to flood like a torrent. They were ugly thoughts. Fearful. Grotesque and dirty. Images of a miserable life without respect. Undisciplined lust for those he couldn't have. This man's name – Jarren. The painful blows of his cruel father. The bitter cold of long and hungry winters. These sensations were pulled from somewhere deep within the fat man and rushed into the mind of Elyn in a flood.

"What are you doing?" the man named Jarren shrieked in his shrill voice as he stepped back again. His former smug arrogance now vanished to reveal the weak little thing that he was. "She's in my head! Stop this magic! Stop it!"

The thoughts rushed quicker now. Her mind flared like the sun. Beyond the thoughts of Jarren she could hear the minds of hundreds of others, like voices in a crowd. Men, grandmothers, terrified children running in fear for their lives, a soldier running to defend his town. Her mind was racing even faster. It was like she could hear the town. Then the Outer Wild. Then all of Kovalith. Vale was there. Everyone was there.

"*Elyn!*" It was Vale's mind screaming for her. She could feel it latching onto her. It felt warm and familiar in this moment of confusion. It felt very familiar.

"*Elyn, please stop this. You're showing too much power. The Ageless will sense you.*"

Elyn knew that Vale was making sense, but she couldn't stop it. The flood of power and feeling was sweeping her mind away. She reached out for Vale – a steadying hand amid the chaos. Elyn gripped Vale's mind tighter than she ever had before, and with that action, she lifted a curtain between them to unveil a plain truth. A terrible truth that struck both of them as both impossible and inevitable. They weren't sisters. They weren't even copies. They were more than that. They were the same person. The same woman somehow existing in two different places at the same time.

Vale was suddenly silent. The obvious truth also laid bare before her.

Elyn couldn't accept it. She didn't understand how this was possible and yet she knew that it was true. The strange bond. The feeling of kinship. A deep familiarity. Unnaturally deep.

"*This can't be real,*" Elyn said.

"*Elyn,*" replied Vale, her composure returning despite the revelation. "*We... we can deal with this later. You need to stop what you're doing now. Can't you feel them coming?*"

Vale was right. Elyn could feel a presence inching along their connection. Something foreign had become attracted to her display of power like a moth to light. It was coming closer. Elyn tried to shut down her feelings but she couldn't. It wouldn't stop. Desperation turned to a sudden stab of panic and the power flared even brighter.

"*Elyn, please!*" Vale screamed but it was no use. The unseen presence was reaching backward along their connection, searching for them both like a hand groping in the dark. Then it found her.

"*Elyn. At last.*"

Yvorre's black thoughts snapped onto her with a sudden cold grip. Elyn tried to push her away but her control was strong.

"*Oh please, don't pull away, young lady. Not after I've spent so long looking for you.*" Her thoughts were slick and oily in her mind. "*Elyn. Why did you assume that name? I always thought the name Vale suited you so much better.*"

"*Let go of her, Yvorre!*" Vale shouted.

"*Ah, my young Vale as well. So, my suspicions were correct. You've found each other at last, and you were so deceitful in keeping it from me. Bythe's broken daughters reunited. This is indeed a glorious day. I almost feel proud,*" Yvorre crooned with an affectionate mocking.

Elyn reeled. "*No!*"

"*I'm afraid it's true,*" Yvorre persisted. "*I've searched such a long time for you, Elyn. Your father doesn't even know you exist, but my mind is far sharper than his. I know why Vale has been such a failure to him. The answer is in you Elyn.*"

"*What are you talking about?*" asked Vale.

"*You still cannot see the truth even when it stares right back at you? Your mind is as dull as your father's. You are broken child. Your very soul is split in two. That is why you've never fulfilled your potential.*"

"*You're lying!*" Vale's accusation was faltering. In her heart, Yvorre's words were finding their mark.

"*No, I am not, but you need not fear. I will mend what was broken. Return to me willingly and I will reward you. You will have a place at my side when I claim your father's empire.*"

"*You're mad, Yvorre,*" Vale replied. "*You're not overthrowing my father, and I'll be damned if I let you do to Elyn what you did to me.*"

"*I'm not talking to you, Vale. You've always been mine. I'm interested in your better half.*" She paused before continuing in a lower tone, "*Elyn, if you make me come for you, if you make me fight to claim you, then your inevitable servitude to me will be on far less charitable terms. Give yourself to me now and spare yourself the terror to come. Do it.*"

"*NO!*" Elyn's scream was desperate, full of fear and rage. It seared through the minds of Vale and Yvorre and sent them spinning into the mental void. Elyn and Jarren also flew to the dirt. The images and sensations stopped and, for an instant, Elyn found herself stunned. As a result, she was confused and vaguely wondered why the Northmen standing over her seemed to be no longer looking at her. She noticed the distant screams had changed in tone and were now guttural and savage. Then she saw a flash of green and the nomad was backing away from her, his axe drawn as if he was retreating from some foe Elyn couldn't see. There was another flash of green, and she realized that a tall figure in a billowing green cloak was standing beside her.

The Ageless.

She watched as the robed figure advanced calmly toward the nomad. The Ageless produced a wooden staff from within his robes and held it in front of him. Then he seemed to crouch – waiting for the Northman to attack. He did not have to wait long. The brute in front of him quickly charged with his axe held high, but when he brought it down the Ageless moved with speed. Suddenly he was no longer in front of the assailant but at his side with his own weapon raised. The blows were a blur to Elyn's eyes. The attacker reeled from a flurry of strikes that seemed almost invisible. His axe fell into the dirt as he staggered backward under the unyielding assault. Within seconds, the Ageless used his staff to knock the man into the dirt and then thrust the end into his unarmored throat in a fatal blow.

Elyn got to her knees and looked around in disbelief. There were several Ageless in the street around her, some in green robes, others in dark purple. All of them were attacking the invaders with brutal swiftness. The second nomad that had been threatening Nadine was now brandishing a sword and charging a purple-robed figure. He thrust his weapon forward into the magician's robes with a deep roar of triumph, but the sword passed into the folds of purple without resistance. The eyes of the Northman widened in confusion as a hand shot out from within the robes to grab him by the face. He shrieked and dropped his sword in a vain attempt to pry the hands away, but before he could reach them, his body spasmed and stiffened then crumpled to the ground lifeless. Jarren cried out in fear. His cocky bravado evaporated, and he turned and fled along the street. Several of the Northmen exchanged worried glances and started to retreat. Cloaked figures ran after them, striking them down as they gave chase. Another crash to Elyn's right heralded the arrival of the town guard. The square was filled with men in the blue livery of Fairhaven clashing with the few invaders who had very unwisely chosen to remain. The outcome was swift and brutal, between the furious soldiers and the lethal magicians, the Northmen's resistance was brief. Within minutes, the invaders lay slaughtered and the soldiers quickly ran to attend to the injured men and women lying strewn like scattered leaves.

Elyn saw little of this. She vaguely knew that the fighting has stopped. That a man in blue crouched beside her, speaking words and trying to get her attention. Elyn's gaze was fixed on the body of Leon that lay alone and untended in the middle of the square. Blood had pooled under him, staining the dirt. The spear still protruded from his stomach like some obscenity. Elyn wanted to pull it out. Why wasn't anyone pulling it out? Why wasn't anyone helping Leon like they were helping the others? She got to her feet. The man beside her was still talking but his words made no sense. She walked toward her father like it was a dream. She needed to get to him. She needed to pull the spear out, and Leon would open his eyes and look at her with that rascally expression of his. And then they would go home and it would be alright again. It would be like this never happened. She had to get the spear out. She was almost there. Then she felt a hand on her shoulder and Jason's face was before her. Jason looked strange. He had blood on his face and on his tunic. He didn't look like Elyn's best friend, he looked heartbroken, empty. He looked like a soldier. Elyn looked at him in confusion. Why was Jason there? Couldn't he see that Leon needed help? She brushed past him and walked over to where Leon lay, the blood staining Elyn's boots and pants as she kneeled down beside him. But Leon didn't move or open his eyes. There was no rascally smile, and it was at that moment that Elyn knew she would never look into those kind eyes again. She felt something hot surge in her throat and her cheeks were wet. A low wail started rising unbidden from her mouth. It raised in pitch until it turned into a racking sob that shook her entire body. She felt hands around her shoulders. Nadine and Jason beside her, crying themselves. She sensed the growing crowd of onlookers gathering around them – stricken at what had unfolded here today. She couldn't have seen the robed figures in green standing behind her. She couldn't have known that despite all appearances, they were not standing vigil over her fallen father. She was completely unaware that their eyes – hidden under dark hoods – were fixed on no one but her.

CHAPTER 10

"Yvorre had risen quickly in the favor of Bythe. She was rumoured to have once been a witch from Kardak, whom Bythe had bested in personal combat and then brought to the Ironhelm in chains – but this may be nothing more than a story. Cunning and devious, Yvorre wasted little time in establishing herself as a trusted advisor before finally obtaining the status of Mistress of Spies and Assassins within the Iron Union. There were many voices within the walls of the Ironhelm that quietly questioned her motives; however, those voices found themselves – one by one – silenced over time."

~Aleasea of the Ageless

The camp was celebrating, yet Vale could hear none of it. She stood alone in her command tent, the night air drifting in through the open flap bringing with it the scents of campfire smoke and cooking meat and the raucous cries of happy men. And Vale could think of only one thing.

Yvorre.

Yvorre had found her. She had found *them*. She knew. Her mind had set to work immediately. Pieces of information were sorting and then re-sorting themselves in her mind. Elyn was Vale. Vale was Elyn. They were the same person – two halves of the same woman coexisting in different parts of Kovalith. How was this possible? It didn't matter, not yet. Vale knew she didn't have enough information to answer that question, so she set it aside for now. There was a more pressing concern. Yvorre knew. She knew and she'd been keeping this from Vale her entire life. No doubt controlling her advance within the Iron Union. Why? She paced in a circle around the map on the table in the center of the tent. Elyn was in danger. Her mind had lit up like a flare during the tragedy and Yvorre had heard. She now knows where Elyn is. Fairhaven. Running a hand through her hair, Vale sighed and closed her eyes again.

"Elyn? Elyn! Answer me!"

Nothing. She could feel nothing, as if a wall had now arisen between them. On one hand, Vale was relieved that she had exclusive access to her own head once more, but the fresh concern she now carried for Elyn eclipsed this relief.

She'd barely had time to relish today's victory before she'd felt Elyn's distress. Moving back to her tent she'd only been able to watch in horror as the events unfolded and Yvorre was all but summoned to witness.

Now Vale realized that her life had changed forever. She couldn't make things go back to the way they were before, even if she wanted to. Yvorre was coming for her. Yvorre had always controlled her like a puppet master – and now Yvorre had simply stepped out from behind the curtain and shown her the strings. Vale faced an agonising moment of indecision. Should she try to resist Yvorre and fight her way through to the Ironhelm, to try to seek an audience with a father who had probably forgotten she even existed? Vale allowed herself a moment of fantasy before realizing that it would be impossible. Yvorre's influence throughout the Iron Union was far greater than Vale's. There was no chance that Yvorre would allow Vale to even get a message to her father, let alone physically reach the Ironhelm. Vale realized that she had one option. She had to turn her back on her career and on her position as the daughter of Bythe. She had no choice but to discard it all for the one slim hope of learning the truth about herself. She had to find Elyn.

Now she knew she had little time. She returned to the map and scanned it for a moment. Her brow furrowed in frustration as she ripped it up from the desk, threw it to the floor and reached for another map which was rolled among others in a basket at the foot of the table. The tent flap opened, and Ethan hesitated only a moment before stepping inside. He was still dressed in his armor of black iron, the silver edging catching in the light of the many lanterns scattered around the tent. Vale didn't even notice him.

"My lady?" Ethan asked somewhat tentatively. Vale looked up and allowed her face to break into a harried smile.

"Ethan. Are you alright?"

"Not a scratch, my lady. The men of the Union were unbreakable today. You led us well."

"Oh no, Ethan, you led your men well today. Thank you for everything," Vale nodded at him before returning her attention to the map. Ethan smiled at the praise, but his face was etched with concern. He walked closer to the table, his eyes following Vale's to the map before them.

"Vale, I heard there was trouble with Morbus today. Is that why you're not out there? Are you alright?"

Vale looked up at him as if she'd not quite understood what Ethan had been saying. "Morbus?" she repeated. She hadn't given the Bureaucrator any thought after the attack on Elyn, now this was an added variable to an already complex equation. "Yes, Morbus. He'll use my actions today as an excuse to assume command, won't he?"

Ethan nodded, unsure whether Vale was addressing him or merely talking to herself. "It's likely, my lady." He stepped in closer and lowered his voice. "Would you like me to take a pre-emptive measure here? Morbus can easily become the victim of a Rak'Tunga rogue looking for vengeance. It will not be questioned. Your men are loyal to you and to you alone."

Vale smiled grimly. "Thank you, Ethan, but no, I won't put you in that position."

"We can't just stand by and let him move against you."

"We won't," Vale replied, her eyes still on the map. "As Bureaucrator, he has been deputised with authority to oversee my assault on the Rak'Tunga." She pointed to a scroll with the wax seal of Yvorre lying discarded on the far table. "He loves to remind me of the terms of his power, but it doesn't give him authority to remove me from command."

"Vale...that's a technicality. Besides, it'd only take a new order from Yvorre to have you removed from command at her request. In fact, I'm sure he's already sent a messenger to her, asking for exactly that."

"I know. That's why I'm in here. We don't have a lot of time." She smiled suddenly and leaned in closer to the map before them. "There!" she said, stabbing a finger at a small marking. Ethan bent over to see what she was looking at.

"Fairhaven?" he asked.

"It's where the Ageless are."

Ethan looked shocked. An expression so unlike him that Vale was tempted to smile. "How do you know?" Ethan asked.

Vale looked at him and, in that moment, she wanted to tell him everything. She wanted to trust him with every secret she had, but she knew it was an indulgence she could not afford. Instead, she prepared her list of lies and misdirections.

"I'm the daughter of Lord Bythe." It felt so strange to say it out loud, to almost say it with pride. "I can feel the presence of my enemies. You have to trust me, Ethan. I know that's where they are."

Ethan nodded slowly.

"I'm going to take them, Ethan. My father's gifts have shown me where they are, and Yvorre's efforts to keep me sidelined have placed me in their path. Look!" She pointed to their location at the northern end of the Great Southern Wastes. "The Helmsguard are engaging Maelene's armies to the west of us, where the front has formed between Azure's Towers and the coast."

Ethan nodded. "That's where their forces are concentrated. Once they break through, they'll have a clear path into the heart of the Outlands."

"Yes, but Fairhaven isn't in the heart of the Outlands," Vale pointed out almost triumphantly. "It's nestled in the northwest against the mountains, not more than a few weeks march from here."

Ethan looked at the map and nodded. "Does Yvorre know this?"

Vale hesitated, wondering how much truth to reveal. "Not when she sent us out here, no. But now...yes, I think she does." Vale looked at Ethan imploringly. "We can't let her take this chance from us, Ethan. She's done everything in her power to prevent me from success and you know it. This is it, Ethan. This is my last chance to stamp my mark in the Iron Union. Once she sees this opportunity, she'll take advantage of it for herself and have me court-martialled for what I've done to Morbus."

All of this was true, of course, and Vale felt only a slight pang of guilt at her lie of omission. She couldn't tell Ethan that she needed to reach Fairhaven before Yvorre did. She couldn't tell Ethan that Yvorre would be furious at that very moment, realizing that her own forces were locked in a slow land war far from Fairhaven, while she had inadvertently placed Vale within striking distance of Elyn. Her first priority would be to restrain Vale and prevent her from taking any action. She couldn't let Yvorre do that. She had one chance to find Elyn and try to get answers. If Yvorre found her first, this chance would be lost forever. Vale had to take this risk.

"But, Vale," Ethan answered, moving around to study the map. "Fairhaven's deep within forested mountains, we can't move an army through there, certainly not in a few weeks, anyway. And even if we could, the Ageless would see us coming and be more than ready to repel us."

"I know. That's why we're not taking the army."

Vale called to the guards outside and ordered them to find Salus. They nodded and left without a word. Vale quickly walked over to the table packed with scrolls, found a writing quill, and began scribbling.

"Vale, what are you doing?" Ethan asked.

"Hurrying," she replied as she cast about for a wax stick and a candle. Locating both, she took a final look at her writing. Satisfied with her work, she used the candle to melt a small pool of red wax onto the scroll, then she removed her Royal Seal from a pouch on her belt and set it into the red mess.

"Done."

The tent flap was pushed aside by a young soldier and the portly form of Morbus moved into the tent. He had changed into his usual garb of over-fine black silk with a white cravat accentuating the already bulging folds of his neck. He wore a smug look as he appraised both Ethan and Vale in one glance. The young guard that escorted him wore an expression of intense discomfort, as if he'd rather be anywhere else than there.

"Commander Vale!" Morbus's voice dripped with arrogance. "The men told me you'd hidden yourself away in here." Vale could see that Morbus had misread her actions after the battle as contrition. It seemed that this had emboldened the bureaucrat.

"Why are you here, Morbus?" Vale's question was direct. The time for games was over. Morbus smiled.

"I'm here to offer you the chance to do this the right way, Vale." His eye's fell upon the wax seal on the paper in Vale's hand and a satisfied grin grew on his face. "And I see you've come to the same conclusion. Very good, young Commander. I see you still retain some good sense."

Ethan looked from Morbus to Vale and then back. "What does he mean?" he asked Vale. It was Morbus who replied.

"She will hand over command to me and await orders to return to the Ironhelm to face official review and potential sanction for her actions today. I trust that is the order in your hand?"

Vale didn't reply. Her eyes were fixed on Morbus's. She wondered how much this fat man knew of Yvorre? How much he'd been part of her plan to keep Vale controlled? How long had Morbus spied on her and betrayed her in subtle ways over the years? Her thoughts were interrupted by the tent flap opening again and the entrance of Salus. The old General paused as soon as he entered, as if sensing the tension within the tent. He eyed Morbus warily before turning his attention to Vale.

"My lady, reporting as ordered."

Vale let her eyes linger on Morbus a moment longer – enjoying the game – before turning to Salus.

"Yes, General. I have orders for you." Vale stepped forth and handed the scroll to Salus. Morbus's face twisted from arrogance to confusion and then finally to fury. He snatched the paper from Salus, scanning it with his pudgy eyes. Salus looked ready to strike the Bureaucrator, but a gesture from Vale stayed his hand.

"You're delegating command of this operation to Salus?" Morbus spat with disbelief. He looked back at Vale with the sneer returning to his round face. "This makes no difference. While you may think yourself clever, Vale, you haven't the wit for games you think you do. For example, did you know that while you were hiding in here that I had *already* dispatched word to Yvorre?" He paused dramatically, waiting for a reaction. Vale refused to provide it. "So, you can try to neutralise me with procedural tricks all you like, but by tomorrow, fresh orders will arrive from Yvorre herself and those orders will place me in command."

Vale nodded. "He's probably right. I'm sorry, Salus, but I'm afraid your command of this operation may be very short-lived; however, I want you to manage the casualties and the processing of prisoners until new orders arrive."

Salus saluted with a fist across his chest. "Of course, my lady...but," he added uncertainly, glancing at Ethan before continuing "...shouldn't command fall to Baron Ethan before me?"

"I'm afraid Baron Ethan also has new orders." Vale reached under the reams of maps on the table, retrieved another scroll – also bearing her royal seal – and handed it to Salus. "I have exercised my authority of Commander of the Iron Union to commission my own operation. A small one Bureaucrator, only five hundred men, well within my authority to authorise in the course of field operations."

Morbus seemed confused by what was happening before him. "You're sending Ethan on another operation?" he asked.

"No, Morbus, I'm leading an operation personally. I've received intelligence regarding the location of the Ageless, and I intend to exploit this advantage while it exists. I leave immediately."

Morbus was outraged. "You can't!" he roared. "You're in command of this entire army. You can't just walk out!"

"Oh, I'm not walking out, Morbus. As you just pointed out, it's completely proper to delegate command of an army to an underling like yourself; however, I think that General Salus is far more qualified for field operations, don't you?"

"Don't be so smug!" Morbus was yelling now. "This will destroy your career, Vale. There's no justification for this."

"No justification?" Vale's own feelings were again like the calm surface of a lake. She always was most effective like this. "I have knowledge of the location of the Ageless. Intelligence which Yvorre herself now shares. Confirm this with her if you like. I have been given the opportunity to strike at the heart of our most hated enemies. Are you suggesting that I should not act? If we hesitate like we did two days ago, then an opportunity will again be lost forever. How will you explain *that* to Lord Bythe once he learns of it? My father may even ask you to explain your hesitance to him personally."

It was a dangerous gambit, invoking her father. How much did Morbus know of Vale's estranged relationship with their god? Vale was gambling on Yvorre's petty need for secrets and she was right. Morbus's confidence began to falter in the face of Bythe's name.

"Then confirm this with Yvorre! Seek her counsel before approving any changes to our plan. It'll take only a few days for a messenger to reach her." Morbus predictably played his last card. Vale was ready for it.

"No, Morbus. I've made my decision." Vale's voice was firm now, the voice of a commander. "Every day I waste deliberating is a day that further closes my window of opportunity. This is the reason why I'm given such discretion on the field – to seize any initiative in the service of our Lord Bythe. I failed to do this two days ago, at your insistence, and my men paid the price today. I will not make that mistake again. I leave at once."

"No! I won't allow it!" Morbus bellowed, furious at seeing his chance for glory slipping away. He turned to the young guard at his side. "Arrest Vale at once!"

Silence fell within the tent. No one moved.

"Bureaucrator," Vale looked down at the floor of the tent, her voice was almost a whisper. "You have just attempted to remove me from command in front of these honored officers of the Iron Union. Under which regulation do you justify this?"

Morbus knew he had stepped too far. Sweat broke on his brow as he considered his dilemma. Too late to reverse his position. He was committed.

"Desertion! Dereliction of duty to Lord Bythe under Article Seven!" he finally blurted.

Vale smiled and shook her head. "I'm so sorry, my Bureaucrator," she said, gesturing to the papers before her with the wax seals. "Article Seven relates to the express disobedience of an order. These are new, legal orders, correctly documented and well within the powers of my duty, well within the bureaucracy." She emphasised the last word to drive home the point. "My adherence to the rules of duty is sound and witnessed. You, on the other hand, have acted most improperly. Attempting to remove a Commander without cause and without proper process is classified as Insurrection under Article Fifteen of the Helmsguard Officer Code. A grievous crime."

Morbus paled. "I misspoke," he whispered, now appreciating the limits of the corner Vale had placed him in. "I was merely suggesting you needed to rest before..."

"Remove him and place him under arrest under charges of Insurrection," Vale intoned formally. She needed to make sure she did this right. She couldn't give Morbus even the slightest chance of escape through bureaucracy. It was bad enough that Yvorre's orders would be arriving soon – possibly as soon as tomorrow. She had to leave. Almost as if reading her mind, Morbus smiled.

"None of this matters, Vale. Soon, Yvorre's orders will be here and I will be placed in charge. You've bought yourself a day or two at most before I hunt you down like a dog."

Vale walked up to the Bureaucrator and stared down into his ugly face. "Tell me, Morbus, did you also report to Yvorre that you were about to have yourself arrested for Insurrection, and that you would need a pardon from her as well as a promotion?"

Morbus froze. The smugness evaporating for the last time.

"No?" Vale continued. "That's a shame. Any officer facing active charges must immediately be removed from any and all command responsibility until the charge is resolved, as clearly stated under Article Three. Am I correct Salus?"

"Indeed, you are, my lady," Salus replied with a smile.

"I expect this will create a procedural dilemma for you, Salus, I'm sorry to say."

"It will no doubt take us some back and forth to sort out, my lady," Salus replied, glaring at Morbus. "In the meantime, your standing orders will prevail."

"Quite right," Vale smiled and nodded for Morbus to be removed. She watched the defeated man as they bustled him from the tent under the control of Salus and the guard. Ethan turned to her once they were alone.

"Vale, you know I'm always with you, but what are we doing?"

Vale looked at him and felt genuine guilt. "I'm sorry, Ethan. I'm doing the only thing I can. The only thing that's left."

"Morbus is right. They're going to come after you sooner or later. What are you going to do afterwards? What happens to you when you come back from Fairhaven?"

Vale stared at the markings of Fairhaven on the map and felt a certainty. It didn't really matter what Morbus or Yvorre planned to do to her once she came back from Fairhaven. After the revelations of today, she now knew better. It was an odd sensation; it should have alarmed her – but it didn't. It gave her a strange sense of satisfaction. A sense of certainty. Of peace. Deep in her soul, she knew that – no matter the outcome – Vale would not return from Fairhaven.

BOOK 2
RETRIBUTION

CHAPTER 1

"While the Ageless are revered throughout the Outlands, there is a common misconception that they serve as leaders to the Outland settlements. This is not true. The Ageless have little interest in administration. The settlements are led and administered as each town decides for themselves. In the town of Fairhaven, the townspeople routinely select a nominated Council to oversee the practical daily operations of the town. However, while the Council may wield administrative authority, they will always yield to the will of the Ageless."

~Aleasea of the Ageless

The days that followed were black and full of grief. An entire city mourned. Dozens of innocents had lost their lives on that afternoon. Captain Lewis was said to be furious. It was rumoured that he didn't sleep in the week that followed, so great was his desire to root out the cause of this evil. The city was completely locked down in curfew for three days. No one was permitted to leave their homes for all but the most serious of reasons. The Council demanded action and answers. It was ultimately discovered that the invaders had gained access to the city via an old and disused hatch in the western wall. Once it had been used to transport goods and stock through to the city stable grounds; however, it had long since been barred and sealed after the last nomad raids. Somehow the hatch had been breached, and the Northmen had chosen the cruellest of moments - the day when all the city was united in celebration - to commit their murder.

Lewis was preparing for a swift reprisal. He ordered every cadet and soldier to report for immediate duty. Lewis intended to scour every rock of every mountain until the raiders were killed and their bodies burnt.

Funerals began immediately after the curfew had lifted, as families began the grim chore of laying their dead loved ones to rest. The Temple was filled with mourners for days and nights, people seeking solace and offering prayers for Maelene to watch over the victims and the living. Priests clad in black tended to all who came, and the entire temple seemed shrouded and subdued by some oppressive air. The Ageless had not been seen since.

Elyn was alone in her grief, even denying Vale entry into her mind. She refused to deal with the lies Yvorre had shown her the day the Northmen killed Leon. Elyn had decided that – for all she knew – Vale was a part of the deception, and so she resisted the pressing intrusions into her mind. She hadn't been able to do that before, and she didn't know if the grief had strengthened her or if Vale was simply respectful. She actually didn't care which was the reason. Although Jason and Nadine both had tried to console her in the days that followed the tragedy, she had likewise been unwilling to accept their sympathies. Yet in their case, she wasn't sure why. She only knew that her life had now changed and that theirs remained the same, and this somehow made her resentful. While Nadine had stayed with her for the first night after the murder, Elyn had found that she just wanted to be alone and had asked her to leave the following day. The parting was tense and Elyn realized that she'd probably been a little rude to her friend, but she found herself now resentful of the beautiful young woman with a perfect life.

There was a certain peace that could be found in solitude. A certain comfort that comes from knowing that you are alone and quiet and shielded from the world around you that seems filled with pain and disappointment. Leon was cremated in the Temple as soon as the curfew had been lifted. Elyn had been eager to move through the pain as quickly as possible, and she found the thought of unfinished farewells to be far too much to bear. She had stood in the gloomy chamber at the head of the congregation as they blessed and praised her father for all he had achieved in life. A large number of people had turned out to respect Leon – so many that Elyn was surprised. She hadn't known that Leon had been thought of so highly. But this realization only made her feel worse, and she found herself slipping further into a depression that had been growing steadily deeper. As soon as the ceremony was completed, she retreated back into

Leon's home. She continued to ignore Vale's pleas for counsel. There had been no word if Elyn could remain there now that Leon was dead, but Elyn didn't think about it. She just wanted to be alone.

• • •

Jason came to visit a week after the attack. Elyn had been sitting in Leon's old armchair staring into the fire, which was permanently alight. She didn't rise when Jason let himself in, instead she merely acknowledged him with a wan smile.

"Hey, Elyn, how are you feeling?" Jason asked as he closed the wooden door behind him.

"Fine," Elyn mumbled, returning her gaze to the fire.

Jason took stock of the room. It was dark, and the curtains remained closed despite the strong early afternoon sun outside. Layers of dust lay across the furniture and swam in the sunbeams. A handful of unclean plates lay in a pile on the table and the water buckets were empty. The room smelled stale of human odors and other scents that Jason couldn't place – nor did he particularly want to.

"Nadine's been asking about you. She wants to know if you need anything."

"No. Not really," Elyn felt a stab of pain at this lie. The truth was she'd wanted Jason to be there more than anything, but the fact that he had taken so long to come made her feel even more resentful.

"Have you seen her?" she asked.

Jason suddenly seemed awkward. "A couple of times, yeah. We see each other around."

Jealousy flared within Elyn.

"Elyn, you need to come out of here. This isn't good for you," Jason said, changing the subject.

"I want to stay right here," Elyn replied quietly.

"Well, you can't." He crossed the room and pulled the curtains apart. "I know this is rough, but we need you on your feet."

Elyn didn't reply and Jason pulled a chair to sit opposite.

"Look, they're sending me into the mountains."

Elyn glanced at him in surprise and noticed for the first time that Jason was wearing the pale-blue livery of the town guard.

"Yeah, that's right, they've drafted me, along with about forty or so others. Lewis wants every trained man or lad to be doing his part. Even some of the girls are getting called up. Looks like I'm going to get to be a soldier a lot sooner than I thought."

"I think you became a soldier a week ago."

A silence hung in the air. Jason seemed unsure of what to say.

"I killed a man. I didn't think I'd have to do that yet. I thought I had more time." Jason looked away to the window, his eyes seemed strange. "It wasn't hard, y'know? Just like they teach you in training, you swing your weapon...and then it goes in, and he falls...and after a bit...he's gone."

Elyn listened in silence. She felt a mild horror at what she heard, not just at the words but at the realization that it was her best friend who was saying them.

"We're going to head north into the mountains and take the fight back to them. Lewis thinks he knows where they are. I'm going to kill again, Elyn. I reckon I'll be pretty good by the time I get back."

Now it was Elyn who wasn't sure what to say. She didn't dare voice the obvious fear that Jason might not return.

"Be careful," she ventured lamely. Jason just returned a grim smile.

"I leave two days from now. That's why I've come. I need to make sure you're on your feet before I go."

"Why?"

"Because I can't just leave you like this! Come on, Elyn, I know what happened is terrible, but you need to get back up on your feet."

"Why? Does the Town Guard need someone like me now? Have they gotten that desperate?" Elyn replied with a little too much self-pity for her own ears.

"Yeah, they do actually. Maybe not to fight, but there's a lot you can do to help." Jason leaned forward in his chair. "Everyone's scared, Elyn. We've never had an attack like this before and no one knows why they did it this time. People are talking. They're saying that this could be the beginning of a new war, that there's a new warlord in the north who's taken command of the wild men. I don't know if it's true, but it's frightening people."

"Then it's great that you can do something about it." Elyn looked Jason in the eye for the first time. "You've always been useful, Jason, you've always landed on your feet no matter what happens to you. Now look at you, you're a soldier already, your parents are proud. Look at me! I don't even have a father to be ashamed of me anymore."

There was a moment's silence before Jason replied in a low voice. "Leon was never ashamed of you."

Tears flowed down Elyn's cheeks. She turned her head in a futile attempt to hide them. Jason wasn't sure how to respond.

"I don't know what to do now, Jason," Elyn's voice cracked, faltered, and betrayed her. It wasn't just the death of Leon; it was Vale, it was Yvorre, it was everything. She tried to keep the emotions in check, but it was getting too hard. She wanted someone to hold her. She looked over at Jason and met his eyes.

A sharp rap at the door startled them both. Elyn wasn't sure what to do for a moment, but it was Jason who got to his feet and answered the door. Both of them were surprised to find a young messenger standing officiously in the doorway.

"I come seeking Elyn, daughter of Leon," he declared, using Elyn's official designation. Jason turned to look at Elyn, who was already on her feet and walking to the door.

"I am Elyn," she answered as she approached, attempting to tidy her appearance. The man turned to address her.

"The Council of Fairhaven orders you to report to the Council Chambers immediately and with all due haste."

Elyn turned to look at Jason in surprise only to find that Jason was returning the puzzled look. She turned back to the messenger. "Why?"

The messenger looked offended. "One does not question the Council's demands, young lady. You will report to the Council Chambers with all due haste. They are in session now and have demanded your presence in the chamber." He then glanced down at Elyn over his long nose, turned, and left without another word. Elyn and Jason were left looking at each other.

"What should I do?" asked Elyn.

"Well, you should go, I guess," Jason answered.

"Yes, alright… I guess I will."

Elyn suffered a deep sense of foreboding. What did the Council want with her? She turned to face Jason. "How long will you be gone?"

Jason shrugged. "I don't know. Maybe a few days, maybe a few months. It all depends on what we find up there and how it all goes."

"Be careful, Jason," Elyn said with sincerity. She stood there for a moment and allowed herself to hope that the brotherly bond he felt toward her would finally change into the love she'd been feeling for him. She ached to be held by him just for a moment, to have him run his hands through her hair and tell her that everything was alright. She needed that now more than anything else.

"Hey, you don't have to worry about me. I'm the Champion Ascendant remember?" A touch of his usual mock bravado returned. "But I want you to take care of yourself, Elyn. Please go to my parents if you need anything or talk to Nadine. Just don't sit inside by yourself, please. No good is going to come from that."

Elyn nodded in return. She let her fantasies evaporate.

"Now you'd better go and find out what the Council wants with you, and if it's about the incident with the Ageless in the laneway, then you'd better not mention my name or I'll come after you!" Jason gave his surrogate sister a playful nudge on the shoulder then turned to leave. "I'll see you soon, Elyn, and I'll have some stories to tell you."

Elyn said goodbye and closed the door after him.

. . .

Minutes later, she was hurrying through the town toward the Council Chambers in the center of Fairhaven. Worry lay on her mind. She didn't know why the Council would summon her, but she had a rising suspicion. Did they finally know about Vale? Was her mental flare detected by the Ageless as well as Yvorre? She could still hear the wild man Jarren in her head. Who else had taken note of what she had done? The Ageless had been there, and Elyn knew that it was unlikely that they had taken no notice. She hurried past the bustling traders and shoppers up through to the large building with an ornate balcony standing near the river. Large stone steps covered by a deep red carpet marked the entry. Elyn skipped up the steps two at a time and half-jogged into the large foyer decorated with blue banners and two large chandeliers. A formally dressed doorman regarded her with curiosity.

"My name is Elyn, daughter of Leon. I was summoned by the Council a few moments ago."

The doorman nodded curtly and pointed to a large set of wooden double doors at the end of the room. She walked through them and found herself in another room, smaller than the first but far more impressive. Twelve large padded and wooden high-backed chairs were arranged in a semicircle on a stage facing an audience of wooden pews, all equally elegant and plush. The walls and ceiling were high and lined with more dark wood, all engraved with the most intricate images of trees, leaves, and other images of nature. Upon the chairs on the stage sat twelve men and women – the Council of Fairhaven. They had fallen silent and turned to regard Elyn as she slowly made her way into the chamber. She appeared very awkward and self-conscious and stood still for a moment hoping that she had not done the wrong thing by walking in unannounced. It was an older man with finely groomed hair and a moustache who broke the silence.

"Elyn? Is that you dear? Come here, come here. We've been waiting for you."

Paeter gestured for Elyn to come forward and Elyn obeyed, walking until she stood directly before the raised platform. She had forgotten that Nadine's father had gained himself a position on the Council, and the sight of his kind face relieved her.

"Thank you for answering our summons so promptly, Elyn. On behalf of the Council, I extend my deepest sympathies to you in this time of grief. Leon was a good man and counted as a friend by many of us here, and we grieve with you."

There were nods and murmurs of assent from the remaining members. Elyn hadn't expected the gesture and was caught by surprise at the silence that followed. Slowly, she realized that she was expected to say something in reply.

"Thank you, sir."

Silence followed her absurdly short and inarticulate response. Elyn cringed inwardly as more silence followed, and the Council waited to see if she had anything more to add. When it was obvious that she hadn't, Paeter continued.

"Elyn, we apologise for this disturbance in your time of mourning, but these are strange days, and much is happening now that has not come to pass in many years. Indeed, some events are transpiring that have never happened in my lifetime." Paeter glanced down at his hands for a moment then looked up straight at Elyn. "The Ageless have come to us, Elyn, and they have requested we have an interview with you."

Elyn felt her stomach drop. With this one statement, he confirmed her worst fears.

"The Ageless do not *request*, Councillor Paeter, they instruct," corrected an older woman seated at the far side of the platform. Paeter nodded in reply.

"Why have they done this?" Elyn ventured although she knew the answer. The woman replied in a cold voice.

"The Ageless have declared that during the Wellspring Festival, you were witnessed to be performing some kind of dark ritual on the Northmen. Is this true?"

"No!" Elyn answered. "No. I don't know any dark magic. I don't know any magic at all. I don't know what happened, but I didn't do anything...intentionally."

"But something did happen?" Paeter asked, his face grave. Elyn was trapped. She tried to think of an explanation that would satisfy them without betraying her link to Vale.

"I don't know what happened, sir. All I know is that the man killed Leon, and then he looked at me, and then something happened in his mind, I'm not sure what, and we both collapsed."

Silence held in the chamber for a few moments.

"Black magic!" the woman snapped. Her thin and wrinkled face was now dark. "This girl is lying to us. She practices some dark rituals in secret and would have us believe that she now knows nothing of her powers?"

"Councillor Morag, please!" Paeter interjected. "This is not the appropriate forum to discuss such matters."

"Oh, but it is, Paeter. The girl has admitted to practising her dark powers on the very day the Northmen attacked. You think that mere coincidence?"

Several other councillors were starting to nod their head in agreement. Elyn began to feel a panic rising within.

"Captain Lewis is yet to determine how the invaders opened the gate in the city wall. I believe that we may have our answer standing before us," Morag continued, her tone becoming slightly shrill. "Tell us, girl, was it the wild men that taught you their magic? Were you sent here as a spy from Outpost? Is that why you were out past curfew a few weeks before the attack? Were you plotting that day with your conspirators?"

A noose was beginning to tighten around Elyn's neck. She felt trapped. It seemed that all the recent events of her life were conspiring against her.

"Councillor, you are out of order! I have known this lady many years, and she is no conspirator!" Paeter rose to his feet. Morag mirrored the gesture.

"No, I am not out of order. I speak common sense. She is suspect by her own admission! She must be seized and taken to trial immediately!"

Several other councillors now joined in the argument, some agreeing with Morag, others siding with Paeter. Voices were raised now, and the meeting had descended into chaos. Elyn didn't know what to do. She felt the urge to run while the councillors were distracted with each other, but she knew that would just compound her problem and it would convince them of her guilt. She had a sudden urge to call Vale for help but also knew that it would be a very bad idea under the circumstances. Her head swam and she felt a wave of nausea.

"Silence!"

The command echoed from the stalls in the rear of the chamber. Elyn put her hands to her ears as it felt like the words had sliced through her temples and into her mind. Given the abrupt silence among the councilors, it seemed they were likewise afflicted. The figure in green appeared to rush toward them out of the gloom as if coasting on a gale. It towered over Elyn and addressed the assembly thundering and terrible.

"We did not have you summon this girl to have her subjected to your bickering!"

The gathering was speechless.

"Forgive us, Master," Morag recovered. "We...we did not know you were here—"

"The fate of this one does not rest with you, nor with any in this room," the Ageless interrupted her coldly. It was difficult for Elyn to identify the voice, it seemed without gender but weighted with authority. Shrieking yet also cavernous and deep, it seemed as if it spoke with more than one mouth.

"We did not seek to disobey you," Morag rushed to explain. She seemed distressed and her cold eyes were now laced with a slight desperation. "We only seek to safeguard the city from any possible harm. The actions of this girl are—"

"None of your concern," the Ageless finished for her. "You will leave her to us."

Elyn didn't know if this was at all reassuring.

"Leave us now," the Ageless continued. "Bar the chamber doors. None may re-enter here until tomorrow."

The councillors rose and began to file out of the chamber. Paeter offered Elyn a quick glance - whether from sympathy or fear, Elyn couldn't be certain - but then he too was gone, and the giant wooden doors boomed shut behind him. The hooded figure turned to face her. From this distance, Elyn noticed that the darkness of its hood was impenetrable despite the nearby lamps. She also realized that whatever manner of creature lay under those billowing robes, it was likely as much a mystery to the councillors as it was to her.

"Be seated."

Much to Elyn's surprise, the words were not unkindly, so much that it almost sounded like a request rather than an instruction. Regardless of the phrasing, Elyn obeyed as rapidly as was possible.

"Be at ease, young lady. You have no reason to fear us." The voice was no longer cutting but warm and almost feminine. "The councillors overstepped themselves. You were not summoned to us for an interrogation."

"Thank you," Elyn replied, using the only phrase that came into her bewildered mind.

"The time for thanks is not yet come. We have called you here as your actions during the Wellspring Festival did not go undetected by my order, and the Ageless have an interest in such matters."

Dread filled Elyn. "What does that mean?"

"That depends on the secret behind your actions, Elyn. Are you naturally gifted, are you a chance recipient of fortune, or are you an agent for a higher power, or a darker one?"

"I'm no agent!" Elyn rushed to respond.

"But if what you say is true and you have no insight into what happened that day, then how can you answer that question? There are forces in this world that can drive a person without her knowing. Can we risk that you may be an agent for such a force?"

Elyn saw the heart of the problem. She wondered how much the Ageless already knew.

"The truth, Elyn, is that there are many ancient powers in this world that you cannot possibly comprehend. We cannot let this development pass unscrutinized, for the good of the town and all who dwell here."

Elyn let the words sink in before answering, but before she could, the Ageless spoke again.

"Very good, Elyn. Calm and careful consideration of your thoughts before you give voice is a practice most wise. This is the first time I believe I have witnessed you exercise such restraint."

Elyn was mildly shocked at the compliment, but it put her at ease nonetheless. "What do you want of me?" she asked.

"Nothing against your will, Elyn. This is true. Despite my instructions to the Councillors, you are free to leave this chamber now and return to your home. We will not interfere. However, we will likewise refuse to interfere in whatever actions follow. As you have already witnessed today, there will be those who will not feel comfortable with your deeds and the powers they betrayed in you. You will have to deal with them and their desires for you – both good and ill. I fear that your life has changed forever, and there is no power we possess that can reset things as they once were."

The words held more truth than the speaker intended. First Vale's incursion into her mind, followed by Leon's death and now this. Elyn's life one week ago now seemed years away, her problems which had seemed so great then, were now trivial and laughable by comparison. She wanted to go home and shut out the world again, but she now understood that she had to be stronger than that. Her problem had to be faced and she had to stare it in the eye. It would make Leon proud.

"If I go home, then Councillor Morag will never give me peace, will she?" Elyn asked, looking up into the deep folds of the green hood before her.

"No," came the sharp answer. "And even if your supporters like Councillor Paeter could keep her in check, you would doubtless find other enemies outside the Council. You would be forced to deal with those as well."

"Then my options are limited, aren't they?" Elyn asked rhetorically. "Exile out there, or exile with you."

"We do not offer you exile, Elyn. We offer you the opportunity to explore your abilities. We can help you."

Despite her suspicion, Elyn realized she had little choice. The Ageless couldn't know that Yvorre was also out there looking for her. By now she might even be watching the gates, waiting to see if Elyn would unwittingly deliver herself by trying to flee.

"What do you ask of me?" Elyn repeated.

"Come with me into Sanctuary of the Temple. There, I will present you to my associates who will look deep into your being, Elyn. They will determine the truth about you."

She was shocked at the magician's words. No one was permitted to go into the inner chambers of the Temple and to do so was an offence punishable by death – presumably at the hands of someone like the figure standing before her.

"And what if you don't like the truth you discover in me?" she ventured.

A silence gripped the chamber again. Elyn held her breath.

"I will not lie to you, Elyn. If your heart is black, then actions will be called for. What these actions may be, I cannot say. But if your heart remains true, then we will offer you more than has been given to any other outside our order. This is indeed a rare honor for you."

Elyn sighed. She didn't know if she had the power to hide her secret from the Ageless, but there were few alternatives now. She was tired of secrets. She was tired of what they'd done to her life. She wanted to tell somebody. She needed help. And if they judged her as an agent of evil, then at least she'd have some certainty back in her life.

"Very well then," she spoke aloud. "I accept your offer. I will come with you."

The cloaked figure did not immediately reply, regarding the young woman in silence for a moment.

"Follow," it finally commanded and then turned to glide back up the passageway between the rows of seats. Elyn did as she was ordered and walked a few paces behind the robed figure as it approached an alcove in the rear of the chamber. The back section of the small hollow seemed to fall away, revealing a narrow passageway beyond. The Ageless did not break stride as it entered the doorway, and Elyn allowed herself a moment of doubt before plunging ahead into the darkness. Inside, the passage was cool and dimly lit by several small lamps – the like of which she had never before seen – embedded into the wall. It was unclear whether the lamps were glowing with flame or some other element, but Elyn didn't have time to investigate as the Ageless was gliding down the corridor so fast now that she had to struggle to keep pace. The corridor sloped downward and twisted this way and that at unexpected intervals. The cracks in the stone made Elyn wonder at the age of the corridor – hundreds of years she guessed, possibly as old as the city itself. After a few minutes of walking, the corridor ended at the head of a winding stone stairway that led down into the bowels of whatever part of the city they had now travelled to. The hooded figure now turned to face Elyn.

"Wait here until I return."

It then mounted the stairs with the same fluid grace and descended without another word. Elyn waited. Minutes dragged by and seemed to turn to hours. She couldn't be sure exactly how long she waited there since the only light came from the alien lamps that cast their strange and steady glow. Finally, the stairway darkened with the shadow of the green robed figure as it silently ascended and turned to face Elyn.

"I have spoken to my associates and they are ready to meet with you, Elyn. Are you prepared?"

"Yes, I am," she lied.

To her surprise, the Ageless moved toward her, raised its hands – delicate and pale Elyn now noticed – and pulled back its hood. The unnatural darkness behind the hood dissolved to reveal the features of a pale and beautiful woman, her face framed with long golden hair which now fell around her shoulders. Her eyes were slightly slanted and colored the most beautiful shade of green, and her ears were so delicate they looked to be crafted from porcelain. Never in her life had Elyn beheld such perfect features, the gentle curves of the cheeks and the nose and chin so delicate as if they had been carefully sculptured from ice. Yet it was the woman's eyes that captivated her. Those eyes so beautiful and deep enough to drown all the sorrows of the world. They betrayed wisdom and strength that her fragile features belied. Elyn gasped in astonished delight. The woman smiled warmly.

"My name is Aleasea, and I am an immortal servant of Maelene. Does my appearance surprise you?"

Elyn took a moment to gaze at the beauty of the face before her. "Are all the Ageless women?" she blurted out.

Aleasea crouched so their eyes were level and fixed her with a steady look. "Elyn, I need you to be sober and vigilant. This could well be the most important moment of your life. I am about to present you to the Assembly. Such an event has not happened in hundreds of years, and not all of my colleagues welcome this. Do not fear," she said, sensing Elyn's alarm. "No harm will come to you – I will not allow it – but you must understand that what comes from this will be determined by everything you say and do from the moment we enter that chamber. Do you understand me?"

"*Make Leon proud of you!*" Elyn thought. She nodded in silence.

Aleasea rose to her full height and hooded her face once more. Without another gesture, she began a second descent with Elyn close behind. The staircase was longer than she expected, and it took another few minutes before they landed at the bottom. When they arrived, Elyn was completely unprepared for the sight that awaited her.

CHAPTER 2

"Maelene, the Blessed Mother, created the immortal Ageless as her first act upon arriving in Kovalith. Although at first there were only a handful, over centuries she created more beings of different race, color, and species. For Maelene loved all forms of life and the creation of more and different beings gave her immense pleasure. Now with the passing of Maelene, there are no longer any new Ageless to bless our world. We have always served as the protectors of the Blessed Mother, a role we continue to fulfill even long after she has fallen."

~Aleasea of the Ageless

Elyn stood in the rear of a large cavern dominated by a giant statue of a beautiful woman – Maelene. Her arms were outstretched, and water cascaded out of each palm into a reflecting pool several dozen feet below. The statue and the rest of the cavern seemed to be illuminated from below by the same unnatural light; only this time it was far more powerful, casting large shadows up into the cavern's walls. She had never seen anything so grand before. The ceiling above the great space seemed to be embedded with hundreds of small crystals that reflected the light and gave the illusion of a field of stars bathing the area in a warm glow. Elyn saw these crystals reflected dozens of times in the eyes of the hooded figures massed before her. They stood silently watching her take the final steps into the chamber and then regarded her as she stood before them. Elyn had no idea how many there were – certainly dozens – all robed in green or purple, some normal height, others much larger, all of them with their hoods raised but their faces visible to her. Elyn speculated that the hood's concealment was something they might activate at will. Their expressions were impassive. They regarded her with nothing more than a professional and respectful curiosity, or at least so it appeared.

"Who is this?" a voice like gravel barked. The figure in dark-violet robes stood on a raised platform of stone several feet above the others. Elyn felt Aleasea's hand press her forward, and she slowly walked into the mass of figures as they parted to allow her through. She noticed a peculiar mix of emotions as she walked through the throng of robed men and women. Fear, trepidation, and excitement all competed within her. She swept the group with her eyes and as she did so, her mind unexpectedly did the same. It quested out as if to link with a kindred soul, scanning and searching the hearts before her. This time a wave of calm emanated from the gathering. Elyn couldn't trust it. She somehow knew she would never be safe now, that blind trust was behind her. Every inch of her being was instead open to pure instinct. The room was a banquet filled with a feast of feelings and egos – of stable emotions and fractured minds.

Elyn realized she could feel them all.

She pulled her focus back to the moment and the sensations receded. As she approached the dais, she saw that – even without the platform – this Ageless above would tower over the others. The figure turned his head and Elyn saw a face like coal peering back at her. His head appeared to be carved entirely of rock, his eyes were red burning embers, and there was something ancient about him. Silence filled the cavern.

Aleasea stepped forward and addressed the congregation in a powerful voice.

"Brethren, give me your attention. I bring you Elyn, Daughter of Leon. She has come here freely and of her own will to be tested by us." She reached back and grabbed Elyn by the shoulder, gently propelling her ahead. "She stands ready and I hand her over to you. May our collective wisdom prevail."

Elyn was staring at the Ageless impolitely but found that she could not tear her vision away. The red eyes seemed to hold her in place, burning deep within and scratching away at her soul. Elyn was relieved when the figure finally spoke.

"My name is Veroulle. You are wondering about me, are you not? About what I am? My age? Where I come from?"

"I'm sorry, but I've seen no one like you before."

"Ah, but do you question the appearance of the world as much as you question the appearance of me?"

"I...I'm sorry, I don't understand?"

"No, you do not, how can you? Forgive me, it is not normally my way to be so dramatic, but my days grow long. I am tired and perhaps now even a little unsure. Come forth, Elyn!"

Elyn took an uncertain step forward, so that she stood apart from Aleasea.

"Elyn, daughter of Leon," Veroulle spoke in a clear voice that rang across the space. "The Sacred Order of the Ageless has stood watch against the forces of Bythe, the Lord of Deceit, for centuries. We alone guard the free women and men of the Forge against his evil. This duty was charged to us by our Blessed Mother Maelene, and it is a task that each of us perform every day for the length of our mortal lives."

"For we honor Her." The chant had been taken up by every person in the chamber save Elyn, and the resonance caught her off guard.

"We work here to guard not only this city, but the Outland Alliance against forces that are sleepless in their efforts against us. These forces plague from without and from within."

With these last words, he held Elyn's gaze firmly so that his point was not lost.

"I have been watching you," called another man from behind, his dark-violet robes were slightly different to the others and Elyn noticed an almost regal bearing as he approached the dais. "I have sensed something unusual in recent days." He reached up and swept the gold-trimmed hood back in one graceful gesture, revealing the same slender features that Aleasea had revealed to her. Only this man had dark hair swept back over a sharp and smooth face. Like Aleasea, his features also seemed perfect – as if carved from marble – and Elyn judged that his age was impossible to guess. "And the source of that disturbance appears to be you."

He levelled a cold stare at Elyn that set her skin tingling. Not with fear, but with an unusual sensation. Elyn realized that she could sense nothing from this man. None of the other emotions that bubbled and popped among the throng were present in him. His dark eyes felt empty. He was completely *blank*. Elyn hesitated.

"Ferehain, now is not the time," Aleasea interrupted.

"Yes, Aleasea, it is," the man named Ferehain continued. "I have served our Mother as a member of the Ageless for over six hundred years. Many of us have done so. It is my life honor, but I would gladly lay down that life for the good of the people I serve, knowing the purpose that I fulfill. This woman is dangerous. If she holds power, then she also holds no strength with which to wield it. I have watched this one, and she is weak. I do not believe our order can benefit from such weakness."

The feelings around Elyn became stronger now. There were hints of agitation and spices of anger bubbling up and popping here and there throughout the crowd. Alarm filled her yet she struggled to remain calm.

"She is clearly unique among her kin," Aleasea said with a casual elegance. "We all know this. We cannot turn her away until we understand her gifts. We must be fluid and adaptive in this, as our Blessed Mother taught us."

Ferehain looked at Aleasea with an impassive expression. The ripple of reaction from the gathering buffered Elyn. Glances were exchanged and expressions altered. Surprise. Curiosity. Indignation. Their scents glided to her as if carried on an unseen breeze. The smooth veneer of emerald and violet had begun to rustle and flow with excitement.

"Enough!" Veroulle said, his voice as cavernous as the room itself. "As our senior ranks cannot agree, then I will exercise my right to arbitrate. We shall take Elyn to the Arcadia, and the three of us shall judge her accordingly."

Elyn suspected that this was an unusual declaration for the Ageless. Indeed, the implications for her own life were only now starting to register in her mind. Aleasea and Ferehain both nodded in silence, and Aleasea gently took Elyn's arm.

"Come with me now," she said. Veroulle and Ferehain descended the dais and led the way. They skirted the massive stone statue and walked to the far end of the cavern where several archways led away from the chamber. They chose one, and once again, Elyn walked steeply downward along an underground passage, only this time the passageway was honeycombed with intersecting paths. Some they ignored while others they took, but the result was still the same to Elyn's eyes and the passage remained almost unchanged.

"These are unprecedented times, Aleasea," Ferehain's sharp voice drifted back to them. "Who can say what our Mother intended with this one? We were all born into this order, chosen by Maelene herself, we were all of us different. This girl is the first to come to us since our Mother's fall. Who are we to establish new laws in her absence?"

"We should honor the traditions set by Maelene's example. Treat her as we were treated. It is the Mother's will," Aleasea replied.

"We have no right to presume her will. We must be careful not to confuse divine intention with our own imperfect desires," Ferehain said.

"We do not have the wisdom to foresee what the Mother had intended for this one," Veroulle broke in. "However, we know she has not come to us by the same path taken by the rest of us. What right do we have to try and set her on that path? Who here can foresee the consequence of such an act? Who here possesses such wisdom?"

Both of the others fell silent and Elyn started to appreciate the authority Veroulle carried. After several minutes, they emerged into an unexpectedly large room. Like most of the other rooms in this place, its entrance was a massive arch, but unlike the others, the arch led to a small platform at the head of three steps. Beyond these steps lay a round room that was immense. It was capped with a domed ceiling high above. Beneath this cupola, floating over an ornate ring carved into the floor, a large glass ball of pulsating light hovered in the center of the room. It towered over Elyn and she could feel something within calling out to her. A strange altar with two faded globes of glass stood toward the entrance to the chamber, beyond this a plain timber bench was set on the platform next to the ball of light. A faint violet phosphorescence seemed etched into intricate engravings into the dome above them. They halted before the bench. Veroulle turned his gaze back to Elyn and held it for a long time. Elyn started to feel very uncomfortable again, as if the eyes were finding a passage into her heart and to her thoughts.

"Where have you taken me?" she asked.

"We call this the Arcadia. It is the soul of our Sacred Heart and is the source of our great power. This room was infused with the sacred blood of Maelene herself when she built this place, and it is blessed with her nature. It will read the soul of any being – man, woman, or beast – and it will pour out their true nature to any who bear witness. It will reveal your secrets, Elyn."

Elyn felt dread.

"There is a strange force about you, Elyn, one that is not natural," Ferehain said, regarding her as if from a distance. "Your father was stubborn when I called upon him before the festival. He would not reveal the secrets of you which I knew he kept."

"My father didn't keep any secrets from me."

Ferehain raised an eyebrow the merest fraction, yet on his implacable face it had a striking effect. "You are an unusual one, Elyn, you seem to be completely without courage and yet you followed me into the alley that day. That is a thing few grown men would dare do. It gives me hope that you may yet have potential."

Elyn was stunned. The twin revelations that it was Ferehain who she had followed in the alley and that it was Ferehain who had visited Leon left Elyn's mind in disarray. How much did they know? She considered confessing everything right then, just spilling it all out in a mad moment of panic, but she also realized the Arcadia would no doubt do that for her in a matter of moments. She drew in a breath and remained silent.

"Come, Elyn, be seated," Aleasea whispered. She guided her up the steps and into the ornate ring carved into the wooden platform. Aleasea and Ferehain each took up positions next to the two globes on the altar. Elyn took a breath and lowered herself onto the bench which gave no sigh or protest under her weight.

"Are you ready?" asked Veroulle.

Elyn nodded and closed her eyes. She sensed something tickling around the edge of her thoughts, like something pulling at her attention, a vague distraction, only the annoyance became more assertive. It started to burrow into her mind like a parasite, cracking through her train of concentration so that her thoughts seemed to change direction midstream. It seemed difficult to focus. Whenever she tried to hold a coherent thought it was buffeted away like someone had smashed it from her hands. She was trying to recall where she was. She was talking with Aleasea. She had been told to sit in the chair. No. Aleasea was leading her down a corridor away from the Council. Then she was about to tell her to sit in the chair? Then another shove and Aleasea dissolved to be replaced with Leon. He wasn't breathing. Blood was pooling under his head, staining his hair. Elyn's cheeks were wet and the Ageless were watching. Then there was another violent shove within her mind and the Helmsguard were watching. They were going to attack Elyn at Outpost. She had to run! She was running through the town. Running faster than she ever had. The surrounds were a blur. She lost track of where she was. She felt panic. Fear. It was cold in her stomach. Ice. She rounded a corner and faced herself.

Don't say her name.

She was staring at herself intently. Why was she wearing a black robe? Elyn looked at herself and realized she was similarly dressed, only in a white robe. This never happened. Elyn approached her twin and her twin approached her – like a reflection in a mirror. She held up a hand and extended it. Their fingers slowly met, then at that instant her twin started to collapse, as if she was made of paper. Her skin began to darken and rumple, blackened as if in a fire. Her eyes were empty sockets and her face became shrunken, jawbones and cheekbones protruding through the black skin before the face itself folded inward. Elyn watched in horror as her image spasmed and convulsed, then folded inward – arms, legs, and neck – all snapped into her body and then imploded into an inky blackness. The blackness grew and Elyn was instantly surrounded by nothing. She couldn't see. Panic overwhelmed her and she felt a desperate urge to cry out, to scream for help, but she couldn't see or hear anyone. She suddenly realized that she didn't even know where she was, and the feeling was suffocating. The deep surge rose within her and broke free of its own will. Elyn screamed. She yelled and thrashed about, trying to tear down the very darkness itself. There was another shove in her head but this time she turned and caught it in her grasp, like she had stopped a blow and now held the fist in her hands. She pulled and the woman in green came sharply into focus. Everything about her came into focus. Her name was Aleasea. She was alone and afraid. Her friends were dying or going mad, and she was no longer sure of the road ahead. It hadn't always been like this. Once she had been young, strong, and reckless. Her allies could not be numbered. Once she had stood alongside Maelene herself and fought the armies of iron from the west. Now she feared she did little more than hide in a cave and dream of days that would never come.

Aleasea cried out and Elyn received another push, this time more forceful. Ferehain's face filled her mind. His impassive features were now dark with emotion. He pushed Elyn's mind again – hard – and the scene in front of her dissolved. She was back sitting in the wooden chair in the Arcadia. Aleasea had recoiled and was looking at Elyn in alarm. Even Veroulle, while still composed, now wore a look of concern on his ancient face. His burning eyes were narrowed and fixed on Elyn. Ferehain was watching Aleasea with a look of faint apprehension, before also turning his attention to Elyn.

"What did you do to Aleasea?" Veroulle asked in a quiet voice.

"I don't know," Elyn answered. "She was in my head...pushing me. I didn't like it, so I think...I tried to push back." Aleasea looked at her and couldn't hide her surprise.

"Was that bad?" Elyn ventured.

"Not necessarily," Veroulle replied. "However, in doing this you have reached into the mind of my brethren. This has never happened before."

"Alright. So it's bad," Elyn murmured to herself.

"The Arcadia has betrayed her. She is weak, panicked and without discipline," said Ferehain.

"No," Aleasea interrupted. "Her mind is searching for something. Her very soul is searching for something. That is what I felt when she reached into me."

"She may possess power, but she is broken," said Ferehain. "If we permit her to remain here, she will be nothing but a threat to us."

"She's missing something," corrected Aleasea. Elyn remained silent. She knew they were referring to Vale, but if they couldn't find her within Elyn's mind, despite all of their power, what did that mean? Veroulle was still gazing at her. The red eyes burning. Impassive. Elyn could feel herself fighting the unnatural discomfort that Veroulle seemed to inject into all those around him.

"What happened to you at Outpost?" Veroulle spoke at last.

Elyn paused a second too long before answering.

"You know what happened. We were invaded by the Iron Union. We had to flee here."

Veroulle took a step forward and repeated his question. "What happened to you at Outpost?"

With a cold shock, Elyn realized that Veroulle had not been speaking aloud. Somehow the old sorcerer had managed to reach into Elyn's mind and place the words there like books on a shelf.

"We have many talents," Veroulle continued in the same unnatural manner. "There is little you could hide from us should you try to do so. I assure you it would be utterly pointless."

Elyn could feel incorporeal tendrils working into her mind. Veroulle. She tried to push back, to clutch into that invisible fist the way she had done with Aleasea, but this was different. Veroulle's mind was as much like a rock as his skin. Elyn rallied her will against the invader yet it scattered like water against stone. Two red eyes were burning inside her mind now. They enveloped her vision and blotted out everything else around her.

"There is an emptiness in you, Elyn. There is something missing, and I suspect you may know what this is. I suspect you discovered this in Outpost."

Elyn started to buckle under the strain. She was vaguely aware of Aleasea's protests, but she was too far away to help. Everyone was too far away. There was only Veroulle and his scalding eyes.

"*Back, child!*" a voice from within Elyn spat.

Silence. The eyes were gone. Veroulle had taken a step backward, something akin to surprise was etched upon his face. Elyn trembled. Even Ferehain and Aleasea were looking at each other in confusion. The voice hadn't been hers. It wasn't even Vale's. Elyn felt sick.

"She is dangerous," Ferehain said. "She is far too unstable to remain here."

Veroulle said nothing. He only stared at Elyn in confusion. For a moment it seemed as if he were about to ask Elyn a question, then he remained silent.

Aleasea looked uncertain. "Are we to abandon her?"

"She is keeping secrets from us," Ferehain replied, his eyes never leaving Elyn's. "Whether intentional or not, we cannot tell. But we cannot risk exposing more of ourselves to one that we cannot trust. She should be imprisoned until we can learn the truth."

"Ferehain, no!" said Aleasea. "We need to help her."

"She cannot stay with us," Ferehain repeated.

"No," Veroulle spoke with quiet command. "No, she cannot. We need time to consider what has happened here." He glanced at Ferehain then seemed to regain his previous composure. "Aleasea, send her back. Although there are many questions here, we know for certain that Elyn cannot be trusted."

Ferehain gave Elyn a satisfied look. Aleasea seemed about to argue but fell silent after meeting Veroulle's eyes.

"What about the people up there? They don't exactly trust me either, do they?" Elyn asked.

"You have secrets that you think are worth protecting, hopefully those secrets will return the favor," Ferehain replied with a touch of sarcasm.

"Either way, your welfare is not our concern. We have far greater problems before us, and we have already wasted enough of our attention with you."

Nothing more was said. Even Aleasea was looking at the timber floor in silence. Veroulle raised his gold-trimmed hood and the mysterious darkness enveloped his features, Ferehain repeated the gesture, then finally – almost reluctantly – Aleasea did the same. The two purple-robed figures turned and swept out of the chamber as if Elyn were no longer even present.

"Follow," the cavernous and shrieking voice of Aleasea seemed all the worse now that Elyn knew the tender face behind it. The Ageless moved to follow the others out of the Arcadia. Elyn obeyed. As suddenly as it had been offered, the hope of refuge and answers had been cruelly withdrawn. Elyn felt emptiness return as she slowly ascended the steps to the city above.

CHAPTER 3

"The Outland settlements of the Outer Wild always enjoyed a loose alliance against the tyranny of Bythe, however such an alliance was easier when Maelene had served as their protector. Now these alliances seemed trivial, like childhood promises rendered foolish by time and by change."

~Aleasea of the Ageless

Elyn had never tasted beer this early in the day. She liked it. Given that she seemed to have few options available to her now, she had decided to indulge. The Last Jar was a rustic tavern with a lively clientele. Elyn had walked past many times and often wondered what it must be like to sit in its dusky interior and drink like so many others. Now that she did, she could see the appeal. The ale was already starting to have its euphoric effect on her, and the cheerful voices of the tavern were becoming more enjoyable to listen to as every moment passed. Elyn drained the last of the amber fluid from the glass and set it down to reveal the two concerned faces peering at her from the other side of the table. The news of Elyn's audience with the Ageless had spread throughout the town in the days that had followed; however, what could have been a powerful boon to her reputation and ego had quickly turned into a savage blow.

When Elyn had emerged from the temple, her hand shielding her eyes from the sunlight, she had stumbled down the massive stone steps, completely unsure of what to do next. In the hours that followed, she had walked aimlessly throughout the town, trying to shield herself from the feelings that drifted to her unbidden and unwelcome. It was in the afternoon when she found Nadine and Jason sitting together on the wall over the river. They had been shocked to see her. She could feel their surprise, along with something else. Agitation, shame, and an unusual amount of guilt. She sensed the feelings of others as well, those who looked at her with growing recognition. Their emotions as plain to her as a scent on the wind. She decided she couldn't handle it. Turning around in the street, she made her way to Leon's house as quickly as possible. Jason and Nadine had followed, but she refused to talk to them. She didn't want to answer their probing questions or face their disbelieving expressions. In the safety of her home, she found that she still didn't want to talk to her friends. Instead, she returned to her station in front of the fireplace and resumed her vigil.

Hours passed. Nadine and Jason came and went and came again. The hours bled into days, and she seemed safe from the town full of emotions waiting for her outside the door. Finally, on the morning of the last day before Jason was rostered to leave, her friends let themselves into Leon's home and forced a confrontation. Elyn gave up. She realized that eventually she was going to be interrogated and scrutinised before the entire gaping populace of Fairhaven, and a nihilistic impulse surged through her.

She decided she wanted to drink.

"Would you like another one, sweetheart?" came the greeting. It was a response to the call of Elyn's empty glass hitting the table. He had the handsome face of a young man, yet his dark eyes betrayed a masculinity that made Elyn's heart stir whenever she met them with her own.

"I think I will, Dex," she replied with a strange confidence. From the beer or something else, she couldn't tell, but the smile she received from the young man was proof that this confidence had its distinct advantages.

"I'll be right back then," he smiled and strode back to the bar. Elyn watched him leave.

"Elyn? Do you want to come back to us now?" Jason prompted her.

"Sorry," Elyn smiled and returned her attention to her two friends. "What were we saying?"

Nadine was incredulous. "You were saying that you've been interrogated by the Ageless! That they seem to have something against you. Elyn, what are you going to do now?"

"I'm going to leave," she replied simply. She hadn't mentioned anything of Vale. She still didn't want to. It didn't seem to matter that Vale hadn't entered her mind since the day of Leon's death. There was something strange about her two friends, as though they were harbouring a secret. The thought made her petulant. "Just like we left Outpost, I'll have to find somewhere else to go. Tell me what options do I have?"

"Elyn, no," Jason sighed. "You can't just leave. Where are you going to go?"

Elyn shrugged and looked out the window at nothing in particular. "I don't know. Probably further east toward the coast. There's still plenty of free settlements that are far enough away from the fighting. I'm sure I can find some sort of refuge there."

"Refuge? To do what? You haven't thought this through. You're still grieving from Leon. Don't make any decisions now."

Fear and agitation emanated from him. Elyn glanced back toward the bar and then back at her friends. "And what do you say, Nadine?" she asked.

Nadine shook her head. She was still grappling with the events that had apparently taken place. Elyn must have seemed strangely different now. "I don't think this is a good idea, Elyn."

There was an awkward pause. Nadine seemed to find something unusually interesting on the floor that captured her attention. Uncertainty started to ripple. Elyn was now sensing it, like sampling new flavours for the first time. Nadine's usual calm poise was absent and in its place was a most unsettling sensation.

"What's the matter, Nadine?" Elyn asked.

Nadine lost interest in whatever was on the floor and looked at her friend directly. "I don't understand what you mean when you say that you were inside the head of that man," she paused before continuing, "the one who killed Leon. What does that mean?"

Elyn let out a long breath. "I can't explain it," she replied carefully. "It was like a part of me reached out and grabbed him like I pulled him into me, or like I pulled myself into him. I'm not sure, but it was strange. I don't know how I did it."

"Have you been able to do it again?" Nadine asked.

"I can't seem to switch it on and off at will. I think it only happened because of what he'd done, because of what he made me feel..." The burning emotions of that day started to swell back into her chest. She tried her best to push them away. She felt a hand on her arm. Jason.

"Don't think about it."

His voice was like a balm. She chose to focus on it and let the rising feelings recede.

"So, what does this mean?" Nadine asked. "Are you some sort of sorcerer?"

The word sounded like an accusation, and for the first time, Elyn could see the seed of mistrust in her friend's eye.

"No, I'm not a sorcerer, Nadine. I don't know what I am, but I don't think that the Ageless will help me work this out. So, who else is going to?"

A filled glass was set in front of her with a knock.

"I can help you, beautiful," came Dex's deep voice. "This will make everything better, I promise."

Nadine rolled her eyes and looked away but Elyn didn't notice. She had arrested the opportunity to look into the dark eyes again, and once again, she could feel the alcohol having its effect.

"I think you're the one making me better," she replied. Jason glanced at her in faint surprise.

Dex smiled in a well-practiced fashion. "How about your friends? Would they like anything?"

Nadine grunted to express her revulsion at the concept, and Jason shook his head.

"Well, you know where to find me." He winked at Elyn and returned to the bar.

Elyn smiled. More people had filed into the tavern as the trio sat there, Elyn didn't need to turn in her seat to know this. She sensed them as they walked past her, indifferent at first, but after they took their seats, that indifference turned into something else. Flashes of surprise, curiosity, even fear. People were talking about her.

They knew who she was.

For Elyn, this was an unusual revelation, a feeling so unfamiliar it was almost a novelty. Celebrity wasn't a feat she had ever hoped to achieve, much less notoriety. Elyn savoured a mouthful of her drink while her mind tasted this new sensation. She glanced again at Nadine and saw that lingering uncertainty still directed at her. Jason fed her no such hesitation, only the warmth of genuine concern. All this validated her decision to keep these new sensations to herself. Her being was starting to alter, as if the pebbles that built up her very body were shifting inside, but the end result was beyond her wildest guess. She chose her words very carefully.

"People are going to mistrust me," she said, carefully avoiding Nadine's eyes. "They're doing it right now, in this room. Haven't you seen them glancing at me? They already know what happened. I don't think there's a future here for me anymore. I don't really think there ever was."

"You don't need to run. We care for you, Elyn, I care for you. People should never be afraid of who they are." Jason had leaned forward in his chair. Elyn thought for a moment that she felt a thread of love.

"And what if this is who I am? What if really underneath all of this, I'm some kind of creature with more in common with someone like Bythe than with someone like you?"

The thread snapped. Jason's face betrayed a flicker of alarm, as if his sister was drifting from him. Elyn took another sip. It was good to finally own something that was hers, truly hers. If it was going to destroy her then so be it – at least she would have something to define her.

"Elyn," Jason's voice cut through her thoughts. "Come talk with my father. He'll know what to do. He can help you."

His plea was almost unheard. The drink was starting to seep into her thoughts and with it came another feeling. A familiar one.

"*Elyn.*"

Vale's voice was pressing into her mind. Stronger now and far clearer than it had been.

"*Elyn, let me through.*"

She tried to push the voice away. She certainly didn't need Vale in her head now that she knew the Ageless were suspicious, but for some reason it now seemed to be a much harder thing to do. Elyn couldn't be sure if it was the drink lowering her defenses, but somehow Vale seemed more present. Closer.

"*Elyn. I'm coming.*"

Elyn stiffened in her chair.

"*What do you mean, you're coming? Coming here?*"

"*Yes. You're in danger.*"

"*Yes, I know I'm in danger. I'm in danger because of you!*"

"*No. You're in danger because Yvorre is coming for you. She's coming for both of us.*"

Vale's voice was strong and with it came Vale's memories of the past week and all that had happened to her since they last shared contact. Elyn felt her own memories flowing into Vale's mind and she resented it.

"*You went to the Ageless? Do they know...about us?*" Vale asked.

"*What about us? Do you even know? What the hell are we, Vale? How can you and I both exist at the same time? Answer me that!*"

There was a slight pause.

"*I don't know, Elyn, but I know that we can't let Yvorre, or anyone, get to you before we've had a chance to figure this out. How much do the Ageless know?*"

"*Nothing. They suspect I'm hiding something, but they don't know what. But it's only a matter of time.*"

"*Don't trust them.*"

Frustration surged. "*Don't tell me what to do.*"

"Elyn? What's wrong?" Jason asked, and she realized that she had stopped answering their questions.

"Don't tell me what to do, Jason!" she snapped. Jason pulled back and Nadine stared at her. The renewed contact with Vale made her feel uncomfortable. Strangely unsettled. She looked hard at them both. They were still her friends, and she loved them both, but she knew that they couldn't help her. She had to act for herself.

"I'm going to leave," she replied. "I can't just stay here and wait for things to happen to me."

"Elyn no—" Jason began, but she cut him off.

"It's my decision. You've always told me that I need to take control of my future and do what I want to do. Well, this is what I want to do now."

He looked angry. "And have you asked Nadine? Is this what she thinks you should do?"

"Do you really think that little of me?" She spat the words with more venom than she intended, and she saw her own surprise mirrored on Jason's face. "Why do you have so much trouble accepting that I've made a decision that you don't agree with? Do you really think I'm just that weak that I can be manipulated by anyone, everyone, even you?"

"Elyn, he didn't mean that," Nadine interjected.

"Didn't he? What about you, Nadine? You're afraid of me, aren't you? I can see it. I can feel it. Does that scare you, knowing that I can feel what you're feeling?"

Nadine seemed to struggle for an adequate reply.

"What's wrong with you?" It was Jason who now resumed the offensive. "Why are you doing this? Do you want to drive us away? Is that it? Do you really want to push away your only friends?"

"*Elyn, calm down,*"

Elyn drove her eyes back to him and she felt them go cold.

"My only friends," she smiled bitterly to herself. "Yes, you're right, aren't you? Poor lonely Elyn without any friends. What can she possibly achieve by herself?"

"Stop doing this," Nadine had found her voice, and it was now impatient. "You're just dwelling on pity now. Look, you know that we don't think of you like that. We're trying to help you."

"I don't want to be helped."

It was true. Elyn just wanted to tear down anything that was good. Anything that was happy and joyful so all that would be left around her was misery.

"What's wrong?" Jason's voice was still kind. He still wanted to help. Part of her felt her heart break with empathy while another part wanted nothing more than for him to understand the same hurt that she was suffering.

"I want to be apart from everyone. I'm sorry," Elyn replied as she raised her eyes to meet his. "Jason, you know how I've felt about you for a long time. I know you do."

Jason suddenly looked uncomfortable and even Nadine shuffled in her place. Somewhere far away Elyn was shocked at what she was doing, but the feeling was so small now. She was surprised at the impotence of her own humiliation.

"You don't have to apologise," Elyn continued. "But you're never going to feel the same way for me...are you?"

"*Elyn, this isn't the time,*" Vale insisted.

"Elyn...I..." Jason stammered.

"Please," she interrupted him. "I'm not trying to make you feel bad, but you have to understand that what you're asking me to do is impossible. What do you want me to do? Stay here and be hated by most of the town..."

"*Elyn!*"

"...with my only friends being the man that I've always been in love with and my best friend, who he loves instead of me."

"*You're an idiot!*"

The deconstruction was now complete. The truth was that she hadn't really been sure of this until she'd voiced it, but their reactions rewarded her instinct. Both Jason and Nadine looked away in opposite directions, as if ashamed to be there. Elyn merely glanced from one to the other, curious as to which of them would speak first. Neither did. The sun had tipped through the midday point and was now beginning its inexorable decline into darkness. Afternoon sun began to leak through the windows at the far end of the tavern. Vale was trying to say something but Elyn pushed back at the voice. She needed to get away. She pushed back her chair suddenly and rose to her feet.

"What's wrong?" asked Nadine.

"Nothing," she lied. "Nothing. I just think that maybe I've had too much beer."

"Do you need to visit the outhouse?" Jason asked, making strange hand gestures around his mouth that Elyn presumed was supposed to represent the act of vomiting.

"Yeah, I think so. Maybe some air."

Elyn had the urge to get away from them for a few minutes and clear her head. She mumbled another excuse and walked away from them toward the bar, carefully plotting a course that would take her away from their eyes at the same time.

"Oh, beautiful, what's wrong? You don't look good!" Dex's deep voice drifted from behind the bar, causing her to hesitate. She risked a glance in his direction and saw him smiling back at her as he wiped a white rag over the benchtop.

"Why don't you come over here and talk to me," he called with a playful grin. "I get lonely over here by myself."

Elyn glanced from the exit to Dex. She faced the agonizing choice of offending him with either unintended arrogance or legitimate social awkwardness. She chose awkwardness.

"I think I need some air," she attempted to say casually while making her way toward him. "I might have had a little too much."

"Too much?" Dex laughed. The sound was deep and somehow very alluring. "Sweetheart, you've only had two! You're not very good at this drinking thing, are you?"

Color flushed Elyn's cheeks, and she found herself wishing that she had chosen arrogance after all.

"Well...no," she admitted. She leaned on the benchtop and as she did so, a ginger cat leaped up from under the bar to greet her. She purred affectionately and rubbed her head against Elyn's arm in the universal greeting of feline diplomacy and attention-seeking.

"Hello," Elyn greeted the animal with mild surprise, gently stroking her behind the ears. "Marking your territory? I swear we're just friends."

Dex smiled at her. "You're cute." He stretched over to grab a used mug and place it under the bar. "I don't often see cute girls in here – just more of the same tired drunks."

"Well, I'm not sure if I'm cut out to be a regular."

"Good," he whispered in a conspiring tone. "I'd hate to see you grow up like them." He jerked his head toward a group of three middle-aged women behind him, all of them laughing a little too loud and acting a little too friendly with another group of men sitting at the same table. The women were dressed in a vulgar attempt to reveal certain body parts, as if this would compensate for their lost youth, and the similarly aging men were looking at them all with an undisguised, selfish lust. The scene struck Elyn as somehow very sad this early in the day.

"That's the end result of a lifetime of well-practiced drinking," Dex added.

"Yeah, I don't think that's me."

"Noooo…" he answered in a playful voice. "I hear you're very special." Elyn glanced at him in surprise. "Oh, don't look at me like that, it's no secret. Half the people in this room have heard, and the rest will know before their third drink."

"I don't know what to tell you."

"You don't have to tell me anything. I'm just impressed to have you here. I've never served a magician before."

"Well, I'm not entirely sure that I'm going to be a great magician. I'm aiming to be an average one for now."

He laughed again.

"Fair enough. I'm only aiming to be an average barman."

"Oh, I don't know about average."

The tease came without thinking, but the genuine smile she received in return dispelled any doubts she may have had about her bold choice of words.

"Why, thank you. Well, I happen to think that you're a very beautiful woman."

A customer started hammering on the other end of the long bar.

"Don't go anywhere, please," Dex said with a wink before turning to attend to the drunk patron. The cat gracefully leaped down and followed him. Elyn smiled. She'd never had this much confidence flirting with anyone before. She'd certainly never been able to do this with Jason. Whether it was the drink or her recent experiences, she couldn't tell, but she was satisfied with the outcome. She glanced around and noticed that she had walked around to the other side of the room where she could no longer see Jason or Nadine. She sensed Vale pressing into her mind again and she pressed back hard.

"*Leave me alone!*"

The shove she sent was almost physical. Vale's presence was the last thing she needed. She just wanted to feel normal again and to try and forget everything that had changed. Dex had busied himself with customers on the opposite side of the bar. Elyn admired him from behind with a sense of growing confidence. She set her mind on the task of finding the right balance of playfulness and modesty when he returned.

"Well, look at this. Already starting out on the new job?" Nathan's voice was like a stone through glass. Elyn saw her confidence drop away only to be replaced by the familiar flood of icy fear.

Nathan had walked up behind her with another friend – who Elyn didn't recognise – in tow. "I guess this is the best place for a whore to find work, isn't it? Although you may need to wait for these guys to get a bit more drunk before they're desperate enough to pay for you."

Elyn glanced at Dex, who still had his back to her, then turned to face her tormentor.

"What do you want, Nathan?"

Nathan smiled at the reply. His cheeks were flushed with the telltale signs of beer.

"What do I want?" he mocked with fake sincerity. "I want you to give me a discount for old times' sake." He stepped forward intimately and placed his hand on Elyn's breast.

Elyn watched the confidence starting to rapidly fade as it usually did, like water through her palms.

"*I'm with you.*"

The fear stopped. It was as if she could hold the emotion in her mind and look at it. Now the fear seemed so small. It occurred to Elyn that it was strange that a mood like this had bothered her so much before.

Nathan pressed his face in close so that Elyn smelled the alcohol on his breath. "You've always had an attitude like you were too good for us. Now look at you. Your father's dead and he left you whoring in a bar. That's fitting."

Nathan's friend giggled in the repulsive manner favored by all sycophants. Something about the giggle disturbed Elyn, something brought back memories of another sickening and weak laugh. Elyn couldn't help but look at him with disgust.

"Who's your friend, Nathan? Do you keep him on a leash like your other dogs?" Again, Elyn wasn't quite sure where her words came from, and judging by the expression on Nathan's face, neither was he.

"What did you say?" Nathan was desperate to regain control of the situation, to save face. Elyn still felt Vale's confidence start to surge, she was looking at Nathan's servile friend now with a sense of growing hatred.

"I said that your friend here will do whatever you tell him to, won't you?" Elyn directed her question at the boy who seemed confused by the sudden transfer of power. "That's the sort of friend you like, isn't it? Someone weak. Someone like you."

"I'm not..." Nathan's crony began in protest, but Nathan cut him off with a gesture.

"Don't worry, Brian, I'm not gonna let this little whore speak to us like that. Get outside now." Nathan grabbed Elyn's arm.

"Outside?" Elyn turned her attention to her tormentor and sensed anger laced with indecision bubbling within Nathan. He wasn't sure how to handle the situation, and the time had come to exploit it. "What's wrong with right here, Nathan? You're always saying you want me. What's taking you so long? Afraid you won't be able to perform? Or do you need a real man to show you how it works?"

Elyn didn't need her new senses to read the disbelief that was now radiating from Nathan. He tightened his grip on Elyn's arm as he turned to pull her toward the door, but instead Nathan lost his grip as he fell backward onto the floor. Elyn was a spectator in her own body as her own right leg swept the floor in front of her and effortlessly knocked away Nathan's footing. As he fell, Elyn watched Vale guide her own hands to grasp Nathan's wrist that had been latched onto her arm. Elyn then took a single step behind Nathan, bending his trapped arm behind him at an unnatural angle. Nathan lay on the floor like a broken puppet whose marionettes were strangely twisted in Elyn's possessed hands.

Elyn felt both euphoric and terrified at the power surging within her.

"*What are you doing?*" Elyn asked.

"*I'm not letting this creep lay a hand on you again,*" Vale replied.

"*Let go of my body!*" Elyn insisted. Panic was starting to rise within her like it had in the Arcadia.

"*Elyn, stay calm!*"

"*Let me go!*"

Elyn pushed with her mind and this time something happened. Something physical. It was like a whip snapping out from her body, crackling and made of light. It coursed out with the same frustration that Elyn felt. It writhed a beautiful arc around her for a moment and then it was gone. Nathan's friend yelped and leapt backward, almost tripping over Nathan's prone form as he did so. The tavern had fallen silent.

"*What did you do?*" Vale asked.

Elyn couldn't reply. She had no idea what had just happened, but she noted that she had control of her body again. It was then she became aware of the voices in the room. Hostile voices. She looked up to see half-dunk men unsteadily rising from their tables with faces reddened by ale and suspicion.

"The strange girl."

"...dirty immigrant."

"...witch..."

She looked about and saw that Jason and Nadine also stood among the faces. Nadine seemed torn between helping her friend and dealing with her own fear. Jason looked stunned at what he had witnessed. Elyn realized that she was still gripping Nathan's wrist and released it. Nathan rose to his feet a little unsteadily, but quickly gauged the mood of the room around him.

"What did you just do to me, witch?" he said. Vale was trying to say something but Elyn wouldn't hear it. This whole thing was getting out of control. The drunken men were closing in on her. She needed to get out of there. Elyn turned to leave but felt a hand grab her elbow. Nathan or someone else – she couldn't tell. Elyn tried to pull her arm free but the hand held fast. There were more men between herself and the door. Her heartbeat started to race and her breath became shallow. In the din of voices, she heard Jason shout and she thought she could glimpse him trying to press through the crowd toward her, but things were happening too quickly. Another set of hands gripped her shoulder and from nowhere a palm slapped her across the cheek. A woman screamed. Elyn's vision shook for a moment. Someone threw ale at her shirt and another man spat. Wet phlegm broke on her cheek. In the back of her dazed mind, Elyn experienced a surreal sensation of destiny. As if she was witnessing the preordained moment of her death. Tragic. Wasted. Killed in a bar by drunks. A burst of wind hit them. Savage and cold. The doors behind Elyn had been flung open and a shrieking gale assailed everyone in the tavern. Everyone stopped. Elyn wondered why. She turned her head and saw a tall figure in a flowing violet robe. A golden edge lined the hood.

Ferehain?

In an instant he was inside the tavern. Robes billowing. The inside of his hood was midnight black. An arm shot out from his robes and seized the throat of a balding, middle aged man who held Elyn's right arm. The man gurgled an incomprehensible cry as Ferehain lifted him into the air with one hand and simply tossed him toward the bar as though he were a pitcher of ale. His skull cracked on the timber with a sound that matched the breaking wood. Elyn felt several hands release their death grip on her as the crowd of drunken men and women seemed to recede like a wave retreating into the ocean. Ferehain loomed tall and terrible before them and – although the room had been full of riotous shouting mere seconds before – there was now not a single person who dared make a sound.

"You do not touch her!" Ferehain commanded in the same unnatural voice that Aleasea had used. "She is under the protection of the Ageless. Anyone who harms Elyn of Outpost will face our judgment...they will face *my* judgment."

The tavern was a tableau of frozen bodies, their reddened and drunken faces wearing expressions of sheer terror. Nathan had retreated into the protection of the crowd. Even Jason has stopped in his place, his own expression disbelieving. Ferehain turned his faceless hood toward Elyn.

"You will come with me."

Without waiting for an answer, Ferehain turned and moved toward the open door. Elyn offered a quick glance toward Jason before following. Outside in the bright sunshine, Ferehain moved gracefully across the street toward a faded, green door in a small stone building. Opening the door, he moved inside and Elyn hurried to follow. The door swung closed behind her and the darkness of the room seemed impenetrable after the light of the street. It took a moment before Elyn could make out the space around them. To her surprise the building was cavernous on the inside and intricately decorated with stone columns and engraved edgework on the walls. Elyn realized the floor had been excavated and was sloping downward into the ground where it seemed to extend into a lengthy tunnel that vanished into darkness. This allowed the deceptively small building to hide its true purpose, which Elyn deduced as one of the access points the Ageless used to move from Sanctuary to the town. Ferehain was standing in the center of the room. His hood lowered and his black eyes regarding Elyn with an intensity that made his gaze impossible to meet.

"Thanks," Elyn offered meekly. She realized she didn't know what else she could say.

"Are you trying to get yourself killed, woman?" Ferehain's eyes did not leave Elyn's face. Elyn shrugged.

"Nathan's always had it in for me."

"Is he worth dying over? I do not think a fool like that is worth such a sacrifice."

"Ferehain, I didn't go looking for trouble. He came up to me."

"I was not referring to the instigation, Elyn, I was referring to your chosen method of defense."

Elyn was still. Agonising moments passed and yet Ferehain said nothing, staring back at her with a constant intensity. "What do you know?" Elyn asked at last.

"I know that you are hiding something from us. I know that you are holding back. This is not wise." Ferehain stepped forward, so he now seemed to loom tall over Elyn the same way he had loomed over the people in the tavern, but when he spoke his voice was not unkind. "I know that I spoke against you in Sanctuary, but it was precisely because I expected a day like this would come. You have power beyond your ability to contain and control."

"You rejected me. You and Veroulle and even Aleasea."

"No, Elyn, we did not reject you. Once Veroulle saw into your heart he agreed with my counsel. I understood that you would not accept our help openly and without reservation on that day. You needed to see the consequences of your decisions for yourself before you would ever appreciate your true predicament."

"You've been watching me? Waiting to see if I'd lose control?"

Ferehain did not reply.

"Well, you were all wrong. I was going to leave. I don't need anyone," Elyn said a little too sullenly. Ferehain's face did not change.

"No, I do not believe that was likely. I believe that you would convince yourself of that intent, but you would not have the courage to see it through."

"Why should I listen to you? You wanted to lock me up a few days ago."

"Grow up, Elyn." The rebuke was so sharp and unexpected, it was like a slap. "Do you think you can fool yourself with petulance? Some could survive on their own out there, but not you. Like it or not, your life has changed forever and there is no going back to yesterday. People are going to want you, to harm you, or to use you to their own ends, but like us, you are different. Do you want to face this alone?"

"I could get by."

"You know that is not true. Yes, some could, but not you Elyn. You will not be safe by yourself and believe me," Ferehain's glare hardened, "you will be alone."

Elyn knew the truth in the words. Even if she decided to stay in Fairhaven and managed to avoid the mobs, Nadine's family couldn't protect her from Councillor Morag and her like. She looked up at Ferehain.

"What are you suggesting?"

"The Ageless are still prepared to help you, Elyn, but you *must* help us in return."

Elyn was silent.

"You must open yourself to us, Elyn. You must tell us what you are hiding. We cannot help you otherwise."

In a crushing moment, Elyn was weary. She was tired of secrets. Tired of hiding. She wanted to share this with somebody. She needed to. She was tired of confiding in nobody but a strange inner voice.

Vale?

Elyn reached out but couldn't feel her. It was at that instant Elyn realized that she hadn't noticed Vale in a while. In how long?

"What did you just do?" Ferehain asked. "I felt you."

Elyn flushed with the shame of a child who had been caught sneaking cookies from the kitchen.

"I was reaching out for…something, but I can't feel it anymore."

Ferehain nodded, seemingly satisfied. "Sanctuary has many safeguards that protect us from foreign power, even here in the outer passages. It would seem that these are effective at restraining you. This is positive."

Elyn reached out again, and again she sensed nothing. Vale was no longer there. She looked up at Ferehain and made a decision.

"There's a…presence in my head. I can feel her sometimes."

"Who is she?"

"I don't know. She reached out to me … in my head, a few weeks ago," Elyn lied. Ferehain's eyes narrowed slightly but he said nothing. "The bond's been getting stronger since then."

Ferehain nodded. "Some of us sensed it. This is what drew my attention to you."

"Is that why you went to my father?"

Ferehain nodded. "He appeared to have no knowledge of your transgressions; however, I doubt that he would have aided me even if he did. The conversation simply reinforced my suspicion that you are clever and cunning."

Elyn realized that Ferehain knew she was holding back. She hoped that this down payment of trust would be enough but couldn't risk too much truth yet. She suspected that Ferehain wouldn't be too charitable if he learned that she somehow shared her very existence with the daughter of Bythe. Elyn realized that she needed to play this carefully.

"I'm worried about this," she continued truthfully. "I don't know what's happening to me or how to control it. I've been trying to work it out on my own, but I don't think I can."

"No. You cannot."

"Can you help me?

Ferehain didn't answer immediately. He continued to stare at Elyn with impassive eyes.

"Clever and cunning," Ferehain repeated. "You must open yourself to us Elyn, open yourself to me."

Elyn looked away. She realized that too little information was as dangerous as too much.

"Her name is Vale. I think we're connected but I'm not sure how. That's all I know."

Ferehain continued to stare at her.

"Look, are you going to help me or not?" Elyn asked. Her frustration was finally starting to boil over. She wondered if she should take her chances with the town after all.

"Yes, Elyn. I will help you."

Elyn was surprised. She hadn't really expected Ferehain to let her off so easily.

"I will help you – not because I believe your story but because I believe you need help. Perhaps over time, we can learn to trust one another," said Ferehain.

"I'd like that," Elyn replied sincerely. Ferehain turned and spread his arm in a welcoming gesture toward the descending passageway that lay beyond.

"Now?"

"Yes, Elyn."

"But Jason and Nadine? I really should..."

"Your friends will be fine without you. I shall send word of your whereabouts so that none miss you."

"But my things? I don't have anything with me."

"You have yourself, that is all you need. We shall provide the rest for you." He gestured toward the passageway again. "Come."

Elyn glanced up at Ferehain then down the passage. It seemed that it was calling her, almost daring her to enter. She looked back at the outline of daylight against the door and knew that behind it lay Vale. Vale from the Iron Union. Vale the daughter of Bythe. Vale coming for her. Behind that door, the townsfolk were coming for her. Before her was Ferehain – also come for her. Every option presented danger. Every path led to someone who wanted her for their own reasons.

To hell with them all.

If the Ageless wanted something from her, then at least she could extract a price in return. She returned her gaze to Ferehain.

"I want you to teach me. Teach me and I'll share what I can."

Ferehain nodded toward the passageway before them. "Then begin your journey."

Elyn strode past him and marched into the passage without further hesitation. Ferehain followed in silence.

CHAPTER 4

"One hundred years ago, the Outlands were all but impenetrable. With the help of Maelene, the Ageless coordinated the Outland settlements into a formidable alliance of fighting men. In addition to this, Maelene's power over the forces of life gave us a natural defense against the foreign invaders of steel and hate. Many invading armies found themselves drowned in the swamps of Outpost or hopelessly lost in the forests of Greenridge as nature itself conspired against them. Sadly, this defense was lost to us when our Blessed Mother fell."

~Aleasea of the Ageless

The men were tired. They'd been marching hard for almost a week since leaving camp, but they'd covered a lot of ground. Ethan had hand-picked five hundred of his best men and had them ready to depart the very next morning. All infantry but for two units of scouts. Cavalry would be all but useless in the foothills and mountains. They had all accepted the new orders without question and by midafternoon, two columns of iron-clad soldiers were snaking across the plains of brown wild-grass. Within two days the plains had given way to undulating rises and crests, which themselves eventually broke into foothills of deep green. From there, the marching became harder as they left the relative ease of open land behind them and contended instead with the increasing density of trees that seemed to stand stoically in their path. Wardens of the wild who silently judged the metal soldiers as unwelcome interlopers. It was among these seemingly hostile trees that Vale had given the order to camp. She had estimated that they were now only two weeks from Fairhaven, an estimate confirmed by the late afternoon sighting of a hazy grey line of mountains on the horizon.

Vale reviewed the map for what must have been the twentieth time today, then – satisfied that nothing had changed and that they were still on course – she returned it to her pouch and continued looking into the campfire. It had been a long time since Vale had led a mission like this one. No bloated army with supply chains and logistics to manage. There was a degree of freedom to it. She might've been happier if her life had just been like this. No vast responsibilities. No armies to command. No world to conquer. No god to please. Just herself and a small command. She sighed and pushed the useless thought away. It did no good.

"*Elyn.*"

Nothing.

Nothing since their brief contact yesterday. Brief but strong.

My gods, it was strong. I was in her body. I could feel what she felt. The closer we get, the stronger it becomes.

But then it was gone. The Ageless named Ferehain had arrived and Elyn was again beyond her reach. This was bad. If the Ageless discovered their connection, there was no telling what they'd do. Imprison Elyn? Kill her? Or could they figure out a way to use the connection to get to Vale? So now there were two threats. Yvorre and the Ageless.

I suppose it changes nothing. Find Elyn and eliminate the Ageless.

Vale laughed and spoke out loud.

"Eliminate the Ageless, just like that?"

"That's our plan, isn't it?" Ethan answered as he walked into the campfire light. Vale felt a slight start at the surprise. She'd been so preoccupied that she hadn't even heard him approach. Ethan lowered himself onto a stool next to the fire, carefully settling his armored legs into a comfortable position.

"You remembered to bring the stools, Ethan," Vale said. "I wouldn't have thought of that."

Ethan smiled. "It's the reason we're conquering the Forge, isn't it? While the rest of the wilderness quibbles about the big issues, we remember the little things."

The stools may have appeared to be a luxury, but the Iron Union realized a long time ago that they also allowed a soldier to remain fully armored while eating by a campfire, therefore transforming a resting soldier into a battle-ready soldier.

"I could never understand how the outland colonies never worked this out," Vale said as Ethan opened his own pack and felt about for his rations.

"It's the difference between us and them, isn't it?" Ethan replied after successfully retrieving a small parcel of dried meat from what must have been the deepest crevice of his pack. "They just don't believe in the craft of production. They don't seem to approve of our god's gift to the Forge."

"Crazy," Vale agreed. "When they've seen all we can do, and they still reject it on principle."

"It's why they're losing. They can have all the principles in the world – it doesn't help them when they're facing a hundred thousand iron troops all armed with weapons they can only dream of."

"Well, they're not completely defenseless, Ethan. I don't want you getting overconfident."

Ethan smiled. "No, my lady."

"Have we had any sightings of the enemy?"

Ethan gave Vale a wry look. "Do you mean the Ageless or our own forces behind us?"

"Both, I suppose," Vale sighed.

"The rear scouts continue to report no sightings. It looks like your little ploy with Morbus has worked for a while. That was very clever of you."

Vale nodded absently. "And in front of us?"

"I've had some reports, but not of rebel outlanders."

"Who else? Northmen?" Vale asked.

"Correct. We've had several reported sightings over the past two days. They've always fled at our approach, but we've seen them far more frequently than we expected."

"What are they doing this far south? I thought they were a spent force these days."

"I don't know, but it's a little worrying. They seem to be a stronger presence than we believed."

Vale recalled the Northmen in Fairhaven. Killing innocents. Murdering Leon in sport. She felt a cold chill of revulsion.

"Show them no mercy. They're to be engaged and killed on sight if the opportunity presents."

"Yes, my lady," Ethan replied. His face betrayed a slight surprise at the decisiveness of the order.

"Northmen," Vale repeated. "Which god created them out of the filth?"

"I don't remember. Whoever it was, he or she has long since left them."

Vale grunted. "They've all gone. All but ours. You think that'd tell them something, wouldn't you?"

Ethan shrugged. "I suppose sacrifice and martyrdom can be a powerful motivation for your followers."

"More powerful than a physical presence?"

"Maybe? Who knows? It seems as if Maelene's spirit lingers even though her body's long gone."

"Maybe," Vale conceded. "It still doesn't explain the Northmen. They didn't worship Maelene. Why haven't they faded into the background like the Paephu or the Rak'Tunga?"

"I don't know, but it troubles me."

They were both silent for a time. Vale stared into the fire while Ethan finished his dried meat. When he had finished the last piece, he tossed the greased paper into the fire and turned to his friend.

"Vale, why are we going to Fairhaven?"

Vale looked at him and their eyes met over the light of the fire.

"There's somebody up there. Someone we need to find. It's very important that we reach her before Yvorre does."

"Who?"

Vale hesitated. She wanted to entrust everything to her only friend, but she knew that would be foolish. Even worse, it could put Ethan at risk, but at that moment she was tired of her solitude. Like Elyn, she also needed to vocalise her anxiety. There was only so much introspection she could take before she started to go a little crazy.

"She's important. I believe that she could be the missing piece in the mystery concerning my father...and me."

Ethan looked at her with incomprehension evident on his proud features. Vale closed her eyes and started to speak. She spoke about meeting Elyn in Outpost. She spoke about their connection. She told him of Yvorre and her clear desire to find Elyn. She spoke of the revelation that Elyn and Vale were the same person – one in the Iron Union and the other now in the hands of their enemies. When she was finished, Ethan was staring in the fire – the incomprehension still plain on his face.

Ethan looked up at his commander and his friend.

"Vale... I've never understood the gods. I've never pretended to. I'm a soldier. All those affairs are just beyond me. I was never meant to understand the things that you do."

Vale laughed bitterly. "You think I have some kind of understanding of all this? I don't, Ethan. I'm just like you. In fact, I think that's the problem."

She stood up and started pacing in front of the fire. The movement helped her to reflect. It felt so good to express her thoughts aloud; she was surprised at how much she was relishing the exercise.

"I don't know what to tell you. That I'm split across two people? That there may be more copies or versions of me out there? Is that woman up there really me, or is this some kind of trick? I really don't know."

Silence.

"It would explain a lot, you know?" Vale turned from her pacing and walked over to return to her stool by the fire, her armor plates gently grating as she did so.

"What do you mean?" Ethan asked.

"It would explain...us. Me and my father. I mean, we were never exactly close."

"Bythe isn't exactly close to anyone. Nobody's even seen him in years. Your father seems to love staying inside the Ironhelm." Ethan reminded her. Vale smiled faintly.

"Yes, that's true," she paused for a moment and then continued in a rush. "I can't really remember him well. Did you know that? My own father, and I only have vague memories of him."

"What do you remember?"

"A god," she answered simply.

They were both quiet for a while, then the silence was broken by a painful admission.

"Did you know he never told me why he sent me to Yvorre?"

Ethan didn't answer.

"At first, I thought it was nothing strange, but as I got older, something happened. I somehow knew that I'd missed something, something that I should have been given. I don't know how to explain it."

"What do you think it was?"

"I'm not sure. I immersed myself in Yvorre's training and the studies grooming me to be a leader somewhere in the Iron Union. I tried not to think about it, but it was always there, tapping away at the back of my mind. Why had he sent me away? Why did he never formally recognize me as his daughter, his heir? What was wrong with me?"

"There's nothing wrong with you, Vale. He's got no intention of dying, that's all. Gods don't need kids to carry on their legacies like the rest of us do. I didn't know you had such a sensitive side." Ethan's tone became playful. Vale smiled in reply.

"Well, maybe now we know what it is. I mean, I'm a fine officer and an impressive fighter, but I'm hardly a god myself, am I? Look at what my father accomplished, building the Iron Union with his own hands over centuries, and yet I've just grown like a typical mortal."

Ethan barked a curt laugh in reply. "Well, that's not unusual, Vale. We all know the stories of the children that were sowed by the gods with mortal women and mortal men over the centuries. They don't grow up to be powerful little godlings. Imagine where that would get us. We'd be neck deep in gods and demigods."

Vale laughed despite her mood. "Still, it seems that this aspect of mine has inherited the powers that my father was expecting to see in me. I need to reach her."

"And then what?"

Vale looked at Ethan. "I don't know. At the very least, we ambush the Ageless and cripple their leadership. As for me..." she trailed off. She dared not voice her nihilistic suspicions. It seemed that the closer she came to Fairhaven, the stronger the obsession became.

Ethan seemed to misplace Vale's hesitance as self-concern. "If we cripple the Ageless, then I reckon that even Yvorre won't be able to touch you afterwards. Don't worry, Vale. You're going to find Elyn and we'll get your answers. Then we'll march back to Bythe himself if we need to. To hell with Yvorre and Morbus. It's going to work out. You'll be legendary within the Iron Union by the time this is over."

Vale looked at her friend and smiled at the irony of his words.

"Yes, I think you're right."

CHAPTER 5

"The Ageless make use of the many crafts gifted to them by Maelene. While they can channel the life energies of the Blessed Mother that still exist in this world and affect life in various ways, they also rely on the fundamental physical defenses employed by all living beings."

~Aleasea of the Ageless

Daylight never penetrated the ancient halls and corridors under Fairhaven. It was impossible to tell whether it was daybreak or dusk, whether the sky was brilliant and blue or dark with clouds. The constant alien phosphorescence lit the passageways and rooms with the same queer glow, every minute stretching into every invisible day. Time was granted no passage into the lives of the Ageless.

Elyn had long since become accustomed to the apparent absence of day or night in Sanctuary. The labyrinth of passageways of the Ageless reached out throughout the entire city like the tendrils of some curious living thing that was bent on infecting every corner. Elyn had only explored a handful of them in the weeks she had lived there, she was discouraged from curiosity and saddled with a constant array of duties, tasks, and assignments to occupy her wandering mind. Today her task was to learn. She stood in the center of another large stone room; however, this one was different to most others. It served as a training hall and small armory, and its walls were lined with racks holding an array of various weapons crafted from wood and stone. Ornate staves of differing lengths lined up like soldiers on parade. Spears with sharp stone tips were racked alongside elegant hatchets likewise crafted from natural elements. The absence of metal was a striking contrast to the lethal nature of the band of instruments on display – but Elyn had learned that the Ageless would never use the weapons of their hated enemy even if they had the resources to do so.

Elyn herself wore a white cloak not dissimilar to the cloaks worn by her mentors; however, her hood was lowered betraying a face transfixed with concentration. The focus of her attention stood across the room facing her, dressed in the usual dark green. Aleasea also wore her hood lowered; however, her slender features were set in an expression of complete tranquillity. In her hands, she gripped two small wooden staves only a foot in length. Elyn held identical weapons, but her grip was significantly less confident.

Aleasea moved forward. Slightly. Deftly. Elyn tensed and prepared herself. She sent a tendril of feeling out to her opponent to try to gain an advantage, but she could only sense stillness. It was strangely soothing. Aleasea started moving her sticks in an elegant pattern around her body. Elyn had seen this maneuver several times already. She was trying to keep Elyn off balance so she wouldn't know where the strike would come from. Elyn reached out with her feelings again. Still nothing. Giving up, she slowly moved toward Aleasea. As soon as she had closed to striking distance Elyn leaped forward and lashed out with her right arm, aiming for Aleasea's outstretched hands. Aleasea rotated her wrist with the smallest and most graceful of gestures, and Elyn's strike passed harmlessly through the air. Aleasea's rebuttal, however was not as harmless and the rap she chose to place on Elyn's outstretched wrists was jarring enough to almost make her lose her grip on her weapon.

"Patience," Aleasea scolded. "A defensive posture yields a far greater chance of success than an offensive one."

They slowly circled each other. Then came a feint of a strike. Then another. Elyn knew this game – Aleasea would try to test her discipline. She held firm and resisted the offered advances. Her guard up and held tight. Her hands gripping the batons fiercely. Another potential blow flew at her left shoulder but – correctly judging it to be offline – she let it pass without a movement. Her teacher smiled faintly.

"Better," she said.

The next series of strikes were for real. Elyn barely had time to deflect the sticks with her own as she took several steps backward to give herself distance. She tried hard to control her breathing, like she'd been taught, as she looked for the chance to make a counterstrike. Aleasea would always offer one, that was the point of the lesson. Elyn merely had to discover it. They circled again and the game began anew. A series of feints followed by a strike aimed at Elyn's head which she deflected with a little more comfort this time. The next blow was slower than the others and she noticed.

This must be it.

She parried the strike then moved in with a strike of her own. Her left hand provided the feint and the right baton was thrust straight forward to her teacher's stomach, only it never reached its mark. Instead pain flared in Elyn's left hand as Aleasea parried her attempted feint with unexpected vigour. The shock of the blow was so fierce it not only disrupted Elyn's attack, but it also forced her to lose her grip on the weapon and it clattered to the floor. She looked up in dismay just in time to see Aleasea's second stick sweep around and strike her firmly on the side of her head. The blow wasn't hard enough to stun her, but it was certainly hard enough to bring tears to her eyes. She stepped back and rubbed her temple.

"Ow."

"What have I told you?" Aleasea demanded, the frustration evident in her tone.

"Avoid getting hit in the face?" Elyn replied sardonically.

"Elyn!" Aleasea's voice became firmer.

"Alright. I was gripping my sticks too tight, wasn't I?"

"Yes, Elyn," she replied with a calmer voice. "We have discussed this. The tighter you grip your weapons, the less control you actually have over them."

"I know." Elyn fumbled with the collar of her cloak. It seemed stifling. "I can't breathe in here. Can we take a rest, please?"

"Of course," she nodded. Aleasea watched her with those strange, almond-shaped eyes as she crossed the room to sit on a bench. After a few moments, Aleasea also crossed the room and sat down next to her, the green robes spreading out gracefully over the bench they shared.

"What troubles you, Elyn?" Her voice was tinged with genuine sympathy. Elyn didn't need her senses to confirm this. She had grown to know Aleasea over the past weeks and knew the concern was sincere.

"I'm just not picking this up, Aleasea," she replied. "It's been weeks and I'm still struggling with the basics of this – and not just the kajik staffs either. I've struggled with the axe, the quarterstaff, even the unarmed combat you've tried to teach me. I'm just not learning it."

"That is not true. I have seen you make progress in all of these fields. Elyn, you expect far too much from yourself. Look at me."

She turned to look into Aleasea's face of paradoxical beauty – both youthful and ancient at once.

"We have lived for centuries, all of us. We have had decades to learn the arts that we are now passing down to you. I can slow the passage of time for brief periods if I need an edge in battle; however, it took me years – no – decades to master such an act. Indeed, most of us will have forgotten how much time we spent mastering these arts in the beginning. I know that I sometimes have difficulty recalling those days." She looked into the distance over Elyn's shoulder as if trying to evoke an early memory.

"You were servants of Maelene," Elyn answered. "She chose you and trained you personally. I'm just a woman, barely a woman, and she certainly didn't choose me."

"Did she not?" Aleasea returned her gaze to Elyn's. "You have gifts that others do not possess. How do you explain this to me?"

"There are a lot of mysteries in this world," Elyn hedged. She still hadn't revealed more about Vale, and to her relief, they hadn't asked.

"No," Aleasea contradicted. "There are only facets of truth that we do not fully understand and all of those are divine in their nature. This world was created by the gods; they left their mark on this world in many ways. All of your mysteries are simply elements of their unrealized plans and designs."

Elyn was silent for a moment, wondering how she could ask for secrets without giving away any of her own.

"So, I may not be a disciple of Maelene? Maybe I'm just a by-product of one of the battles between Dazh and Narak that levelled the Great Southern Wastes?"

Aleasea smiled. "Dazh and Narak could only destroy, never create. I remember them only too well. You were certainly not created by them."

"You know what I'm trying to say."

"Elyn, you are with us in the heart of the Outer Wild. This is the empire that our Divine Mother created for us. Nothing in here grows without her blessed consent. I believe she still watches over us, and I do not believe she would let you in here if it were not her will."

Elyn sighed. "My gifts are improving, I can feel that at least. I still can't quite control it, but it's getting easier to draw upon now. It's been getting easier every week."

"Good," Aleasea nodded. "It is going to take some time for you to discover your abilities, Elyn. Please try to be patient."

"I know, it's just that..." she hesitated a moment. "I guess I feel the need to show you all something, to prove that I'm deserving of the attention you're giving me."

Aleasea gently placed her hand on her shoulder.

"Elyn, it is we who should be feeling indebted to you. We have fought so long and so hard against Bythe that decades have long passed without any sign from our Mother. Although there are those that continue to foretell her return to us, some of us were beginning to wonder if we would ever hear her call again – it has been so long..."

Aleasea removed her hand and averted her face. The sudden pain in her voice seemed to crack her beauty and yet strengthen it. She drew in a long breath and when she spoke again her voice was calm.

"You have come to us at a time when I needed hope the most. It is you who has delivered us this most precious gift. Anything we give you in return is a poor exchange."

A silence hung in the air for a long time. Elyn experienced renewed guilt at her words. She couldn't snuff out Aleasea's hopes by confessing to her that – instead of serving as an agent for Maelene – she actually shared her existence with the daughter of Bythe. She wondered if Aleasea might help answer her own questions.

"Can you tell me what happened?" she asked.

Aleasea gave her a questioning look. "What are you asking?

Elyn felt very awkward, like she was asking a most personal question. It was very likely that she was.

"Can you tell me what happened when Maelene fell?" she replied.

"Surely you must know the story of her fall by now?"

"Well, of course I know the proclamations and the prayers." Elyn began to recite from memory. "'The Mother was finally betrayed by the Lord of Deceit and was put to death.' I also know that she was attacked and slain at the chasms we call Maelene's Fall, but none of the songs and the teachings tells us what actually happened."

Aleasea paused for a moment. "Is this some kind of morbid fascination?" she asked at length.

"No!" Elyn rushed to answer. "No, not at all. Please. It's just that there's always been so much mystery and secrecy surrounding the Mother, I suppose it's only natural to be curious." She paused for a moment to search Aleasea's face for any objection – and after finding none she ventured further. "And I thought that, now that I'm here, I might be able to learn a bit more."

Aleasea was silent again for a moment.

"Very well." She fixed Elyn with a stern gaze. "Many here would not approve of what I am about to do, but I will trust you, Elyn. Do not betray me."

"I promise."

She sighed. "You know that Kovalith and all the creatures in it were created by the old gods thousands of years ago?"

Elyn nodded silently.

"Then you also know that in the ages past, many gods walked across these lands and forged them according to their will. There were dozens in the old times. Dazh and his brother Narak. There was Lubalt-Teb who was fascinated by love in all of its forms. It was said that he lay with over nine hundred women in a single year to explore and perfect his art."

Elyn took the meaning of her words with a slight feeling of embarrassment, but Aleasea paid her no mind.

"There were so many. Basalt the Wanderer, Nishindra the Crafter, and of course, Bythe the Steelmonger – who became so enamoured with his metals and all that can be produced with them. All of them used Kovalith as a plaything to amuse themselves. They named it the Forge and set about creating life, destroying life, warring, feuding, and celebrating. However, as the centuries passed, the gods grew tired as immortals are wont to do and, one by one, they departed their Forge in favor of their natural homes. In the end only Bythe and our Mother remained, and it was then that the Great Deceiver's true nature was revealed."

An expression of discomfort passed over Aleasea's features, as though the very act of voicing the events was taking considerable effort.

"With all other obstacles removed, Bythe chose to move against our Mother and wage a war upon all of her creations. He wanted complete control over everything in his Forge. His greed and his lust for control knew no bounds. The war was terrible for us, for we were a peaceful collection of races, not an army bred for war. Bythe's forces carved through us and many lines were driven to extinction on the tips of his spears. So many young and so many innocents were slaughtered. It was not until he had swept through the Great Marshlands and driven us back as far as Azure's Towers that our Mother was able to use her crafts to rally a defense."

She paused again and when she resumed her voice was harder.

"We learned how to use our gifts to defend ourselves. Nature can be as wild and as savage as she is beautiful, and we taught the Helmsguard this lesson well. We used stealth, deception, poisons, and confusion to slowly weaken then strangle the invaders. We united all the races of the wild and pushed them out of our lands, we tried to push them back into that dreadful furnace of industry where they were conceived, but alas we discovered that – much like us – their defenses grew stronger the closer we struck to their heart. They eventually reinforced their armies until our offensive was impotent and then pushed us back in turn. And so, on it went for years and then for decades. One side would push the other as far as it could, only to be pushed back in turn, and the cycle would reverse."

"The Anarch?" Elyn asked.

"Indeed. Much was lost in those fifty years of war, much life and even more of Kovalith. I fear that we fought for so long that a madness began to touch us on both sides. It had to end and end it did. A truce was brokered, and our Mother agreed to meet with Bythe to negotiate an end to the war. It was agreed that both Bythe and the Mother would meet at the mid-point between our two kingdoms where our conflict had stalemated. Each would only bring a personal guard of fifty troops. Maelene honored this agreement, Bythe did not. He concealed five hundred men in the surrounding hills and only when our Mother had willingly placed herself at her most vulnerable did he strike like a coward."

Her voice had descended into malice. It did not suit her.

"Were you there?" Elyn somewhat carefully asked. Aleasea smiled grimly.

"No, I was not. Others were. Few survived that day; most gave their lives defending our Mother. Indeed, it was only by the grace of Maelene herself that any of them lived."

Aleasea's voice became so quiet that it was almost a whisper.

"Her fury at the betrayal was said to be terrible," she continued. "None had ever seen her act with such... vengeance. She is said to have slaughtered the Helmsguard that tried to seize her and then launched herself at Bythe, ordering her own guardsmen to flee. Of course, none did. They stood their ground in the face of overwhelming numbers and fought until they died. Maelene fought Bythe with such a fury that the very ground shook and broke beneath her feet. A great chasm rent the land so large that it swallowed all of them. Helmsguard and Ageless alike all fell to their doom."

Elyn let a respectable pause linger before voicing her inevitable question.

"And Bythe?"

"It would seem that the gods reward evil in the Forge. Bythe alone climbed out of the pit and returned to his towers in the Ironhelm. He had won. We were leaderless after that."

"And you've been trying to hold the Iron Union at bay ever since?"

Aleasea shrugged with a barely perceptible gesture. "They have continued attacking us, but it would seem that our Mother protected us even with her last act. The chasm of Maelene's Fall is so vast that it proved to be a very effective barrier against Bythe's armies, and those that have managed to make the long journey around have found themselves hampered by our other defenses." She paused and drew in a breath before continuing. "But I fear that even those defenses are proving too few and too futile for Bythe's armies. The truth is that we have been steadily losing ground since we lost our Mother."

"Isn't there anything we can do?"

"There are those among us who believe that Maelene will return to us. They have foretold of a night when the Temple will blaze with her power and she will return to guide us in our darkest night. They claim to have seen it in visions."

"Do you believe it?"

"I would dearly like to; however, most prophecies are never fulfilled, and some are given to us only to provide hope."

Elyn nodded quietly. Aleasea hadn't answered the question that burned most in her mind. She decided that she needed to risk voicing it.

"Aleasea, who is Yvorre?"

Aleasea looked at her sharply. "Where did you hear that name?"

"I heard it in Outpost. I think she was with the army that invaded," she lied.

Eyes of compassion turned to ice, and the change in Aleasea's expression was utterly intimidating. Elyn was forced to look away.

"Elyn, your games need to come to an end. We know that you are hiding from us, and it is only through the patience of Veroulle that we permit it. He believes that you will open to us of your own volition, given time and trust. But while we may be ageless, you may discover that our patience is not." She stood up with a rustle of fabric. "Come, we have tarried here too long. I have business far from here that I must attend to urgently, and there is still much that you need to do today."

She motioned for Elyn to follow as she gracefully walked through the exit. Elyn complied but, in her mind, she was still processing all that she had just learned, and it seemed that her questions had now spawned and multiplied. Elyn reflected on the frustration Aleasea displayed and decided that she'd asked enough questions. She found herself thinking of Jason and Nadine and wondered if they were still alright. There had been no further attacks in the past few weeks; however, she'd had had no word on her friends or how they had been managing in the city above. Jason had almost certainly become a soldier by now and Elyn tried not to think about the dangers that he could be facing. It only made her feel worse. Yet, a small and ugly part of her gloated at this, at the risks he was now facing. After all, Jason had fallen for Nadine despite everything Elyn had felt toward him. It was fitting that Jason was now thrust directly in harm's way. It was just. Elyn flinched and shook her head to rid herself of the dark mood that had ambushed her. The action caught Aleasea's attention.

"What troubles you?" she asked without stopping but still regarding Elyn closely.

"Nothing," she quietly replied, ashamed and unwilling to give voice to her selfish fantasies. Aleasea noted her reluctance to answer and didn't press the issue, leaving them to walk in silence for the rest of their journey together. After a moment, they reached a small chamber where several passageways converged. Elyn had learned that Sanctuary was full of these hubs and it had taken her quite some time to memorise them. Aleasea suddenly turned to face Elyn with a conflicted expression.

"Elyn, you trouble me. There is something familiar in you that I cannot place," she said.

"What?" Elyn asked.

Aleasea studied her for a moment in silence. "I feel a kinship with you, but I do not know why."

Elyn shrugged. "I just feel...frustrated."

Aleasea reached out and gently placed her palm upon Elyn's forehead. Elyn resisted the impulse to pull away. Aleasea locked her eyes on Elyn's, and the strength of her gaze was both intense and intimate. For a brief moment, she caught a sensation of a young girl filled with hopes for a better world before centuries had worn away her ambition. Then this feeling was washed away and replaced with a warm surge of complete happiness. It seemed to flood in through her palm, and the emotion Elyn felt was utterly euphoric. The spite she had carried moments earlier was washed away in that torrent, and when Aleasea removed her hand, the anger was all but forgotten. Elyn looked at Aleasea and, to her surprise, she saw weariness on her face. On some level, Elyn knew that this had cost her, that the happiness she felt hadn't come from nowhere – it had been gifted from her teacher. Elyn was humbled.

"Elyn, I need you to be strong. Whatever conflicts rage within, you will need to overcome them soon. I have to leave you for a time, so I will not be here to watch over you."

"Am I in danger?" Elyn asked.

"No. Veroulle will never allow harm to come to you in here. But time is growing short. We believe Fairhaven is in great danger."

"The Northmen?"

Aleasea nodded thoughtfully. "Perhaps. Perhaps there is more at work. That is what I need answered. If you want to repay the trust we have extended to you, then I suggest you start by confessing to Ferehain or Veroulle all that you know."

Elyn stood there in silence. Sheer emotional war raged within her, yet she couldn't bring herself to act. She wanted to confess her secrets, but she was terrified of their consequences.

Aleasea gave her a look that might be described as affectionate if it were seen on any mortal woman's face, then placed a hand on her shoulder. "I can stay no longer. Trust yourself, Elyn. It is all you can now do."

Without further comment, she was gone and Elyn was standing alone.

CHAPTER 6

"Little is known about the Render in the south. It is said that when the gods first created Kovalith, they started with the Render and that the lands there were greater and more magnificent than any mortal could imagine. As the gods journeyed to the north, they had perfected their art of worldmaking, and the life and lands of our kingdoms became far more stable. However, many in the Fareaches must keep an ever-watchful eye to the south, for even the most mundane of the creatures that dwell in the Render are much unlike the men and women of the northern lands."

~Aleasea of the Ageless

The wind was a fierce mistress that could cut through you in the northern mountains. It was like every inch of warmth was intentionally stripped away from you, as if she held the very clothes you wore in complete contempt and laughed at your feeble attempts to stave off her touch. She was a fierce and cruel mistress, and in the altitudes high above Fairhaven, she was supreme. Jason had learned to respect her in the past few weeks. At first, he was so shocked by the relentless cold he feared that it would end him as he slept through the frostbitten nights. But he survived. Sergeant Barnes made sure that all his men survived.

"It is not negotiable," he would repeat time and time again, and after a while Jason began to believe him. Barnes had been Jason's first commanding officer on the day he reported for duty and they had been in constant company ever since. Indeed, the entire troop of seventy-five men had eaten, slept, and fought together almost every day over the past three weeks. They were a family now. Barnes was their father. He was in his early thirties but carried himself with the confidence and experience of a man far older. The men gravitated to him naturally. He was their alpha. Strong, fit, and with that assuredness of conviction that seems to gift some men. Jason had liked him instantly and Barnes seemed to respond to the competence and capability that Jason had offered him. His reward had been genuine acceptance into the family, which was not a gift offered to all cadets. Most had been sent back to Fairhaven after one or two patrols.

It was not an easy calling, but Jason had thrived, proving his value on several occasions. He had fought again as he predicted he would. Hesitantly at first, and even then, only to support his fellow, more experienced soldiers. However, on his second patrol he had been thrust into the midst of an ambush. That day he killed three nomads without thinking about why. That made it easier. From that day onwards, he never thought about killing the same way he had when he was a boy. It was just a job now, no different from setting up camp or mucking out the stables. Just a task.

He watched his brothers now as they hiked up the thin dirt track they had been following for three days. The elements had hardened their features so much that they had all begun to resemble each other, brothers now in appearance and in solidarity. All of them now had beards. Even Jason – who had never grown a beard before – now wore a shallow coat of rough white hair along his jaw. None of them spoke. They never uttered a word when they were on a forced march. It was as if every ounce of strength had to be conserved and treasured, like a resource that was suddenly in high demand and short supply. The mountain air was instead filled with the crunching sound of leather boots on gravel and the rustling of cloth packs with their contents lightly dancing about within. The sun was beginning to fall toward the peaks of the mountains on the horizon, marking the unspoken signal that it would be time to set up camp and make preparations to defend themselves against the night's uncompromising cold. Jason placed his hand under his shirt and felt for the shape of his father's watch. It hung there on a chain around his neck, cool against the heat of his chest. He found the soft vibrational ticking reassuring when he felt like he was a long, long way from home. It was like he was still in his father's workshop watching the cogs and gears dance their intricate and never-ending routine. It was soothing.

"Alright, men, form camp!"

Barnes's command carried clearly though the air. The order was repeated and rippled down through the Corporals so that it seemed to pass over him like a wave.

As he rounded the nearest bend in the track, he could now see that the path widened out into a clearing which – while hardly ideal – would be their best option for the night's accommodation. A thick collection of trees bordered the space, and the imposing granite wall of the mountainside continued its seemingly endless climb a mile to their left. As the line of men reached the campsite, they, one by one, set about their duties in an orderly and almost mechanical fashion. Jason was no different. Within an hour the fires were lit, patrols were stationed, and rations were being prepared as the sun was beginning to slip beneath the mountains, causing large shadows to creep across their sanctuary. Jason had completed his duties and now sat with two other men whom he barely knew. They were both full soldiers and several years older than him; nevertheless, they accepted his presence without discrimination or prejudice. He was family to them now.

"So's been a week without a sight of 'em," said Edward, a short and stocky young man who was breaking up a piece of his trailbread by hand.

"Maybe we've scared them off," wondered Walt with a slightly sarcastic tone in his voice. He was an amiable man of average height and unremarkable appearance who always smiled in that awkward way that people who are unsure of themselves normally smile.

"Yeah, that's it, I'll bet," Edward answered with a mouth full of bread. "They've heard you were comin' and all packed up an' gone home."

"They're bloody cowards mostly, anyway," answered Walt. "Every time we send our men into these mountains, they just turn tail and run. They don't have any guts unless it's for killin' innocent women and kids while they're just goin' about their business."

Edward spat in the dirt. "That's the truth. For the life of me I can't figure out why we don't just slaughter every last one of 'em. Men, women, even the kids. Seems to me like every ten years or so we kick their sorry arses back to where they came from, only we just stand by and let them breed and breed until they get cocky enough to come and have another crack at us. I mean, what? We got to wait until they come and kill our kids before we do something about them? Why not just take the fight to them and finish them all off once and for all?"

Walt shrugged in reply.

"Don't seem right to me," Edward continued his quiet tirade. "So now we gotta come up here week after week and try to hunt 'em all down. To hell with it. Let's just go to war and don't stop until the job's done. Where'd they all go runnin' off to, anyway? It's freezing up here and I want to get back home."

"You just want to get back to some whores," Walt said with a smile. Edward offered a dignified shrug.

"A man has his needs, and they certainly ain't filled by sleeping on frozen rock every night!"

"Well, it's been so long for me that a frozen rock is starting to look pretty good."

Both men laughed at the collegial sharing of personal desire that was the hallmark of male friendship. Jason found himself thinking of Nadine. He had discovered that she had been encroaching upon his thoughts every time he trekked out on patrol. It was as if the continual threat of death demanded an equal measure of affection and intimacy in return. Their relationship up until this point had been a rather strange one. He knew of her attraction toward him just as he felt it in return, yet neither seemed to have the opportunity or the will to act upon it – largely out of respect for Elyn. Now that Elyn was with the Ageless, things seemed different. He had had only a brief chance to see Nadine before he had hiked out, and that had only been a stroke of fortune. They had spoken to each other like shy and awkward children who were deeply ashamed that some passing bystander might recognize the passion that was stirring within them and then call it out for all to see. He'd promised to be careful and in reply she asked him to call on her upon his return. Then there was the briefest brush of soft lips to his cheek and she was gone, leaving only her lingering scent.

"Well, maybe it's the kid hero here that's scared the bastards off?" Walt smiled, nodding to Jason who started with the realization that the conversation had turned toward him.

"Could be." Edward nodded in reply and turned to face Jason for the first time tonight. "He's making quite the name for himself, isn't he?"

"That he is. They'll probably be sending him off to fight Bythe soon if he keeps this up." Walt spoke to Edward as if Jason were not present.

For his part, Jason ignored the patronization, good natured as it was, and instead remembered his place as a junior member of the unit. He focused instead on carving off the smallest portion of dried meat from his rations and storing the rest away like precious cargo. Meat was always a rare delicacy among field rations, and Jason was trying to make his last as long as possible.

"I simply try to serve my sergeant as best I can," Jason finally answered when he realized that they weren't going to be satisfied until they had a response to their jibes.

"Well, you're serving Barnes pretty well. At least a lot better than most of the other cadets we get," Edward addressed Jason directly for the first time. "How many kills you got now?"

"I'm really not sure. Two or three, I think," Jason lied.

"Crap!" Edward spat. "You're doin' better than Walt. I know you are."

"I don't know," Jason hedged, unwilling to embarrass his senior comrade-in-arms.

"It's alright," Walt came to his rescue. "You're a natural talent boy, a rarity. You don't have to worry about offendin' or pleasin' us. You just keep doin' what you've been doin' and you're going to go far."

"So, has there been any sign of the Northmen at all?" Jason was desperate to change the subject. He was all too aware of the added pressure that always accompanies the scrutiny of fame and reputation.

"Don't think we've even seen a clue," replied Edward.

"Bloody cowards, all they want to do is kill our women and kids," repeated Walt from his earlier posturing. Edward nodded.

At that moment, a tall and broad figure strode into the circle of the campfire light and smiled at the group with genuine and uncontrived affection.

"How's the food, boys?" Sergeant Barnes asked in his usual charismatic tone. All three of them hurriedly moved to stand but Barnes cut their move off with a gesture.

"As you were, soldiers, as you were."

They arrested their mark of respect and resumed their seats.

"Care to join us, sir?" asked Edward.

"Have you eaten?" said Walt.

"The answer is yes to both questions," Barnes smiled as he rested his large frame on a rock next to Jason as easily as someone might sink into an armchair. He had a large face obscured by a thick brown beard and an even thicker mane of reddish-brown hair. His bright blue eyes peered out from the depths of that forest in a way that seemed to size people up immediately. It was this thoughtful gaze that now swept over the three men before him, pausing at Walt.

"Walt, right?" he guessed, pointing at him.

"That's right, sir, good memory," Walt replied.

"My memory's bloody awful, but I'm working on it," he admonished himself with a grin. "So, who else do I have the pleasure of sitting with?"

"My name's Edward, sir. Edward son of Harl." Edward replied with none of his former bluster. His contrite manner was almost comical by comparison to his behaviour a few moments earlier.

"A pleasure." Barnes smiled back then turned his gaze to Jason. "Ah! The cadet! So, this is where you've been hiding yourself. Tell me, how have you been enjoying our little mountain tours?"

"They've been....emotional, sir," Jason answered with a small grin and Barnes barked a short laugh in return.

"Emotional indeed! But you seem to have been handling it better than most boys of your age."

Jason started to mumble a noncommittal reply when he was thankfully interrupted.

"Sir!" interrupted a young soldier who came running over to where they sat.

"Yes, Corporal?" Barnes turned to face the man.

"Sir, three scouting parties haven't returned."

"How long have they been gone?"

"They were each scheduled to report fifteen minutes ago, sir. There hasn't been a sign of them from any of the company."

Barnes's face darkened, and he rose to his feet. The other three men instinctively followed their leader's movement.

"Put the company on alert immediately and arrange a search party..."

His words were cut off by a cry of alarm further along the campsite. Another cry echoed in the opposite direction and suddenly chaos broke loose. Men with faces covered in colored scarves were rapidly streaming into the camp like a torrent of water from a cracked dam. Arrows flew through the twilight air and screams pierced the night where they fell. The Northmen had found them.

"Rally!" bellowed Barnes in a voice that seemed far too big for him. "Rally on me!"

Several men came running to his call, but too many more seemed unable to hear it. Jason could see dozens of the Northmen running into the camp in a blind frenzy, slashing and killing wherever they could. In all of their patrols into the mountains, Jason had never seen so many attacking in such a concentrated force. He reached for his sword and glanced about him. Walt and Edward had drawn their weapons and were rushing to support their sergeant. Jason rushed to do the same, and he joined Walt as they formed defensive positions around Barnes.

"Rally! Rally to me!" Barnes shouted, but it was in vain. The sheer tumult around them drowned out his words, and the handful of men realized that they were going to have to depend only on each other. All around them the camp was starting to become obscured in a fog of dust, flame, and fading sunlight. So many of the enemy were pouring into the camp, it became difficult to see any of the fellow soldiers. The Northmen were savage, dressed in crude armor plates of hardened leather and even of black metal, they brandished axes, spears, and swords with obvious hatred.

Jason barely had time to notice their equipment as the first wave of Northmen rushed at them. Jason held his sword firmly with both hands angling the top of the blade skyward and waited for the enemy to come within range. A moment later, the group of nomads were upon them, and Jason could stop thinking, the sword-strokes coming to him unbidden by any conscious will. He parried the overhead blow of the red-swathed man in front of him and sidestepped to his left to deliver a lethal thrust into the exposed ribs of his enemy. He fell screaming, and Jason quickly stepped over his dying form.

"Fall back!" came Barnes's cry, and Jason realized that the enemy had pushed his allies back several feet through the weight of their numbers. More soldiers had come to join the fight, but the small group of allies was breaking apart. Jason started toward them but stopped when he saw Walt's body lying in his path, his unseeing eyes staring upward into the dying sunlight. Jason stared for a moment. He had seen death before, but the sight of his companion lying in the dirt before him struck him very differently this time. He felt alone and didn't quite know why. Another cry broke his thoughts, and he saw another of Barnes's defenders fall beneath the blade of a Northman. He realized that within minutes all the men would be dead.

Jason lofted his sword and ran toward the cluster of struggling nomads. He didn't flinch as two turned to face him. Raising his sword even higher, he screamed an unintelligible cry and brought his blade down with all the strength in his body. The shock of his blow shook his arm up to the shoulder, and the raider fell without a sound, Jason's sword stuck firmly between his neck and shoulder. The second attacker swung his heavy axe at Jason's head, and he barely had enough time to duck before it cut the air above him. Jason desperately tried to remove the sword from the body of his fallen enemy, but it had become stuck fast in the corpse. He looked up to see the Northman coming at him with a second strike and rolled to his left as the axe split the dirt where he had been crouching seconds earlier. Jason's mind raced, searching for an escape, but could find none. The enemy now stood between him and his weapon. The Northman seemed to notice his victim's dire predicament and said something guttural in his own tongue – ugly sounds muffled beneath his mask and the din of battle around them. They were the last sounds he ever made as Barnes ran him though from behind, throwing his body to the ground before stepping over it and helping Jason to his feet.

"Well done, lad!" Barnes shouted, and Jason only then realized that Barnes's men were now beating back their assailants. His charge had provided them with the distraction they had needed to turn the tide – at least for the moment.

The camp was now overrun, and soldiers were fighting in disorganized clusters, each trying valiantly to stave off the attackers that now outnumbered them. Barnes surveyed the scene for a moment with a furrowed brow.

"Alright!" he shouted above the noise. "We fall back to the southern entrance and establish a line there."

His next words were drowned out by a loud crack, and a flash lit the clearing as though daylight had returned for an instant. When Jason's vision returned, he saw that the Northmen near to them had fallen and three green-robed figures were now visible within the chaos, attacking the nomads with supernatural speed.

"Blessed Mother be praised!" Barnes cried as he watched the Ageless set to work on the enemy. Although they were only three, the shock of their appearance and the ferocity of their attack gave the appearance of far greater numbers. Jason paused for a moment as he watched the nearest magician dance around his enemy. The Ageless dealt strikes and blows with such furious intensity that they almost helped the nomad stay upright while he made his slow descent to the ground.

"Rally to me!" Barnes's voice rang out once more, only this time, it seemed to carry across the entire field of battle. "To me, men! Rally!"

One by one, men came running out of the chaos to join them and within moments, Jason stood among a unit of at least two dozen men. Now some Northmen charged again but this time the men of Fairhaven were ready for them.

"To me!" Barnes bellowed again and again as more men came running to join the defense. The Ageless continued their attack, using their surprise to sow more confusion among the enemy. Another loud crack followed, and another flash heralded more screaming Northmen falling about in confusion. Jason stood by the shoulder of his sergeant and together they fought hard against wave after wave of attack. Jason lost count of the number of foes that fell against their blades as much as he lost count of the passing of time. His father's watch seemingly suspended between moments against his chest. Finally, the enemy seemed to waver; the attackers lost their momentum, and the flood of nomads started to trickle and then to ebb.

"Forward!" came the order and the men obeyed. Slowly now, they inched forth. Jason reckoned their number must now have been fifty or more. Moving as one methodical unit, the men began to push the attackers back against the surrounding trees. It was at this time that Jason realized one of the Ageless had come alongside him and was now addressing Barnes through the din. Jason peered over to the green clad figure but could not discern any face beyond the black recesses of the hood. Barnes's face seemed grave and Jason realized that something was very wrong. At once, the Ageless pointed to the cliffs above them and by the fading daylight Jason could see his sergeant's face go pale.

On the ridgeline above them stood more fighters – hundreds upon hundreds – and at the lead stood a man clad head to toe in white. Tall, almost impossibly tall, with his face covered in a white mask. As Jason watched, the figure silently raised his right fist then brought it down in the same action. On this signal, the Northmen unleashed a horrendous cry of fury and began descending the ridge in an almost chaotic rabble. The silent figure in white descended effortlessly to the bottom of the cliff as if stepping from a footstool. From its shoulder, he unsheathed a sword unlike any weapon Jason had ever seen. He hoisted it high with both hands and started striding straight toward them. Armored nomads were streaming through the trees around him.

"Leave!" The bellowing shriek of the Ageless rang clearly over even the new clamour. "Retreat now!"

It took Jason a moment to realize that it was addressing them, not the Northmen. The figure in white was almost upon them, and its reinforcements were already sweeping into the tired defenders, who were trying to mount a fresh resistance against a now overwhelming number. The figure in white swung his sword once and two soldiers fell to the ground screaming, their midsections severed by the single stroke. As he stood there prone with his sword extended a third soldier stepped in to exploit the perceived advantage, but the creature in white simply stepped away from the soldier, dropping his greatsword and gripping the soldier's extended arm. The creature then savagely guided the soldier's weapon back against its master. In seconds, the creature's massive sword was back in his hands, and he resumed his relentless march toward Barnes. Jason noticed that his movements were strange, smooth and fluid yet somehow stiff and unnatural. Somehow familiar.

"Leave now. Run!" The Ageless ordered again then leaped through the throng in one movement toward the enemy. Brandishing a wooden quarterstaff, it let fly with a series of blows. Again and again the creature in white was struck on the face, chest, and legs yet he did not break stride for an instant, instead he hefted his sword and brought it crashing down onto the magician's staff, smashing it into pieces. The Ageless fell to his knees – the green hood cast back to reveal the slender features of the male underneath – and raised his hand toward his foe as he spoke some unheard words of power. The white assassin raised his weapon and brought it down upon the sorcerer.

His death cry was terrible. As if a thing truly unique and beautiful had been ripped from life and crushed from existence. It stunned the soldiers nearby. No one had ever seen one of the Ageless die.

Barnes started to lead his men on a slow retreat across the clearing, but the creature in white was rapidly closing the distance between them. The Northmen rejoined the combat as they surged forth in numbers. Another Ageless appeared before Jason. It raised its hands high then brought them down with a shout. An almighty crack rent the air and Jason was flung back a great distance. When he opened his eyes, he saw that he must have lost his senses for a time as some moments seemed to have passed. A thick smoke now shrouded the clearing and there were men running in all directions. Jason strained to make sense of the scene before him but was unable to discern any order. He staggered to his feet and tried to clear his vision, only to see a masked nomad running straight toward him. Jason tried to command his body to move but he was too slow. The Northman raised his axe and brought it down in one savage movement.

Jason flinched and tensed for the blow, but it did not land. Instead the Northman seemed to slow in mid-strike until he was all but frozen in place. The scene would have looked comical had it not been so deadly. Only then did Jason notice a robed figure in green emerge from behind the nomad. It had extended its arm toward the Northman and the attacker was slowing as if it was stuck in time. Without waiting, Jason cleared his head and stepped forth, thrusting his sword deep into the man and watching him slowly fall to the ground. The Ageless stepped forward and moved around Jason.

"Flee, all is lost here," it thundered in that unnatural voice as it passed, then it paused, turned its hooded head in his direction and seemed to stare at him. Jason didn't move. A piercing scream from the battle behind them broke the moment and the Ageless looked about.

"Come with me, Jason," the figure ordered and then turned to leave. Jason hesitated, torn between his duty and self-preservation. The Ageless appeared to understand this conflict and repeated the instruction more forcefully.

"You will follow the orders of the Ageless, cadet. Come with me now."

Jason would never admit how relieved he felt at receiving such an incontrovertible order. He complied and dived into the trees, leaving a massacre behind him.

CHAPTER 7

"Many creatures walk this world that would seem incredible to the mortal man. Most of these creatures were created by the gods of the past, and they now find themselves wandering alone without a master or mistress. However, I believe that it is the creatures who still have someone to serve that we should fear the most."

~Aleasea of the Ageless

"Imbatal?" Vale could barely believe her own question, but the answer was confirmed by Ethan's face.

"Yes. We've questioned three prisoners now and their stories all match. It would seem that Imbatal is here and he's leading the Northmen," said Ethan.

"That creature doesn't *lead* anyone. This is Yvorre's work."

Ethan nodded.

Vale swore and glanced northward. From her camp atop a hill she had a clear view of the foothills as they rose and fell in increasing frequency. The mountains that had been a grey smear on the horizon weeks ago, now loomed strong and bold before them.

"We can't be more than a few days from Fairhaven," said Vale.

"No more than three, but if the prisoners are to be believed then we've got a problem."

It had been yesterday when the scouts had returned with the first of the prisoners. It had been a Fairhaven soldier, a young man with dark hair and a haunted face. What remained of his once-fine blue uniform had been stained brown with blood and dirt. He had been wandering blindly when the scouts sighted him. Vale had been deeply surprised at the state of the man, not only due to his appearance but also because he seemed genuinely relieved to have been captured by the Helmsguard. Within hours they had discovered two more men in separate locations but in similar states. Vale had then started to realize something was wrong. When she ordered the soldiers questioned, they were surprisingly compliant and surprisingly consistent, yet their testimony chilled Vale more than they could have realized. Not only their accounts of the ferocity of the Northmen, but their unerring description of the warrior leading them.

"It would seem that Yvorre's been far busier than we thought," said Vale with a humourless smile.

"How did he get here?" asked Ethan. Vale only shook her head.

"I don't know anything about that man. I've only seen him a handful of times in my life," Vale replied, recalling her beating at the hands of Imbatal two year earlier.

"I've heard...stories."

Vale nodded. "I've witnessed them."

Ethan glanced at her, clearly eager to hear what his friend had to say. Sensing the unspoken question, Vale continued.

"When I was fourteen, I led a small unit of two dozen men to put down a petty rebellion at Coalpont. It's a tiny village north of the Ironhelm not even mapped. It turns out that a handful of drunken men got some ideas about self-governance and succession from the Union. Yvorre sent me to quell the insurrection. She also sent Imbatal with us."

Vale paused for a moment as the memory broke free of its moorings and floated to the surface of her mind like a bloated corpse in water.

"They were just drunken fools in some insignificant village. There was one man who'd learned to read, and he was the one with the ideas. You should've seen the looks on their faces when we arrived, Ethan. They had no idea what they'd gotten themselves into." Vale cleared her throat before continuing. "But we did as we were ordered. No prisoners. The village was to be an example to any other educated peasants with bold ideas. The first dozen or so men who tried to fight us were dead within minutes. It took us another ten minutes to catch those who had tried to run. Imbatal was ferocious. I think he killed more than the rest of us combined. When all the rebellious men were dead, we moved on to the other men and executed them. No prisoners. When that order was fulfilled, we stopped."

"And Imbatal?" Ethan asked.

"No. Imbatal didn't. When there were no more men, he moved onto the women and cut them down. He murdered them even as they kneeled before him, then he moved onto their children. I ordered him to stop, I screamed at him to stop – but he just didn't listen. We all stood watch, but no one dared to try and stop him."

Vale paused and Ethan waited for the inevitable confession.

"I was terrified of him, Ethan. I think we all were. We watched him walk from one hut to the next and emerge with more and more blood on those white robes."

Ethan bowed his head and muttered a brief prayer of mercy to Bythe.

"Then...when there were nothing more than chickens and goats roaming loose in the street...only then did he stop. And then he just left. He walked straight past us as if we weren't even there and headed back to the Ironhelm. He didn't say a word."

"Why would he do that?"

"Because Imbatal is Yvorre's attack dog. She sent him to Coalpont that day to break the spirit of anyone who might oppose her. She's sent him to Fairhaven now to have the same effect."

"The Northmen are under Yvorre's direction?"

"The Northmen lost their god a long time ago, like you said. They've been wandering abandoned for centuries. They'd be a ripe tribe for spiritual cultivation."

"Yvorre's no god." Ethan spoke as if the thought were sacrilege.

"No...not yet, but I've been wondering if she's trying to change that."

"You mean Elyn?"

"I mean Elyn and me. If we're two halves of a broken god..." Vale let the idea trail off. Ethan stared at her in open disbelief.

"What are you saying? That once you're united with Elyn...you're going to...change? What's going to happen when you both meet?"

Vale turned to him with an expression of complete exhaustion. "I don't know, Ethan. I've turned it over in my head every hour of every day and I just don't know. But Yvorre is desperate to find Elyn, and I can see now that she's been keeping me close to her throughout my entire life. I don't think it's a co-incidence that my father handed me over into her supervision. She arranged it."

"Why?"

"Don't you see, Ethan?" Vale suddenly felt frustrated that her friend could never seem to grasp the solution as quickly as she could. "Yvorre's not loyal to my father – she never really has been. She's a twisted witch or maybe some mongrel demigod who's sold her soul for power. She created a monster like Imbatal! Gods only know what other secrets she's kept over the centuries. She's clearly been harvesting worship from some of the outland races and building her own little army."

Ethan smiled. "An army of Northmen still won't be a match for the Iron Union. I'm sorry, Vale, but your theory has holes. She already has a far superior army in the south at her disposal. Why bother with the Northmen?"

"That's not her army in the south, it's Bythe's army." Vale fixed him with an intense stare. "Think about it. She needs to capture Elyn. The Northmen are closer, the Northmen are loyal only to her – why wouldn't she use them? And once she's caught both me and Elyn in her noose, she'll have the power of a god under her control."

"She can take your power and finally come out of hiding," Ethan finished.

"Gods damn me for a fool!" Vale whirled about and kicked the small footstool with her metal boot. The unfortunate piece of furniture was shattered into firewood. "Why didn't I think of this earlier? I thought I was so clever. I thought I'd finally outsmarted her. Instead, I've broken away from one trap and marched right into another. She must be laughing at me right now."

They were silent.

"Turn back," Ethan said at last. "If this is where she wants you, then don't play into her hands."

"That won't work," Vale sighed. "She's already bolted the door behind me with Morbus. If I go back to Morbus now, I might as well march up to her chamber and hand myself over to her personally."

Ethan looked uncertain. "Should we flee eastward, toward the coast?"

Vale laughed. "What would we tell the men? That we've abandoned our mission to attack the Ageless and decided it's a good time for a little fishing and relaxation instead? If I fled with my men, I'd be leading them into open insurrection. You'd all become fugitives from Bythe just for following me. I won't allow that."

Ethan stepped forward and, for a moment, his face betrayed an intimacy that Vale hadn't consciously expected.

"Vale, the men will follow you. I'll follow you. You know that don't you?"

Vale met Ethan's eyes briefly then looked away. Her confidence and poise as an officer were brutally stripped from her in that look, and she suddenly felt naked before him. Vale had never taken lovers. There had been few opportunities although she was often the sole woman within ranks of men. Neither romance nor even physical need had ever been taught as a valued priority for her. She turned her face away and let the moment pass in awkward silence. Ethan sighed and started collecting the broken pieces of wood, throwing them into the fire one by one. As she watched her would-be lover complete this menial chore, she settled on her course.

"There's only one way forward. We have to find Elyn before Yvorre does. Without Elyn, her plan falls apart. Yet if we find Elyn, we finally start to get some answers."

Ethan returned to where their map lay among the remains of their meal. He dusted it off and started examining it.

"I don't think it's wise to continue our approach. If Imbatal and the Northmen are nearby, then we need to be very careful. They're going to outnumber us."

"You're right," Vale replied, walking over to join him but now keeping a professional distance from his body. "We should circle to the east around Fairhaven and see if we can get some intelligence on where they're positioned."

"If they're massed in the numbers reported by the prisoners, then they shouldn't be too difficult to spot." He turned to look into her eyes again.

"See to it," Vale ordered bluntly. Ethan saluted and turned to leave, but uncharacteristically hesitated.

"Vale?" Ethan asked. "Do you think Elyn *wants* to be found by us?"

Vale pushed away the uncertainty. "She will. She has to. Once she understands the true nature of the Ageless, I'm afraid she'll be like me – she'll simply have nowhere else to turn."

CHAPTER 8

"Though few outsiders understand this, there are two unique schools within the Ageless. Most of us favor the path of the Entarion - a school of open thought and communion with the energies of the Forge. We understand how to manipulate and wield the forces of our Blessed Mother for the defense and understanding of the world. However, Maelene also foresaw the need to defend her people with a more militant attitude, and from this need she created the Violari. Robed in purple, these Ageless dedicate their calling to the defense of Maelene, Sanctuary, and the Outer Wild at all costs. Over time, the Violari has gained more membership and influence within the Ageless. After Maelene's betrayal, we found ourselves turning to them more often for guidance. Ultimately, we turned to them for leadership and placed Veroulle as the most senior of our brethren."

~Aleasea of the Ageless

Elyn was alone.

She had realized this as soon as Aleasea left. Until that point, Aleasea had been her primary tutor within Sanctuary. Now she'd also left her behind. Like Leon. Like Nadine and Jason. It seemed that everyone close to her would - sooner or later - melt away into their own world, leaving her behind.

That morning, Veroulle had ordered that Elyn be trained by the Violari. The Violari were Ageless that had a talent for more militant and martial skills over their green-robed brethren, and Elyn needed to understand the unique role they performed. She had made the trek into the depths of Sanctuary. A place where the passageways were so ancient that Elyn was certain this must have been among the oldest halls of the labyrinth, possibly carved by Maelene herself. She had walked with increasing trepidation toward the vast cavern that housed the Violari. It was a dark place. Darker even by the standards of the Ageless, who seemed to prefer the soft glows of indirect light everywhere throughout Sanctuary; but here, the massive cavern seemed lit by little more than candlelight. Toward the back of the cavern lay a small rockpool with the ubiquitous statue of Maelene positioned in the center of the water. The Violari had stood in a semicircle in the center of the stone floor – seemingly there to welcome her. Their hoods were lowered, and their smooth faces were turned in her direction as she entered. Elyn had approached, slowly, respectfully, and a little timidly. She had stopped a short distance from the group and bowed her head.

"Masters, I've been ordered by Veroulle to attend you for training." She looked at them and smiled. "I want to thank you for this opportunity. It's a great honor to learn alongside the Violari."

The Ageless in the center of the group spoke. He looked young, barely a few years older than Elyn. His short black hair was slicked back, and his skin was a deep brown.

"Yes, it is indeed a great honor. Which is why you are completely unworthy of it." His words were sharp and low. Elyn felt the hopeful smile fade from her face as she began to appreciate the veiled hostility before her. She hadn't known what to say in reply. While she cast about for words, the young Ageless spoke again.

"Veroulle has ordered you to attend us, but that does not mean we must train you. We do not nursemaid young girls who are thrust upon us for day care. Especially girls tainted as you."

Elyn instinctively took a step backward. A soft ripple of laughter emanated from the group. She had never heard the Ageless laugh. It sounded unholy.

"But no, you must not run back to Veroulle. We will honor his order and keep you here for a time." The young Ageless turned and gestured to the pool where the statue of Maelene stood. "Our blessed Mother becomes besieged by moss and other excrements of the life that dwells in these caverns. You may serve her by cleaning this."

The youthful face twisted into a sneer and Elyn's heart sank. She realized that she couldn't return to Veroulle and complain. It would prove the Violari right – that she was little more than a petulant child, in need more of a wet-nurse's care than a warrior's training.

"Come, chosen one, your chosen tasks await you." The Ageless pointed to the pool.

Elyn turned from them and slowly walked to the edge of the water where she found a bucket filled with foul-smelling rags and a coarse brush. She hefted the bucket, scooped up the brush with her spare hand and stepped into the water. The pool was on the point of freezing. The cold sent a pain slicing through her feet and into her legs as she waded into the dark liquid toward the statue. The Violari watched her in silence as she set to her humiliating task. She had no idea how long she had worked in the freezing dark. At some point the Violari had lost interest and melted away, although now and then one would appear briefly in the cave before vanishing back into the dark. It seemed that even as an amusement, Elyn's usefulness was short-lived.

She was alone.

Elyn scrubbed the putrid lichen and slime from the base of the statue without complaint. She had started to shiver and had long ago lost feeling in her legs. It was when the misery had dissolved into a sense of numbness on her mind – that Ferehain's sharp voice surprised her.

"What are you doing, Elyn?"

Elyn turned, the freezing black water sloshing around her waist. Ferehain stood in his purple robes, his hood lowered and his black eyes flashing even in the dull light of the cavern.

"I was told to clean the statue," replied Elyn through lips so numb that her words came out dull and misshapen.

"You were ordered here for training. Get out of the water now!" The command was so sharp that Elyn started and made her way awkwardly to the edge of the pool. Ferehain did nothing but watch as Elyn extracted herself from the water and stood before him in a shivering puddle. Ferehain stared at her in silence for a moment longer, then he turned his face to the darkness and spoke in a voice that filled the chamber.

"Kaler! Where are you?"

In an instant, the apparently empty chamber was filled with purple-robed figures. The young Ageless that had assigned Elyn her duties stepped forward with an air of solemnity and subservience.

"I am here, Master Ferehain," he whispered.

"Do you think this a game, Kaler? Were you not given an order by Master Veroulle himself?"

Kaler seemed to grow pale and assumed the look of one who realizes that a clever idea has gone unexpectedly wrong.

"Master, we thought that you did not approve of—"

"You do not speculate on my feelings, Kaler. None of you do! You follow the Violari, and we all follow Veroulle."

"But Master, Veroulle now leads all the Ageless, both Violari and Entarion alike. You are the true leader of the Violari now."

"Master Veroulle leads all Ageless, both peaceful and militant," Ferehain replied.

"But Master, he has softened since his ascension to leadership. We require a firmer hand if we are to—"

Ferehain's blow struck Kaler's cheek so quickly that Elyn could barely see it. Kaler staggered back a step. The entire cavern was silent but for the gentle lapping of water from the pool.

"I give you your firm hand, Kaler. You will not question me." He turned to the larger audience and his voice rose once more. "None of you will question my will, nor the will of Master Veroulle. You have disgraced the Violari with your actions today. You have disgraced me with your treatment of Elyn."

Elyn looked up at Ferehain in surprise.

"Our Blessed Mother has placed this one in our path and you dare to question her will?" Ferehain levelled a look of pure disgust as his gathering. "I had thought better of you. Clearly, I have succeeded in teaching you strength but failed in teaching you wisdom. Perhaps some of you are better suited to green robes?"

It seemed as if Ferehain had now struck the entire assembly in the same manner he had struck Kaler. Expressions of shock and shame flitted across the faces in the dark. Ferehain turned back to Elyn.

"Get out of those wet robes, Elyn. Kaler, bring her towels and dry clothes immediately, then strike a fire in the retreat. Hopefully, you will not have killed her with a sickness."

"At once, Master." Kaler bowed low and shamefully, then was gone. Elyn slipped the freezing robe from her body and stood naked before the gathering.

"Come, Elyn," Ferehain said, pointing toward an archway in the far end of the cavern. "You have endured enough humiliation this day."

They walked in silence through the archway where Elyn found a small room with a brazier filled with wood in the center. Quietly, Kaler entered after them and presented Elyn with a bundle of towels and brown robes. Elyn took them without a word, and Kaler busied himself with setting the fire in the brazier as Elyn dressed herself. When the fire was burning, Kaler bowed to Ferehain who dismissed him with a nod of his head. Elyn moved to the fire, grateful for the warmth now seeping into her fingers and toes. Ferehain positioned himself on the opposite side and looked at her across the flames.

"Elyn, know one thing. I am not Aleasea. I am not your friend. As you just witnessed, I am nobody's *friend*. I will not consider your hurt feelings or wounded pride in my efforts to make you the strongest Ageless your limited talents will allow you to be."

Elyn slowly nodded. She regarded her teacher cautiously.

"We need to understand you. You are a mystery to us, and we cannot tolerate mysteries in our midst. Not now, of all times."

"What am I doing here?"

"I believe that the Violari can carry you further in one week, than the Entarion can in six months of blundering guesswork. We seem to have uncovered the nature of your gifts – you are seeking something; your mind is seeking this other being you commune with. Indeed, you do not have any of the gifts that I have seen our Mother bestow upon her children; however, you seemingly take from others that which you cannot create yourself."

Elyn thought back to the other occasions when she had used her power and the theory now seemed to make sense. She had been questing. Searching. Taking what she could from others and absorbing it somehow into her own being.

"I can help you. We can use your gifts to their natural advantage. I believe I can teach you to use your power to read the skills that I have acquired over centuries. In effect, you can use your power to tap into mine."

Elyn looked up at him in surprise. "You would let me copy your powers?"

Ferehain nodded. "If it helps you to become a stronger warrior, then yes. There is something coming. I can sense it, as do some of the others. You can sense it also, can you not?"

"Yvorre," Elyn spoke the word as if it were a curse.

"We do not have the luxury of time that most of us seem to think that we have. We must all be ready and at our zenith when the threat is upon us. You are no exception, Elyn; indeed, I feel that your preparation is the most important of all."

Elyn felt hope for the first time since her father died.

"Thank you, sir."

Ferehain looked at her with faint surprise. "Do not thank me yet. I fear your part in the journey ahead will far outweigh the contributions of us all." He stood and walked to the archway. "Warm yourself here for a time and wait for my return, but I warn you to be ready. I do not train my students with the same patience that Aleasea is gifted with."

Elyn nodded and watched Ferehain leave the room. She stretched out her hands and the fire warmed her frozen body. As she felt the first tingles of feeling return to her fingers, she allowed herself to wonder if her solitude was to be broken by the most unlikely of allies.

CHAPTER 9

"Although the Ageless defend the Outer Wild, very little was known about them before the Siege of Fairhaven. It was during the terrible events of this time, that the existence of Sanctuary was revealed along with many other secrets that had been held for centuries."

~Aleasea of the Ageless

"Eat."

The Ageless threw a small parcel of bread and nuts at Jason as he settled down in the hollow of a large tree. They had been running for days now, maybe a week. Days with little food and even less rest. Their flight from the battle had been fraught with peril and there were several moments when Jason had thought they'd be captured, but the sorcerer's knowledge of the wild seemed almost omniscient. He would blindly follow his guide as it threw itself into a dense wall of shrubs and undergrowth to elude their pursuers, trusting that the sorcerer would lead them to safety through the bewildering maze. Throughout the first night they ran without pause. The Ageless picked out small paths and goat trails that wound down the mountainside in the most unpredictable fashion until finally they had reached the flat and stable footing of the valley floor. There they rested only an hour before they were forced to move again, the Ageless somehow sensing pursuit at their backs.

And so it went for days.

Following the course of the valley they moved westwards rather than risk following the valley east as it would take them closer to the heart of the Northmen's homelands. The west path – while safer – took them a great distance away from Fairhaven but would circle back around southwards and hopefully bring them out deep in the woods of Hare-Min to the west of Fairhaven. They still sat in the shadows of the mountains, which had now given way to low foothills, revealing the first sights of the ancient forests beyond.

Jason opened the small parcel and began to eat, carefully watching the sorcerer as he did so. The Ageless was now standing completely still some distance away, staring from its vantage point toward the south, its cloaked head tilted slightly as if listening for something as its unseen eyes probed the distant horizon. Jason had observed this ritual several times now over the past few days. The Ageless seemed to sense the surrounding environment, convincing the land and the trees to give up their secrets and to tell them what they knew about the pursuing nomads as well as what lay on the paths before them. Eventually, the cloaked figure righted itself and turned to walk back to where Jason sat.

"Would you like some?"

Jason made his customary offer to share his food knowing full well that it would be declined this time, just as it had been every other time he had made the same offer. He had never seen the sorcerer eat during their ordeal, and they had endured some exhausting trials. Yet it had never seemed to tire for want of food and water. In fact, the only reason they ever rested seemed to be due to Jason's physical needs.

"No, Jason," came the unsurprising reply. It glided near to him with the eerie, billowing cloak then sat down on a large fallen log. Jason had now become accustomed to the strange movements of his new companion, a vast change from the fear he felt when he first watched the Ageless up close in the alleyway with Elyn that day. It seemed like years ago. Jason thought of his old friend for the first time in a while and he immediately felt guilty. Guilty for neglecting her in his thoughts and guilty for choosing to ponder Nadine in her place. He felt the urge to make some sort of amends to his conscience, driven as he was by this misplaced sense of shame. He looked at the Ageless and wondered if it knew of Elyn. Was it acceptable to ask? He decided not to risk it.

"How far are we from Fairhaven?" he ventured.

There came no immediate reply. Instead the Ageless sat there in silence, swaying very slightly. This strange behaviour gave Jason an uneasy feeling.

"Are you alright?" Jason asked.

"Yes," the Ageless replied. It paused for a moment and then continued. "We have journeyed further west than I had hoped, it will take us at least two more days before we can return home."

Jason felt his heart sink a little.

"Do not trouble yourself, Jason," the Ageless spoke as if reading his feelings. "We have made good progress; I am doubtful that our pursuers will catch us now. We need only to keep our wits and, with the Mother's help, we should return without harm."

Jason nodded, and they both sat in silence for a moment.

"I feel like I should thank you," Jason mumbled. "I want to thank you. I don't want to sound ungrateful, but..." he was unable to finish the awkward question. If the magician knew where the words were leading, it gave no indication. Instead, it sat there. Jason decided that he had eaten enough and wanted to distance himself from the figure opposite. He got to his feet and walked to where the Ageless had been standing moments earlier. Jason realized that from that spot he could see the vast expanse of the ancient forest reaching southeast in the distance. The mountain range was behind them and the landscape directly ahead rolled in gentle peaks and valleys. Jason observed the scene while his mind struggled to overcome the clash of feelings inside. Why had the Ageless taken him away from the battle instead of leaving him there? It didn't seem to need his help; indeed, Jason thought the magician's journey would be far quicker alone. But the most pressing question Jason faced was why did he agree to leave? Yes, a soldier of Fairhaven must follow any orders of the Ageless, but that wasn't the whole truth of the matter. Deep in his heart Jason knew that he had wanted to leave – he had embraced the opportunity to flee.

So, am I little more than a deserter? Am I really a coward?

He suddenly resented the sorcerer for rescuing him.

Why didn't you just let me die with the men? Why did you give me this option?

The wind brushed Jason's face and with it came a desire to confront his saviour with this self-righteous charge. He turned but his accusations died in his mouth as he saw the Ageless sprawled on the ground. He cried out in alarm and ran to the side of his fallen comrade only to stand awkwardly with no idea what to do next.

"Are you alright?" he asked stupidly. When no reply came, he continued. "Can you hear me?"

No response came and the great emerald cloak bled out over the ground before him. Jason noticed for the first time how that once pristine cloak was now stained and ragged from their ordeal as he kneeled down and extended his arm. He touched the robe and felt the mass of a body concealed beneath, then quickly withdrew his hand as though a bolt of lightning might shock him at any moment. The great hood was no longer dark and billowing but now lay flat over the clear shape of a human head. Jason found himself torn with conflict. He wondered if he should remove the hood. He didn't need to remind himself that such an act was clearly unthinkable, that death – a most horrible of deaths – would serve as punishment to the poor fool that tried such a thing. Yet there seemed no other option. They were days from help with the enemy at their heels, and too many men and Ageless had died already. He lifted his hand and cast back the hood to reveal a beautiful young woman with golden hair and slender features.

"A woman?" Jason whispered to himself in awe. He now recalled the perfectly sculptured features of the male Ageless that fell before the Northmen several nights earlier, and he realized that in the madness of the time since, he had forgotten the revelation. He turned his attention back to the woman before him. She was beautiful even in her current state of injury, and her skin seemed to almost shimmer in the sun's light. She was breathing, which gave Jason some measure of relief. He reached for his water canteen and gently cradled her head with his left hand as he guided a thin stream of water over her lips. She stirred and her eyelids flickered open to reveal eyes of deep emerald green. They were confused eyes that sharpened into focus.

"Jason!" she hissed in a delicate voice devoid of its usual grandeur. "Jason, what have you done?"

"I've tried to help you," he snapped, irritated by the accusation in her voice. She waved away his offence and tried to sit up only to find she lacked the energy.

"Rest for a second," Jason ordered.

Aleasea obeyed. She lay there for a moment, her eyes fixed on Jason, seemingly regarding him and weighing possibilities and alternatives behind that stare. Jason wondered at the look and the thoughts that were driving it. He could not help but marvel at her beauty and the perfection of her face. At length, she sighed.

"The gods have set you firmly in my path, Jason. I cannot fault your actions."

"Fault my actions?" Anger crept back into his voice.

"The removal of my hood. The forbidden enquiry that should never be excused. You knowingly brought death upon yourself this day, Jason."

"Well it seems to me that death has been brought to all of us, both Ageless and soldier."

Aleasea smiled ruefully at his response. "Indeed, you speak wisely for one so young. You are right of course and acted justly. I suspect that many saw my brethren fall before Imbatal. I fear the time for subterfuge and secrecy may now be behind us. No, you were right to act as you did, and I thank you."

Jason nodded in reply and helped Aleasea as she again struggled to sit up, this time with success.

"Are you injured?" Jason asked.

"No, I am unharmed. However, such prolonged and severe use of my power can leave me drained and fatigued. I will recover presently. Do not be alarmed."

"Oh," Jason replied with some surprise. Aleasea studied the response.

"You thought us all-powerful?" She smiled and Jason felt a little foolish.

"Do not feel ashamed, Jason," she reassured him. "Indeed, it is what we would have you believe, but no we are not all-powerful. We draw life energy from the natural world around us as do all other living things, and like all other living things, we too have our limits. You seem to be learning much of the limitations of the Ageless in a short space of time, are you not?"

Jason nodded.

"Does this mean you're going to kidnap me into your sanctuary too?" Jason meant the comment as a joke, yet he could not quite keep the edge of concern from his voice. Aleasea smiled.

"No, I am afraid you will not be reunited with Elyn in the near future, least of all now."

A silence hung in the air. Aleasea waited for the question that was clearly in his mind.

"How...how is she?" Jason's question was quiet, almost solemn, as if they were speaking of the dead.

"Elyn is safe and well," she answered. "I cannot share the secrets of her activities with you, but she is safe under our protection. However, she seems ... troubled."

"Troubled?"

"Yes, Jason, I can sense her confidence growing, but with it comes something else. Tell me, Jason, you know her intimately, do you not? Have you sensed this?"

Jason was put off balance by the question.

"Intimately? We're friends... I'm not sure that I'm that close to her..."

"Elyn is becoming a strong woman. I sense she is even more powerful than she knows, and yet she is still fragile. She will still need love and support. Do you understand this, Jason?"

"Of course," he replied defensively. Too defensively. Aleasea studied him again with those deep green eyes and he felt exposed.

"You have taken advantage of her nature, Jason, you know this," she said. "She has long harboured deep feelings for you, and you have chosen to ignore them."

"That's not true, I never—"

"You may try to lie to me, but do not lie to yourself. It does not serve your character. You pretended that you did not notice her feelings because her attention flattered your ego. You told yourself that she was little more than a sister to you, and yet you knew that you meant far more to her."

Jason cast his eyes at the ground but didn't reply.

"You have taken far more from her than you have offered in return, and you now owe her a debt."

Aleasea's words were like the pronouncement of a sentence. Jason opened his mouth to argue but silenced himself as he considered her words.

"You're right," he said at length. "I've always loved her like a sister, but I knew that, for her...it was more than that. I should've said something earlier. It just felt good to be adored like that. I guess I didn't want it to stop."

Aleasea looked at him thoughtfully. "You have a good heart, Jason, and I do not wish you to agonise over the natural follies of your youth, but she is going to need your support in the days to come. She will need the true loyalty of a friend, not the childish emotional games of adolescence."

"But I can't see her."

"It will not always be this way," she sighed and started to rise, only making it as far as the log before seating herself again. "I do not have the wisdom to see all paths. I only act as the Mother guides me. When I beheld you in the forest, I knew that this was no coincidence or random turn of chance. Strange fate brought us together. I could not deny the gods that which they place in my path. You will play an important role in what is to come. I believe this as much as I believe in Elyn."

"But you don't know for sure." It was almost an accusation. Aleasea shrugged.

"What is known with certainty? Not even the gods can answer that. Much lies outside their own influence. And I am no god."

"The gods have left us," Jason muttered as if to himself.

"No," Aleasea replied quietly. "Bythe remains."

Silence reigned for a moment as if uttering that name ushered a stillness that had to be respected. Jason felt like Bythe was now privy to their conversation and wanted to change the subject.

"Imbatal," he recalled the name from earlier in the conversation. "Was that the name of the...thing that attacked us? Imbatal?"

"Yes, we believe that is his name." She paused for a moment and seemed lost in thought. When she spoke, it was almost as if Jason weren't even there. "But why is he here?"

"Who is he?"

She looked at him as if reminded of his presence. "We do not know. He is the favored assassin of one of Bythe's witches. Yvorre. And this is the second time I have recalled that name in recent days. The other person to mention her name was Elyn."

Jason stared at her blankly. "She never mentioned her name to me. I've never heard of her."

"Few have, Jason. She is a relatively new figure in Bythe's empire, but she seems to have risen in influence very quickly in recent years. We believe she ordered the assault on Elyn's hometown of Outpost."

"I heard that it was some young Commander who took Outpost."

"On the surface it was Commander Vale of Bas-Tyra – daughter of Bythe – who led the attack, but we believe she did so on Yvorre's orders. Yvorre seems to be quite well established in such a short time. Besides Imbatal, she appears to also command the daughter of Bythe himself."

"Imbatal," said Jason. "He tore us apart like we were straw men, and..." he left the words hanging in the air unspoken. Aleasea finished his thought for him.

"And he killed two of the Ageless. Yes, once he is committed to a task, he appears to be all but unstoppable. It is a rare circumstance when Yvorre unleashes her deadliest weapon; yet whenever she has, there has been but one result – the destruction of whatever target she has given him."

"You don't know if you can stop him." The realization dawned on Jason. Aleasea did not answer.

"What was he doing with the Northmen?" Jason asked.

"I do not know. We did not expect to find him here or we would have come better prepared to face him. We did not track you high into the mountains in order to contend with the likes of him."

Jason turned her words over in his head, weighing their implications for him and his companions back home.

"Why were you tracking us?" he suddenly asked. Aleasea stiffened slightly at the accusatory nature of his question.

"Mind yourself, Jason," she cautioned. "Circumstances may call for some concessions in our formality; however, you do not question the Ageless and you certainly do not question our intentions."

"Yes, master," Jason's response came so quickly it was like a physical reflex. He wondered then how much conditioning he had been subjected to on this matter over time. Aleasea glanced up at him and sighed with what seemed like a hint of apology.

"We train you too well and it distresses me. We were not always this way. The Ageless have become far too militant for my tastes in recent years. I do not believe the Blessed Mother would approve of the path some of us have chosen since she fell. Forgive me."

"It's alright," Jason replied. "I forgot my place."

"Your place?" she repeated with a touch of sarcasm. "Your place is wherever you choose to be. The Ageless were supposed to be your protectors, not your wardens. I fear we have taken our role too seriously. Mother guide me, please."

Jason had no idea how to reply.

"We were also concerned about the increased aggression from the Northmen, and we have been using every tool at our disposal to learn the cause," Aleasea continued. "We have been using much of our craft and skill to divine the answer, as well as more practical methods such as our own reconnaissance. I fear that our latest attempt has now given us some of the answers we sought." A strange look of exertion passed over her face as she slowly rose to her feet. "We must delay no longer, Jason. I am certain that Imbatal still tracks us and our brethren must be warned of – "

She broke off suddenly as her head snapped to her left, her eyes fixed on the nearby trees.

"What is it?" Jason asked following her stare.

"Mother curse me!" she hissed in a low voice. "We are discovered!"

Jason reached for his sword. He could not see their enemy, but this did not lessen his faith in his companion's judgment. His nerves lit afire with anticipation as he stepped backward to stand close to Aleasea.

"Can you tell how many?" he asked.

"No, but I know there are several. They approach from the east. I did not expect them to flank us this way. These are tactics most unusual for them."

"Can you fight?" he asked.

"I still have strength in me," she replied as she raised her hood and cast her features into that unnatural darkness. She drew her kajik staves from within her robes, and they both steadied themselves for battle. Jason locked his eyes on the trees ahead and felt his heart hammering in his breast. The realization dawned that it was unlikely that his Ageless companion would be able to see him through this fight – that this time the probability of death was high. They waited and, for a long time, nothing happened. Jason glanced about, his instincts sensing a trap tightening around him. Even Aleasea seemed uneasy, her head moving this way and that under her concealing robes. Then, one by one, armored men stepped out of the cover of the trees and into the light of the clearing, and Jason recognized them at first sight.

"Behind me, Jason!" Aleasea's order came with the cavernous thunder he had become accustomed to and he again obeyed out of instinct.

The Iron Union here? Why? How?

His mind reeled at the revelation and tried to grapple with the questions in vain. The men before him drew longswords of fine steel in obvious preparation for combat. Aleasea stiffened her stance in reply and stood ready. Jason searched his mind and his surroundings for some kind of escape from this fatal trap. He could find none.

"Yes, there's strength in you – plenty of strength left I'll bet. Let's not test it, alright?"

The voice floated out from the trees behind the other soldiers and it took Jason a moment to place it, but before that moment could come, Vale stepped into the clearing with a strange look on her weary face. No one could tell the manner of expression on Aleasea's concealed face. She simply stood fixed in place. Unmoving like stone.

"On your knees, Ageless," Vale ordered. "You too, Jason."

Jason felt as if he had stepped out of his body. The sight of Elyn standing there in the armor of the enemy seemed unreal, and for a moment he wondered if he'd slipped into a dream. He looked to Aleasea for guidance. She simply continued to stand there as if carved from rock. After seeing no response, three of the Helmsguard took a step toward her but they halted at a signal from Vale. Then they all stood there unmoving as if in some kind of strange tableau.

"Help me here, Jason," Vale called out. "We don't want to kill her, but we will if she forces us to."

"Elyn?" Jason found his voice. The face of his friend smiled grimly.

"No, Jason, but if you want to help Elyn, you'll convince your mistress to surrender to us."

Jason struggled to comprehend all that had happened in the past moments. He again looked to Aleasea, awaiting a signal, any signal. He decided that he would live or die by her next actions. He would follow her lead no matter the end.

He waited.

They all waited.

And at length, Aleasea slowly lowered her weapons to the ground.

• • •

Elyn was learning.

She sat in her meditative position in the enormous cavern in the depths of Sanctuary. Ferehain sat opposite. They were practising a ritual that Ferehain had been teaching her at length over the past week. They focused on words of power. Words – Elyn had learned – unlocked the keys to the fabric of the world. Reality was defined by the words we chose. While it had taken Ferehain years of his life to learn these words, Elyn discovered she could lift them from his mind if Ferehain allowed it, like reaching into a compartment in his psyche. This had been difficult but Ferehain had helped. Together they had meditated in silence as Elyn allowed her power to reach into Ferehain's mind and find the words stored away on a shelf of his thoughts – powerful words stored there after decades of practice and conditioning. She was practising this exercise now.

Concentrate.

Elyn reached out with her mind and into Ferehain's. She felt Ferehain guiding her through the maze of thoughts and consciousness to the waiting compartment. She opened the box and found the words there, taking them one at a time and placing them into her own mind. When she did, the effect was as incredible as it had been the first time she used it. She rose like smoke on the wind, watching Ferehain's silent and still body below her as she floated upward. She was now floating outside her own flesh. Elyn noticed her vision start to dim as she reached the ceiling and fought back the mild sense of panic as her consciousness dissolved and spread out throughout the dirt beyond the underground walls. She felt herself spreading thinner and thinner as she reached out through the ground, touching dirt, rocks, roots, and the trees they nurtured. She sensed the life of the city of Fairhaven, not just the trees and the plants, but the tiny pinpricks of feeling that were men and women. Thousands of them, like pins and needles crawling across the back of her head – if she had had a head at that moment, the sensation would have been almost euphoric. Elyn spent minutes – or perhaps hours – soaking in the sense of complete symbiotic connection to the life around her. It was bliss. Finally, as she always did, she noticed Ferehain tugging on her mind and pulling her back into her flesh and blood confines. She opened her eyes and it took her a moment to realize where she was. Ferehain was watching her with an expression that was almost admiration.

"You have done well," was all he said, but coming from Ferehain it was high praise.

"Thank you, Master," Elyn replied.

Ferehain rose to his feet, his robes of deep purple moving with a life of their own. Elyn had learned that the cloaks the Ageless wore were enchanted to follow the will of the wearer, that they could conceal or reveal as much of their identity as they wished. Ferehain was letting his face be known to Elyn today as was the polite custom within Sanctuary.

"I believe it is time to demonstrate this to my brethren," Ferehain continued. "You have shown much progress over the past several days, and I believe it is fitting that we share this. It may have a bearing on our judgment of your standing among us."

Elyn felt a surge of satisfaction and pride.

"Thank you. I'll try not to let you down," she answered.

Ferehain walked over to Elyn and fixed her with an appraising stare. "I have told you before that we do not have the luxury of time. I do not do this for you, Elyn. I do this for the entire order." He walked past Elyn and glanced up at the colossal statue of Maelene. "There is a threat approaching. By telling you this, I breach confidence; however, I believe we no longer have the time for discretion. The Northmen are coming for us in strength. We believe this is Yvorre's work. While others of my brethren may disagree with me, I believe that she may even be coming for you."

Elyn immediately felt guilty. Did they know about Vale? She tried to push the thought away in case Ferehain could somehow sense it.

"How long do we have?" she asked.

"Days. Possibly only hours. Their army has breached Haere-Est, and Captain Lewis is preparing for siege. We need every resource to help."

Elyn had noticed a sense of anticipation in Sanctuary in the past week. She'd also noticed the number of Ageless starting to shrink. It had started with Aleasea several days ago, and now it seemed that every day, more Ageless were vanishing from this place and going who-knows-where to do gods-know-what. Now she realized the truth – they had been going to defend the town against Yvorre. They were actually defending her – whether they knew it or not. Elyn felt a touch of guilt.

"Elyn, I need you to help. We need to harness your gifts to use against Yvorre; however, there are limits to what I can achieve alone. I require Veroulle and the Entarion to lend their power to what I propose."

"What do you need from me? Tell me and I'll do it," Elyn replied.

"We need to impress Veroulle with your potential. Should we succeed, I will petition to have you immediately promoted as an Initiate member of the Violari. I will then be permitted to grant you access to the life blood of Sanctuary itself – a far greater source of power. If you can access this power the same way you access my mind, the results could be enough to hold even an army at bay."

Elyn was stunned with a surge of pride. To wear the purple was an honor in itself, but to be given the chance to prove her worth to the Ageless in this way was far beyond anything she had expected.

"Master, yes! Of course!"

"We will commence at noon tomorrow. Train, meditate, and be ready, Elyn. This will be the most important test of your life so far. Do not fail us."

"I will not, Master."

Ferehain glided from the chamber without another word, and Elyn watched him leave with a feeling of enormous gratitude. For the first time in months, she had hope. She finally had an answer. She could help the Ageless defeat Yvorre, and in return they would then drive Vale from her mind and fight back against Bythe and his Iron Union. It was a way out of this mess. She allowed a faint hope that Aleasea would return to witness the achievement.

CHAPTER 10

"The Siege of Fairhaven came without warning. While Captain Lewis had increased patrols into the mountains in an effort to stamp out the Northmen, he had no inkling of the sheer force of numbers that had amassed on his doorstep. The Northmen swept over the lowlands like water from a ruptured dam, forcing the town's gates to be barricaded within hours of the first sighting. So rapid was their advance, many farmers and fieldworkers were caught unprepared and could not return to the safety of the walls before they were locked and barricaded. It was reported that they were shown no mercy when the vile and savage Northmen arrived to find them huddled in fear outside the town gates."

~Aleasea of the Ageless

The fires burned like hundreds of tiny lights reflecting off a large but distant lake. Some lights were larger than others. Some were clustered into knots while others seemed to float alone in a vast expanse of darkness, many others winking in and out of sight while moving along a slow course. It was beautiful to behold from a distance, a serene spectacle for the casual observer, strangely contradicted by the lethal truth behind its beauty. The fires burned in and around the homes of people. The lights were that of a war machine come to kill. Fairhaven was burning.

Vale studied the scene for a moment before returning her gaze to the figures standing before her. She stood in her private campsite with her two prisoners and Ethan. All other security had been dismissed out of casual earshot – but Vale knew they'd be at her side in seconds if someone shouted the command. Jason still regarded her with a look of bewilderment. Aleasea – Vale recalled the name from Elyn's memories – wore an expression of complete and total indifference. The Helmsguard had cautiously lowered her hood once they'd restrained both prisoners, but the face that greeted them was as impassive then as it was now. After capturing them, Vale had moved her team a short distance to the east, mounting a ridge that would give them a view of Fairhaven while keeping them well concealed from any wandering Northmen. It was nightfall when they arrived. The vantage point they had sought now granted them a clear view of Fairhaven's unexpected peril. Vale had stared at the scene for a long time as she considered how this changed her plans. A direct attack of any kind was no longer an option. Vale had weighed her choices and then decided that the time had come to talk to her prisoners.

Jason looked at his hometown burning in the distance, then looked again at Vale.

"Is this your work? Are the Helmsguard doing this?" Jason asked.

Vale shook her head but remained silent. Jason considered for a moment.

"The Northmen? In those numbers?"

Again, Vale didn't answer. A truth discovered for oneself was always far more powerful than a truth learned from another. Jason turned to Aleasea for confirmation, but she stared directly in front of her – seemingly oblivious to all that was transpiring. Vale knew better.

"My gods," Jason whispered. "How many are there?"

"We don't know," Vale broke her silence. "Too many. Far too many for your kinsmen to resist." She paused for a moment then rested her eyes on Aleasea as she made her next move. "And they haven't yet seen Imbatal."

Aleasea's eyes flickered toward her, and in that simple movement, Vale knew that she had her.

"Yes, Aleasea. We know Imbatal fights alongside the Northmen." Vale noticed her eyes widen at the mention of her name. Aleasea stared at her openly now. Her stoic expression hardened.

"I concede that your use of the Northmen was a brilliant tactic, Commander Vale. We did not think them capable of an alliance with the Iron Union. It would seem you have well earned your reputation."

Vale inclined her head in acknowledgement. "I appreciate the thought, Aleasea, but I'm afraid your intelligence was correct. The Northmen have always been at odds with the Union. They've never acted for us."

"Lies," Aleasea replied as a simple statement of fact. "Imbatal serves your mistress Yvorre. Do you think us blind?"

Vale eyed her carefully. As much as she hated the Ageless, she realized she would need this one for her plan to work.

"I really don't care what you believe, Aleasea, the fact remains that Fairhaven is under siege." She turned from them to stare out at the distant battle. It seemed calm, but it was much like the storm that was brewing in her mind. Tumult turned to tranquillity by the grace of distance. "It's not going to stand, even with your magic to protect it. The numbers of the Northmen are far too great."

"So, what do you want with us? Are you here to gloat to her before you kill us?" The courage behind Jason's interruption was a surprise to Vale. She turned back to them.

"No, Jason, that's not why I'm here."

"How do you even know who I am?" Jason asked. "And why does she look like Elyn, Aleasea? Didn't you realize that Elyn looked like Bythe's daughter?"

"While we had heard of Commander Vale, we had no knowledge of her appearance," Aleasea replied in an even tone. "We still do not know the face of Bythe's daughter, even now. We have no evidence that this woman is who she claims to be. Do not fall into her trap, Jason. This is nothing more than Bythe's deception and treachery."

"Bythe's treachery?" Vale's voice rose with slight incredulity. "How dare the Ageless lecture anyone about treachery! How many innocents have died from the village wells you poisoned? How many families have starved when their crops were blighted by your magic? How many children have died when you burned their houses to the ground?"

Aleasea's eyes were cold. "We have a right to take back the land you stole. Why did the Iron Union place innocents in harm's way?"

"You murdered peaceful civilians!"

"You murdered our Blessed Mother under the promise of peace!"

"Stop!" Jason commanded. His face was dark, and Vale noticed he looked like a man twice his years. "I don't care about any of this. Not now. I care about Elyn and I want to know why you wear her face."

Vale drew in a breath and regained her center. She hadn't expected the Ageless to draw out such emotion in her.

Is this Aleasea's doing or is this something else?

She glanced at Ethan who stood behind the two captives, then she decided.

"I know Elyn well, just as Elyn knows me. We share a connection."

Aleasea eyed her with intensity. "Then it is you? You are the presence we sensed?"

Vale nodded.

"What do you mean that you share a connection?" Jason asked.

"It's more than a connection, I believe that we're the same. We're one person."

Jason looked at her with complete confusion. "That makes no sense! How can you be one person when you're standing before us right now?"

Vale clenched her jaw. "I can't explain it. I don't have all the answers, but somehow Elyn and I are...I don't know how to say it."

"You are complementary aspects of one person simultaneously coexisting in the material plane," Aleasea said. "Is that what you would have me believe?"

"More or less, yes," Vale answered.

"And you will use this pretence to infiltrate my order? It is a clever and untried idea, much like using the Northmen to flank us. Once again you have my respect. But no, I will not play into these lies."

"It's not a lie, Aleasea. I'm not here to infiltrate your order, not anymore. It's clearly no longer practical with the Northmen at your doorstep."

"So why are you here?" asked Jason.

"I need to find Elyn. She's in danger."

"Indeed, she is in danger because you seek her, and she will be in more danger if you find her," Aleasea observed dryly.

"She's in danger because Yvorre wants her."

"And you serve Yvorre, and Yvorre serves Bythe," Aleasea countered.

"No," Vale readied herself. After she played this card, she could not return. "Yvorre serves herself. She commands the Northmen, and she wants Elyn for her own twisted reasons."

Aleasea looked at her. An ancient mind processing the information. Ancient eyes scanning her for signs of deceit. Finally, she spoke.

"She wants Elyn because she believes that you are both two halves of Bythe's daughter. A broken god?"

"Yes."

"And she now seeks both you and Elyn?"

"Yes."

"What are you talking about?" Jason interrupted. "Elyn's not Bythe's daughter. She has a father...she had one."

Vale spoke to Aleasea in reply. "You know there's power in her. Your lot must've sensed it."

"We knew there was power, but we were unsure of the source. There were...competing theories among us." Her face began to darken as if a sudden thought had dawned on her.

"Think about it, Aleasea, and you'll see that I'm not lying. If this was a trick, why wouldn't I come with more men? If I was in league with the Northmen, why aren't they here with me now? I could use Imbatal's help at the moment. No, I'm here because I need to get to Elyn before they do. Like it or not, we have a common interest tonight – to keep Elyn safe from Yvorre."

"And what of Bythe?" Aleasea asked.

Vale sighed. "He doesn't know about any of this. He doesn't even know I'm here. I've fled from Yvorre. I need the truth."

Aleasea seemed to consider this. "What do you want from us?" she asked.

"I need your help to get into Fairhaven. After I've found Elyn, I give you my word that you'll be released. I think I'm being extremely fair under the circumstances."

"Lies," Aleasea muttered under her breath.

"Alright, Aleasea, what will it take to convince you? Should I tell you about how I learned your name? How you came for Elyn in the council and took her into Sanctuary. Should I tell you about Veroulle or Ferehain? How you all tested her then feigned disinterest in her? How you toyed with her and almost got her killed in a tavern?" Her heart was racing with remembered feelings. She whirled around and glared at Jason. "Should I tell you of how hurt Elyn felt when she realized you'd chosen someone else over her? Should I share the depths of her pain to both of you? Or should I tell you of how deeply her world descended into blackness on the afternoon she watched Leon die on the road? I was there too that day, Jason. I felt Elyn's life shatter. And you, Ageless," Vale found herself pointing accusingly at Aleasea, "while my father was dying before me you simply stood there and watched."

The campsite was silent. Aleasea's eyes were downcast and even Jason looked ashamed. When Vale spoke again her voice was low.

"You need to help her. We all need to help her."

Jason was shaking his head. "I can't understand this. Elyn can't be the daughter of Bythe. She grew up in Outpost. She was Leon's kid."

"I don't understand how this happened, but I know in my heart that it's true. I don't have any of the answers, Jason. I'm trying to find them just like you," said Vale.

Aleasea's face had continued to change. Her features slowly melted from confidence to uncertainty as her mind digested the news.

"Prove it to me," she declared abruptly.

Vale was caught off guard. "How?"

"Open your mind to me," she answered.

"What are you suggesting?" Vale asked.

"If you wish to prove your words true to me, then you must let me touch your feelings as I once touched Elyn's. Only then will I know, and only then can I begin to trust your word."

"Vale, no!" Ethan broke his silence and stepped forward. "It's a trick. You can't let the witch inside your head. She'll take control of you."

Aleasea glanced at Ethan with a look of pure disdain. "I cannot control her will. Your superstitions are absurd."

"Vale, you can't risk it! You have no idea what she can do to you. They're savages," said Ethan.

Vale didn't take her eyes from Aleasea as she considered her offer carefully. She decided it was time for truth.

"I don't think I'm going to make it through this, Ethan," she said at length.

Ethan glanced at her in alarm. "Don't talk like that, Vale!"

Vale smiled and turned to look into his eyes. "It's true. I've suspected this for days, and the feeling only strengthens the closer I get to Elyn. It's a sense of foreboding that I just can't shake."

"What are you talking about?"

"I need to find her. I can't go back to the way things were – I just can't. I need to know what's wrong with me. Whatever happens, it'll be worth it because it will give me these answers." She finally offered him the look of uncompromised affection she knew he longed for. "Do you see, Ethan? There's little I have to lose right now. Even if this Ageless hurts me, it'll do nothing more than rob her of the same answers." She turned her eyes back to Aleasea. "But I don't think you will. I think you need to know the truth almost as badly as I do."

Aleasea was watching her but said nothing. Vale smiled.

"So yes, I'll submit myself to your test, Aleasea. I'll even give you the chance to kill the daughter of Bythe, if it means you might help me...and help Elyn in return."

"Vale, if she even tries to harm you, I'll kill her where she stands!" growled Ethan.

Vale held up her hand for silence before crossing the campsite and untying Aleasea's hands. "Well, Aleasea? Do what you must. I'm at your mercy."

In reply, Aleasea reached out a hand and gently placed her palm upon Vale's forehead. Vale resisted the impulse to pull away. Aleasea locked her eyes on Vale's and the strength of her gaze was both intense and intimate. For a brief moment Vale caught a sensation of an ancient woman filled with pain and weariness, then this feeling was washed away and replaced with emptiness. The feeling was so complete it seemed to drain every living feeling from within her heart. It was a barren, sterile, and hopeless sensation, as if there were nothing left in the world that could provoke a sense of joy or delight. It reached through her, stretching into her toes and fingertips with a chill that was absolute and seemingly final. Then Aleasea removed her hand and the feeling was gone. Vale looked at Aleasea and to her surprise she saw compassion on Aleasea's face. On some level, Vale knew that this had cost her, that whatever she had seen within her soul had vindicated her and shocked Aleasea. Vale felt relief.

"He knew. Somehow, he knew," Aleasea whispered, her face changing from compassion to uncertainty to alarm.

"Who knew?" Jason asked.

"Ferehain. I knew he suspected something, but he would never disclose his thoughts to me. I knew that Elyn was tormented, but how could I have known this was the reason? But Ferehain...he must have suspected this. I can see that now...Oh Mother, forgive me."

"What's wrong?" Vale asked. An uneasy feeling swelled inside her at the grave look on Aleasea's face.

"If what you have shown me is indeed true – if Elyn is the daughter of Bythe – then I have left her in the care of a man who will hate her the most!"

CHAPTER 11

"While the Violari began as militant members of the Ageless, their views and behaviours became somewhat more extreme following the death of Maelene. They broke with our long-standing principled refusal to use the iron and steel of our enemies. Instead, they believed that using a foe's own weapons against himself was the most fitting form of justice."

~Aleasea of the Ageless

Elyn stood in the enormous cavern in the middle of Sanctuary. The statue of Maelene towered before her with those infinite streams of water pouring from her hands. She stood at the foot of the stone steps that would lead her to the top of the plinth she mounted on her first day in this place, and like that day, watchers again surrounded her. Not as many as had attended her first appearance, but still enough to make her self-conscious. They wore mostly purple robes. There was a distinct lack of the usual emerald green in the room this time, but that was not altogether surprising. It made sense that Ferehain's Violari were present to show support for this unexpected development.

She was ready.

After today, the Ageless might accept her as an Initiate, no longer a simple acolyte. Ferehain would invite her into the ranks of the Violari, and then she could tell them about Vale. They would help her. So much progress in such a short space of time. She waited in silence at the foot of the steps. Veroulle stood to her right, his purple hood cast down and his burning red eyes locked on Elyn. Ferehain stood beside him, hood raised but with his eyes still faintly visible beneath. She wondered what it would be like to wear that uniform.

"Elyn," Veroulle spoke. "Are you ready to begin?"

Elyn almost didn't hear his words. Her only focus was on the trained reflex action inside her mind. Ferehain was there. Ferehain would guide her as a mental template. Silence filled the chamber. It was time.

Elyn lifted her right leg and began the ascent up the stone steps, one at a time. Each step inching her closer to a destiny to which she now seemed increasingly entitled. Eventually she stopped. There were no more steps. She was at the pinnacle of the platform and there was nowhere left to hide. She was tired of running. Maelene appeared to watch her from above, her massive features fixed in a permanent state of serenity and yet seemingly fixed on Elyn. She thought of her first moments in this chamber and wished that Aleasea was present. It would have been fitting. She hoped she was alright. It had been a long time since Elyn had last seen her. Soon she'd be able to help her.

Focus! Push the distractions away.

She breathed out gently and tried to cast the stray thought out of her mind. She had been preoccupied in recent days, like something was unsettling her, gnawing at the corners of her concentration. It seemed to be getting harder to focus, possibly because of the pressures of her lessons with Ferehain, but then possibly not. So many faces watching her. Some concealed, others not.

Focus!

Elyn reached behind her head and drew the white hood over her features. She decided that if she was going to be tested as a sorcerer then, pass or fail, she was going to damn well look the part. She extended her hands before her – fingers splayed apart – closed her eyes, and started to breathe. Magic started with breathing. Breathing cleared the mind and focused energy. She forced her breathing into the correct rhythmic pattern then started to reach out with her awareness. Her tendrils of thought reached out and searched for Ferehain. He was close by and it took seconds for Elyn to find her teacher. Just as they had practised, Elyn reached into Ferehain's mind and found the shelf where she had stored this ritual. The box was opened, the words poured out and the mirror reflex in Elyn's mind was activated – euphoric tingles ran along her spine as the surge of power flowed along every pore and through every vein. Elyn could feel her mind rising and took heart from the clear expression of surprise on Veroulle's ancient face. Her consciousness hovered above them like an ethereal phantom, and, for a moment, Elyn knew that she was next to the statue of her goddess. She could feel a kinship with her at that moment. Was Maelene watching over her now? Taking pride in this achievement with her? Elyn willed her mind to the next level of consciousness, yet she found she couldn't leave Maelene's face. She tried again, and yet she still remained where she was. Transfixed by her it seemed?

Beautiful, wasn't she?

Ferehain's voice in her head was as unexpected as it was distracting. Why was he doing this now? She had to remain focused.

She was the most beautiful creature I had ever beheld. Would you like to see how she died?

Something had gripped inside her chest and was now pulling her downward into herself. Her vision faded and the dark chamber was replaced by a searing sun in a blue sky. She stood on a broad plain, the air choking with dust and screams. All around her were men in the black armor of the Helmsguard, swords drawn and slashing violently. There were hundreds of them. Murderous. Vengeful. Victorious.

It was like this. They came at us from the hills, hidden within the rocks for days before we arrived. It was a trap as brilliant and as treacherous as your father!

Elyn felt sick. Ferehain knew. He knew Elyn's secret and this was his opportunity to expose it. Elyn realized that she was watching Maelene's Fall, and she was watching it through the memories of Ferehain. He had been there? Ferehain seemed to sense the questions in his mind.

Yes, I was there. I will never forget this day for as long as I continue to live. This was the day that I failed her. This was the day we all failed her.

Elyn realized that there was a figure in tattered purple robes fighting desperately a few feet in front of her. His hood had been cast back in the battle and his head was bleeding, his face was a mask of rage matted with damp crimson. Ferehain. He wielded his kajik staves with blinding ferocity, felling three Helmsguard as Elyn watched, but for every enemy that fell there seemed to be an endless supply of replacements. It seemed obvious to all but him that this battle was doomed.

I wanted to die protecting her. I wanted nothing more than to get to her side, but I could not! You know how that feels, Elyn. To know that the one person you love above all else is dying within feet of where you stand, and yet you can do nothing to stop it.

Elyn tried to vocalize a response but found that she couldn't. Instead she only watched in mute witness as Ferehain was forced back by the unrelenting onslaught of the black armored figures. He moved with supernatural speed, darting from one adversary to the next in a vain attempt to regain the advantage, but it was having little effect. The sheer number of the enemy was neutralizing any magical advantage Ferehain tried to employ. Then there was a cry so full of despair and rage that it obliterated the sounds of the battle itself, and for a moment, all on the battlefield seemed to pause in awe of that sound. Then the air seemed to split with a thunderous crack and a wave of force rushed over them all, knocking them into the air like leaves. Elyn wasn't sure what had happened as the air filled with dust so thick that it seemed to block out all light. Then it was black. The silence was punctuated after a moment by Ferehain.

I lay there for days and when I awoke, she was gone.

The darkness dissolved and was replaced by another image. The battlefield returned into view, only now it was rent by a split in the ground itself. Where there had once been a flat plain, there was now a chasm, wide and black and stretching far into the distance. The dead lay around the landscape in the hundreds, no one moved but for one purple-robed figure.

I searched that chasm for weeks and found nothing. Not Bythe. Not my Blessed Mother. Nothing! My kin were left to rot on the field and yet there was not a trace of my Mother. What happened to her, Elyn? What did your father do to her?

Elyn tried again to make some sort of reply, but Ferehain had her tightly in his grasp.

You see what you bring here? What sort of death you carry with you? Did you think I would let you walk in among us and spread your disease to us even further? You have your father's black soul and you speak to him. Did you think I was blind to this? Did you think I could not sense your dialogue with Bythe himself? Show him to us! Show us all who you really are.

Panic started to rise in Elyn as she perceived the trap that she had willingly walked into.

Yes. You are an even greater fool than I thought if you believed for a moment that I was ever going to help you join us. You have no one here to coddle or protect you anymore. Leon is gone. Aleasea is gone. Yvorre comes to help you, but she will arrive too late. I will have broken you and taken what we need, then we shall use it against that witch.

Elyn tried to scream. She tried to yell, shout, or somehow let the others know what was happening to her but she couldn't. Ferehain had trapped her with his mind and all the training and apparent bonding were now revealed for what they really were – an opportunity to learn Elyn's mind and to break through her defenses. The panic rose in pitch and then rapidly subsided in order to give way to humiliation, then anger. She was tired of the abuse. Tired of the bullying and the mistreatment, of the unfairness of it all. It wasn't right. She tried to scream again, only this time she channelled her hurt and her rage into that one powerful shout. She heard it faintly at first, as if she was screaming from somewhere far away, but then it grew louder and then louder still until the scream seemed to be so great that it shook her vision. The image of the battlefield dissolved, and the blackness of Sanctuary once again saturated her vision. She was kneeling on the cold flagstones on the dais, her rage still pouring from her mouth and echoing off the cavernous walls far above her. Veroulle was looking up at her with concern on his face and beyond him the sea of purple figures was rippling in agitation. It took Elyn a moment to regain her bearings, and then she was moving. Pure rage propelled her down the steps in leaps, and when she found the floor, she threw herself at Ferehain like an animal. Guttural sounds emanated from her throat as she flung her outstretched hands toward her enemy, the enemy who effortlessly sidestepped the attack leaving Elyn to grapple with empty space.

"Coward!" Elyn bellowed as she swung around, looking for her betrayer. "Come back and face me!"

The chamber was buzzing with excitement, but Elyn was unconcerned. Her only focus was to find Ferehain and to hurt him.

"Elyn!" It was Veroulle that called her. "Elyn, control yourself. What is wrong?"

"She is her father's daughter. She is the corrupt offspring of Bythe himself. Behold her true nature. Are you convinced now?" Ferehain's voice rang out from the darkness.

"Liar!" roared Elyn. "You betrayed me!"

Elyn wheeled about violently, searching for Ferehain among the hooded figures around her.

"Elyn, please!" Veroulle walked over to her, his face a mask of alarm and his palms extended in a conciliatory gesture. "Maintain control of yourself."

But it was impossible. The rage was welling in her and it would not be contained. She could feel it poisoning her reason, but she didn't want it to stop. It felt good. It felt powerful. Finally.

"You see, my brethren, it is as I have always predicted. This girl is corrupted and twisted. She is the agent of our enemy brought to Fairhaven to undo us. She has called her allies and now they are at our doorstep. Do you need more evidence than this?" Ferehain reappeared among the Violari, standing alongside the smirking figure of Kaler, and Elyn appreciated the depth of the ruse.

"Ferehain, enough!" Veroulle snapped, turning to face him. "This is not the time for this discussion."

The distraction was momentary but enough. Having sighted her enemy, Elyn reached out toward him with her feelings. Only this time – instead of a thin tendril of consciousness – Elyn could feel an uncontrollable torrent of pain, despair, and hatred gushing out of her like a flooded river. The wild snake of emotion thrashed and flayed about her with a mind of its own. It hit Kaler first and felled him instantly with its potency, then it flayed about the room in a wild and random dance, striking down random Ageless where it happened to touch them. Even Ferehain's expression changed from sneering triumph to disbelief as he watched the now-visible crackling energy tail surge throughout the chamber in a wild flurry of destruction.

"Elyn, stop!" Veroulle called through the din, but it was pointless. Elyn seemed to have completely lost control of herself. Years of pent-up emotions were breaking within her and the consequences were a nightmare.

"Seize her," cried Ferehain from within the crowd, and several figures started to move toward her. Elyn wanted nothing more than to turn her power toward Ferehain and drain him of all thought, but she knew that this was beyond her. The power was out of control and she had to shut it off. She had to get out of there. Find a hole, some dark place, and just bury herself. She could see more figures closing on her from her left, and she realized that she didn't have much time. With another cry of rage, she wheeled the arc of light around her in a magnificent circle, throwing down several of her would-be attackers and causing the others to quickly retreat. Then in the instant of their hesitation, she sprang from her feet and bolted across the chamber into the sanctuary of a dark passageway. Again, she was running. Like that night months ago, running for her life. Only now it seemed as though she was running away from her life. Away from everything. Into the blackness that forgave and forgot all.

•   •   •

Aleasea crossed the campsite. Confusion and distress marred her face.

"Ferehain had sensed Elyn's abilities almost as soon as she arrived at Fairhaven. He could feel you reaching out to each other, but we had no way of knowing who she was or what this meant. We had become concerned about Bythe's new witch and the recent success she had brought him. Everywhere, our allies were falling back before Yvorre's forces, and now one of the refugees from her onslaught had betrayed a kind of power we had not seen in a long time. There was division among us on how to proceed. The Violari suspected a connection to Yvorre and wanted her imprisoned and interrogated. The Entarion wanted to reach out to her to see if she was a kindred power gifted to us by Maelene. As you have seen, Vale, it was Veroulle who decided on our actions. Elyn was to be extended every courtesy unless it could be proven that her power was corrupt."

"But you took her in and trained her?" Vale asked.

"Yes, and the Entarion were sincere in our offering of assistance; however, I suspected that Ferehain and his Violari still refused to surrender their position. Somehow, he must have known about you both. If that is true, then he was merely using this as an opportunity to expose Elyn's parentage and to do so convincingly."

"What would Ferehain do?" Vale asked with anxiety creeping into her voice.

"I do not know. We were once very close; however, after we lost...so much... he changed. Like so many of us changed. He is a hard person to understand now. He was there when Maelene fell, when Bythe betrayed her, and out of all the Ageless, his hatred of Bythe now burns brightest of all."

"Will he kill Elyn?" asked Vale.

"I do not know. Even Veroulle would not abide the daughter of Bythe to live. Gods help me, I did not intend this." She turned back to face Vale and Vale saw tears in her ancient eyes. "I looked into her heart and I saw such tenderness there, such a capacity for love and kindness. I just wanted to protect that. It seems that kindness and compassion are no longer useful qualities in the world we have built. I could not believe she was evil."

"She's not evil!" Jason spoke with such vehemence that Vale realized they had all but forgotten him. "I know, Elyn, I sure as hell know her better than both of you. She's good. She's kind. She's too kind. You said so yourself, Aleasea."

"And what do you know of her?" Vale asked.

"I know that she won't even raise a hand to protect herself, let alone hurt anyone. She's always putting others first, even when she should be sticking up for herself. Her kindness frustrates me because you're right, Aleasea – it's not a good thing in the real world. I try to toughen her up, but she won't listen. She said herself, she's just not capable of it."

Aleasea stared at Jason for a moment as if she hadn't understood his words, then she looked at Vale as if seeing her for the first time.

"She is incapable of violence and yet you have mastered it. She is capable of such kindness and compassion that you feel drawn to her for fulfillment."

"What are you saying?" Vale asked, but she already knew the answer.

"You are split. You are one woman torn in two. You each have an immense capacity for love, for anger, for violence, and for compassion; yet these abilities are split unevenly between you both."

"How has this happened?" asked Vale.

"I do not know."

The campsite was silent for a moment before the peace was broken by quiet laughter. All turned to look at Ethan, who seemed mystifyingly amused by what he had heard.

"I'm sorry, Vale, but I can't accept this," Ethan said. "Your immense capacity for anger? Violence and aggression, yes, but I don't think I've ever once seen you act in rage. Man or woman aside, you're the coldest killer I've ever known."

Aleasea shook her head gravely. "You do not understand, soldier. I did not say that Vale had capacity for great anger."

"Then you meant Elyn?" Jason asked. "I'm sorry, Aleasea, but you're wrong again. Elyn's never lost her temper in her life."

Aleasea sighed in frustration. "How can you know her so well, yet so little? Do you think she shows her anger? It is buried deep within, hidden so deep that she barely knows it exists, but it burns in her heart and feeds on itself. I have sensed it once and felt it rising. At that time, I did not know why, but now I do."

"Because of me," Vale said.

"Yes. The closer you both become, the more you destabilise the other. You are both feeling emotions that are foreign to you. In your case, Vale, you are feeling empathy and compassion like you have never known."

Vale closed her eyes. "And for Elyn?"

"Her own anger. Her father's capacity for hate. She is finally setting it free."

•   •   •

Elyn burst from the dark of the tunnel into the cool night air. Her heart beat fiercely in her chest and her lungs burned, but she was certain that she hadn't been followed. She paused for a moment to gasp for the breath that she'd denied herself for the past twenty minutes of desperate flight. She wasn't quite sure where she'd wound up – somewhere near the walls of the Old City she guessed – but she didn't really care that much. Something sick and heavy welled deep in her belly, like an infection that was growing and threatening to choke her from within. She started to walk blindly down the street before her, oblivious to where she was going, contemptuous of where she had been. She could taste the poison within her. She realized she should ignore it, but she didn't – she couldn't. She wanted to dwell in the misery, to feed it. And the more she fed it, the more it grew and the more it demanded in turn. Elyn recognised this in some logical part of her mind, but she couldn't pull herself away from the destructive spiral. Instead, she embraced it. These people had betrayed her. Ferehain had betrayed her. Aleasea was nowhere to be found – even she had abandoned her. Dimly, Elyn noticed a sound. A distant roar, only she couldn't tell if it was real or in her head. She rounded a corner and found herself in a street along the river. Pausing, she rested her hands against the low stone wall that followed the water and tried to stem the rage building within. It was welling. Seething. She wanted to break something. Across the road, a tavern disgorged the last of its drunken patrons into the night. Their garbled shouting pierced the night air and added to the rumbling in the air – or was it in her head? It didn't matter, she needed to contain her feelings. Bottle in this rage. Don't let it—

"Oi! Who the hell is this?" Nathan's drunken voice slurred through the din like a knife. Elyn didn't even need to turn to recognise it.

"It's the end of the world and the gods have given us Elyn for our last night. This is perfect."

Laughter from the group. Four or five maybe? They were walking over in her direction, no doubt having finished another night of drinking and seemingly oblivious to the threat of the Northmen. Their timing could not have been worse.

"It's the end of everything, you little slut," Nathan continued. "Let's have fun like there's no tomorrow."

Nathan's beer-drenched voice sounded louder now. They were only a few feet behind her. Again, that rumbling echoed somewhere in the distance.

"Leave me alone, Nathan." Elyn's voice grated through clenched teeth. "Just go."

"What happened to the smart mouth? Remember when you said I couldn't handle a woman? How about I prove it to you right here?"

The voice was over Elyn's shoulder now. She felt the rough hands on her waist and breasts as Nathan pulled her around to face him. As he did, his mocking look that greeted Elyn froze on his face.

Elyn was never sure exactly what expression she wore at that moment, but it was clearly the sort of terminal intent that has to be respected. There's a look or a tone or an action that commands universal respect when a person sees it in another. It may vary from person to person but it's a constant in human emotion, and tonight Nathan beheld it for the first time on the most unlikely of subjects.

It was likely that it was the last thing he saw.

•   •   •

"We have to help her!" Jason demanded.

"That's exactly what I intend to do, but I'm going to need help," said Vale while looking pointedly at Aleasea.

"You want me to help you gain access to Fairhaven?" she replied.

"I know the Ageless have the means to access the town, even under these conditions."

"You expect me to betray the secrets of the Ageless to my enemies?"

"Aleasea," Jason interrupted, "we're beyond that now. By morning, there may not be any secrets of Fairhaven left to protect."

She considered for a moment then nodded. "Very well. However, the passages I will show you will not accommodate an army, Commander Vale. You must leave them behind."

"No!" demanded Ethan. "Vale, this is a trap."

"No, it isn't," Vale answered. "She makes sense. You know I can't take a hundred men into Fairhaven without detection. Stealth will be far more effective than force."

"Then at least take me with you."

"No, Ethan, I need you here to lead the men. I've got a far more important task for you."

"Please don't ask me to leave you, Vale. You'll be trapped."

"No, I won't." Vale turned and called over her shoulder. "Tell me, Ageless, what do you think will happen once I find Elyn?"

Aleasea fell silent for a moment. "I cannot know."

"You can guess," Vale replied as she turned to confront her.

"If you accept each other and reconcile, you may have the ability to shape the Forge as the gods do, to remake the parts of this world that are within your power. Like life to our Mother. Like steel to Bythe."

"I could become one being as I was meant to be?"

"It is possible," agreed Aleasea.

"And then she would have the power of a god?" asked Jason.

"It is possible," repeated Aleasea warily. "The ancient gods all chose their gifts. They chose which elements of the Forge they would have mastery over. Vale may be no different."

"In that case, Ethan, I will be far from defenseless," said Vale.

Ethan shook his head and took her hand. "It's too great a risk. Come back with me, Vale. We'll go straight to the Ironhelm and to Bythe himself. He's your father after all!"

"And what about Elyn?" Jason asked. "If you turn your back on her and head back to the Iron Union, what becomes of her?

It was Aleasea who replied.

"If we do not help her now, it is clear what will become of her. She will lose control. She will become the worst parts of her father."

．　　　．　　　．

The rage consumed Elyn. The terrified remnants of Nathan's group were desperately seeking shelter in the tavern from where they'd only just emerged. Two of them lay stupefied on the road. Nathan now knelt before his intended victim, his eyes wide with terror. Elyn was oblivious to this. Her heart beat loudly in her ears and she could feel fury coursing through her entire being. It flowed along the veins in her arms and fired in the pit of her stomach. Her breath was rapid and her hands trembled, but she would not notice. All she focused on was the act of ripping Nathan apart. To grasp him violently by the face and slam his head against the ground until it shattered like an egg.

These thoughts pleased her.

They swam though her mind like a drug, blinding her to all other sensations. She was vaguely aware of distant shouts and screams. Someone was telling her to stop and the distant rumbling returned, louder this time. Much louder. Elyn no longer cared what happened to her. All she wanted was to watch Nathan die. To murder him with as much brutality as she could. She sent her psychic tendril spearing into Nathan like a weapon and it hooked deep within his mind. Nathan's mouth opened in a silent scream and a look of sheer terror shot across his face, sparking a smile of malicious satisfaction on Elyn's. A smile that wasn't hers yet at the same time felt strangely familiar. As though it had been lost to her and now was returned.

• • •

Barnes never thought that he'd be a soldier. He always thought that he'd follow his family into some kind of well-to-do trade. A financier like his older brother, perhaps? Or maybe a trade broker? They all certainly expected it of him. But no, there was something about the call of a military life that was irresistible to him. The images of the officers dressed in finery. So proud. So honorable. The dreams of honor and earned dignity fanned his flickering interest into a flaming desire. Earned dignity. Not the kind that was bought from a family fortune or a wealthy dowry, but real dignity. Where was that dignity now? There was very little dignity in his behaviour over the past few days. How many men had died serving him? Men that he had sworn to protect, now dead. He lurched forward on unsteady feet. The city couldn't be far now. He'd spied it from the ridge yesterday – or was it this morning? He couldn't tell anymore. Jackson would remember.

"Jackson."

The words barely left his lips. He had so little energy left. Where was Jackson? He stopped for a moment and looked about him. Jackson was nowhere around. Then he remembered. Jackson hadn't woken up from their last rest. He'd been brave. Determined to get home and warn the others, to hell with his injuries. Again, Barnes focused on that sound that he'd first heard a few hours ago. It was a roaring in his ears. Hysteria no doubt setting in through dehydration or blood loss, only now it was becoming intolerably loud. The Northmen had swarmed through them and ripped them apart like they were a gang of kids. It was unbelievable. That demon in white had cut through them like a farmer scything the field – had that been one of the Ageless he'd cut down, or had the Ageless cut the demon down? The memories just weren't clear anymore.

Again, there was that roaring sound. Where was it coming from?

He stumbled up the rising slope that would break over Fairhaven. He could then report to Lewis. Lewis had always liked him; they'd shared that kindred bond of two natural soldiers. Yes, the Captain needed to be told what had happened; he needed to be warned. Then he'd know what to do.

But the Captain already knew, didn't he?

Barnes knew this the moment he crested the rise and the roar swept over him, the moment he beheld his city for the last time, the moment he saw the sea of thousands of lights – torches held by Northmen – marching on his city. Barnes knew that it was over – his career, his home, and now his life.

Barnes never thought he'd be a soldier. He certainly never thought he'd die as one watching his city burn.

But fate can be cruel.

And the wandering paths of many men's lives often twist and end in strange locations, far from where they expected. Very far from home.

BOOK 3
RENOUNCEMENT

CHAPTER 1

"No god has ever returned to us from the beyond. It would seem that once they leave us, they are incapable or uninterested in returning to the world they have created.

However, there are those among us who believe otherwise. They believe that our Blessed Mother will return to us when we face our darkest moments. They tell us that the Temple will blaze with her glory and herald her return. They tell us that this light will bring change and will finally drive away the darkness of Bythe.

They tell us such tales and yet the fact remains – no god has ever returned to us."

~Aleasea of the Ageless

It was nearing midnight as they walked along a subterranean passage that was older than Vale could fathom. It was dark, no natural light penetrated this deep underground nor followed them this far from the concealed entrance. The dozen or so turns and abrupt bends in the passage had defeated any such pursuing light over the past hour, leaving small sputtering lanterns alone to fight the absolute dark that encroached upon the party from all sides. The party was smaller now. Vale had taken twelve of the best men leaving Ethan in command of the rest with strict orders. Lanterns were raised high by the guardsmen in front. Four of them, two with the lanterns and two armed with swords drawn, were cautiously leading the group into Sanctuary. Another three formed a rear guard and the remaining five kept a close formation around Aleasea. They barely took their eyes from her as they walked. Every single man was ready for trouble. Each one was looking for the slightest hint of betrayal or an unexpected movement that would give them permission to send her into the arms of her precious Mother in whatever afterlife was waiting for her.

She gave them no such justification.

Vale was uneasy. She disliked that Aleasea had agreed to their plan almost at once. Why wouldn't she? They were taking her home into the heart of her own defenses. With every step, her position became stronger while theirs became weaker. It was surely only a matter of time before an opportunity would present itself to her, and she would not hesitate to take advantage. Vale knew this was an incredible risk, but she had to find Elyn.

Jason walked behind Aleasea like a man in shock. No doubt the revelations of the day had almost overwhelmed him, and now he walked with his head bowed and his eyes distant. He was disarmed, of course, but while the guards kept watch on him, it was obvious that he would offer little serious resistance in his current state. Vale looked at him and wondered what circular thoughts and arguments must rage in Jason's mind right now. What must he be going through? This empathy was a strange development for Vale, but it wasn't an unwelcome one. She stepped over and fell into pace with Jason, who looked up at her with slight surprise and a trace of expectation on his face.

"Why aren't you a full soldier in your army?" Vale asked after a moment. "I've watched you through Elyn's eyes. You seem capable."

Jason hesitated for a second as if he would not answer. As if his code of acting as a loyal prisoner of combat forbade such causal discourse with the enemy. But then defiance faded from his eyes, and he seemed to surrender even this token resistance.

"I've only just joined the service. Normally, I'd serve a few tours as a cadet before I became accepted as a full soldier."

Vale nodded. "But you've seen action?"

"Yeah. Much more action than a cadet would usually see. I have the Northmen to thank for that." They were silent for a moment before Jason spoke again. "You sound exactly like her, you know?"

"Elyn?"

"Yeah, it's strange. I just feel like I'm talking to her, only... you're evil."

Vale laughed. A genuine ring of humour that was out of place in this grim underworld. "Is that what these sorcerers teach you, is it? That we're evil?"

Jason shrugged.

"The Ageless have always been deceitful," Vale continued. "They play at acting as the defenders of the free and the just, but they really just want power like the rest of us."

"Like the Iron Union," Jason countered.

"Yes, like the Union, but at least we're open about it."

"I'm not sure that justifies everything you've done."

Now it was Vale's turn to shrug. "Bythe brings order. That's what we do. Before Bythe, the Union was a ruin of warring tribes and savages. Bythe united them under one banner and one order. There's been peace and stability in our lands for centuries. This offends the Ageless and they've spent their entire existence trying to disrupt it."

Her last comment was louder than the rest and clearly intended to reach Aleasea's ears. She didn't react.

"But there's more to it than that," Jason continued, feeling a little more confident. "The Union's been aggressive so many times, you can't pretend that it's all out of concern for our best interests."

"I never said that," Vale replied as they rounded another bend in the tight corridor. "I said that Bythe brings order and control. The places we annex are far stronger as a result. Look at your town for example." Vale gestured upward to the unseen city now directly above them. "Your town is under siege by chaos. You have an army, but it's pitifully small and now it's being overrun, all because your leaders thought that concealment would protect you. It won't. It can't."

"We've been caught off guard—"

"Exactly!" Vale almost sounded happy as she interrupted. "The Iron Union would never allow that to happen! We're strong and we're united, and we make sure we protect any of the lands we bring under our control. When has the Helmsguard ever been caught off balance?"

"I seem to recall some examples," Aleasea's voice drifted back to them.

Vale smiled. "Probably true. The Ageless enjoy bringing terror, don't you? That's what your Violari do."

If Aleasea replied, the words never reached them. Instead a loud rumble swept down the corridor shaking the walls and loosening dirt from the roof of the passage. Everyone halted.

"The city's getting torn apart," Vale said. She looked over at Aleasea. "How much further before we can get to the surface?"

Aleasea looked upward as if she was staring at something past the stonework walls. "We have already passed two exits into the city, but I thought you would like to reach closer to the temple and my kin?" There was a hint of sarcasm in her tone.

Vale felt an intense stab of anger and remorse. It was a reaction not her own, yet one which was instinctively familiar to her. It was Elyn. Elyn was free of Sanctuary, but she was now surging like a flaming beacon. Something was wrong.

"We need to get up there. Elyn's not in the temple."

Aleasea looked at her. "Are you sure?"

"I'm very sure," Vale answered. "I can feel her again. She's up there in the city."

Aleasea looked confused. "That cannot be possible."

"Something's not right, Aleasea. She's lost control. How do we get up there? Show me now!"

Aleasea gestured up the passageway. "Seventy feet on your right, there is a stairway."

Vale started back down the passageway at a run, leaving her guards struggling to hurry after her. After a short distance, she began searching the featureless walls of the passage.

"Where?" she shouted in frustration.

"Here," replied Aleasea, who leaned over her and gently placed her palm onto a large stone above Vale's head. The wall fell away to reveal a large alcove concealing a circular stone stairway leading upward. Vale couldn't wait and she threw herself up the stairs as quickly as her grating metal armor would permit. As Vale climbed the stairs, the distant sounds of battle became louder and more distinct. Within minutes, smells joined the sounds – burning wood and the sharp smell of exploded powder. When she reached the top, she could feel Elyn close by and it was a strange notion. A calling. It made her somehow happy, and the closer she came, the stronger the sensation.

"My lady, please," called the captain of Vale's guards as he bounded up the steps behind her. "Stand behind us. We don't know what's going on out there."

Vale begrudgingly let three guardsmen shoulder past her into the night air. She followed, emerging into the all too familiar chaos of a battlefield. All about her was smoke and ash, thick like a winter morning fog only lit up in shades of orange by the sickly glow of burning lives. They had emerged in the warehouse district of outer Fairhaven, and while the current fighting seemed to be taking place elsewhere in the city, it had not spared the area its ravages. Several warehouses were burning, and three bodies lay in the roadway in front of her. Their remains became the subject of the Helmsguard's interest for only a moment before they turned their attention to securing the street ahead. Vale turned her attention to the buildings encircling her. Elyn was near, frustratingly close yet the emotions were all but screaming at Vale, overloading her mind and making it impossible to pinpoint the exact location.

Aleasea and Jason emerged from the passageway that had been fashioned into a seemingly innocuous stone wall and walked over to stand near Vale. Aleasea fought hard to maintain her composure but her eyes betrayed the grief she was suffering at the sight of her city burning. She glanced once at the orange glow in the distance then back to Vale.

"Where is she?" Aleasea asked.

"I don't know." Vale looked about in frustration. "She's close and she's in pain, but I don't know where!"

Jason looked around, trying to get his bearings through the smoke and the darkness. "We're outside the Old City, near the markets. Why would she be here?"

The captain returned to them, having satisfied himself that his guards had the street protected for the moment. "We can't stay here for long, sir. The fighting's a few miles over near the north wall, but it looks like the nomads have broken through here once already and they could come back through anytime."

Vale continued looking about in vain.

Jason stepped away and looked keenly into the darkness. "I think I have an idea where she might be."

"Where?" asked Vale.

"We're near the markets, the square. Elyn hasn't been here since that day...you know...when Leon...".

"When my father was killed," Vale finished his sentence softly and walked off toward the marketplace.

•   •   •

Elyn was cold.

She stood in the darkened marketplace store where she had hidden at the Wellspring Festival, when the nomads had streamed in from nowhere and changed her life forever. Flames lit the night sky and the sounds of distant death were all around her, but here it was a tomb.

Leon's tomb.

It had been the most tragic of deaths that any daughter could experience. Not that she was Leon's daughter. She felt that now more than ever. Leon would never do the horrible things that she had done tonight. Nathan's screams still echoed in her head and she could still hear his mind breaking, like the sickly, crackling snapping of an insect slowly crushed underfoot. It made her ill to think of it now.

What am I? A murderer? An animal?

Elyn couldn't answer. She wished that Jason was with her. Even Nadine. She wanted someone to comfort her. Anyone.

"Father, why did you leave me?" she asked the night quietly, tears filling her dark eyes. "I need you now and you're not here."

Leon would never answer her again, but it didn't stop Elyn from hoping. Everything had gone so wrong. Couldn't it just go back to the way it was? She hadn't known despair this black since her father died.

"Elyn..." Jason's voice came tenuously through the night air. Elyn turned to see her friend standing in the door behind her. For a moment, they both just stood there in silence, each disbelieving the sight they beheld, each regarding the change in the other. So much had passed in such a short time, they were barely recognizable to each other now.

"Elyn," Jason repeated and stepped toward her. "It's alright."

Elyn merely looked at him in reply.

"What's happened?" Jason asked with genuine concern in his voice. "You look terrible!"

Elyn shook her head slowly as if trying to clear the fog that had settled over her mind these past few hours.

"I don't know, Jason." Just speaking those words, simply interacting with another person helped Elyn start the internal process of lifting her dark mood. She realized the destructive cycle that this solitude was producing, and she reached for Jason like a lifeline out of a torrent. "I think I need help."

At these words, Jason closed the space between them and took her into his arms. It was the first time they'd ever shared such an intimate expression of affection, and yet it was shared with no sense of hesitation or reserve. Elyn released her tears like the breaking of a dam, and the sobs that emanated from her were unbidden and raw. For his part, Jason stood there immovable and stoic, ready to be the rock that she needed. He weathered the onslaught of Elyn's grief and held her upright throughout. It took full minutes to pass, and in the end, they both stood embracing in silence. When it was over, they separated without a word. Elyn took a deep breath and exhaled, feeling the nerves and adrenaline starting to leave. Then she looked at Jason and immediately questions started to form in her mind.

"Jason, what are you doing here? We're under attack. Shouldn't you be doing...I don't know...something?"

Jason smiled. It was strange how quickly they reverted to their old mannerisms. "I am doing something; I've been trying to find you."

Elyn eyed him cautiously, abruptly on guard. "Me? Because of Nathan?"

Jason's face betrayed confusion. "What? No, of course not." Jason paused for a moment, sensing Elyn's anxiety. "What happened to Nathan?"

Elyn walked away from him and sat down on a nearby crate. For a while she said nothing, and then when she started to speak, everything came out in a rush. Jason listened in silence as Elyn explained everything that had happened over the past few weeks, the teachings by Ferehain, the test, the betrayal, and finally Nathan's assault. Now it was Jason's turn to be silent.

"Did you kill him?" he asked after a while.

"I don't know. I think so. If I didn't kill him, then I've crushed his mind. I've got no idea what that does to someone."

Jason walked over to Elyn and crouched in front of her so their eyes were level.

"Elyn, listen to me. I don't know what's happening to you, but this isn't your fault. There's something wrong here, things we didn't know about...you."

Elyn looked at him with suspicion again in her eyes. "What do you mean?" Elyn's mind started to race. "Wait, why were you looking for me, how did you even know where to find me?"

Jason paused. "This is difficult to explain. I'm not even sure how to say it. Something's happened over the past few days. Things have changed..." Jason let his voice trail off as he fumbled for the words. As he did, Elyn began to feel the familiar awareness of someone else close but out of sight, someone familiar but also altogether foreign. She immediately stood up and turned to face the door through which Jason had entered.

"*Elyn, I'm here.*"

Jason was continuing to talk but Elyn couldn't hear him. She was focused intently on the doorway and the figure now standing beyond. It was as if the door frame were edges of a mirror and the woman within was some bizarre reflection of her. Some kind of parody. A hint of what she might have been had she lived another life. Elyn stood watching her walk toward her as if transfixed. The movements were so like her own and yet so completely different. The black armor, the blue eyes, the confidence in her walk, and the secure way she carried herself were all so alien to Elyn, but her face – that face was hers. Without a word, Vale had walked to stand in front of Elyn and the two regarded one another in silence. Aleasea had also entered the room and stood beside the door, observing the scene with an excitement she rarely displayed. Jason had stopped talking and watched. Both Elyn and Vale stood before each other without word or motion, both fearful of what had happened last time they had met. Elyn tried to reach outward with her feelings but nothing answered her call, it was as if the violence of the past few hours had stunned that part of her into shock and now, she could feel nothing.

"I understand what's happening to us now, Elyn," Vale said quietly. "You're searching for me. Your mind is searching for mine."

"I know," Elyn answered.

"We were never meant to be broken, Elyn. I don't know how it happened, but it was wrong. It needs to end."

Elyn looked at her twin. Strong and confident. Her weapon hung at her side as naturally as if it were a part of her. A killer. Like her. Elyn felt cold.

"I want nothing to do with you," Elyn whispered. "I hate what you've turned me into."

"Elyn, that wasn't me. That's you. That's part of who you are, who we both are."

"Shut up. You're not me. I'm nothing like you."

"Yes, you are. Can't you see? We're the same, Elyn. I'm a part of you that was taken. That's the reason you hate me.

"I hate you because you destroyed my life. You rode into town with your mistress, Yvorre, and you ruined my world. I was happy in Outpost. I was happy with my life then, and you came and took everything!"

Vale felt a surge of frustration at Elyn's petulance. "You think it's all about you, Elyn? I've been used too. My whole life, I've been used. At least you had a father and a home for a time. I never had any of that."

Vale clearly remembered her upbringing, her years of gruelling training and conditioning in the Ironhelm. She collected the memories as vividly as she could and pressed them into Elyn's mind. They remembered lonely nights in the city staring up at that grotesque and monstrous citadel of black metal, an ornament to industry and the strength of their father's wars. They remembered the private quarters where Vale slept as a child – sparse and functional. They remembered the nursemaids with their cragged faces and unsympathetic eyes. They remembered the physicians and witch-doctors and their regular visits. The examinations and the pain. Elyn grunted in disgust and turned away.

"Stop it! Just leave me alone. What do you want from me?" she asked.

Vale looked at her in surprise. "Elyn, we're not supposed to exist like this. We need to be reconciled."

Elyn recoiled. "I'm nothing like you, Vale, stay away from me. What are you going to try to do?"

"Elyn, be calm," Aleasea said. She moved from her place at the door and crossed the floor to stand beside Elyn. There was a strange look on her face. "I will not let anyone harm you. There is nothing she can do to you without your willing help."

"What do you mean?" Elyn asked.

"I am so sorry, I failed you. I understood your gifts far too late. I should have seen this earlier, back in Sanctuary when you first invaded my mind." She looked from Elyn to Vale and back again. "When you were divided, your gifts were split between you both. Elyn, you have power, so much power, yet you have no strength to control it. And you, Vale, you have inherited the strength of a disciplined mind designed to harness a power that you have simply never possessed. Yet between you, there is more. There is another force at work that I did not fully perceive until you both stood before me. Now I sense her completely."

"What are you saying, Aleasea, that I have the power of Bythe?" Elyn asked.

"In part. You have raw ability. The potential. But without the will of a god you are unable to use it. Instead it uses you. It is searching for something. Searching for something it needs, something it has lost."

"Searching for me," said Vale.

"Yes," answered Aleasea. "Elyn, your mind is capable of reading others, taking what it needs. What it needs is now standing before you."

Elyn looked at her sister. "You mean that, if I reach out to Vale..."

"Yes," Aleasea confirmed. "You will find your answers. You will become the person you were meant to be. You will reconcile. You will become the daughter of Bythe, and now I suspect you will become something much more than this."

"And Vale can't do this?"

"No," Aleasea said. "For all her skill, she has no power. Only you can take this action for both of you."

Elyn looked at Vale.

"Then I refuse," Elyn said flatly. "You can keep your answers. I don't need them."

"Elyn—" Vale began but Elyn cut her off in a voice heavy with fear.

"Stop it. I'm sick of this. I just want it to stop. You want to change me. You all want me to change. I don't. I don't want to lose what's left of me. I don't want to become someone else."

"Elyn, I know you're frightened but you need to be strong," Vale cautioned.

"Strong like you? Your strong body and strong mind." Elyn turned to Aleasea. "Tell me Aleasea, who will be dominant if I allow myself to reconcile with Vale? Which mind will prevail when it's done?"

"I cannot know, Elyn. I am merely speculating," Aleasea answered.

"Then speculate now! Which is more likely? Will I come out of this as I am, or will Vale's stronger mind assert dominance over the weak-minded Elyn? Tell me which is more likely."

"Elyn, we must seek out the counsel of Veroulle. There is another force at play now. I did not realize that—," Aleasea answered.

"You're avoiding the question," Elyn said, cutting her off. "My raw power and untamed emotion harnessed by Vale's stronger mind? I'll cease to exist, won't I?"

"We don't know that, Elyn," Vale replied, yet her face betrayed a twinge of guilt. "Look, come with me and we can sort this out. We need to get away from here before the Northmen break through. Yvorre wants you too, and she won't indulge you with a conversation."

"I'm better off without you, Vale."

Vale took a step closer to Elyn. "Do you really believe that? She'll find you, Elyn, and then she'll hunt me down too. I've got nowhere left to run. She'll take us to her dungeons in Kardak, and she will see you writhe in pain until you beg to give her what she wants. You won't have a choice."

Elyn opened her mouth to mount a futile argument but her words were drowned out by a scream. Vale was instantly alert with her weapon drawn. Aleasea moved in front of Elyn and readied herself in a combat stance. One by one, three black-armored men came through the door and hurried to take up a protective formation in front of Vale, their sabers pointed toward the empty doorframe.

"Ageless, my lady!" the captain said breathlessly. "It's killed the others. Stay behind us."

"Aleasea..." Vale began, but before she could finish the words, the doorframe and the surrounding timber wall of the marketplace exploded into thousands of splinters. The force sent everyone flying backward in a cloud of dust and confusion – all but Aleasea, who remained in her stance as the shockwave swept over her.

Vale was momentarily dazed before the screams of her soldiers brought her mind sharply into focus. With a reflex action she was back on her feet – her sword never having left her grasp – and was instantly assessing her surroundings. Elyn lay a few feet behind Aleasea, stunned but shielded by Aleasea's magic. Jason lay further behind, and Vale hoped he was only unconscious. Aleasea remained unmoving while she watched the purple-robed figure of Ferehain sweep through the room. He killed two of the remaining Helmsguard before they could even rise. Ferehain was bent over both of his victims as the Helmsguard captain got to his feet behind him, swinging his saber at Ferehain's exposed back. Ferehain extended his left arm blindly and the captain froze mid-swing, allowing Ferehain the time he needed to pivot in place and sever the captain's head from his neck.

There had rarely been moments in Vale's life when she had been shocked into inaction. Shock was an unprofessional liability learned at the youngest age. Yet Vale had never witnessed the full fury of the Ageless. She had never truly understood the brutal efficiency with which they could kill. As she stood in the shattered ruins of the marketplace, watching Ferehain wipe the blood of her kinsmen from his blade, she learned this lesson well. Ferehain stood before them, his hood was lowered, and his eyes blazed with the fanaticism of a zealot as they locked on Vale. Vale readied her saber and became aware that Elyn was now standing at her side.

"Ferehain, hold!" Aleasea commanded. Ferehain did not take his eyes from Vale as he replied.

"So, you have found both of them. I congratulate you, Aleasea. Do you now congratulate me also? Do you accept that I am right, now that the truth stands in black iron before you?"

Aleasea moved to stand between Vale and Ferehain. She looked into her kinsman's eyes with a mixture of defiance and desperation. "Yes, Ferehain, you were right. She is touched by evil. She is a fractured aspect of the daughter of Bythe. Yet you still must listen to me. There is more to her than darkness. I sense more. I now realize that I have always sensed it. We must consult with Veroulle immediately."

"Why our brethren indulge your sympathy is something only The Blessed Mother could comprehend with her infinite compassion. If only they had listened to me, we would not be here now."

"Ferehain, enough!" Aleasea raised her hand to interrupt him. "We should not be out here. This is dangerous. Why did you drive Elyn away from Sanctuary?"

"You know the answer to that. She is the spawn of our enemy. Evil. Corrupt. No good will ever come of her."

"You tried to hurt her?" Aleasea's voice was almost a plea.

"She has tried to destroy us, Aleasea!" Ferehain replied. "Look at the city collapsing above you. Imbatal himself is here. Do you think this is all coincidence?

She stepped in closer to his body and for a moment their manner almost became intimate. "Don't you see?" she continued in a quiet voice. "The love and sensitivity I can feel within her, this cannot come from her father. We did not understand why so many of us felt a solidarity with her, but now I do. We are so close to unravelling this mystery, Ferehain. Now is not the time for dissension."

"Indeed?" Ferehain paused as he regarded both Vale then Elyn in turn. His impenetrable black eyes peered curiously into theirs. "So, Elyn, now you hide from me behind your illegitimate sister. I see that your rage has deserted you again in favor of cowardice."

Elyn's anger flickered but it was Vale who spoke on her behalf.

"Leave her be," she demanded.

Ferehain raised an eyebrow but the rest of his face remained as stone. "So, Aleasea has brought Commander Vale, the hollow godling herself, here to reclaim what she had lost?" he sneered.

Elyn could feel Vale's rage start to kindle within her also, a fire which was immediately fed by their shared memories of all that this man and his Ageless had done to both of them. They were lock-step in mounting fury.

"I've come myself, of my own will, to get my own answers," Vale replied. "I'm here for Elyn. I'm certainly not here to answer to you."

Ferehain smiled coldly. "Oh, you will most certainly answer to me now. Did you think that the daughter of Bythe could walk into Fairhaven and ever walk out again? You have always been a failure to the Iron Union. I understand you are much like your sister, a disappointment. Only you choose to hide your weakness beneath your father's armor."

The crack of Ferehain's jaw was the sound that Vale remembered most. She remembered Ferehain trying to step back once he sensed Vale's impending strike. Indeed, Ferehain's reaction was so immediate it would have been almost imperceptible to anyone standing nearby, and yet to Vale it was infinitely slower than it needed to be. Vale had felt Elyn's own anger fuse with her own, and they used that focus to send their mutual adversary crashing to the ground.

For a moment nobody moved. Nobody seemed to be capable of understanding what they had just witnessed. Ferehain lay sprawled on his back in shock, and everyone stood rooted in their place as if transfixed. Even Aleasea looked at Vale with an expression of outright disbelief. As for Vale, it took her a moment to comprehend what she had done. For the briefest of moments, her own anger had synchronised perfectly with Elyn's, and in that window, she'd discovered an intensity unlike anything she had ever experienced before. It was a strange mixture of euphoric confidence. For only a moment, she truly felt like she could achieve anything, as if no feat was beyond her.

And it felt exceptional.

Now the sensation was passing, and Vale perceived the real threat emerging as Ferehain slowly raised himself from the ground. Blood trickled from the edge of a mouth twisted into a sneer of pure hatred. Aleasea reacted before all others.

"Ferehain, stand down!" she commanded with surprising authority.

"You grant the daughter of Bythe clemency even after she has attacked one of your own?"

"People have struck you before, Ferehain. Even I have struck you. You will let this pass; the stakes are far too important!"

"*You hit Ferehain?*" Elyn's surprise was obvious in her unspoken message to Vale. "*How could you do that?*"

"No," Vale replied. "*It was both of us. I could feel your strength, your anger. You gave me the means.*"

Ferehain's eyes swung to Vale then back to Elyn. "I see," he whispered. "They are fusing even as we stand here. Aleasea, your naive charity has gone too far even by your standards. You've brought an unstable god into our midst."

"What does he mean?" Elyn asked.

"I mean that you're fractured, cracked, broken." Ferehain spat the words disdainfully. "Perhaps the term 'damaged' is most appropriate? And yet your spirit has already begun to repair the damage of its own accord."

"No!" shouted Elyn. "Aleasea, you said I could control this! You said I had a choice!"

"You can. Remain calm. But we must get you to Veroulle immediately."

"What makes you think we can trust Veroulle?" asked Vale

"Listen to me, both of you!" Aleasea's voice was commanding. "There's more at work here than Bythe's magic. You're reconciling because of where you are – you're near Sanctuary."

"So?" asked Elyn. "What does that matter? I've been in Sanctuary for weeks."

"Not with Vale nearby." Aleasea stepped forward and grasped Elyn firmly by both shoulders. "Elyn, the reason I have felt such a connection with you is the same reason your power is beginning to flourish now. Not because of your father, but because of your mother."

Ferehain's face twisted into shocked revulsion. "Aleasea, you are mad..."

Aleasea shook her head. "No, Ferehain, I am not. I do not know how it is possible, but I know it in my heart to be true."

At that moment, when Fairhaven faced its deepest peril, the night was split by a splinter of daylight. The light streamed upward from the center of the town. The Temple of Maelene was ablaze with a brilliance none had ever witnessed before. The light lanced skyward and for a time, everyone paused to watch – both attackers and defenders alike. The light illuminated everyone in the town. It illuminated Ferehain's face, which had changed from disgust to disbelief and finally to joy. Tears welled in his eyes and he stepped backward as he openly marvelled at the sight before him – and at its significance.

"Blessed Mother be praised," Ferehain whispered to Aleasea. "Can you feel it? I had never believed it possible."

Aleasea stood beside him, and her face was also lit with tears. "Nor I, my brother, and yet it has happened, just as they prophesied. I can...feel her presence."

Ferehain did not take his eyes from the light. It had completely transfixed him. "The Blessed Mother has returned to us."

Aleasea nodded and turned to face Vale and Elyn.

"And she calls her daughter home."

CHAPTER 2

"The gods are not all powerful. Certainly not within the confines of the Forge. Each god must choose an aspect of Kovalith over which they will claim dominance. Nishindra the Crafter devoted his power to the creation of artefacts both wondrous and terrifying. So great was his power, that it was said he even had created the means to peer through time. In the end, he became so mistrustful and protective of his creations that he locked himself in his Tower and was never seen again. Maelene similarly dedicated her power to life and the natural world. She used her immortal blood to grow Sanctuary and from this blood would spring the fruitful bounty of her work. Bythe discovered the power of metal and spent his energies perfecting it. And so, did all the pantheon of gods carve out sections of our world to claim as their own."

~Aleasea of the Ageless

A soldier of the Ironhelm stood in Sanctuary. Hours ago, it had seemed unthinkable, but so much had changed in those few hours. As had been prophesied by the most hopeful and the most desperate of the Ageless – the Blessed Mother Maelene had returned to her people.

Once the Temple had called to them, Ferehain and Aleasea wasted no time. All debate was over. Their duty was clear. Vale realized her opportunity to take control had evaporated in the light of the beacon. United in elation, Ferehain had carried Jason in his arms while Aleasea guided Elyn and Vale back to the hidden passageway from which they had earlier emerged. From there, they had all but run toward Sanctuary. Even Ferehain managed his burden as if Jason were an infant. Vale could do little more than attempt to memorise the various turns in the subterranean labyrinth in the slim hope that she might later manufacture some form of escape. But she realized that the hope was slim indeed.

Vale and Elyn now stood side by side in the massive cavern that served as the main gathering chamber within Sanctuary. Aleasea and Ferehain were helping Jason regain his feet. The tiny crystal lights that had pinpricked the ceiling of the cave before now shone like thousands of beacons screaming wild light. The dark and sombre cave was now lit with an exuberance to match the illumination. Dozens of Ageless gathered with their hoods lowered so that nothing could mask the joy openly worn on bared faces. The cavern was a chorus of song as every Ageless rapturously exalted a chanting, rhythmic hymn that Elyn recalled from the Temple services. She had heard the people of Fairhaven raise their voices for this song, but it was a poor counterfeit compared to the soaring tones and impossible harmonies that touched her ears tonight. The Ageless were rejoicing.

"Aleasea. Ferehain."

A gravelly voice cut through the melodies, and the five newcomers turned to see Veroulle stride through the crowd toward them. To Elyn, it seemed as if the ancient face of obsidian was almost smiling. There was a relaxed quality to the burning eyes that Elyn had never seen before.

"We received your command, Veroulle," Aleasea bowed, her face still brilliant with joy. "We have brought them both home."

"Excellent," Veroulle replied and turned his gaze to both Vale and Elyn. "This is truly a joyous day, my brethren. Aleasea, we owe you thanks. Only your wisdom has foreseen this."

"*They believe Maelene is our mother?*" Elyn's silent incredulity rang out clearly in Vale's mind.

"*I know, but I can't believe it,*" Vale answered. "*I don't understand how that's possible. She died decades before we were born.*"

"*But do you remember who our real mother was?*"

"*No,*" Vale silently conceded. "*Do you?*"

"*I only remember Leon – no one else.*"

Veroulle turned his gaze to them. "Your bond continues to grow stronger I see. I can feel your connection." He walked over to stand before the two young twins. "Elyn of Outpost and Vale of the Iron Union, if only we had known the truth about you sooner. Never mind. It matters little now."

"Are we your prisoners?" Vale asked the question directly in the manner of a soldier. Veroulle focused his burning eyes on the young Commander, and Elyn saw her sister stiffen under the intensity of his gaze.

"I understood you made the long journey to Fairhaven to find the answers to your questions. This was your own free will. Are you really prepared to leave, when these answers are now within your grasp?"

Vale wrestled with the contradiction. Every instinct borne out of her military training screamed for her to make an escape, yet another part of her yearned for the truth. She knew she would never find peace if she left without answers.

"She waits for you," Veroulle continued.

"Maelene?" Elyn asked. "She's actually here?"

"She is, and she has asked for both of you," answered Veroulle. He waited while Elyn and Vale shared an uncertain glance.

"Will you keep her waiting?" Aleasea asked with a smile.

"No," Elyn said after a pause. "Take us to her."

Veroulle nodded and motioned for them to follow him through the throng of joyous bodies. Jason moved up to walk alongside Elyn. He seemed stunned by everything that was unfolding around him. Elyn gave him a sympathetic glance and a reassuring hand on his shoulder as they walked on in silence. Within seconds they had cleared the room and all six of them moved through the passageways of Sanctuary. Elyn recognised where they were heading.

"The Arcadia," Elyn said quietly. "That's where you're taking us."

"Your instincts are sound," Veroulle replied. "Yes, that is how our Blessed Mother has returned to us."

"I don't understand," Elyn said, but Veroulle raised a thin black hand for silence.

"Your chance for questions will come, for both of you. For now, you must have patience and faith." They remained silent as they walked the rest of the way through the dull glow of Sanctuary. Within minutes, they passed through the massive archway that led to the platform that both Vale and Elyn recalled from their shared memories, but the room had now changed. Where the platform had ended in steps leading into the Arcadia, a curtain of light that ran the length of the platform now blocked the steps. Beyond the shimmering curtain lay the round room with a domed ceiling and pulsating glass ball of light that was now almost blinding. The strange altar with its two globes were vaguely discernible through the wall of light, as was the wooden bench; but what seized the attention of the sisters was not the bench within the Arcadia, but the figure seated on it. A slender figure with golden hair was seated with her back to them. Both Aleasea and Ferehain immediately dropped to one knee and bowed their heads in respect. Vale and Elyn both resisted an awkward compulsion to follow the example.

"She appeared to us after you left, Elyn," Veroulle said in a voice that was almost a whisper.

"Why is she in the Arcadia?" Elyn replied in an equally low tone.

"It is as we have told you. The Arcadia was one of our Mother's most powerful creations. In life, she imbued the artefact with much of her blood and power. It is not surprising she would use this path to return to us."

"How did it happen, Veroulle?" Aleasea asked with the excitement of a child.

"I could feel her approach," Veroulle said. "It was as if I was recalling the feelings of an old friend from long ago. The scent, the ring of a voice. These feelings drew me here while all else were engaged in argument over how to defend the city or whether to pursue Elyn. When I neared the Arcadia, the Temple became lit with the power of our Mother, announcing to all that she had returned. I understood then, at that moment, that destiny was to be fulfilled, and as I crossed the threshold, I beheld the curtain of light blanketing the Arcadia, and I beheld the Blessed Mother Maelene."

"Has she recognised you?" asked Ferehain.

"Indeed, she has," Veroulle replied with a touch of humility. "She greeted me by name and commanded me to bring her daughters before her. It was at that moment, Aleasea, that I realized why you had felt such a strong connection to Elyn."

Vale walked over to where the curtain of light hung in the air. She stared at the petite form still sitting on the bench, expecting her to move. "You can't go in there can you?" she asked at length.

Veroulle inclined his head in agreement. "That is correct. Our Mother does not yet exist in this world and the curtain separates us from her presence; however, I suspect the children of Maelene face no such barrier."

"*They expect us to go in there,*" Elyn communicated.

Vale stared at the figure on the bench. "*Do you really think she's our mother, Elyn?*"

Elyn walked over to stand alongside Vale and looked through the curtain. "*I don't see how it's possible, but you said you wanted answers. I think this is the best chance we have of getting them. Maybe our only chance.*"

Vale nodded. She felt Elyn's power searing through her. It was becoming stronger with every passing moment. Their shared thoughts were effortless now, as if they were of one mind. Elyn sensed it as well and shot Vale an uncomfortable glance.

"*If we're going to do this, then let's get on with it,*" thought Elyn. She turned back to Jason who was standing, all but forgotten, toward the rear of the room. "Jason, we're going to head in there. Aleasea, I'm trusting him to your care. Make sure he's kept safe."

"Of course, Elyn, but you have nothing to fear. No harm can now come to you or Jason. Maelene has returned," said Aleasea.

Elyn said nothing. Instead, she turned to face Vale, who nodded in confirmation to an unvoiced question. Jason and the three Ageless stood watching them expectantly as they both turned to the pulsating curtain and stepped through.

Once they passed the light, the Arcadia vanished. Gone was the huge space under the ornate dome, replaced by a flat stone platform. The cupola above them had been replaced by a night sky, dark and punctuated with hundreds of stars. Stretching out before them lay a blanket of mist followed by a patchwork of intermixed mountains, rivers, and oceans. The landscape seemed to shift and swim before them as they watched, never remaining static for more than a few moments. Before them, a young woman stood staring out at the strange scenery before her. Her hair was long and golden and when she turned to face them, the simple movement betrayed a grace and elegance that neither woman had ever beheld. Her face was radiant. Beautiful. And she looked at them both with an expression of unconditional love and acceptance.

Maelene.

Mother.

It was Elyn who first stepped toward her, the movement almost involuntary. Maelene regarded her with an expression of immense joy and pride, then turned the same expression on Vale, who returned it with a more cautious reaction. Undaunted, she walked across the gap between them and – starting with Elyn, then Vale – brought them both into her embrace.

"I have missed you both so very, very much."

Her voice was soft, almost a whisper, and yet both daughters heard every word. She finally pulled away to look at them both with eyes that seemed rimmed with tears. Vale stood as if in shock. It was Elyn who asked the most obvious of questions.

"You're my mother? Our mother?"

Maelene nodded in reply. Elyn felt the strangest emotion roiling within her as her own eyes started to swim with tears. There was a strange kinship with the beautiful woman standing before her, an unmistakable bond of recognition. Elyn felt no doubt that she was standing before her mother. Silence fell upon them all for a time.

"And...?" Vale finally spoke up with an edge of irritation. "Are you going to add anything to that? It's a little difficult to accept."

Maelene looked at her and smiled again, but this time the smile seemed touched with a trace of despair.

"You carry much of your father in you, Vale. So much, but I suppose that is to be expected."

"What does that mean?" Vale shot back. "Are you here to speak in riddles to us?"

"Vale, I have been gone a long time. You know this. I have been called back because I am needed. I believe that you and your sister have called to me. I am here to give you the answers that you seek of me, the answers that you seek of yourself, and together we can end this bloodshed."

"Fine," Vale snapped and walked away from her. "Then explain to me – explain to us – how you could possibly be our Mother. You died a hundred years before we were even born."

Maelene walked over to Vale and extended her hand. "Come with me and I will show you."

"How?" Vale asked.

"We are in the Arcadia; it was made by my hands and with my blood. You have access to its power because you share my blood, because you are family."

"Can the Arcadia take us to where you are?" asked Elyn.

"Not physically, no," she answered "But our shared energies can be used to explore much of the past and the present in this place. The power of family is strong. Vale, you can finally have the answers you have sought for so long."

Cautiously, Vale nodded and took her hand. Maelene turned and made a similar offer to Elyn who accepted without hesitation. Together, she led them all to the edge of the platform so they could all see the swirling imagery beyond. She disengaged her hands from both daughters and extended her slender arms in one graceful gesture. The mists surrounding the platform parted to reveal the narrowest of steps leading downward at an alarmingly sharp angle.

"Follow me," she commanded and with that she walked down the impossibly steep staircase. Elyn and Vale looked at each other with unspoken uncertainty.

"It is alright," Maelene called back without breaking stride or even turning her head. "Your own mind cannot harm you in here."

Elyn took the first step causing Vale to quickly follow. The descent was harrowing for both of them. It seemed to Elyn as if the slightest gust of wind would send them tipping, but no wind came, not the slightest breeze despite their incredible heights.

"If you want the full answer to who you are, I will need to take you back years before you were born." Maelene's words drifted back to them without so much as a movement of her head in their direction.

"Is there another way to do this?" Elyn asked, and Maelene's laughter was like wind chimes.

"I told you that you do not need to fear. You are exploring our shared knowledge, nothing more."

The staircase ended at an intricate balcony made of white marble overlooking a vista that was clearly impossible, a view of what seemed to be the entire world stretched out before them like a map. Two great wings of land separated in the middle by the huge wedge of the Bitter Sea. Elyn realized that she could make out the vast expanse of the Outer Wilderness in the east while Vale similarly focused on the mighty towers of the Iron Union to the west. All was visible before them.

"It is indeed beautiful, is it not?" asked Maelene as she walked over to rest her hands on the marble edge of the balcony. As she stood admiring the view, her daughters quietly followed her. "Do you know how Kovalith came into existence?" she asked, and then without waiting for an answer, continued. "The ancient gods created this world as..." she paused, as if searching for the right words "...an experiment. I believe that we wanted to create life, meaning, or some sense of purpose. Some of us wanted to be worshipped; others wanted to use this place as a means of competition, to resolve petty disputes and squabbles. Regardless, we all agreed there would be a benefit to the creation of such a place, and we all invested our immortal energies into its creation. And this was the result. We named it Kovalith; however, over time, most of us came to call it the Forge."

She gestured to the world before them and smiled fondly.

"For a time, it was good. We created life. We created civilizations and empires. We were worshipped and fought and played like children for centuries. But then all things pass and even immortals desire change, and one by one we slowly lost interest in Kovalith and decided that it was time to leave."

She sighed and turned to face them, her back now to the world.

"We all came together in the Render, beyond the lands where men cannot tread, to determine what should become of us and of this world. We argued back and forth; however, we could not reach an agreement. Many of us wanted to leave Kovalith and take back what they had given it. A few of us wanted to remain and take responsibility for the life we had created."

"I don't understand," said Elyn. "What was there to discuss? Why not just leave, if that's what you wanted? You're gods – who tells you what to do?"

"Elyn, it is difficult to explain an immortal existence to one so limited by the tactile world; however, all things are connected, and matter cannot be created from nothing. When we all agreed to create this beautiful world, we all invested something of ourselves in the process. A part of us. We all paid a price to create this place."

"And some of you wanted that back," concluded Vale.

Maelene nodded. "This world was woven by immortal craft; our energies flow through the very fabric of this realm. Now that they had grown tired of this place, my brothers and sisters wanted to take that energy back."

"You mean destroy our world and everyone in it?" asked Elyn.

"Yes. You have to understand that Kovalith is but a trifling amusement to most of my brethren, a petty distraction for a time. Now that their Forge was no longer exciting to them, they would simply like to see it over. I disagreed and I had but two allies in my argument – Bythe the Steelmonger and Nishindra the Crafter. Together we made a compelling case for the ongoing existence of Kovalith and all of its life, and eventually, we won a concession. We agreed that Kovalith would be left in peace for a time and that any gods who wished to remain behind to guide the people might do so;however when this time is over, it was agreed that all gods shall return and pass final judgment on their Forge."

"And what is a final judgment?" asked Vale coldly, clearly suspecting the answer.

"If Kovalith and its people are not found to be worthy of a continued existence, then the Forge shall be broken," replied Maelene in an equally cold voice. "All the gods then departed but for the three of us. We found that we then bore the responsibility for the fate of this entire world. Of course, we three could not agree on how this salvation was to be achieved."

Maelene turned back to the world before them and pointed to the west. The views of the Ironhelm and its cities of tall iron burst into clear view.

"Bythe believed in the power of strength and that men should be prepared to defy the gods through strength when they return, to prove their worth and right to exist. He travelled west to establish his empire of might and used his powers to build the immense cities you see here with their intricate defenses and, before long, became absolute ruler of his western empire."

She moved her hand from left to right and the images of the Iron Union were replaced by scenes of lush greenery, trees, and rolling landscapes stretching into the distance.

"I believed in the pure and unspoiled beauty of the world that we had created and that Bythe's imposed militarized order did nothing but undermine that perfection. I travelled east and set about creating Sanctuary along with the Ageless to serve me in my quests. I charged them with the duty of ridding the world of destructive creatures that would stand against the spread of natural beauty, and they were successful. The endless gardens they created were as glorious as they were wild and vicious, any man that wandered into the east with malice toward nature in his heart was quickly dealt with. And so, as if guided by fate, we were both set on our own respective courses."

"Those respective courses led to war," said Vale.

"Yes," agreed Maelene. "It was not long before we came into indirect conflict, then the indirect became explicit, and then, without knowing how, we were at war with each other. Bythe would use his might to smash into the east, but our forces would strangle and hamper his men until I forced him to retreat, and we would wage our counter assaults against his iron walls. Back and forth we raged for tens of years, laying waste to so much, as our frustrations turned to rage and then ultimately to hatred. Nishindra had long since grown tired of our bickering and vanished into his Tower. There were only two of us left."

She sighed and then walked to the far end of the balcony where the staircase continued downward.

"Come," she said. "There is more you must understand."

She turned and descended the steps, passing out of view almost immediately. Vale and Elyn followed and were again confronted with the sickening sight of steps leading sharply downward into darkness. Vale showed no apparent fear as she mounted the first step and Elyn tried her best to compete. After an unbearable minute, the impossible staircase ended and all three of them were standing in the edge of a large circular room. Maelene stood in the center of it wearing a travelling cloak, her elegant hands extended in front of her. She seemed to be staring off into the distance at something the others couldn't see.

"Where are we?" asked Vale.

"Somewhere no mortal has ever tread," answered Maelene. "This is The Tower, one of the last Constructs of Nishindra and his most powerful. It was said that he housed many secrets in this place. Once, I sought him out for help against Bythe, but I found his Tower empty."

Elyn looked around at the bare room furnished only by a series of strange markings on a floor as black as obsidian. Maelene tensed and the room around them began to gently flex, distort and eventually dissolve into another scene. It was a landscape of utter desolation. They were all looking out over a grey wasteland of sand flowing over bent iron towers and ruined cities. The vision seemed to take in the land from a great height, as if seen from an eagle at impossible speed. The image of Maelene sighed and closed her eyes. Again, the scene warped and dissolved and was replaced this time by another landscape ravaged by fire and broken, twisted earth.

"All the gods chose a purpose when they came to this life. A focus. It was Nishindra's gift to create incredible objects. At first, he impressed us by creating items that would defy gravity or the elements. In the end he was able to build The Tower and use it to even peer through time itself – as time exists in Kovalith," Maelene explained.

"He could journey through time?" Vale asked.

"Not travel, no. I do not believe his power reached that far. But he could peer into the futures, discern glimpses of what might happen. He felt it was his greatest achievement. When I failed to find him, I took advantage of his absence."

"You wanted to discover how to defeat Bythe," said Vale.

Maelene nodded. "I admit, that was my initial goal. My hate burned bright in those days, and I was anxious for any advantage against Bythe. I spent many years in this place as I slowly uncovered The Tower's abandoned secrets. However, when I eventually learned how to peer into the possible futures, I did not like what I learned."

Elyn walked closer to where the image of Maelene stood and watched the surrounding visions.

"You're looking at the destruction of the world, aren't you? In every future, you're seeing nothing but death."

Maelene nodded.

"The Tower believed that this was the ultimate outcome of my struggle against Bythe. That our war of decades would escalate in violence and intensity to the point that we would quite literally break the Forge instead of saving it."

Elyn looked at her mother and then at Vale, who mirrored her own confused expression. Maelene simply nodded toward the visions before them. Image after image of destruction and total ruin flashed before them. Sandy plains littered with rent bodies or city streets lined with rotting carcasses no longer recognizable as human. Then – after a seemingly endless parade of similar images – a picture of order hazed into view. Maelene jolted in her trance and the image came sharply into focus. It was a landscape of low buildings made of dark metal overshadowed by a soaring black fortress. It was a scene that Vale instantly recognised. It was her home.

"The Ironhelm," she muttered.

"Bythe's fortress," Elyn recalled from her own shared memories. "That place was your home."

"For a time."

Vale said nothing more. The image dissolved again and reformed to show a young woman in ornate Helmsguard armor sitting atop a large black throne. The young woman looked similar to both Elyn and Vale, but not exactly like either of them.

"For years I searched through every vision The Tower would give me, and then I discovered this. This vision is what started it all," continued Maelene. "The Tower's revelation that my daughter held the key to the salvation of this world."

"Your daughter on Bythe's throne?" asked Vale sceptically.

"The offspring of myself and Bythe on the throne," she answered. "It was the one and only path that I could find in our future that would avert total war and disaster between us. I did not want to believe it. I left this place full of anger and bitterness. I felt that I had been cheated of my rightful path to victory."

"You didn't want peace?" Elyn asked.

She turned to Elyn and her expression became distant. "I have forgotten what it is like to walk as a mortal on this world. The decisions that I made as a creature of flesh and blood are...strange to me now, as though I remember them as the actions of another. I can no longer quite understand how I felt then, but I know that I felt rage. Hate. I was irrational and did not want to abandon my dreams of victory, but time has a way of winning all arguments, and over many more years of fruitless bloodshed, my hate descended into hopelessness."

Maelene refocused on her daughters as if remembering they were there. She turned and walked back the way they had come, gesturing for both of them to follow. They returned to the staircase and continued their descent. This time the darkness parted quickly, and they dismounted the steps onto the firm and reassuring security of the solid ground. Elyn felt relief flood through her. They were now standing on a dirt road with scrub-covered countryside behind them and a towering wall made of dark colored rock and reinforced iron before them. It was night.

"I know this place," said Vale.

"You should," replied Maelene. "This is where you were born."

Vale looked at her sternly. "We're outside the eastern walls of the Ironhelm," she said.

"Yes, we are," Maelene agreed. "This is where the two of you came into existence as you are now, first inside those walls then beyond them."

"I don't understand," said Elyn.

"You will," Maelene reassured her and walked over to the wall, staring up at it as if she expected it to speak to her. There was an expression of pain on her face that looked ill-suited to her otherwise benevolent features. She stared at the wall for a moment longer and then she started to speak.

"After fifty long years of war, my rage was finally starting to weary me. The visions of The Tower had worn heavily on me, and I decided that I was ready for peace. Sending word to Bythe via an emissary, I told him of the visions in The Tower. I told him we were on a path to destroy Kovalith, yet our unborn daughter might save it. I told him to meet me on neutral ground between our two empires and we could end this chaos. I was tired of war, I was tired of everything. And in my sullen mood I acted too quickly."

Elyn glanced at Vale. They both understood where this part of the story was going.

"I was betrayed by Bythe. He had decided that the only peace he could accept would be bought with my capture. When I met Bythe with a small guard in good faith, I was ambushed by his forces and overcome...but I did not die as my followers believed. That was not Bythe's plan. I was taken back into the Ironhelm and held captive in the heart of Bythe's empire."

Maelene's voice started to tremble and falter at these words. Her daughters remained silent.

"Bythe," she continued, her voice now barely a whisper. "Bythe interpreted The Tower's vision in a very different way. He believed that his daughter borne of me would rule his empire, uniting the world and that this would be the key to Kovalith's salvation when the gods finally returned to pass their judgment. He demanded this of me. I refused."

"And so Bythe held you here?" Vale asked.

"Yes, for over a hundred years. I refused to give him what he wanted, and he refused to take it by a mortal man's force – he at least had that much respect for his brethren. But in the end, I became tired. I was tired of this world. Tired of the games. I wanted to return home and I had but one way to do this – give Bythe what he wanted. In the end, I agreed."

At this, she fell into silence again. Her face had become a strange mask of vaguely remembered guilt mixed with pain. Elyn couldn't understand why it felt so uncomfortable to look at her this way. She walked over and offered a consoling hand on her mother's shoulder, as if that act might somehow lift the weight of tragic events from long ago.

"You gave birth to us, to twins?" Elyn gently asked.

Maelene raised herself up to her full height again as if the question had suddenly reminded her of where she was.

"No. I bore only one child."

"Then what happened?" Vale asked.

"That is what you are here to witness," Maelene answered. "After giving birth to a daughter, I found new meaning in my life. I no longer wanted to pass out of the Forge. I desperately wanted to protect you. I knew that I had been a fool to trust Bythe, and I was not prepared to allow him to corrupt you as he corrupts everyone around him. I lulled everyone into thinking I was weak and defeated, then waited for my chance."

As she spoke, the hooded figure of Maelene appeared from a hidden alcove in the wall. She was dressed in a black robe, her face hidden, and an infant child swaddled in her arms.

"I used what little power I had left to take you out of the Ironhelm. It was no easy task, but I succeeded. For a short time, I had you all to myself."

She moved closer to the scene involuntarily, an old mother trying to reclaim the lost years with her infant. They were all silent for a moment, and it was then that Elyn noticed that the silence had become intense, almost palpable. Not just among themselves but all around them there was not a sound. The stillness was unnatural.

Then came the scream.

A faint sound from within the city walls seemingly miles away, a distant cry of rage and dismay that carried through the total silence of the night. The image of Maelene looked about. The wail did not relent. Instead, it slowly started to rise as it drifted across the night toward them. Rising slowly in both volume and pitch, echoing off the towers within the walls and escalating in its intensity and its rage and its pure fury. The scream climaxed in a primal and terrifying passion that was as deafening as it was dreadful. Elyn again felt ice flood throughout her veins. Vale clenched her jaw in obvious discomfort – the closest Elyn had seen to an emotion resembling fear on her face. Then just as it seemed the screaming would crack and splinter their skulls in its fury – it stopped, and the virgin silence returned. The image of Maelene straightened and looked behind her, the infant was unmoved.

"My act was discovered. My plan had failed," Maelene whispered.

Out of the stillness, a blast of wind slammed into the figure of Maelene and sent her reeling. It shrieked from the south and pushed her toward the walls, drawing her backward toward the city she was so desperate to flee. The infant was crying now. They could hear her pain and fear even above the wind, and it seemed that the image of Maelene was desperately trying to keep her grip on the child. She stumbled to her knees, holding the baby aloft with both hands before trying in vain to regain her footing as the wind became stronger along with the child's cries. The infant began to shriek now, not just a cry of complaint but the primal screams of a creature in fear of its very existence. The type of cry that turns the stomach. And with the scream came another burst of wind so great that Maelene knelt as the infant was literally ripped from her hands. The scream became a chorus. Not one voice but two cried out in pain, and even as Maelene gripped little Elyn with all of her strength, she watched in horror as something tore itself away from the child and was sent screaming along the wind. It cried horribly as it flew over the black walls and back toward the Ironhelm and the terrible wind seemed to leave with it.

Then the silence returned.

"That was me, wasn't it?" Vale asked at length. "The... thing that was carried away on the wind, that was me?"

Maelene didn't answer immediately. She seemed lost in her own thoughts, staring after her daughter as she drifted away from her. "Yes," she replied.

Vale looked back at the tower in the distance. Elyn looked at her and then at Maelene, who was watching her own infant daughter. Then she spoke.

"Bythe tried to reclaim you. He discovered the treachery and used every fibre of his being to find you while you were close, but a father cannot forcefully claim his own daughter, no matter how much he might desire to. You are both the union of your father and your mother – Bythe could only lay claim to the parts of you that were his and nothing more, but from that moment onwards you were torn into two."

Elyn looked at the image of Maelene as she checked the infant for harm.

"But you didn't know what had happened," Elyn said. "Vale had been delivered to Bythe and you still had me."

"Correct," Maelene said. "Bythe was searching for you and I was weak. I managed to get myself to a safe location under disguise. I hid you among the smugglers and criminals of the Ironhelm while I went in search of aid, but when I returned to you, those same criminals had stolen you away from me."

Elyn stared at Maelene in confusion. "But what happened? How did I get to Outpost? Where did you go?"

Vale stepped in front of Elyn. A strange look was on her face.

"They're excellent questions, Elyn." Vale's voice was hard. "I have a better one. How did Maelene take refuge with the criminal underworld of the Ironhelm? They're a notoriously mistrustful group. You have to be if you're going to operate under the nose of Bythe."

"Vale, what's the matter with you?" asked Elyn. Vale turned back and smiled at her twin.

"Nothing," she replied, then turned back to Maelene and without warning, slapped her violently with the back of her hand. Maelene staggered back with a cry.

"Vale!" Elyn screamed.

"I have to give you credit," continued Vale in a conversational tone as she advanced on the retreating woman. "You had me wondering at first, I really wasn't sure if it was you, but that slip in the end was very sloppy. I've been trained to detect deceit. You taught me far too well, Yvorre."

Maelene stared at her with a look of shock. A thin trail of crimson bled from her mouth. The shock melted from her face and was replaced with a thin smile.

"I had hoped to do this differently, but you were always such a difficult one, weren't you, Vale?"

"I can't really hurt you in here can I?" Vale asked as she stopped advancing. "The lie was good. I think most of it was true, wasn't it?"

"As I always taught you, a lie is most convincing when it is barely a lie."

Elyn grappled with a swell of disbelief and confusion. She stared at Maelene. Her beautiful face, now deprived of its loving warmth, had grown cold and hostile. "Yvorre is Maelene?" she asked.

"Yvorre *was* Maelene," Vale corrected. "You were betrayed by Bythe, but he didn't imprison you for all of those years, did he? He twisted your mind until you broke, and you became another of his servants like the rest of us."

Elyn realized the image of Maelene and her daughter was still playing out before them. As Elyn watched, the robed figure braced herself against another gust of unnatural wind as she made her escape. The wind tore at her robes, but it was weaker this time. All it could do was force the robe's hood back from her head. Vale and Elyn both saw the twisted and sunken features of Yvorre already marring the once beautiful face of Maelene.

"It was as I told you, my child," Maelene replied in a voice worn with bitterness. "Bythe corrupts everyone around him, even me."

"You were trying to escape him that night," said Vale.

"Yes, that was true. I'd be damned if I was going to let him harness your power. You were mine. I timed my deception perfectly and stole you away so cleverly that no one had the slightest idea who it was who had taken you. But as you witnessed, Bythe discovered the crime too soon and I knew that I couldn't get far with a baby in my arms before I'd be noticed."

"Leon?" Elyn asked, suddenly inspired.

"Very good, Elyn," Yvorre said with a teacher's approval. "You have strong instincts. This is promising."

"Stay away from her," Vale demanded much to Elyn's surprise. "I won't have you messing with her head the way you did with mine."

"Oh, Vale, I was merely rewarding your sister's curiosity," Maelene said patiently before returning her eyes to Elyn. "Yes, Elyn, you have no idea who your surrogate father really was do you? Leon was an excellent smuggler in his youth, one of my network of spies in the underworld of the Ironhelm. Once I realized that the entire force of the Helmsguard would be searching for us, I had to hide you for a time. I went to Leon and demanded he keep you safe until I returned for you."

"You knew that your absence would implicate you. You had to return to Bythe to play the innocent servant, didn't you?" said Vale.

Maelene smiled.

"Leon was a criminal?" Elyn asked.

"Oh, he was an excellent smuggler," Maelene said consolingly. "But don't worry, my child. As I soon discovered to my dismay, he also had a heart and a conscience. When I returned to Bythe to discover his daughter was apparently safe and well in the Ironhelm, I had no idea what had happened. I did not know if Bythe was playing a ruse to draw out the kidnapper, or if Elyn had already been retrieved from Leon in my absence. It was not until years later that I deduced the truth, and by then, Elyn, you were far out of my reach."

"What happened to Leon?" Elyn asked.

"Bythe's anger is legendary, even among the gods, but I had never seen him in such a state. He was furious at the betrayal and devoted his strength to uncovering the culprit. He interrogated hundreds, both innocents from the city and his own officers and bureaucrats. So many of them died under torture. So many people were falsely named by their accusers as a means of escaping death. Bythe stacked the bodies high as a monument to his determined rage, but through my cunning, I remained hidden from his wrath."

"But then you weren't able to retrieve Elyn," Vale concluded. "It was too great a risk while the city was being searched for any conspirators."

"And Leon fled?" Elyn joined. "Once he realized that caring for an unexplained baby would draw suspicion?"

"I knew that Bythe suspected me and was watching every action I took. It was several months before I could return to Leon. I never discovered exactly what happened during my absence, but by the time I was able to safely return to collect you, yes, he had fled the Ironhelm forever."

"And you began searching for him," Vale said. "You never stopped searching for him."

"In the months that followed, I searched for Leon as discreetly as I could without drawing too much attention to myself, but that was fruitless. I abandoned hope again for several years and returned to my role as Bythe's loyal servant until something extraordinary happened – or should I say something extraordinary *didn't* happen."

Vale's jaw clenched again.

"Yes, my child, you were a mundane disappointment to your father and that was my insight. I finally realized what had happened when you were ripped in two that night and how your power was broken between you." Maelene's face began to twist in malevolent pleasure and her cheeks sunk inward. Yvorre's skeletal features began to emerge as she spoke. "I was reborn with new hope. I convinced Bythe that The Tower's vision was wrong. That he had already conquered me and the world without the aid of his daughter and that perhaps that was the true meaning of the vision. I convinced him that you were a failure, not worth his time, and to entrust your education to me. He agreed, and once I had you under my control, I set out scouring the Iron Union for your sister."

"But you couldn't find us, could you?" asked Elyn.

"No," said Maelene. "Unfortunately, Leon was indeed an excellent smuggler. There was no trace of his passing no matter how many agents I dispatched to find you. I searched the entire Union over ten years and found no trace. It was then I realized Leon was in the Outlands. But I would not desist. I was forced to use military campaigns as a pretext to search for you outside the borders of the Union. It was easier now that the Outland alliances were collapsing, but when I finally reached Outpost, my patience was rewarded, and then I missed you both by pure chance."

"The day you surprised us at Outpost," Elyn said. She looked at the ground for a moment, then back at Maelene's ugly form. "Did Leon know who I was?"

"How could he? Vale was at her father's side once more and there was no reason to suspect the child of Bythe had ever been abducted. I have no doubt he had suspicions over the nature of your origin; however, he did not abandon you, much to my surprise and frustration. I suspect it was self-preservation at first. He knew me. He knew if he abandoned you to others less careful than him, I would find you eventually, then I would probably find him. However, who can understand the hearts of ageing men? I do not understand why he kept you close to him. I can only surmise that as he settled into his new life in exile, he grew to look upon you as his daughter over time. You were fortunate Elyn."

Elyn nodded. Her throat felt heavy. "I know he loved me. I had no idea what it cost him."

"And now you know how you came to be here. It has taken much effort to bring you together, but now you see the truth. Will you help me?" Maelene said soberly.

"What do you want, Yvorre?" Vale spat. "Stop this charade. Show us plainly who you are."

Maelene jerked and stiffened. Both Vale and Elyn stepped backward as she doubled over in immense pain. The surrounding images of the Ironhelm stopped, splintered, and cracked, and light flooded in like water. Elyn shut her eyes against the piercing brightness and when she opened them again, she found herself back in the Arcadia. She spun her head to her left to look for Vale, but she found her sister standing protectively before her. Elyn turned her head to her right and looked at a person she had thought was Maelene. This figure was bent over and twisted, shimmering in a manner slightly incorporeal, and yet Elyn fancied that she could smell the death on her.

"Stand back," ordered Vale.

Yvorre slowly unfolded herself and rose to her twisted and wretched full height. Her skeletal arms hung too long at her sides, and her sunken eyes stared out from the pits in her face. It was obvious that she still wasn't physically present – the faint shimmering like a heat haze around her body was evidence enough of that – and yet she was here in the most sacred of places. Elyn tried to step back as her gaze locked with Maelene's, only she realized to her horror that her legs were frozen in place.

"*Run, Elyn! I can't move,*" Vale ordered.

"*Me too.*"

"My patience is ended. I have tried diplomacy, now I shall use force," Yvorre croaked in a voice that somehow reminded Elyn of dust.

Elyn became aware of other muffled noises. Shouts distorted. Yvorre's sunken eyes moved past her daughters and met those of her disciples.

"Veroulle. Aleasea. Ferehain," she muttered as if distracted. "Now you come to me?"

Elyn found that she could move her head, and she watched Yvorre step past her to stand before the shimmering curtain of light. She gestured with a bony hand and the wavering curtain seemed to settle. The Ageless could now be heard distinctly, but Yvorre cut them off.

"Spare me your pleas and outrage, my children," she said with sarcasm. "You come to me too late."

"Mother," gasped Ferehain. His face was frozen in shock. "Mother, what has happened to you?"

Elyn realized that they had witnessed everything that had happened in the Arcadia. Yvorre had shown this to them intentionally. Their entire purpose had been shattered in that cruel instant. This was her vengeance upon them.

"And now you are concerned for me, Ferehain?" she smirked. "Where was your concern all those long years while I rotted in that tower? Where were you all while I stood in chains waiting for you to come? Wishing you would come for me. Night after night while Bythe tortured me." Yvorre's voice seemed to crack and falter as she spat out her litany of hate. "Why wouldn't you come? I waited for you all. I waited!" The last words were an ugly shriek that echoed though the silence that followed.

"Mother," Veroulle said. "Mother, we did not know you lived."

"You did not care! You did not even search for me. I tried to call for you, but you were not listening."

"Mother, no!" Ferehain was begging. "Mother, please believe me, I tried to find you."

"You did not try enough. You failed me, all of you." Yvorre smiled a leering smirk that radiated contempt, condescension, and triumph. "Oh, how I have tempted myself to return to you like this over the years once Bythe granted me my power, just so I could have my revenge on you. But over time I came to realize that you were also my failed children, no different to my daughters. You are simply not worthy of my time."

"Mother, why did you not return to us sooner?" Veroulle asked in a broken voice.

"Did you not hear me?" she snapped. "I had no wish to ever see any of you again unless it was to burn this place to ashes. I no longer have need of my failed disciples; my real children will provide me with the family I need."

"Please, Mother, let us in. Let me in. Let me talk to you," said Ferehain.

"I will not. You cannot enter the Arcadia. None but family can pass through this curtain and you are not of our blood. The magic I have given you is useless here."

"Where are you, Yvorre?" asked Aleasea. "You are not physically here."

"I am far from here, Aleasea, but that does not matter. While I cannot transport myself to my old home, I can send my energies through the Arcadia, and I can also send a proxy in my stead."

"Imbatal," said Aleasea.

"Correct," said Yvorre. Her grotesque smile split and twisted her wasted face.

"We do not fear Imbatal," said Veroulle at length. His voice was flat, without emphasis or emotion.

"You mean that you do not fear Imbatal, Veroulle, as you do not fear death, but you cannot speak for the others. I can already feel their fear. Death is finally coming to claim them after centuries of falsely earned immortality." She took in the entire room with her cold stare and no one challenged her. "They know that Imbatal is coming for my daughters and he will quite simply kill anyone if they intervene."

Aleasea narrowed her eyes. "You're bluffing, Yvorre, even your demon doesn't have the strength to challenge all the Ageless. You're not going to risk losing your best soldier on such a gamble."

Yvorre smiled again.

"You will find that Imbatal has been well rested in preparation for this. I have seen that he will have enough strength to deal with you all, either way..." She paused and looked again at her daughters. "The godling daughter of both Bythe and Maelene? I think we all know that such a prize will warrant a risk."

She waved her thin hand once more and the curtain returned to a shimmering state. The raised voices of the Ageless were calling to her, but they were once again distorted. Elyn watched her as she returned to stand before her two helpless daughters.

"And now it is time to repair that which was broken so many years ago," she said as she extended her hand, palm upward, toward them. For a moment Elyn thought Yvorre was making an offering of some kind. Then she felt the pain. It speared through her from the tip of her scalp down into her bowels. Breathless pain. Pain so intense she didn't cry out, only gasp in disbelief.

"It is best if you do not resist. The pain will be lessened."

Elyn could feel her energy seeping from her body. It was being drawn out of her like blood.

"*What's she doing?*" Vale asked. The bond between them working as strong as ever, despite the pain shared by both of them.

"*She's tapping into my power. She's going to reconcile us. I can't stop it.*"

"That's correct," Yvorre cut in aloud. "In this place I am supreme. I built it for that reason. I imbued it with my blood, my power, and I can manipulate you because you are also of my blood. You cannot stop me from taking your power. It is rightfully shared by us all. We are family."

The pain stabbed again, and this time Elyn had to scream. The sound was shrill, and it seemed to echo in her ears. It took her a moment to realize that she was hearing Vale scream in unison. There was a dull crash followed by the sound of an explosion. Yvorre glanced beyond Elyn for a moment then returned her attention to her offspring.

"Do not worry, my children," she said caustically. "My false children seek to aid you but even the might of Veroulle cannot breach the barrier. We are safe in here."

"I can't stop it," Elyn cried out. She saw the tendril of crackling light emerge from her chest. Yvorre gestured with her palm and guided the light toward Vale as if it were a puppet on strings.

"Help us!" Elyn cried to the Ageless beyond the curtain. "Help us, please!"

Yvorre grunted in disgust. "You are as slow a student as your sister. Even a god's power must follow natural laws. You will know this once I am your teacher. No being is all powerful in the natural world we created, and the Ageless are no exception. I have built the Arcadia to repel any who are not true family. Their greatest spells and artefacts can never breach this place. I have ensured that the three of us cannot be disturbed."

"*Family,*" Elyn thought as she cried out again. She looked over and met Vale's eyes. They were hard with pain, but she saw the recognition in them as Elyn's suggestion was understood.

"Yes, family," Yvorre repeated. "One of my more ingenious spells, I admit, as there are none like us left in the world." With a thrust of her palm she sent the spear of light into Vale's chest. Both of them screamed as the connection between them was completed. For a moment Vale and Elyn were joined completely. They shared one mind. One set of memories. Then they fractured apart.

"I can keep you safe here until Imbatal is ready for you. Then he will bring you to me," said Yvorre. "Stop resisting, both of you. This is the reason you were born. It is time for you to grow up."

Vale looked at Elyn. "*I'm not sure I can do this, Elyn.*"

"*You have to try, you're the only one who can. Take my power. Take it!*" said Elyn.

Yvorre looked from one to the other. Suspicion furrowed her ancient brow.

"What are you doing?" she demanded quickly. Too quickly. Her bravado had faltered, and for a second, they both glimpsed her uncertainty.

Vale nodded to Elyn then turned to her mother.

"We thought that no family gathering is really complete without the father," said Vale through gritted teeth. "Would you like me to summon him?"

Confusion clouded Yvorre's sunken eyes for a moment before they sharpened into realization, then horror.

"No!" she shrieked, but it was too late. Vale had closed her eyes and latched onto Elyn's power. She focused hard on the Ironhelm and shot out her feeling toward it with every piece of shared thought and emotion they could find. Vale focused on her father, the love she had felt for him as a girl, and the hurt, the confusion she felt toward him at his abandonment. She brought the feeling to life from the pits of her heart. Just like the day Leon had died, their power again shone like a beacon in the name of their father.

"Stop it!" Yvorre's voice was hysterical now. She screamed like a mad woman. Her incorporeal form tried to claw at Vale's face in vain, but Vale wouldn't stop. She used a warrior's discipline, all of Yvorre's teachings, to steel her mind as she sent a beam of light spearing from her heart to latch onto something at the summit of the Ironhelm.

The Arcadia dimmed. Yvorre froze. Even the Ageless fell silent beyond the barrier. For a moment there was a heavy stillness in the space under the cupola. A sense of overwhelming dread and oppression. Vale had felt something familiar latch onto her mental signal. The room grew cold. Outside the curtain, a shadow began to form across the barrier. Spots of darkness seemed to materialise on the surface, then moved and coalesced into a larger, cancerous whole. Vale felt the tremendous weight of Bythe's presence working its way down the connection, like he was climbing a rope hand over hand. With each step the darkness grew thicker. The black masses on the barrier had now grown and merged so that everything outside the Arcadia was now obscured by something dark and terrible.

Yvorre shrieked in an inarticulate mixture of desperation and panic as the folly of her arrogance was exposed before her. The black essence of Bythe, the spiritual bond of their family, began to seep through the barrier in drops. The darkness moved slowly through the barrier like mist. As more of the black cloud entered, Elyn became aware of a low rumble, like a constant peal of thunder far away. The air was like ice, and mist formed on her breath as she watched the blackness twist and spread inside the Arcadia like ink in water.

Yvorre looked about desperately, but she was helpless to interfere as the figure of Bythe began to take shape before them. The darkness collected into a dense cloud, large and wide. The rumbling grew louder, and Elyn thought she could hear voices in the sound. A man's voice. Deep and resonant and full of fury. He was saying something but Elyn couldn't yet make it out.

"No!" Yvorre screeched. "I won't let you take us again!"

Bythe began to emerge. Elyn saw a powerful body of massive girth taking shape. It looked strangely familiar to her, and Elyn felt both protected and frightened at the same time. Yvorre turned from him and looked at her daughters with an expression of pure hatred.

"You've achieved nothing from this! Imbatal will still take you, and now I will make you suffer for what you've done!"

Yvorre then turned toward the ball of light at the center of the Arcadia and swung her withered hands into the glass. The ball cracked and boomed and for a moment the entire Sanctuary seemed to heave in pain. Then a flash of light broke from the glass as it shattered into hundreds of small crystals, sweeping through the room in a roar of power and disintegrating the ghostly forms of both Bythe and Maelene in its wake.

"Elyn!" Aleasea's voice cut through the din and Elyn realized the barrier between them had fallen. She could also move again. Aleasea gripped her wrist with surprising strength and all but dragged her toward the entrance.

"Vale? Vale?" she called out.

"I'm here," Vale answered as she sprinted up beside her.

Ahead of them, Jason, Ferehain, and Veroulle were waiting by the exit. Ferehain collected Jason in his arms and vanished through the tunnel.

"Go!" Veroulle bellowed over the noise, and Aleasea led Elyn and Vale into the passageway behind Ferehain. Elyn was vaguely aware of Veroulle close behind them as they sprinted hard through the corridors. The entire Sanctuary seemed to groan and heave. Pieces of rock were clattering from the ceiling like the first rain-spots of an impending storm. The lights of the corridor dimmed, faded, then surged in a random and erratic array of pulsations. Sanctuary was dying.

"Quickly!" Ferehain shouted from somewhere ahead of them. Elyn had become completely lost as they turned through passageways with bewildering speed. Behind them came the sound of crashing rock as the passageway collapsed. She didn't dare turn. She felt Aleasea pulling her faster, almost dragging her off her feet. She had to move faster or they'd be killed. Elyn's legs coiled like steel springs and she pushed herself harder than she ever had before. It felt like nothing – as if she could sprint forever if she willed it. Her muscles felt like they were on fire and her entire body was burning. She moved with incredible speed. They moved with incredible speed. Elyn and Vale were united again in a moment of purpose and single-minded agreement. They ran in unison. Side by side. Elyn shook off Aleasea's protective hand and ran harder. Their shared mind drove their bodies through the passageway like a wildcat, each stride covering three times the distance of a normal person's. Within heartbeats, both Elyn and Vale has passed Aleasea and joined Ferehain at the head of the group. Now unrestrained by speed, Ferehain accelerated and led the flight at an inhuman pace. The surroundings should have been a blur to Elyn and yet somehow their mind kept pace. She could recognise every paving stone underfoot and every bend in the passage. She could even see the gold lining of Ferehain's cloak as it trailed behind him. She could see the look of terror on Jason's face as he lay helpless in Ferehain's arms.

An instant later, the dimness of Sanctuary was replaced by fierce sunlight. Ferehain led them all out onto a grass-covered pathway next to the side of the Temple. Elyn and Vale looked around to steady themselves, but there was no time.

"Hurry!" Aleasea ordered and they fled away from the Temple, finding the stone steps that led down to the river. As they descended the first steps, Elyn heard a tremendous crack. It was as if somewhere an enormous stick had been snapped clean. She wasn't sure what had broken, but she knew that the sound was terrible all the same. With her uncanny strength, Aleasea flung Elyn to the steps, causing them to land awkwardly. Elyn heard another groan, as if the Temple was crying out, then there was the sound of rocks. It started with a few drops, then the noises accelerated like a landslide. Elyn heard the rumbling and clatter of thousands of rocks, boulders, and piles of dirt rushing and crashing over each other somewhere far beneath them. The ground around them dropped suddenly, forming a tremendous crater around the Temple. Elyn and Jason cried out in shock. For a moment, it seemed as if the entire Temple grounds would be swallowed up and cast into the depths beneath them. The Temple seemed to shrink inward as great cracks split its ancient face. The building sighed and sank, as if it had grown weary and decided to lie down. It settled into a ruin, half standing, and exhaled a torrent of dust and debris from its depths like a death rattle.

Vale got to her feet and extended her hand to Elyn, then to Jason.

"Are you both alright?" she asked. They nodded then turned their attention to the Temple. The three Ageless looked at it in absolute disbelief.

"I'm sorry," Elyn offered feebly. It was all she could think of. There were no words for such a moment. There was no time for mourning. The sun was making a pathetic attempt to rise through the air clogged with the scents of thick smoke and death. Elyn and Vale turned to look at the town. The scene was worse than they could have expected. Toward the southern walls of the city, Elyn made out crowds of people grouped by the hundreds, maybe even thousands. They were streaming down the streets carrying bundles of belongings, bundles of children, or nothing at all, as they all took part in a frantic exodus from their homes in a desperate attempt to flee the terrors to the north. They seemed to have realized that their protectors might not save them this time.

Elyn looked north and the reason for their concern was justified.

The once peaceful and idyllic city of Fairhaven was in ruin. Where trees once lined streets in an honor guard of green, there were orange flames and black smoke. Where a proud stone wall once towered over the barracks in the outer city there lay an ugly hole with crumbling debris. Farmlands far beyond the city walls were all burning, and inside, the outer city was flooded with hordes of men swathed in crude armor and headmasks. Elyn realized that the entire northern half of the outer city had been overrun. Even the wall to the Old City that formed an inner ring to where Elyn now stood was under threat. From her vantage point, she could see the invaders were only a few streets away from reaching it. The town guard had formed a desperate defense on this last fortification, and even as Elyn watched, she saw the men in blue scurrying to take up positions in front of the army slowly advancing through the streets toward them.

"They've taken the barracks and the military bases," said Vale in her clinical manner. Elyn sensed Vale assessing the situation and rifling through their library of knowledge to apply potential solutions. "This isn't good. We're not going to hold out for long at this rate."

"Captain Lewis has beaten them before," answered Elyn. Vale quickly sifted through their shared memories like reading random pages in a book.

"Not like this he hasn't. Not with this many invaders."

Jason stepped up alongside them. "I can't believe this. First the Northmen attack us, now the Ageless are crippled. And this is all because of Yvorre, Maelene...your mother?"

Elyn and Vale could sense a cloud of resentment and suspicion return in Jason's heart.

"I'm sorry, Jason," Elyn said. "I had no idea either. You saw that, didn't you?"

Jason nodded and stared out over the burning houses. "I have to find my father. I need to make sure he's alright."

Vale glanced at him. "You're a soldier, Jason. Your family is your unit and your town. That's your duty now. Your father can wait."

Jason returned her look with anger and for a moment, they simply stared at each other. One soldier to another. Yet there was something in Vale's bearing that gave her authority. Something more than just the armor she wore or the sword at her side. She had changed. She was larger. Jason seemed to notice this and dropped his eyes.

"*I see it in you too,*" Vale thought. "*We've changed after the Arcadia.*"

Vale's thoughts were strong. Elyn struggled to distinguish them from her own.

"*The reconciliation started, but it hasn't completed. I didn't want this,*" Elyn replied.

Vale rested a hand on her sister's shoulder. "*You're still you. We can stop this Elyn. I won't let it happen.*"

"What happened to Yvorre? Is she dead?" Jason asked.

"No," Veroulle answered in his harsh voice as the Ageless joined them at their vantage point. "No, our Cursed Mother is far from here. She sought to imprison Elyn and Vale in the Arcadia so that Imbatal could retrieve them."

"And Imbatal is still here to complete that mission," said Vale. "Nothing's changed. We haven't beaten Yvorre. We've only bought some time at the cost of Sanctuary and everything you have."

"We gained valuable knowledge," said Veroulle. "We can deny Yvorre her prize today. Come with us, both of you. We can retreat into the Outer Wild and regroup."

"You should do what he says, Elyn, but I can't go with you," Jason said. "My family's down there and I won't leave them. I need to go now."

Elyn looked at Jason and then at the town beneath them. The words came out of her mouth unexpectedly. Her words or Vale's? It didn't matter. She knew they were right.

"And how many will pay the price for my cowardice, Veroulle? How many innocents will die as I flee into the forest? How many will be raped and slaughtered today just so that I can go on living? Am I really that special? Is Vale? How will I be able to go on living after today, knowing that my survival came at such a high price?"

Elyn knew the truth of her words deep within her heart. If she fled, she knew that she could rationalize it in many different ways, but she also knew that she would not be able to escape the absolute truth that thousands of people died because she had run. She knew that truth would return to haunt her at night when she tried to sleep, then it would follow her into her dreams and be there waiting for her when she woke. She knew that such a horrible truth would ultimately weaken her and then – one day – destroy her. Ferehain was now looking at her with something akin to respect. Veroulle's face hardened.

"You are the daughters of Bythe and Maelene. Yes, you are that special. You could change the fate of us all."

"Or I could just be another illegitimate godling," Elyn replied. "Prophecies and visions be damned. I don't care."

"Enough of this," snapped Veroulle and he stepped forward to seize Elyn.

"You will not touch me!" Elyn commanded in a thunderous voice that filled the air around them. Veroulle paused in surprise. Elyn stepped toward him, her eyes shining with confidence and pride.

"I am the proven daughter of the pure Blessed Mother. You all bore witness to this fact. You are sworn to serve the sacred blood of my Mother, and you are hereby sworn to serve her daughter. Your Blessed Mother has fallen into darkness, and I am all that remains. You swore to serve her blood – well, I am all that's left of her blood. Act against me and you will truly have nothing left. You will only be the servants of Yvorre!"

The crag-like rocks of Veroulle's ancient face did not change. "Do not press me, Elyn," he replied evenly. "It is true that I have no right to raise arms against the daughter of our Mother, but you are also the daughter of our enemy. The truth is that I am torn into two minds over you."

Elyn smiled. "I know the feeling well."

Vale stepped forward and stood beside her sister. "We've made our decision. We're not going to run."

Veroulle gave them both a measuring look. "This is noble; however, it is also quite foolish. While you are stronger than ever, you have not reconciled. You have not yet unlocked the gifts of your Mother or your Father. What exactly are you hoping to accomplish with this act of bravery?"

"You know much, Veroulle, but you don't know everything," Vale replied. "I know a few things that you don't. I know there are other ways to end this conflict that you haven't even considered. I know there's a good chance I can't survive this, but I also know I can end this now, one way or the other. You can help me succeed or stand back and watch me fail."

Vale and Elyn shared a thought. A single hope.

"Jason!" Elyn called to her friend. "I need you with me."

The sisters now knew what they had to do.

CHAPTER 3

"The army of Fairhaven was a proud and effective group. Irrespective of their inferior weapons and armor, Captain Lewis led his men to achieve more than should have been possible in the years that he stood as Fairhaven's protector. It was a point of pride for Captain Lewis that he had successfully defended his people using nought but what they had. His own failure to maintain this standard throughout the siege was something he could never truly forgive himself for."

~Aleasea of the Ageless

Captain Lewis had always been a practical man, never thinking about things that weren't concrete nor factual nor relevant to a task right in front of him. So it stood to reason that he was having a hard time accepting Elyn as she stood in front of him now. It wasn't the fact that she was a female – he had never questioned the worth of a woman on the battlefield. Instead, it was that this was the girl who had cowered before his desk less than a year ago. This girl that had been too absent-minded to find her way home before curfew. This girl whose carelessness had caused the Ageless to come to Lewis in the dead of night – the night he had been outrageously ordered to send out search parties, no matter the risk to the city guard. It had been an absurd situation then – but now? This same girl was now standing there – with a strange twin in enemy armor no less – ready to give orders.

This had to be a ridiculous trick.

They were gathered on a hastily erected wooden platform attached to the Old City wall from one side and supported by timber poles on the other. From this position, Lewis was able to survey and command the battlefield while still enjoying the relative protection of the wall's old but effective ramparts. Elyn, Vale, and Jason had come flanked by their entourage of magicians – now serving them, it almost seemed – and together they stood on this makeshift command post trying to understand what Vale and Elyn intended to do next. It was all too much for Lewis whose first reaction was to try to have Vale arrested. If it hadn't been for the presence of the Ageless, he almost certainly would have succeeded. Veroulle had assumed rank and forced Lewis to be more accommodating.

"*I like him,*" Vale thought. "*He's a solid commander.*"

"*Yeah, well you haven't seen him when he's had a bad night, and I should point out that he's currently trying to have you imprisoned. So maybe we should forget the whole soldierly-respect thing for now?*"

"So, what are we doing, Veroulle?" Lewis looked tired. His blue officer's uniform was bloodied and smeared with dirt and his face was drawn and grey. It seemed to Elyn that all the trimmings and decorations of Fairhaven's field commander had been ripped away by hours of relentless and defeating combat – and yet his eyes had lost none of their steel. "Take a look out there! Look how many there are! We've never engaged this many of them before. The tribes have united against us and they're overrunning us with sheer weight of numbers."

"I understand that, Captain, but things have changed for us," Veroulle's voice was still calm and low in contrast to the slight edge of desperation that colored Lewis's voice. "We may have an...opportunity."

Lewis looked back at the twins. Elyn and Vale were ignoring everyone else and surveying the city that was now a battlefield before them. They moved their heads together in eerie unison. The newer streets outside the Old City walls were more structured than those within, yet they still managed to curve and tangle in a serpentine fashion, and infested within that mass of snakes lay their enemy. They were gathering in groups behind impromptu barricades of crates and wagons. Scattered throughout the streets were occasional flashpoints of sporadic fighting as some soldiers defended the few remaining strong points, but most defenders had retreated to the safety of the Old City wall.

"*The Northmen fight undisciplined,*" Vale observed. "*A fractured army. I've seen this before.*"

"*I know,*" Elyn answered. "*Do you think Lewis can pull this off?*"

Elyn could feel Vale walking through her head again, pulling out memories and facts within seconds. "*I don't know. I don't think so – not without us. We need to act.*"

"They will assault us within the hour, Veroulle, maybe within minutes. I don't have time for this." Lewis's tired and frustrated voice drifted back to Elyn. "And frankly, my lord, I'd hoped that your own people would do more to help us in this hour. We need every able-bodied man and woman to fight, not to stand here and hold a conference with me!" His voice was rising in frustration now, and Elyn could sense his temper fracturing at this critical moment. Lewis wheeled about, looking for somewhere to vent his fury, and he laid his eyes on Jason.

"What the hell are you doing standing here, cadet?" he scalded Jason with words that were now rising to a fever pitch. "There's a bloody war on and you're standing here daydreaming. Get downstairs to Corporal Hanniston right now or I'll have you in the stocks!"

"He stays with us," Elyn commanded. Lewis turned his glare onto Elyn now, but it was simply ignored as she continued to scan the streets that were slowly betrayed by the rising sun.

"What did you say?"

Elyn continued to ignore him. Lewis opened and closed his mouth in silence as he struggled to understand how this arrogant young woman now seemed impervious to the intimidation that had torn her self-esteem apart so effortlessly such a short time ago.

"I don't care what you want, girl!" Lewis's voice was almost shrill now, and he turned to a sergeant at his side. He was about to give the order to arrest probably both Elyn and Jason, when Elyn and Vale stiffened. They saw something in the streets below them. A merciful act of the gods, perhaps? They knew the time had come.

"Captain!" Elyn turned and took in the entire group with a stare that commanded respect, her voice returning to that authoritative rumble that she'd used outside the Temple. The stance made her look more like Vale, and it was becoming increasingly difficult to tell them apart. "It's us they want, me and Vale. We're the reason they're here. Veroulle can explain if you need proof, but for now you need to listen to us."

Vale stepped forth and addressed the audience in a voice identical to Elyn's. "We're going to draw them over to the western wall. They'll target us once we're sighted, have no doubt of that. Once we've drawn them out you need to take advantage of our actions and strike hard."

The platform broke into cries of protest. Elyn listened to none of them. She turned to Lewis who was still shouting something at the Ageless. Elyn's voice cut above them all. "We're out of time! There's something worse than nomad warriors coming. It's after me. It's after Vale. Let it come for us so that your men can be spared."

Everyone fell silent. Comprehension dawned on Lewis's face. Aleasea's was a mask of concern. Veroulle was stone.

"We're going to do what we can to draw it away, Captain," said Vale. "Take whatever action you need to save your people."

Then Elyn swiftly removed the remains of her stained white robes and threw them to the wooden platform at her feet. Standing in her simple clothes again, she turned to look at Veroulle, Aleasea, and Ferehain in turn.

"If you truly want to help the daughter of Maelene, then be at my side by the west wall." She pointed again to the spot she had identified earlier, then turned to leave. A hand stopped her by the shoulder.

"Elyn..." Jason said. "Let me help you."

"No, Jase. I need you to find Nadine and protect her. What happens now is going to be the most dangerous test of my life. I want to know you're both safe."

Jason didn't know how to reply. He felt a sudden mix of affection for his old friend and shame for how he had treated her. Jason removed his sword and handed it to Elyn.

"Try to avoid hitting yourself with it." Jason suggested.

Elyn smiled. "I'll do my best."

As one, Vale and Elyn turned and stepped up onto the ramparts of the Old City wall, the new day's sun catching their twin features as they stared down at an army that had come to claim them. Elyn looked over toward the distant marketplace, now visible in the rising sun. Elyn and Vale closed their eyes and returned to that day. The day Leon's life drained into the dirt. The day a murderer had giggled like a girl while he stabbed a defenseless old man. The day Elyn had felt scalding grief surge into her chest and throat as she witnessed her entire life simply crack before her eyes. She hadn't noticed that her heart had started to race. That dull roar had returned, and her chest clenched like a vice.

Elyn and Vale again felt a unified anger. A unified purpose.

They were moving. In one swift action they both leaped from the heights of the wall to the laneway below. Together they moved with speed. They were predators on a scent. Within seconds, they cleared the laneway and rounded two corners to bring themselves face to face with the target that fate had unexpectedly placed in their path. A squat killer stood there in a small raiding party with three other men. Possibly some of them the same men that had been in the marketplace that day. Who knew? It didn't matter. Within the next minute they would all be dead.

Jarren looked up into her eyes, and Elyn saw several feelings reflected there. Recognition followed by brief elation dissolving into dismay. It seemed that even this man could sense that Elyn was not the same weak young woman he'd met in the market months ago. There was something different about her – many things in fact. Here she stood, tall and proud, her face cold and her eyes colder. He probably wondered what had happened in such a short time to turn the tables so dramatically. How had what was supposed to be his crowning moment of triumph reversed into the worst mistake of his miserable life? It's possible, even, that he felt regret. Elyn never knew which feelings shot across the man's heart in those brief moments; however, whatever feelings surfaced, they were most definitely his last. Elyn had raised her sword and without even thinking, had stepped forth and quite simply severed the fat head from its body in a single, fluid movement.

There had been roars of shock and outrage from the other raiders, but they too were as insignificant as their leader's last thoughts. The killer's body began to teeter and fall, and yet Vale had already moved past Elyn toward the remaining three masked attackers. Their shared will had reverted to the cold and logical mindset that Vale had perfected so long ago. While the raiders were not unprepared for the attack, they were ambushed by the sheer speed of its onslaught. Clearing the distance between them in a single stride, Vale swung her saber in a horizontal arc and sliced through the thin material of the first nomad's unprotected neck. Blood sprayed as a mist, the droplets suspended in time and glistening like rubies in the breaking sun as Vale turned toward the second man. He had started to move toward her, his expression unreadable beneath the black cloth that bound his face and a crude axe raised above his head, but his movements seemed as lethargic as the fall of the blood droplets now breaking gently upon Vale's cheek. She stepped to her left, and the axe swung through empty space. The wielder lurched forward – momentarily unbalanced – which was all the opportunity Vale needed to drive her armored knee forward into the raider's face with a sickening crunch of shattering bone. As he fell to the dirt – far too slowly to Vale's eyes – the final man hesitated. Fear shone from the eyes under the mask. Vale and

Elyn merely advanced as the two men behind them died in gurgling and muffled screams.

The nomad's hand dropped to his belt.

Not for a knife, Elyn noted, but for another far deadlier weapon. Yet Elyn did not move to stop the raider as he unhooked the horn at his side. She could have. The nomad was moving with almost frustrating delay and Elyn realized that she could have severed the man's arm in three places before he'd brought the horn to his mouth. But they needed him to do this. They stood there patiently as the nomad tucked the mouthpiece to the horn under the fold of his mask and blew. The three notes rang out in the morning air. Two high, one low, almost certainly a signal that they had found their target.

Elyn glanced at Vale, then they were moving again.

In a smooth motion, they turned back down the street in the direction they'd come. Already, more swathed faces had emerged at some of the side streets that intersected their path and were peering at them both with curiosity. Curiosity followed by excitement.

"*We have to hurry!*" Vale warned.

Elyn silently assented. Although their skills seemed formidable, they both had no real desire to test them against an entire army. They started to run down the street as the first cries of pursuit rose behind them. The three-note alarm cried out over and over, and with every repetition more attackers could be heard answering the call. With a unified mind, they turned down a laneway that connected two larger streets and started sprinting as hard as they could down the narrow passageway. Vale's metal armor plates creaked and sang out as she ran and yet she barely noticed them. They navigated the laneway littered with empty boxes and strewn garbage and burst through into the broad street beyond.

There were sounds of pursuit.

Elyn didn't need to look back to know that their enemies were marking their movements. The three-note call had been taken up by other horns, and a chorus of them were now sounding from the rooftops around them.

Vale glanced upward to find the line of the Old City wall above the warehouse rooftops a few blocks to their left and began to run along a parallel street, heading what she hoped was westward. The sun was rising at their backs and their shadows hurtled down the street before her. Somewhere, an arrow sang out and buried itself into the dirt several yards ahead of them.

"*Run!*" Vale commanded. "*We're out of time.*"

"*I know!*" Elyn snapped back, and although their pursuers were receding for the moment, Elyn redoubled her efforts and drove toward the western wall as hard as she could.

The street was becoming wider and rutted with wheel tracks. Vale could now see the two watchtowers that flanked the western gate. On that watchtower, she saw something that gave her a glimmer of hope. Behind them the chorus of horns bellowed louder. Now all she could do was pray to whatever gods still cared that her plan might make it to the next stage. They were both breathing hard when they ran up to the wooden double gates that marked the only entrance point to the western side of Fairhaven.

"We need cover!" Vale said and cast her eyes about, scanning and cataloguing every item nearby. She spied a wagon lying maimed against the wall with one wheel ripped away and started for it. She glanced back to see five nomads running toward them with an untold number starting to flood into the street behind.

"*Well, we certainly got their attention,*" Elyn observed.

"*They don't want to kill us, Elyn. Remember that. It may give us an edge.*"

"*That's very comforting.*"

They reached the cover of the wagon and pushed it onto its side against the city wall to form a makeshift barricade. Vale finished her task then turned back to deal with the first assailants – who would be upon them by now – only to find they didn't have to. Three figures were now standing a short distance away with the fresh corpses of the nomads at their feet. Two of the figures wore Ageless robes with Kajik staves brandished. The third wore a stained blue uniform and carried a worn sword of Fairhaven's town guard. They turned and hurried to where the twins stood watching them. Aleasea and Ferehain lowered their hoods as they approached the crude cover of the wagon. Jason was flushed and breathing hard. Elyn felt the urge to say something to her old friend, to admonish him for putting himself in danger like this or to thank him for his loyalty. Instead she met his eyes but said nothing. Words felt inadequate in the face of such defining acts of friendship. Aleasea walked up and stared at them both flatly, her features still serene even in the face of such danger.

Ferehain stood guard at the opening to their barricade. "They are coming," he called over his shoulder. "At least fifty of them. We have less than a minute."

As if to reinforce his words, the horns now sounded again in unison. There was the dull crash of dozens of boots stamping out their disjointed rhythm.

"We've drawn them out," Elyn replied. "They'll divert their efforts to my capture. Will Lewis launch his attack now that they're coming for us?" She tried to keep the edge of desperation from her voice, tried to sound in control. She didn't feel completely successful.

"I believe so," Aleasea answered. "Veroulle remained with Lewis to ensure they can take advantage of what you have done, but you must leave with us now. Lewis cannot save you from here."

Elyn looked to Vale with a mock-serious expression. "That's an excellent point. Who do you think could possibly save us now?"

Vale smiled back. "I might have a suggestion."

A loud groan of timber was followed by a wrenching crack as something large and wooden was ripped from its moorings. All of them turned to watch one of the wooden gates in the outer wall pop away from the frame and collapse inward, landing in the dirt in an explosion of dust.

"Behind me," Vale ordered as she moved to the opening, pushing Ferehain to safety. As she did this, dozens of black armored soldiers began streaming through the open gateway in a tight formation. Elyn watched, feeling Vale's pride ripple within her as the Helmsguard charged forward to meet the advancing nomads. Within seconds, they had slammed into the wildmen who had been expecting nothing more than the mild resistance of a few magicians. The shock of finding themselves colliding with the strength of the Iron Union led to chaos as the Northmen tried desperately to retreat before this new threat. Behind them Elyn could hear Aleasea's sharp intake of breath.

"Vale?" she asked.

"Five hundred of my finest," Vale answered. "I left orders with Ethan that they were to attack from the west at dawn, should I not return." She turned to look at Aleasea. "Did you really think I was going to walk into enemy territory without a plan to walk out, Aleasea?"

She smiled at the genuine shock on Aleasea's face then broke cover and walked toward the five soldiers who had separated from the main group and were striding toward them. They slowed as Vale approached them, their confident movements now betraying hesitance as they no doubt saw the subtle changes in who they presumed was their leader. Ethan stiffened and saluted regardless of his confusion. Vale returned the salute with a gesture. She stepped forward and clasped her old friend's hand. Ethan didn't remove his helmet, but his eyes betrayed his confusion.

"Thank you, Ethan. You saved my life again," Vale said.

Ethan look over Vale's shoulder toward the Ageless, his eyes showing more concern. He raised his arm to signal their capture when Vale interrupted the unspoken order with a wave.

"Stand down. They're not our enemies today."

"My lady," Ethan began, clearly uncertain about what to say. "Did you find Elyn?"

Vale gestured to Elyn and Ethan stared at her in open wonder. "She looks exactly like you."

"Indeed, she does. We've both been through a lot these past few hours."

Ethan took in the changes in his friend. "Are you alright, my lady? You look different."

"I'm fine," Vale interrupted him. She knew that Ethan must be having doubts, but she couldn't give him the luxury of an explanation nor could she afford to give him time to question what was happening. "I saw your sentry on the watchtower. Well done, you arrived just as I needed you."

"We marched here through the night and set a watch to look for you. No one seems to be watching this gate."

Vale nodded. "They're all preoccupied defending the north of the city. We've managed to put everyone in the city off balance for a moment."

"So now we seize Fairhaven?"

"No," Vale answered. "As I said, these people aren't our enemy today, but Yvorre's treachery needs to be dealt with."

"Imbatal?" asked Ethan.

"Yes, he's coming for us with the Northmen."

"But the Ageless?" Ethan asked.

"Yvorre would like to crush them too, but they're not her true target – I am – and that makes the Ageless our allies today, but only for today."

Ethan nodded slowly. Vale knew that he couldn't argue with this logic no matter how much it surprised him, and the anger he felt for Yvorre would no doubt cloud his judgment further. Today, she needed to keep her old friend as imbalanced as her enemies.

"We'll protect you, sir," Ethan said, his eyes sweeping the battle and the surrounding buildings. "We can have you out of here within minutes and I'll commit a rear guard to make sure Yvorre's men are..."

Vale silenced him with a shake of her head.

"The best way to protect me is to make a stand here, not to risk flight with Imbatal at our heels. We have allies here, even if they're only temporary allies, and we need to use them." She turned and motioned for

Aleasea and the others to join him. As they approached, the Helmsguard took a step backward, their hands moving to their weapons.

"At ease, everyone," Vale ordered as the group approached with their own guarded postures.

When they arrived, they stood quietly. Elyn looked from one group to the next and a distant part of her wondered when was the last time Ageless and Helmsguard stood alongside one another like this.

Vale cleared her throat with only a touch of self-consciousness. "I know this is difficult for all of you. We've spent our lives fighting each other but today I need you to put that aside. We have a far bigger problem before us, and it will take our combined discipline and control to defeat it." She looked at Ethan who returned this stare uncertainly. "My friend, I think I'm going to ask the biggest sacrifice to come from you. I need you to take my men eastwards into the heart of the city and link up with the city guard. Find Captain Lewis and submit to his command."

Elyn could see that, even under the armor of his helmet, Ethan looked as if Vale had struck him. He took a small step backward, and when he spoke, his voice quivered with a barely contained fury.

"*Submit* to him? Why? What have I done to you to deserve this, Vale?"

Vale took a step forward and placed a hand on his shoulder. "Remember our battle against the Rak'Tunga? A committee cannot lead an army. You are the finer commander by far, but this is his city, and these are his people. There can only be one leader in this fight, and today, it has to be him."

She was aware that she wasn't lying to Ethan, but she also needed him to feel hurt. It would make it easier for her to do what needed to be done. She needed them to be gone before Imbatal came for them. She ignored that expression in her friend's eyes and turned to Aleasea, Jason, and Ferehain.

"I need you three to get to Veroulle and Lewis and tell them what Ethan is doing, get the message to them quickly. You need to make sure Lewis doesn't attack them along with the Northmen. Am I clear? The only chance we have is for us all to fight as a unit."

Ferehain glanced at Aleasea for a moment. "Five hundred men will not turn this battle, Vale," he said.

Vale rounded on him. "Five hundred of Ethan's men are worth more than a thousand of Lewis's soldiers and five thousand of those savage wildmen! If they fight alongside Lewis, we may stand a chance. If we fight each other, then we're all doomed. Everything is different now, Ferehain, you've seen it for yourself."

Ferehain looked at Vale and the magician nodded.

"Go," Vale ordered.

Ethan saluted in an action that was far too formal, and it stung. Then he was retreating up the street shouting commands to his men who were already routing the Northmen and pushing them back into the city. Ferehain raised his hood and left, ghosting up the street, and then was simply gone from sight.

Jason didn't move, instead he looked at Elyn. "And what are you going to do?"

Elyn didn't reply. Instead, Aleasea broke the silence. "They will wait here for Imbatal."

"No one else will die at the hands of that demon because of me. I'm going to deal with him here," Elyn replied.

Aleasea sighed. "Elyn, you have nothing to atone for, and you need not sacrifice yourself like this." She stepped up to Elyn and touched her face gently, like a mother tending to her child. "Just run away. Do not stay for us – not for the Ageless or for the Union – just leave for yourself. Go away and we will not come after you. I promise you I will stop them."

Elyn felt her resilience waver and for the first time she understood the maternal care that Aleasea had harboured toward her. Elyn's hand betrayed her and involuntarily clasped Aleasea's hand where it met her cheek.

"Imbatal will hunt me," Elyn finally managed to answer.

Aleasea nodded. "Then I will stand here with you."

"Jason," Elyn turned to him. "Go to Lewis. I need you to confirm Ferehain's report."

Jason shook his head. "No, you don't. I realize you just want me gone."

"Jason, you can't fight Imbatal."

Jason shot her a grin that Elyn knew well. "Since when do you tell me how and when to use a sword?"

Elyn smiled back despite her dismay. "Jason, please. Think of Nadine."

"No," he replied flatly. "Vale was right. I'm a solider and my first duty is to my unit – today, that's you. Besides, how do I explain to Nadine that I just abandoned you here? I'm not leaving you, Elyn."

"And neither am I," Aleasea responded.

"You've got loyal friends, Elyn," said Vale.

Unexpected feelings of pride bubbled and rippled through their shared psyche. Together they stood and watched Ethan's forces push the invaders further and further into the city, until they were all but gone from view.

CHAPTER 4

"Of all the Ageless, it is Aleasea who is remembered above all for her actions against Imbatal at the Siege of Fairhaven. We shall always honor her courage and the price she paid."

~Councillor Paeter. Fairhaven Council Proclamation 568.

Time seemed immeasurable that morning, and Elyn had no idea how long they stood waiting. Hours or minutes? The morning air was now thick with smoke as the entire city appeared to be burning. A shrill crack rent the air as another section of the wall surrounding the Old City fell, and Elyn wondered what was happening. Was their plan working or was Lewis attacking Ethan as viciously as he attacked the Northmen?

"*Focus,*" Vale admonished. "*Don't be distracted by trouble you can't influence.*"

Elyn drew in a deep breath and let it out slowly. She tried to rediscover that cold mindset, but it was wavering. She was scared.

"*I'm sorry, Elyn,*" Vale continued.

The thought genuinely surprised Elyn. "*Sorry for what?*"

"*When I came to find you, looking for answers, I didn't think about what you wanted. I just assumed you'd want the same as me. I didn't want to understand why you resisted our reconciliation.*"

Elyn was thoughtful for a moment before making her confession.

"*I was scared, Vale. I still am.*"

"*I know that now.*"

"I don't want to lose who I am. I never even had a chance to know who I am. What would have happened to me if we reconciled? You're stronger than me. Does my mind get swallowed by yours?"

Vale considered this for a moment. *"I don't know, I don't think so. I think we'd both have changed."*

Elyn smiled. *"Well, I've never been good at changing."*

"And I tried to force it on you. I'm sorry, I didn't even stop and think. I was obsessed with finding my answers. Anyway, I think I've found all the answers I need."

"That we're prophesied to save the world?"

"No. I don't believe that. There're no prophecies we need to fulfill, Elyn. Neither of us is broken. We are who we are. I just want you to know that, and I wanted you to forgive me."

Elyn looked at her sister and was grateful for the acceptance. *"There's nothing for me to forgive."*

Jason looked at them both then broke the silence. "I hate to intrude into your mental conversation, but is there anything that anyone knows about Imbatal that might actually help us?"

Vale shook her head and looked to Aleasea. She also shook her head in grim confirmation.

"There is not much that we know of him," Aleasea answered. "We know he is powerful enough to best any Ageless in single combat and that he seems impervious to any attack."

"Well, that's helpful," Jason muttered.

"Weaknesses," Elyn pressed. "Back in the Arcadia, Yvorre admitted that she was taking a risk. That suggests there must be some way of hurting him."

Vale thought about this for a moment. "If Imbatal has a weakness, then Yvorre never discussed it."

"Every time we have engaged Imbatal he has defeated us," said Aleasea. "Our only blessing is that Yvorre has used him so rarely." She looked at Elyn sternly with an edge to her voice. "We cannot win this fight."

"Why does she use him rarely?" Jason asked.

"We do not know, although there may indeed be a secret there." Aleasea again lapsed into silence, considering this.

"Alright, we engage him as a unit," said Vale. "I'll take him from the front; Aleasea, you and Elyn back me up to his sides; and, Jason, I want you on his flank where he's weakest. We'll be looking for any vulnerability we can exploit, a gap in his armor or perhaps a blind spot we can use. He'll have something – we all do."

"I believe I may have skills to slow him," Aleasea offered.

"What do you mean?" asked Jason.

"Jason, you have seen me practice some small influence over the natural flow of time in Kovalith. It is a rare ability even among the Ageless. I believe I should be able to slow his movements for a short while, but you must all take care to keep your distance. If you are too close you will be caught in the effect."

"Nice of you to start sharing your secrets right before we die," Jason answered with a smile then turned to Elyn. "Do you think it'll work?"

"I don't know, but it's got to help us," Elyn answered. "Any other tricks you can use?" she asked Aleasea.

She shook her head. "I have several, but I fear none will be effective. We can assail the mind and body, yet he seemingly has no mind to attack and does not feel the same pains that a flesh and blood creature should feel, as my brethren have learned."

It was Vale who had sensed it first – one warrior detecting another – an almost animal instinct borne from one predator sensing an equal threat.

"It's too late now." Vale said. "He's here."

When Imbatal arrived, Elyn had expected it to be in a magnificent display of strength and power. That he would emerge in a mighty leap over the warehouses, or with the tremendous crash of collapsing buildings in his wake as he smashed through Ethan's line. So when Elyn first saw the lone figure in white emerge from an alleyway in the distance, she was sure that it was no one of importance. But when it slowly and deliberately stepped in their direction, there was something in that single movement that filled Elyn with a slow sense of horror. The figure was human in shape but was covered head to foot in white clothing the color of bright snow, his face obscured with the same plain-white mask that obscured everything but for two blank eye slits. But when he walked, his walk was of a person not quite human. It was a kind of unnatural movement, as if it had been mimicked through observation instead of learned naturally. It was stilted and slightly uneven, the arms jerked as they swung through what should have been their natural arc. It was at that moment Elyn realized that giving Imbatal a gender was probably an unrealistic conception. She felt dread start to creep back into her stomach.

"Hold it together, Elyn. We can do this," Vale said.

But Elyn couldn't feel calm. All she could feel was the power emanating from the figure who was slowly approaching them. The monstrosity of Imbatal now stopped and regarded them across the distance. Behind this creature there was fleeing, fighting, screaming, and death. Elyn realized that death was almost certainly staring at them now. Vale started to raise her saber in anticipation of an attack. Elyn stood beside her and mirrored the gesture. They stood as twins. They shared one mind. Despite their racing hearts, they also felt a strange aura of peace and certainty. It was as though the acceptance of death had somehow removed the fear of it.

Imbatal stood motionless, head cocked to one side, and it seemed to Elyn that it could see the truth behind the two fractured godlings and was fascinated by it. Then Imbatal straightened himself to his full, towering height and took a slow and deliberate step toward them.

"Be ready," Vale commanded to her companions.

Imbatal took another step. Quicker this time. Vale and Elyn tightened grips on their weapons and adjusted their stance.

Then in an instant Imbatal was upon them.

He had charged them with a single magnificent leap that planted him in front of the twins, his gigantic, two-handed greatsword sweeping downward in an arc that would easily cleave a horse in half, but Elyn had swung to the left just as Vale swung to the right. The blade dug into the dirt. Jason and Aleasea had also leaped to opposite sides of Imbatal and were now moving to take up flanking positions. Imbatal seemed unconcerned. He retrieved his blade tip from where it was stuck in the road and turned to swing again. Elyn stepped back and raised her saber with barely enough time to deflect the incoming blade and send it ricocheting over her head. The force of the blow sent shockwaves up her arms and Elyn was reminded of Aleasea teaching her how to keep her grip on her weapon.

She could see Vale moving in toward Imbatal, her own sword flashing in the morning sun followed by the dull ring of metal hitting armor. Imbatal did not so much as turn his head. His blank eye slits remained fixed on Elyn.

"*He's testing us,*" Vale warned. "*He doesn't want to kill you, he's gauging your strength.*"

The creature swung again, quicker this time, and Elyn felt the sword miss by inches. Vale took advantage and swung her own blade, but Imbatal stepped clear before the sword could land.

Jason stood behind Imbatal, waiting for an opening. Only the three combatants had moved with supernatural speed and Jason waited in vain. Eventually, he lashed out with his sword again and again, but Imbatal paid no attention to the ineffective blows. Even Aleasea swept forward in an arc of grace and speed, her staves a blur in the morning light, and yet she was rewarded with nothing but the sound of metal.

They danced, all five of them in a bizarre repeating pattern. Elyn, Vale and Imbatal moving toward and away from each other in unison as they thrust and parried with their swords, while Aleasea and Jason ineffectively tried to break the rhythm.

"*Keep your distance*," Vale thought to Elyn. "*Let me draw his attack.*"

Elyn stepped backward, knowing that Vale would simultaneously step forward. Imbatal turned to deflect Vale's attack, and Elyn was relieved from danger. She watched Vale defending them all and for a moment she saw herself as she might have been. If different paths had been taken and different decisions made. She watched Vale and, in that moment, realized that Vale's selflessness, her maturity, and her apparent wisdom was nothing more than a choice. It was an act of will. She watched Vale and she finally understood the differences between them. She found that she no longer envied her strange twin. She no longer felt the childish need to be distinct and different from her. She knew that the desire to be special was a child's wish. She knew that her time as a child had ended.

. . .

Vale stepped forward and swung her own blade low and cut a ragged gash across Imbatal's stomach; but where steel should have met flesh, it was instead met with more steel and the sword slid harmlessly away. In retaliation, the creature swung his fist backhanded and Vale was sent flying into the dirt. Her head swam and bright sparks danced before her eyes. She tried to focus. She could feel blood dripping over her forehead, and something burned there. All was white before her eyes. Concussion? No. Imbatal filled her vision as the creature stood over her. The point of his sword thrust downward in a terrible stroke.

As the sword tip descended, Vale was aware that Aleasea had said something in the distance. Words of power, of that she had no doubt, but she wasn't sure what Aleasea had said. Imbatal's blade continued downward on its journey that would maim her, if not kill her outright. In that instant, Vale mused that Imbatal may not be that effective at the finer points of carrying out orders. Hands grabbed her under her armpits and in a moment, someone had pulled her clear. Elyn was hauling Vale to her feet as Imbatal's blade continued to stab downward at the place where she had been, only he was now moving much more slowly. Vale looked at Elyn and then over at Aleasea who returned the unspoken question with a nod. Her face was a mask of concentration set upon Imbatal.

"I have slowed the passage of time around him, but it is...difficult. He seems totally unnatural, and he is resisting." Aleasea spoke the words without taking her eyes from her opponent.

"How is he unnatural?" Jason asked but Aleasea was focused on Imbatal.

"You were caught in the effect. We had to get you out," said Elyn to Vale.

Vale nodded thanks before turning her attention back to Imbatal. As they watched his sword stab into the dirt with increasing speed, the creature slowly turned his head to where the sisters were now standing.

"He's speeding up!" Jason warned.

"I cannot hold him," Aleasea muttered. Sweat was beading on her brow, and she looked as if she was devoting every shred of her being to the single task before her. Vale didn't hesitate. Taking full advantage of the situation, she lunged forth and violently plunged her saber, point first, into the heart of the creature. She threw her entire body weight behind the blade and felt it sink into the metal armor of the breastplate under the white robes. She felt the blade strike something hard and for a moment she heard the strange click that emanated from within the giant. Then she felt her sword buckle and crack into two ruined pieces as she fell to the dirt again, her useless weapon falling beside her. She rolled away as Imbatal's boot smashed into the ground where her head had been seconds earlier. It was moving with the speed of a drunk now, like a man half asleep.

"This is pointless!" Elyn spat. Even Vale offered no encouragement, the sight of her weapon now a wreck in the dirt seemed to drain all hope from her. "He's unstoppable."

"Yes," Vale agreed quietly.

Imbatal turned again and reached for Elyn. He was almost back to full speed. There was only one way to salvage this situation now. Perhaps they could still save Jason and even Aleasea. Elyn and Vale knew they had to surrender. Elyn opened her mouth to say the words, but it was Jason who spoke instead.

. . .

It was the click.

It wasn't the sound of Vale's magnificent blade breaking in two or the cry of dismay that rose from Aleasea when Vale fell defeated into the dirt. These sounds would be terrible and would have certainly commanded his full attention – but for the clicking sound that Imbatal had made when Vale struck him. This sound was unnatural, like Aleasea had said – yet it was also familiar. Just like the creature's movements, Jason was certain that he had seen this before. These were sounds and sights he had heard and seen every day when he had been a child. When he had sat in the workbench and watched his father work with a child's fascination.

It was the sound of a clock.

More specifically, it was the sound of the gears of a clock. The intricate machinery within. And Jason now knew where he had seen the movements of Imbatal's gait before. It was the sweeping yet not quite smooth movement of the second hand on a clock face – every care given to replicate smooth, natural movement without quite achieving that perfection.

"It's a mechanism!" Jason yelled. "Whatever this thing is, it's been built by some form of clockwork!"

This was incredible. An intricate mechanism on such a grand scale and attached to some sort of life form. His father would have been thrilled. This was incredible because it lent an explanation to the impossible acts he'd witnessed. And this was incredible because it gave Jason an idea that might also give them a chance.

. . .

A clockwork demon.

Neither Elyn nor Vale had knowledge of any such creature in their shared history. It was an interesting revelation, but it wasn't one that would change the inevitable outcome of this disaster. Not until Jason spoke again.

"Don't you see? All clocks need to be wound up!"

No mechanism was independent of its owner. They all needed to be charged somehow. Suddenly things became clear to Vale. Yvorre's words from the Arcadia recalled themselves to her.

"*You will find Imbatal has been well rested for this...*"

"His power is limited by time!" Vale shouted. How many turns had Imbatal used up already? Now she understood why Yvorre had always held him in reserve. Like a charging bull this creature was unstoppable, but the bull cannot charge forever and when he is exhausted, he becomes vulnerable. Elyn shared an idea and an instant later Vale had a strategy. It was an incredible risk, but it was their only slim hope. Vale stepped backward as Imbatal swung his sword again, almost back to full speed.

"Aleasea!" Elyn shouted across to her. "Reverse your power. Don't try to slow him down, speed him up instead!"

Comprehension registered on Aleasea's face. Increase the passage of time around him and increase the speed of those internal gears and windings. Exhaust him but also make him all the more dangerous until he's spent. She refocused on Imbatal. Again, those strange words emanated from her mouth. Imbatal paused and this time he seemed to twitch and spasm as the time currents around him shifted and gripped his mechanical body. It uttered a strange sound, a terribly inhuman clatter like the wrenching sound of rusted steel on steel. Then it moved faster than Elyn expected.

To Imbatal, Aleasea was the greater threat. Her magic and skills were impeding this beast. That's why his first reaction was to attack her with speed – his own augmented agility now boosted by Aleasea's own work. He moved and in one swift action his sword cut through her robes and severed her extended arm. She fell to the ground without a cry, her eyes half closed and a strange expression on her face. Blood started to pool beneath the crippling injury in an alarming quantity. Jason knelt to her side, desperate to help her and heedless of his own peril. Imbatal raised his blade and swung a second time, only it was Vale who stepped in to meet the blow.

It was a sudden act. Impulsive. Instinctive. She had no weapon. No means to possibly defend herself and yet she could do nothing less. The sword fell and simply broke Vale's body in two. Elyn watched her sister's broken form sink to the dirt with a sense of disbelief while Imbatal raised his weapon's now bloodstained blade from the dirt, his deliberately precise actions betraying some kind of perverse satisfaction with his achievement.

As she watched Imbatal turn in her direction, Elyn felt her anger rise again. She felt the rage mounting and with it came the drumming in her ears.

And then she felt it clear.

She looked down at her dying sister – at herself – and suffered a stab of shame and regret. She realized that she had been trying to hold on to moments that had long since passed. Memories of Leon. Her dreams of Jason. Her hopes that someday the world would stop and recognise her for who she was. It was all trivial in the face of her twin sister's selfless actions. She had believed that her own inaction could somehow prevent change. Watching Vale die, she realized how futile such a delusion was.

The world was going to change, and she simply could not stop it. Vale was going to die. Vale was going to pay the price for her own stubbornness and fear. She couldn't allow that. She couldn't live one day longer knowing that her cowardice had permitted the best parts of her to die, while her own weak shadow would linger. Elyn made a decision. She ignored the horrors around her, turned her mind inward, and snatched an instant of time that seemed to stretch outward for years. She saw herself in Fairhaven. She saw herself grow into a woman. She saw herself return to the Last Jar and resume her flirtations with Dex the barman. She saw them make love. She saw herself in a respectable house near the old wall. She saw their beautiful baby daughter and the love she would heap on her. She watched her grow from infant to girl to woman and she felt the warm glow of bittersweet satisfaction as she drifted away from her to start her new life. She watched the life she would never own and for an instant, she let herself love it. Then she let it slip from her grasp like water through her hands.

Elyn reached out with her mind and felt Vale. She was still there, warm and fading. Elyn gently picked up what remained of Vale's soul and held it close.

"*I'm so sorry, Elyn,*" said Vale from a great distance.

"*It's alright, Vale. I'm here now.*"

"*I didn't want you to do this. It's not fair.*"

"*No, Vale. I've been selfish. I've been scared. Forgive me.*"

There was a pause. Elyn felt her mind overlap with Vale. Vale felt her mind overlap with Elyn. Their thoughts became one. Their two voices became indistinct.

"*There's nothing for us to forgive, Elyn.*"

"*Come home.*"

She did. And they were both changed forever.

• • •

She couldn't quite place the difference. It wasn't something she could define or articulate. In the time to come, she would look back at this moment and try to remember how she had felt before, but she wouldn't be able to do it. She would look at the behaviours of Elyn and Vale as if they were some kind of strange other-person, whose actions she couldn't quite relate to. Now that Vale and Elyn were both truly part of her, she couldn't understand why she had ever felt any other way. Why she simply hadn't been this person all along. It didn't matter.

Imbatal was upon her.

He moved with that same speed, his massive greatsword swinging about him like it was a branch in a storm.

She didn't retreat.

She raised Elyn's sword with both hands and met Imbatal's blade. The weapons crashed together, and for a moment, they both stood there frozen in a mirror image of each other. Swords locked overhead, muscles straining against mechanical gears in silent contest. Then Imbatal disengaged his weapon and swung again. He was fast. His blade struck her on the shoulder and sent her stumbling backward a few steps. She felt blood run down her arm, but her arm was still there. It wasn't severed as it probably should have been. If Imbatal wore an expression of surprise, then it wasn't visible through the blank mask of a face. A face that was now peering slightly upward at her instead of downward. She realized that the world now looked different, she seemed taller, larger. Indeed, it seemed as if her physique were expanding before her eyes. She felt good. She felt strong, and again she found herself wondering why it had taken her so long to accept this. What had been stopping her all those years?

Imbatal was attacking now with an almost manic speed. Although Aleasea might have fallen, her magic was still in effect. The creature whirred and grated with unnatural sounds as it swung the sword again and again. Although she now realized she had new tools with which to handle this situation, she decided to practice caution; Imbatal was still very dangerous. She back-stepped and parried, back-stepped and parried. All the while leading the clockwork demon in their strange dance across the street. She knew that they were both moving with a supernatural swiftness, that she couldn't possibly have matched Imbatal's blows moments ago. But now it almost seemed simple. They danced like this for a time. A minute? Ten? Twenty? It was impossible to say. She continued to predict and block Imbatal's strokes like a teacher training a novice. After a time, she noticed that her sword was buckling under the unrelenting attack of the creature. Then after a final parry the sword broke completely. She let it fall to the ground. She no longer needed it. Imbatal was starting to slow.

The new god skipped backward as the greatsword cut at the air in front of her, then after a time she walked backward, then she eventually paused. Imbatal was moving spasmodically now, trying in vain to lift the weapon above him for one final downstroke. Its gears clicked and grated in a shrill noise that hurt the ears, and it seemed like the closest approximation to a scream this false-man could make. She walked over and wrapped her own hands over the hilt of Imbatal's sword in a gesture that was almost intimate, then she pulled gently, and the weapon came loose in her hands. Imbatal's blank face turned toward her, and she could now see cold blue eyes underneath the hood. The eyes seemed to plead with her.

For mercy?

For release?

The new god granted him this.

With a mighty overhead swing, she sent the sword crashing into the wreckage of the creature before her, sending a spray of cogs, gears, and metal splashing into the dust. She swung again and again and realized she was screaming. Her pure emotion rose from the depths of her stomach and broke free in her throat in a rage she'd never before released. It echoed off the walls around her and rippled through the sickly yellow liquid pooling from Imbatal at her feet. She screamed for as long as she could and when it was over, she felt her entire body sag. She looked at the ruins of the monster in front of her and then at the ruins of her home around her.

It was over.

CHAPTER 5

The legends of that day would live on for years after the battle had ceased. People would speak eagerly of what they had seen – or of what they chose to believe they'd seen – to their children, their friends, or anyone with a passing interest. Some stories would warp with time, others would become completely fabricated, and yet the essence of the legends would remain largely consistent. There were some stories, however, that did not alter with different tellings or through the passing of time. There were some stories that were undisputed, as if their facts had been carved in stone, permanent and unchanging and unmistakable. Chief among these facts was the tale of Ethan and his men, and how of all the people to come to Fairhaven's aid in her darkest hour, it had not been the goddess Maelene, but her deepest enemies who had answered the call. It was said that Elyn herself had led them into the city and dispatched them to aid Lewis's men, while Elyn remained to face Imbatal in combat. Ethan's men had cut through the surprised invaders like a scythe through a wheatfield and sent them scattered on the wind. Indeed, it was only the far-sighted Ageless who sent word to Captain Lewis in time and ordered him against attacking his new and unexpected allies. It was said that Ethan halted his own small force once the armies of Fairhaven were in range and had personally kneeled before an astonished Captain as he offered the services of his men in defense of the city.

The general consensus would be that that was the moment the tide of battle turned for the people of Fairhaven. That the unthinkable act of a commander of the Iron Union willingly submitting his men to the command of his enemy seemed to catch the very attention of the gods themselves. And it was said the gods responded in measure.

Of course, none of those who bore witness had also been present on the day Ethan and Vale had faced the loose alliance of the Rak'Tunga. If they had, then they might have realized it was experience more than the will of the gods that ruled the field that day. Just like the wild men of the wastes, the nomads of the north fought with little discipline and even less honor. Once it became clear that they were fighting a force stronger than expected and once they realized that Imbatal was no longer there to support them, that lack of discipline spiralled into disorder and then into chaos. Ethan's men led the charge – an unexpected spearhead into forces that had moments before assumed they were the aggressors. Vale's estimate of the capability of the Helmsguard was redeemed, and those five hundred men fought as fiercely as thousands of the Northmen. They thrust into the raider's forces, bisecting them and sending them back into the streets and mazes of the outer city where they struggled to regroup. There Lewis's men found them and gave them no respite, harrying them further until they were forced to retreat toward the city walls. It was at that point that command between the tribes appeared to break down, and they defended themselves not as a united army, but as individual units with no regard for each other.

From that point, the retreat of the Northmen descended into a rout as the invaders desperately tried to escape the confines of the walled city they had come to raze. It was said that the Ageless weaved their magic to confuse the already panicked raiders and prevent their escape. The stories would say that many of them cried out desperately for Imbatal before they died, but he would not come. He could not. So they screamed his name in vain as one by one the armies of the Northmen were annihilated. And even before the sun had peaked in the midday sky, they had quit the city and were fleeing eastward in chaos.

It was told that Elyn did not join in this heroic pursuit of the invaders as she had bested Imbatal in single combat and stood gloriously triumphant. A symbol of the might of Fairhaven and the bright future to come.

And while some legends had a basis in fact, others were to be proven myth.

      .   .   .

Ethan watched the blue-clad soldiers of Fairhaven go about their duties with the practised efficiency he had always admired in his own men. They had fought well, much to his surprise. Although they lacked the arms and the armor that he had always taken for granted, they had shown remarkable tenacity and skill defending their homes. Ethan respected that.

His own men, for their part, had shown no hesitation. Even at the unthinkable moment when he had bent his own knee to his enemy and ceded authority, they had followed their orders without question and taken the fight to the invaders with pride. The Fairhaven Captain had used the help well. He was a canny commander who would've been an asset to the Iron Union had circumstances been reversed. Lewis had supported Ethan's men and hadn't abused them as disposable fodder, as Ethan had initially feared. Instead Lewis had treated Ethan's men with the same frugal conservatism as he did his own. Compassion or simply economization of assets? Perhaps a mixture of the two was desirable in the best commanders.

Now Ethan led his men back into the heart of the city as he searched for his friend and commander. They'd suffered surprisingly few casualties – only half a dozen makeshift stretchers would carry the injured or dead away from this place – far, far fewer than the dead they'd leave behind here. He cast his eyes over the city that seemed to glow in the late afternoon sun. The light did little to warm the desolate scene before him. Their city was broken. Ethan looked at it and wondered if it might ever fully recover. Even if it did, it was unlikely to go back to the city it had ever been before. There wasn't just physical damage here – something had changed. A betrayal of the people, perhaps? Ethan could see it in the way the townsfolk now looked at each other, the way they spoke in hushed tones. "How could this have happened?" those looks seemed to cry. No, the consequences of this day would stretch far beyond the replacement of bricks and the resetting of mortar.

Today's dead would not rest easy.

Ethan returned his gaze to the city square before him to see a figure walking in his direction. At first, he gave the soldier only a passing glance before realizing that the soldier was walking directly toward him, and also that there was something familiar about the woman. When the recognition set in, Ethan wondered if the day's supply of bewildering revelations was finally spent. Vale walked toward him, but this was not the same woman Ethan had last seen only hours before – she had changed. No, changed wasn't the word. She was now a different person. She was taller, much taller, and yet it wasn't just her height or her physique that now betrayed the strength of a warrior in peak condition. There was an intangible sense of raw power about her, a new confidence that seemed to emanate from her even as she casually walked across the square. If Ethan or his men had ever doubted that Vale was the true daughter of Bythe, then those doubts were crushed on this bloody afternoon.

"Ethan, thank you so much," greeted the woman once known to them as Vale. The voice was stronger now, slightly deeper yet still feminine, and the eyes that flashed out were of bright, cold blue. Although the face was still familiar.

"My lady...?" Ethan began, but his commander interrupted him with a familiar dismissive wave.

"No more formalities," she replied and with sudden abruptness, she reached over and embraced him. The hug was warm but also awkward. Ethan could feel the surprised stares of his men boring into his back and was conflicted. Part of him had longed for such a moment and yet now that it was here, he found he wanted Vale to regain her composure so things could return to normal.

"Vale, what's happened?" he asked. At the sound of that name Ethan felt her stiffen and then the embrace was broken. She looked at him with a strange expression.

"I'm not sure that I'm that person anymore, Ethan."

"I don't understand. What have they done to you?"

"Nothing," she smiled. "They've done nothing to me. It's as we discussed, Ethan. I've found Elyn and I've found my answers. It seems that I've finally discovered what it means to be Bythe's daughter. Tell me, do you think he'd be proud of me now?"

Ethan shook his head, not in disagreement but in silent disbelief. She guided him by the shoulder, and they walked a short distance away from the rest of the soldiers. Their similar height was now a strange thing for Ethan to behold. "I'm not going to be able to tell you the story I'm afraid, maybe one day I'll get the chance. You're probably going to hear all sorts of bizarre distortions about me but none of it matters."

Ethan halted and turned to face her with suspicion. "What are you talking about? You'll have ample time to tell me everything on our journey back to the Ironhelm!"

She didn't answer. She looked at the man who might have been her lover with a mixture of affection and regret. The look told Ethan all he needed to know.

"You're staying here? You're deserting us?"

A look of pain shot across her features. "No, Ethan. I'm not deserting you, but I can't go back with you either. I told you I'm not the same woman I was when I saw you last. In fact, I haven't been the same woman for quite some time now. I think you've known that."

"Vale, you're not making sense!"

"This is so hard to explain to you, and I don't think I know how to do it. I'm different now, Ethan, I'm still the woman you knew in some ways, but in other ways..." she paused "...I'm becoming someone new entirely."

Ethan took a quick step backward. He felt a strong surge of mistrust for this person before him. "I knew this would happen, Vale. I tried to warn you. Why didn't you listen to me?"

She sighed in resignation. "I wish I could help you understand but we're out of time. You have to leave here before the Ageless decide they don't want you to leave."

Ethan's face hardened. "You've led us into a trap?"

"No, please no! But I don't speak for the Ageless. You're only here by my actions and they don't like it, and now that the threat is gone, they're going to turn their attention to you. You have to leave now."

"And yet they're not going to imprison you along with the rest of us?"

Ethan intended the question as an accusation, but he was shocked as she broke into laughter. Ethan couldn't remember the last time he'd heard her laugh like that.

"Oh, Ethan, I'm the one they're going to want to imprison most of all!"

Ethan paused. Confusion washed over him. "Then why stay? Come with us. Come with me."

"No, I want the Ageless to preoccupy themselves with me while you slip away as quickly as you can. I'm afraid there's only real escape for one of us."

For one of the rare moments in his life, Ethan had no idea what to do or how to react. His mind raced as he tried to piece together what had happened to the woman he had loved, but he simply couldn't. All he knew with certainty was that her warning rang true – the longer they stayed in Fairhaven, the greater the danger to him and his men. If she was deserting them, then what other choice could he make? Attempt to capture her? Looking at her now, he wondered if it would be possible to restrain this new daughter of Bythe, even without enemies surrounding them on all sides. No, he had but one option and that was to retreat as quickly as possible, and on some level, he realized that the woman he loved had already known that was the only possible outcome. Ethan felt used. Manipulated. Betrayed.

He stiffened to attention and saluted, but the gesture was formal and without respect. She opened her mouth as if to explain one last time but closed it again. Perhaps she thought it was easier this way? Perhaps it was easier for both of them. She said nothing more. Instead, she watched the man she wanted to love turn away to start the long journey home.

In the days and nights that followed on the long journey back to the Ironhelm, Ethan would replay this last meeting between them and wonder if he should have said more, should have questioned her longer. Maybe he even could have changed her mind? In the end, he was never sure why he didn't, but then the answer is often much the same with proud men – stubborn courage can shatter in the face of true pain.

•   •   •

She had followed Ethan's party to the west gate and watched them leave safely. Ethan never once glanced backward. Then for no particular reason, she'd chosen to keep walking. Who was she now? Elyn or Vale? She was both and she was neither. She could feel that something had begun, a change that would start to consume her and take her somewhere unknown. For now, it seemed as if her two halves were interchangeable, but they were slowly and irrevocably bleeding into each other. Elyn? Vale? Or another name?

She reckoned that she was into her third hour of wandering. The sun was touching the tips of the Temple and soon night would engulf the town. She mused that it was more fitting that a day like this shouldn't have to suffer light when it seemed so out of place. Better to cover all of it in darkness and let these scenes be swallowed up out of sight. She thought she'd probably covered most of the city during her meandering journey. She strolled through the warehouses of the outer city recalling the time Elyn and Jason had foolishly stalked the Ageless through the alleyways and she smiled at the memory. Her feet then took her south and into the beautiful streets of the inner Old City lined with now empty houses, some with shattered windows that gave them a look of disquiet. It was eerie to stand there in a silent street that should've been buzzing with the sounds of mothers calling children and playful children ignoring their mothers. Standing there, she had also realized that the difference wasn't entirely external. She was looking at them differently now. They seemed smaller to her. Perhaps her new memories of the towering spires of the Ironhelm, along with the other incredible things Vale had seen were casting Fairhaven in a very different light? She shrugged – it didn't matter. She turned away from the row of quiet houses and kept walking. At some point, she returned to where they had fought Imbatal. She was surprised to find the wreckage of the creature still there, and she wondered how long before the Ageless would return to claim it. Imbatal's monstrous sword lay in the dust where he'd dropped it hours before, grotesque yellow liquid encrusting the blade. She hefted it easily in one hand and cleaned the blade with the remains of Imbatal's robes. It was a fine sword and it somehow seemed fitting that it should pass to her. She loosed the scabbard from the remains of the creature's back and claimed the weapon as her own before turning her back on the corpse of the thing that had once tried so hard to destroy her.

"I thought you'd still be healing?" she asked the figure standing in the wall's shadow. Aleasea stepped out into the fading light. Her green robe was loose and hung limp around her shoulders. The remains of her right arm were concealed underneath the cloak. Aleasea's face was pale and now seemed to wear the small lines of age.

"I am not sure any of us are going to be completely healed from what has happened today," Aleasea said as she walked over.

"Your arm...?"

"Yes, it is lost," she said. "Do not trouble yourself, Elyn. You should know that we do not limit ourselves to the mere physical. It will be difficult for a while, but I will adapt to this."

She felt mild shock at how casually Aleasea accepted an injury that would ruin most men. She realized her respect for Aleasea seemed to constantly grow. Aleasea looked at her appraisingly, like a teacher reuniting with an old pupil.

"How do you feel, Elyn?"

She laughed. "I don't know. I don't think that's even my name anymore. Elyn and Vale are both here, but they're also both gone."

Aleasea nodded. "What is your name now?"

She thought for a moment and the name seemed to come to her unbidden.

"Valeyn," she answered. "My name is Valeyn."

Aleasea nodded and smiled. "That seems fitting."

"How do you feel?" Valeyn repeated Aleasea's question delicately. She knew that Aleasea had paid a higher price today. Her grievous physical injuries were almost trivial when compared to the revelations of Yvorre and the destruction of Sanctuary.

"I do not know what they will do," she sighed. "The Temple is crippled but Veroulle may yet rebuild it. Ferehain has already spoken of the need to hunt down Yvorre and have justice...but we are broken."

Valeyn nodded and there was a pause. Aleasea looked at her with the penetrating eye of a teacher once more.

"You will leave." Aleasea said it as a statement, not a question.

Valeyn nodded again in reply.

"I'm the daughter of Bythe and Maelene. My presence caused all of this." She gestured to the ruins around them as she spoke. "Bythe will be coming for me now, and I need to draw him away. You're not going to ask me to trust the Ageless again, are you?"

Aleasea shook her head. "I could not persuade you to follow a conviction that I no longer understand. The Ageless are no longer the family I once loved; I knew this before. Yvorre's actions today have only sealed this decision in my mind."

Valeyn looked at Aleasea, the former pupil assessing the weaknesses of the teacher for the first time. "I'm not sure I can ever accept what your people did, what they tried to do to me."

Aleasea looked at her for a moment before turning her eyes to the horizon beyond. "We acted as we thought would serve the world best. That is all any of us did, even Ferehain. Be careful with your newfound strength my child. Godling or not, you may discover that your wisdom is still as limited as ours."

Valeyn shook her head slowly. "I know I'm being unfair...but this is difficult to understand. I need to sort this out for myself."

Aleasea nodded. "You are right. You need to discover your own wisdom; you do not need more of ours forced upon you."

"Thank you, Aleasea, for everything you did for me. I know you truly cared."

Aleasea returned her eyes for a moment. They radiated love. Valeyn extended her hand to Aleasea, who took it and smiled.

"Take care. You are my child no longer."

They parted without another word. Aleasea walked into the dusk, leaving Valeyn alone.

•   •   •

Valeyn studiously avoided venturing near the old house where Elyn had grown up with Leon. She wasn't sure why – somehow it just didn't feel right. Perhaps she was afraid that if she ventured too close to the path behind, then she might be tempted to turn from the path ahead. It was likely this motivation prompted her to turn in the direction of the marketplace and led her step by step to that terrible spot where her life had changed forever. She stood there again alone – the market seemed far from everyone's attention that evening – and watched the shadows thicken and lengthen across the cobblestones where her father had lain. She wasn't surprised when she heard footsteps behind, and she knew who it was before she heard the voice.

"Elyn? We've been looking for you," Jason's words were tentative but still warm. Valeyn smiled at this. She turned to face him, noticing how much shorter he seemed now – it was odd. Jason seemed to be attempting to mask the surprise he so clearly felt at the change in her. Valeyn was happy to see her old friend again. She reached out and they held each other for a long time. They sat on the cobblestones like children and they talked. They talked for a long time. The sun dipped behind the city walls and the stars appeared in the early evening sky as she told him what she could. She let it all out. She told him everything. He looked very handsome in the soft twilight, listening patiently as she told of how Elyn first met Vale and their strange connection. He had always been a good friend; it was little wonder that she'd loved him. She probably still did, but like everything else it seemed different now. She was glad that he'd found Nadine and that they were starting to find happiness together. They still had a long journey ahead of them, but she knew they had every chance. At some stage as the evening deepened into full night, she realized Nadine had also found them. She'd been standing a respectful distance away at first but had slowly edged closer to hear more of the story and by the time Valeyn had finished she had accepted the unspoken invitation to join their intimate council. After Valeyn fell quiet, the silence held for a long time.

"Aleasea?" Jason asked.

"She'll never be the same, but she's alive."

Jason nodded almost gratefully.

"I don't think any of us will be the same after today," Nadine said. There was silence for a moment before Jason's face softened into a smile.

"So... did you see the moves I used out there today? Not bad, right?"

Valeyn looked at him with a deadpan expression. "You mean the one where you needed me to save your sorry butt from Imbatal?"

Jason shrugged, still smiling. "Hey, I did my bit. Did you see how much damage I did to his wardrobe? He must've been so angry at the amount of needlework I was giving him..."

Nadine laughed at this exchange and all three of them relaxed. For a time, all was forgotten – the fighting, the deaths, the change. They were three friends once more. Jason questioned her about the time in Sanctuary and she answered truthfully. Jason spoke about his time in the mountains and Nadine shared the terror she'd felt for both of them – as well as the frustration at being left behind. They spoke late into the night, until the sky began to soften with the promise of dawn. As the darkness began to recede the conversation started to become awkward, then falter, then finally to pause. It was as if their discussion had run its course and that after a night of conversation, there was now little else to say.

None of them spoke.

It seemed as if they all wanted to hold on to this moment for as long as they could, as if they all knew that the very act of speaking would start the inevitable chain of actions that would lead to what had to come next. They all wanted to hold onto the past for just a moment longer.

It was Valeyn who broke it.

"I'm going to leave."

Nadine lowered her head as if in shame. Jason only looked at her for a moment then answered in a voice that was thick with emotion.

"Why do you have to do that?"

She looked away. "This isn't my place anymore, Jason. I don't think it's ever really been my place. I mean, I've never really felt completely at home here, not fully. You know that I've never really fit in. That's why it was such a relief when the Ageless claimed me. I thought that for the first time, I'd actually found my home." She laughed. It was a short, bitter sound. "Look how that turned out."

Jason stood up and walked a few steps away as if he needed to process the news. That simple act of standing seemed to serve as the catalyst, and within seconds, all three of them were on their feet.

"What about Veroulle and the Ageless? What about Bythe?" Nadine asked. "Won't they come for you?"

"Almost definitely. That's why I have to go now. The Ageless have been busy tonight, but by morning they'll start to recover, and their first order of business will be to secure me one way or the other. I'm not going to turn this city into a battlefield. Too many people have died over this already."

"But they'll come after you?" Jason pressed, the concern in his voice evident.

"I'm sure they will, but I don't think they'll press too hard just yet. They must now know what I'm capable of."

She delivered this last sentence with such cold intensity that Jason's face fell into dismay as he heard Vale's voice clearly for the first time. If he harboured any hopes that his lovable and harmless younger sister still existed, they were erased with these words. Jason had known how she'd felt toward him of course – she didn't need her new gifts to realize this now – but she wondered how he must feel to know that she wasn't his little sister anymore. That she never would be again. She supposed it didn't matter.

"Where will you go?" Jason asked, and she caught a trace of suspicion in his question. No doubt the return of Vale's voice had also unsettled Elyn's closest friend. He was probably wondering if Vale would want to return to her father? Would she betray them? She thought about this for a moment. Maybe one day she would make her way to the Ironhelm. There was no doubt she could sense some kind of destiny tempting her down that path, and she was sure one day she would explore it through till its end. But not now.

"I'm going south," she answered.

"South?" Jason asked in confusion. "What's down there?"

"So much. The Tower – the one Yvorre told us about," she answered. "I can feel it now. It's distant but it's there. I can feel the Ironhelm and what's left of Sanctuary. I think I can feel most of the Constructs of the old gods."

She turned her face to the glowing sky and closed her eyes for a moment. "There's a lot out there, so much we didn't know. So much that's been hidden from all of us. I want to go find it and see the truth for myself. I think I'm the only one who can. I need to understand what it is to be a god. I need to understand what I can do."

"Yvorre?" Nadine asked.

She shrugged. "I think Yvorre now has more to fear from me than I do from her. Bythe will hunt her down now that he knows what she's done, and I'm inclined to do the same. Besides, I have a feeling I'll find her again, when I'm ready.

"And Bythe?" said Jason.

"Father already knows I've awoken. He'll come for me, but I'm not afraid. I think part of me welcomes it, but I can't be here when that day comes. I need to face him on my own terms, and I won't put any of you in danger."

"Elyn, no!" Nadine's voice was pleading now and there were tears in her eyes. "There has to be another answer!"

She realized with genuine surprise that Nadine and Jason still didn't quite understand, and a broad smile broke across her face. The expression bewildered them.

"Nadine," she said as she crossed the space between them and placed her hands on her friend's shoulders. "Nadine, don't feel sorry for me! I'm sad to leave you both, but I'm not sad to be leaving!"

She laughed, a clear sound in the young dawn. She placed one hand on the shoulder of each of her friends and looked at them both in turn.

"You both have no idea how I feel now. I feel...incredible. I feel like I've finally realized who I'm meant to be. I'm not supposed to be here. I'm supposed to be out there. I don't know where my journey's going to end but I know as surely as Leon was my father that my destiny is out there – and it excites me."

She spoke the words with more conviction and passion than she'd intended, and as she did, she was convinced of her decision. A giddy thrill shot through her chest, and she pulled her friends to her in a strong embrace.

"I'll remember you both always, and I promise I'll come back one day," she whispered, and Jason tightened his grip while Nadine let out a muffled sob. Hot tears traced her own cheeks now and she didn't hold them back. They stood there in that embrace for a time and then broke off. She looked at them both. "Don't feel sorry for me. When I come back, I'm going to be a different person."

Jason nodded. His eyes were red, but he was smiling. "You already are. You just have to outshine me, don't you?"

Valeyn laughed and the tears flowed hotter. Jason joined and then they all laughed together one last time. The joy and the sorrow and the pure emotion coursing out of them in scalding tears. It was a sweet moment. They knew they would never be together like that again.

·   ·   ·

As Valeyn walked toward the gates, she felt content. She felt at peace. The dawn was starting to fill the sky with a pink glow hinting at the day to come, and she was reminded that this had always been her favorite time of day – both as Elyn and Vale. She watched a young family refitting a broken door onto the entrance to their home. She saw the surprised expressions as she passed and the gratitude in their eyes. Clearly, the stories had already begun to spread. Their young girl – a child no more than five or six with delicate blue eyes – waved up at her with all the adoration and excitement that only the beautifully innocent can provide. She smiled and waved back, and in doing so gave the girl a story that she would joyfully recount for the rest of her life. She walked past them and felt satisfied knowing that these families would carry on here, that the city would rebuild and find peace again, that her friends would grow and do well, and that she would find her own path and she would likewise grow and flourish and change – on her own.

She walked out of the eastern gate of the city and watched as the first brilliant splash of orange touched the sky in front of her.

And she smiled.

She smiled because she wasn't afraid, and she smiled because she wasn't really on her own. Of course, people like Elyn and Vale – with deep reservoirs of thought and reflection – they could never really be alone. But now, as she sensed Elyn's and Vale's minds shifting and settling within her own, she knew this was more certain than ever.

"*Did you know, I never really liked it there?*" Elyn silently asked herself as she walked into the open fields before them.

"*Believe me, you wouldn't enjoy the Ironhelm either,*" Vale answered distantly. "*I think it's time we found our own place.*"

She nodded. She could no longer distinguish Vale's thoughts from Elyn's, and it felt good. It felt like it was always meant to be this way. A short time ago Elyn had considered leaving Fairhaven like this, but she knew now that Ferehain's misguided advice had actually been true. She had wanted to leave for the wrong reasons that day: she had wanted to run.

She wasn't running anymore.

She felt herself growing with every step and with it came a thrill of excitement – an urge to explore the world before her and to test what she could achieve. She knew that people would challenge her on the path ahead – they might even try to stop her – but she didn't need to fear that anymore. For the first time in her life she knew her strength.

She looked forward to her new life. She knew she would find her place. She would carve it out. She would claim it as her own. She was a new god with all the terrifying possibilities that came with it. She would discover them.

And then what?

Confront Yvorre? Confront Bythe?

Perhaps, but she knew that was no longer important. She had learned a far greater secret. She had confronted herself; the gods could no longer frighten her.

ACKNOWLEDGEMENTS

This book was over fifteen years in the making and so much has happened over that time that it will be impossible to mention everyone who helped contribute.

First of all, my brother Andrew had so much direct and indirect influence on some of these characters. Thanks for taking the journey with me over the years and helping me to bring these people to life in different ways.

Thanks to Reagan at Black Rose Writing for helping me transform this book from another manuscript into a published novel.

Thanks to my mother and stepfather for reading this as soon as the drafts were available and for the support. Thanks also to my online writers' group (especially Tash, AK, Mel, Ally and Andy) who helped me shape the final touches on this book. Thanks to Edwin (@fantasymapshop) for making my world real.

And finally, to my beautiful wife Anya. Thank you so much for encouraging and supporting my writing over all these years. This book is only possible because of you.

The Godless Trilogy

ABOUT THE AUTHOR

Christopher Monteagle is a lifelong fantasy reader and writer of fiction in various forms. Growing up in outback Australia with no running water, electricity, or - needless to say – television, Christopher was introduced to books by Tolkien and Herbert to pass the time. He soon began writing his own stories and became immersed in the worlds of fantasy and fiction. *The Union of Lies* is Christopher's second novel.

Note from the Author

Word-of-mouth is crucial for any author to succeed. If you enjoyed *The Union of Lies*, please leave a review online—anywhere you are able. Even if it's just a sentence or two. It would make all the difference and would be very much appreciated.

Thanks!
Christopher Monteagle

We hope you enjoyed reading this title from:

www.blackrosewriting.com

Subscribe to our mailing list – *The Rosevine* – and receive **FREE** books, daily deals, and stay current with news about upcoming releases and our hottest authors.
Scan the QR code below to sign up.

Already a subscriber? Please accept a sincere thank you for being a fan of Black Rose Writing authors.

View other Black Rose Writing titles at
www.blackrosewriting.com/books and use promo code
PRINT to receive a **20% discount** when purchasing.